MURDER BY MOCHA

Berkley Prime Crime titles by Cleo Coyle

Coffeehouse Mysteries

ON WHAT GROUNDS
THROUGH THE GRINDER
LATTE TROUBLE
MURDER MOST FROTHY
DECAFFEINATED CORPSE
FRENCH PRESSED
ESPRESSO SHOT
HOLIDAY GRIND
ROAST MORTEM
MURDER BY MOCHA

Haunted Bookshop Mysteries
writing as Alice Kimberly

THE GHOST AND MRS. MCCLURE
THE GHOST AND THE DEAD DEB
THE GHOST AND THE DEAD MAN'S LIBRARY
THE GHOST AND THE FEMME FATALE
THE GHOST AND THE HAUNTED MANSION

MURDER BY MOCHA

CLEO COYLE

BERKLEY PRIME CRIME, NEW YORK

THE BERKLEY PUBLISHING GROUP
Published by the Penguin Group
Penguin Group (USA) Inc.
375 Hudson Street, New York, New York 10014, USA
Penguin Group (Canada), 90 Eglinton Avenue East, Suite 700, Toronto, Ontario M4P 2Y3, Canada
(a division of Pearson Penguin Canada Inc.)
Penguin Books Ltd., 80 Strand, London WC2R 0RL, England
Penguin Group Ireland, 25 St. Stephen's Green, Dublin 2, Ireland (a division of Penguin Books Ltd.)
Penguin Group (Australia), 250 Camberwell Road, Camberwell, Victoria 3124, Australia
(a division of Pearson Australia Group Pty. Ltd.)
Penguin Books India Pvt. Ltd., 11 Community Centre, Panchsheel Park, New Delhi—110 017, India
Penguin Group (NZ), 67 Apollo Drive, Rosedale, Auckland 0632, New Zealand
(a division of Pearson New Zealand Ltd.)
Penguin Books (South Africa) (Pty.) Ltd., 24 Sturdee Avenue, Rosebank, Johannesburg 2196,
South Africa

Penguin Books Ltd., Registered Offices: 80 Strand, London WC2R 0RL, England

This book is an original publication of The Berkley Publishing Group.

This is a work of fiction. Names, characters, places, and incidents either are the product of the author's imagination or are used fictitiously, and any resemblance to actual persons, living or dead, business establishments, events, or locales is entirely coincidental. The publisher does not have any control over and does not assume any responsibility for author or third-party websites or their content.

PUBLISHER'S NOTE: The recipes contained in this book are to be followed exactly as written. The publisher is not responsible for your specific health or allergy needs that may require medical supervision. The publisher is not responsible for any adverse reaction to the recipes contained in this book.

FIRST EDITION: August 2011

Library of Congress Cataloging-in-Publication Data

Coyle, Cleo.
Murder by mocha / Cleo Coyle.—1st ed.
    p. cm.
    ISBN 978-0-425-24143-1 (hardcover)
    1. Cosi, Clare (Fictitious character)—Fiction. 2. Coffeehouses—Fiction. 3. Coffee—Fiction.
4. Aphrodisiacs—Fiction. 5. Murder—Investigation—Fiction. I. Title.
    PS3603.O94M85 2011
    813'.6—dc22   2011015824

PRINTED IN THE UNITED STATES OF AMERICA

10 9 8 7 6 5 4 3 2 1

This book is dedicated to the readers.
From the heart . . .
Thank you.

ACKNOWLEDGMENTS

Murder by Mocha marks the tenth entry in the Coffeehouse Mysteries, and it's long past time I acknowledge the reason the Village Blend is still open for business—the readers. I may live in New York City, but the World Wide Web has made it possible for me to converse with many of you throughout the country and the planet. I thank you for your kind support and (yes) love. I send that love back to you with this book.

In particular, I wish to thank a few CM readers by name for their creative contributions to this entry: First, Nancy Prior Phillips, whose signature phrase suggested an entire character. Of course, Clare's new barista is a complete fiction with one exception. On down days, I think we can all use an "inner Nancy." Thanks to pro-baker Paul Yates for lending me his good opinion on the *dieci*; thanks to Alicia Farage for the chocolate cobbler recipe; and very special thanks to Peggy-Jo Schilger and her grandmother for sharing "Mama Bert's" coffee cheese recipe.

For their supportive good cheer, I also thank J.J. and Marcia Pierce, Paul Mulligan, Chuck H., Bob L., Julie and Kerry M., Nurse Judy Mac, Victoria H., Pam F., Lura W., Laine B., Lesa H., Barbara H. (Babs), Lori G., Amy A., Deanna S., Tiffany B., Mason C., Dru Ann L., Nikki B., Nora-Adrienne, Juju, Hai, Geekette, Wendy W., Jung-Min, Kelly Jo B., Erin H., Rhonda, Nicole, Carol, Karen in Pennsylvania, and the awesome Three Lanes of Texas. Mary Tracy I thank for long-standing support, along with the amazing Red Hatter Shirley Jackson (eighty years young).

To everyone else, whom I could not mention here by name, please know that every one of your comments and kind messages has helped keep my spirits up and my pen pressed to paper. My virtual coffeehouse is always open. You are more than welcome to join us at www.CoffeehouseMystery.com.

For background on the culinary aspects of this book, I thank the accomplished chocolatiers of Mast Brothers Chocolate in Williamsburg, Brooklyn (www.MastBrothersChocolate.com). Mocha cheers also to the incoming chair of the Barista Guild of America, Jason Dominy, for sharing his award-winning Mocha Diablo recipe with me. Jason works for one of the top coffee bars in the country, Dancing Goats Coffee (www.DancingGoats .com), and the excellent Batdorf & Bronson Coffee Roasters, based in Atlanta, Georgia.

More java thanks must go to two award-winning coffee roasters: PT's Coffee Roasting Co., based in Kansas (www .PtsCoffee.com); Gimme Coffee, based in New York State (www.GimmeCoffee.com); as well as another of the nation's top coffee bars, Joe the Art of Coffee, based in Greenwich Village, New York (www.JoetheArtofCoffee.com).

For foodie inspiration, I raise a glass to my fantastic fellow mystery writing cooks at Mystery Lovers' Kitchen: Krista Davis, Avery Aames, Elizabeth S. Craig, Mary Jane Maffini, Sheila Connolly, and Wendy Lyn Watson. (Visit us at www .MysteryLoversKitchen.com.) For continually giving me food for thought, I thank Janet Rudolph of Dying for Chocolate (www.DyingForChocolate.blogspot.com); Dave Scott of A Year on the Grill (www.YearOnTheGrill.blogspot.com); and "the Bibliochef" of Cooking With Ideas (www.CookingWithIdeas .typepad.com). A warm, sweet shout-out must also go to the incredibly kind staff of Cops & Doughnuts Bakery, owned by real police officers in Clare, Michigan (www.CopsDoughnuts .com). *Don't glaze me, bro!*

As many of you know, I write in collaboration with my very talented spouse, Marc—a better partner a girl couldn't ask for. He and I both owe a debt of gratitude to our publisher, Berkley Prime Crime, as well as its dedicated staff, especially our amazingly talented editor, Wendy McCurdy; her hardworking assistant, Katherine Pelz; our excellent managing editor and production editor, Jennifer Eck and Patricia Callahan; and our fine copyeditor, Jude Grant.

With the utmost respect, we tip our hats to the NYPD in general and the Sixth Precinct in particular for kindly answering our questions. As to the p's and q's of police procedure, this is a light work of amateur sleuth fiction. In the Coffeehouse Mysteries, the rules occasionally get bent.

Finally, we send a very special thank-you to our literary agent, John Talbot, for his astonishing good nature and unflagging professionalism. Mocha kisses always to family and friends, including the hardest-working mom in the West, Dr. Grace Alfonsi, MD, whom we thank this time out for consultation on matters medical- and zombie-related. If there are errors in this book, they are entirely our own.

When coffee dreams, it dreams of chocolate.

—Starbucks saying

MURDER
BY MOCHA

PROLOGUE

There is a great deal of wickedness in village life.
—MISS JANE MARPLE, *THE THIRTEEN PROBLEMS*
BY AGATHA CHRISTIE

Five years ago . . .

FROM *head to toe, the woman wore black.* Black for mourning, *she thought.* Black for death.

All day she waited, checking her watch, preparing the props, counting down minutes till uncertain light. When the sun sank low and the sky's blues deepened, she made her way to the railroad bridge.

With a quick unzipping, she exposed the belly of the large Pull-man, specially outfitted for this evening's performance. She removed the old pair of white satin pumps, set them beside the four-foot rail.

In the warm purple twilight, yellow bulbs flickered on. "Spots for my stage," *she whispered.* "Kliegs for this Kabuki." *Far below the river flowed, dark and distant as a starless night.*

"My Rubicon . . ."

A popular eatery sat on the river's bank, a scenic patch near the country club stables of Bay Creek Village. She saw those diners, young and old, raising glasses, speaking civilly, adhering to dress codes.

Look at them, pretending to be decent, loyal, kind . . . Liars! Cheaters! Monsters! Hypocrites, every one . . .

Seven years before, her mother's trial had been passing entertainment for all of them, a morsel of scandal to be relished with appetizers, forgotten completely by the second course.

"Hey! Down there! You wanted a look at me? Look at me now!"

Fading back into the shadows, she watched the round white faces moon her way. Seconds later, a brand-new shout echoed along the water, shattering the serenity of the eight o'clock seating. Customers leaped to their feet, knocked over cocktails, stained outfits with wine.

She knew what they were seeing, as they gawked upriver—a woman plummeting off the bridge. Down the body sailed, through violet sky, wedding gown ballooning like a favorite yacht spinnaker. The figure splashed and quickly sank, as if eager to reach the underworld.

"My world now," whispered the woman in black. "Now I am Persephone, queen of shadows . . ."

With a hollow thud, her purse dropped—well beyond any pool of illumination. Inside that bag was an epic tale, scrawled in perfect longhand on neatly folded sheets. Here were the answers to the inevitable question, "Why did she do it?" along with enough IDs to satisfy every last dull, distracted authority on Long Island.

Hurrying toward a thicket of evergreens, she found a new path. At last, her plan was under way, blossoming like Aphrodite's red anemone beneath the dying Adonis.

Sixty yards away, every diner would tell the police they had witnessed a suicide . . .

Well, *she thought*, this is one drowned corpse who's about to be reincarnated. And, in this new life, no one will be judging me or my mother. The turn will be mine to act as judge, jury, and executioner.

ONE

"WHAT'S your pleasure?" I asked, holding open the Blend's beveled-glass door.

Against the pink champagne of the dawning sky, Mike Quinn's grim face gave up a small smile—not that anyone else could tell. Like New York's police commissioner, whose official photo had every cop in the city calling him Popeye, Quinn's smile was more of a wince.

"Got something hot for me, Cosi?"

"Maybe," I said, stifling a yawn. "But you have to come in to get it . . ."

As the corner streetlight flickered off, Mike's broad-shouldered form moved smoothly by, snagging my hand as he went. He'd been a street officer for years before making detective, and he brought that cop authority wherever he went, a quiet, commanding coolness that attracted me from the first moment he'd set foot in my coffeehouse.

While the heavy door swung shut, Mike backed me into the shadows of my empty shop. Flattened against an exposed brick wall, I looked up at him.

"I can't pour from this position."

"You can kiss from this position."

"True," I said, then my arms curled around his neck, and I finally gave the man a proper greeting.

Such was the oh-so-sweet beginning to my morning.

It wouldn't last.

Before the day ended, I would have two dead bodies on my hands—one a likely murder, the other something else entirely. Soon after, I'd have two female NYPD detectives on my case, a half-naked fitness queen ready to kill me, and a member of my staff dizzy enough with unrequited love to commit a felony.

None of the above was on my mind at the moment, just Mike Quinn's sturdy body pressing against mine and the kind of soft morning light that gave everything the illusion of beauty.

When Mike's head finally pulled away, I noticed the gray paleness of his complexion. His jaw felt wrong, too, like sandpaper. And thin strokes of crimson slashed the whites of his midnight blues. The details of his expression implied more than physical exhaustion. He looked mentally worn down.

"So," I said, keeping my tone light, "what kept you up all night?"

Mike's jaw tightened. He glanced away.

"Okay," I said, "come on . . ." Now I was the one tugging his hand, pulling him along. At the espresso bar, I moved behind the counter, scraped my Italian-roast brown hair into a kitchen-ready ponytail, and began turning ordinary cow juice into liquid velvet.

Mike peeled off his rumpled sport coat and took over his favorite stool. Then he trained his gaze on me so he could drink in the ritual.

It occurred to me then, as I fixed his steamer, that most of our days are spent in ritual and routine, at least until some dramatic event jerks us off our hamster wheels, puts us on brand new ones. Nineteen, for example, brought the end of my childhood—with the beginning of my daughter's.

Joy's conception was far from planned. After marrying her father, I developed close bonds with his mother and began working in their family coffee business. Ten years later, my marriage ended, and (much to the dismay of my mother-in-law) I ended my job, too.

Taking custody of my girl, I retrenched to west Jersey, land of safer schools and saner streets. Then Joy grew up.

My daughter's coming-of-age came with her enrollment in culinary school along with a move to an apartment in the city I'd abandoned. At last, she was on her own, and so was I. At thirty-nine, I entered what felt like a second stage of adulthood; and even though I resisted making a change, I needed it.

My freelance food writing kept me far too isolated. Not that I'd been living like a nun—well, *almost*. I'd dated since my marriage ended, but every encounter had left me cold.

My subpar love life aside, Joy and her bubbly friends were no longer around. Without them, my quiet suburban ranch became intolerable. I wasn't simply alone anymore; I was lonely.

Returning to New York's Greenwich Village had its challenges (now there's an understatement), but I'd never been happier. I'd always loved managing this landmark coffeehouse for my mother-in-law, and if I hadn't taken a leap of faith and admitted to her that I wanted my old job back, I never would've met the man sitting across from me now . . .

After texturing the whole milk, I coated the bottom of a glass mug with our newest bar syrup, poured in the thick white milk-paint, stirred everything to blend the shades, and slid my drinkable masterpiece across the counter.

Mike's brow furrowed. "Where are my shots of espresso?"

"You don't need caffeine. You need sleep. I made you a chocolate steamer."

He peered into the mug. "What's a—?"

"Steamed milk with a special syrup. In this case, tempered bittersweet, turbinado sugar, a kiss of sea salt, vanilla, pure almond extract, and *canela*—"

"*Canela?*"

"Mexican cinnamon. Still spicy but with less bite." I angled my head at the chalkboard. "It's the same syrup we use for our new Mexican Choco-Latte."

Mike sipped, and his eyes widened, the shadows lightening a fraction. "Really, really amazing," he said, drawing out the words so suggestively I could have sworn he said, *Really, really orgasmic.*

I smiled. To me, great chocolate was like a perfect espresso—the quickest path between the abyss my customers were stranded in and a sensory experience of transcendent pleasure.

"We just started using a new chocolate supplier," I explained. "Voss, in Brooklyn. They're one of the few artisan bean-to-bar chocolatiers in the area . . ."

Bean to bar was the hottest trend in the confectionary industry, and the more I learned about it, the more I realized how much it had in common with my own seed-to-cup specialty coffee business—from partnering with farms in developing countries to small-batch production and passionate service.

"They even import and roast their own beans like we do."

"Sweetheart, it's heaven in a mug," Mike said. "But I still need the espresso hit. I have a one o'clock meeting with the first deputy commissioner, and I can barely keep my eyes open."

"Then don't. Crash upstairs. I'll caffeinate you in time for your meeting." (The irony of drugging up an antidrug cop didn't escape me, but I could see Mike wasn't up for that particular joke.)

"I can crash upstairs?" he said. "You wouldn't mind?"

"You have to ask? Drink this up and I'll tuck you in."

"Tucking me in. I like the sound of that."

"Good," I said, moving to check the front-door lock. "As long as you understand: *tucking* is not a euphemism for something else."

"It's only one letter."

"You need your rest. You look like hell."

"I feel like hell . . ."

"Then follow me . . ."

I led Mike up the service staircase to my duplex above the Village Blend. (I say "my" because I lived there, not because I owned it.) The apartment was an exquisite little perk that my former mother-in-law handed me with my new employment contract.

Madame Blanche Dreyfus Allegro Dubois had lived here herself for decades when she ran the Blend. Over the years, she'd packed the apartment with imported furniture, lovingly preserved antiques, and an array of paintings and sketches from Village artists (patrons of her shop for nearly a century), which is why she considered me a curator as much as a tenant.

While Mike followed me into the master bedroom, I started some quiet tucking-in-time calculations. The bakery delivery had been made, so I had forty, maybe fifty, minutes to get the truth out of this man before I had to open the shop.

"You want a snack before you crash?" I asked. "I made a batch of my Chocolate-Glazed Hazelnut Bars yesterday. You love those."

"When I wake up," Mike said, letting out a long sigh. "I'll have four."

I stepped close, tugged the knot of his tie. "So . . . are you going to tell me?"

"What?"

"What went wrong last night. It's obviously weighing on you."

As head of the NYPD's OD Squad (a nickname for a much longer, official sounding moniker), Mike supervised a small group of detectives tasked with the job of investigating criminal activity behind drug overdoses.

Like the NYPD's Bomb Squad, Mike's team was based at

the Sixth Precinct, just up the street, but they had jurisdiction across all five boroughs, which meant Mike's workload was heavy, his hours unpredictable, and the mental strain of the political pressure periodically appalling.

For those reasons—and a few others—the man strapped on mental armor daily, along with his service weapon. In the quiet of the bedroom, however, I expected him to loosen that armor, along with his tongue.

"Well?" I pressed.

"You really want to know?"

"You really have to ask?"

Mike didn't answer, just watched me pull his tie free and begin unbuttoning his dress shirt. He stopped my hands, peeled off his shoulder holster, and took his time hanging it off the back of Madame's Duncan Phyfe chair.

"Two of my guys," he slowly began.

"Which guys?"

"Sully and Franco . . . they spoke to a young man earlier in the week, an aspiring artist—"

"Long Island City?"

"Williamsburg. The kid was our key witness in a case against a New Jersey dealer doing business in the city. Looking over his statements, given the ME's findings, I had some concerns. I went with them both to reinterview . . ."

"And?"

"This kid had been working all week on a sidewalk painting. When he was finished, he went to the roof of his ten-story building and dived off."

"Oh God. That's awful . . ."

"His painting was an elaborate bull's-eye. Nobody realized it until he jumped. He aimed right for the center."

Mike moved to the carved-mahogany four-poster, sank down on the mattress. "The morning papers already have the story, which I assume will be the subject of my one o'clock meeting with the first deputy commish. My captain asked me to take the meeting solo. He'll owe me . . . he says."

I sat next to him, touched his shoulder, felt knots as hard

as baseballs. *Oh, Mike.* I dug in both thumbs, began to massage.

He closed his eyes and exhaled. "Thank you . . ."

I worked him over a minute. "So how messed up is your case?"

"Scale of one to ten? *Nine point five.* This kid was the fiancé of the girl who OD'd two weeks ago. You remember the one I told you about?"

"The singer?"

"Yeah, beautiful girl, barely out of her twenties. Came here to be the next Lady Gaga. The boyfriend was the one who gave up the dealer. He'd also been the one buying his girl the stuff."

"It probably made him feel good," I said. "Knowing she needed him that badly."

"Except it wasn't him she needed," he said. "It was the drug."

"Sometimes love is a drug." (I wasn't speaking rhetorically. Given my history with Joy's father, I'd spent most of my twenties making *amore*-addled decisions.)

Mike's gaze shifted, as if looking for a change of subject. He found it. My sketchbook lay open on the bedside table. He leaned toward it, read the large letters I'd scrawled across the top.

"Aphrodite's Kitchen? What's this?"

"Nothing."

I'd been doodling elaborately around the margins: a big, voluptuous Venus emerging from the sea, a spatula in one hand, an oven mitt on the other. He picked up the book, clearly intrigued by my comic rendition of the Botticelli masterpiece.

"Hey, give that here."

He teased it out of reach, scanned my list of recipe ideas. "These sound pretty tasty. Any test batches coming my way?"

"As long as you make it to the launch party tonight. I'll be managing the samples table."

"Samples for?" He tapped his forehead. "Right. That magical mocha coffee."

"Mocha Magic Coffee."

"A rose by any other name."

"When the name is trademarked, there is no other name."

"I remember now. You told me about it a few weeks ago. Some new coffee powder that enhances . . ." He smirked. "What does it enhance exactly?"

"Alicia Bower claims it's an herbal aphrodisiac, but I still have no idea what's in it, other than my coffee beans and Voss's chocolate. She's keeping everything else to herself."

"Didn't you mention she discovered the active ingredients in India?"

"Yes, but I have yet to try it, and frankly, I'm skeptical about its potency."

"Well," Mike said, arching an eyebrow, "I'm happy to be your lab rat. Got any around?"

"I hate to disappoint you, but although Alicia has been hyping this thing online for weeks, the launch party is the first place anyone's going to try the stuff. She has me serving it up as a beverage, and to showcase its versatility as a flavoring agent, we'll have samples of mocha candies and bite-size pastries."

"Now you're turning cookies and cakes into aphrodisiacs?"

"Not me. All I did was share my chocolate and mocha recipes from the Blend. Alicia gave them to her chocolatier to make—Voss, the same Brooklyn boutique we've started buying from."

"I don't know, Cosi . . . sounds like those infamous Alice B. Toklas brownies."

"Don't you go looking for collars on my turf, Detective. Nobody's lacing anything with cannabis around here."

"Is that so?"

"Yes. In fact, Alicia claimed she was so happy with the results of my recipes combined with her product that she treated Madame and me to dinner last night so we could brainstorm more, which is exactly why my sketchbook is full of them."

"Cannabis-free?"

"So far. And by the way, the original Alice B. Toklas recipe was for fudge, not brownies."

"I hate fudge," he said.

"You do not. Your mother told me she made cherry cordial fudge for you every Christmas."

"Oh, chocolate fudge I'll eat. What I can't swallow is fudg*ing*—as in fudging statistics, fudging results, fudging the truth. Mathematicians call it a fudge factor—putting an extra calculation into an equation just so it will work out as expected."

"Fudge factor?"

"Yeah. It's what we law-enforcement types call a scam."

"Oh God . . ." The single word deflated me. "I just hope this aphrodisiac claim of Alicia's doesn't turn out to be one."

Mike paused, studied me. "You're not kidding?"

"What I am is worried."

"Why?"

"Alicia has been using my Village Blend beans, that's why. As soon as her product launches, everyone's going to know it. So if this Mocha Magic stuff tastes like *merde* or doesn't live up to its claims, then it's my rep on the line."

"Oh, sweetheart, no it's not. Your customers know how high your standards are. That won't change."

"Bad reviews can do a lot of damage, Mike, especially if her magic powder lays a big, fat chocolate egg."

"You're not the owner of this place; your former mother-in-law is."

"Madame may own this business, but she's leaving it to me and her son to run—and one day we'll leave it to our daughter. I'm also the master roaster here, not just the manager." I paused, took a breath. "Sorry. I just loathe not being in control."

"I know you do. It's how you're built. It's also why your coffeehouse runs smoother than the purr of a pampered kitten."

"That's nice of you to say, but—"

"But worrying isn't going to change anything, Cosi. You're fully on board with this thing. If it goes bad, you'll figure out the next step. You always do. In the meantime, try to trust the process."

"What I'm trusting here is my employer. I have no choice. Madame is the one who signed the contract with Alicia—months ago, as it turns out, without consulting me or her son. She just roped us into this thing . . ."

Despite my continual, borderline belligerent questioning, Madame had provided very few answers, beyond the vague explanation that Alicia was a dear old friend to whom she owed a great deal. (An NYPD detective I could handle. My former mother-in-law was another matter. The octogenarian took stonewalling to a whole new level.)

"Well, Cosi, like I told you," Mike said, reaching out and curling a lock of hair around my ear, "I'm ready to test the stuff when you are."

I smiled. "You'll get your chance. Tonight."

"Why wait?"

I laughed, but Mike wasn't kidding, and the veteran street cop had some tricky moves. In one fluid motion, he caught my wrist, pulled me flat, and rolled. Now I was pinned on the mattress, at his mercy for a long, slow, delicious kiss.

"Seems to me," I murmured, "you don't need an herbal stimulant."

"Do you?" he whispered, slipping his fingers beneath my henley.

Before I could answer, his mouth was covering mine again, kissing me so deeply that when he undid the button on my jeans, I had all the resistance of self-saucing pudding cake.

About then is when my cell phone went off, abruptly ending our tucking-in time. I might have ignored the darn thing, but the *La bohème* ringtone was adamant. My employer was calling.

"Madame?" I answered.

"Clare, thank goodness you picked up. You must come at once."

I glanced at Mike. "Come where? Your penthouse?"

"No, dear, you forget. After you left the restaurant last evening, I took a room here at Alicia's hotel so I could enjoy breakfast with her this morning."

"What's wrong?"

"Just come to the Topaz, room 1015. I'll explain when you get here. And tell *no one* where you're going, *especially* that nice police officer boyfriend of yours."

"Why not?"

"Honestly?" She lowered her voice. "It's a matter of life and death."

"If that's the case, call 911!"

"There's an issue."

"An issue?"

"Yes, you see . . . the situation is extremely delicate."

"But—"

"No buts. And no more arguing. Keep the *Closed* sign on our door and hail a cab tout de suite!"

Two

~~~~~~~~~~~~~~~~~~~~~~~~~~~~~~~~~~~~~

LEAVING Mike Quinn's big, warm body felt about as right as pouring a fresh-pressed pot of Ethiopian Yirgacheffe down the drain. He felt the same but (being the amazing man that he is) let me go without a grilling. He even agreed to come downstairs to wait for Nancy Kelly to show.

Nancy was my newest barista, an apple-cheeked twenty-something from "all over," as she put it, "upstate mostly"—rural was my guess since she was the only member of my staff who bragged she got up with the sun. (I wasn't about to let my regulars down, so I rang her.)

With the Blend squared away, I hailed a taxi and rocketed north. My neighborhood's sleepy lanes and ivy-covered bricks receded as Manhattan's jungle of glass and steel grew. Soon we were rolling into the maze of cutthroat commerce known as Midtown. We zigged, we zagged, and finally we headed east, toward Lexington.

A less glamorous avenue than majestic Fifth or stately Park, Lex made economic sense for the Topaz, a tasteful enough inn (only a few minutes walk from the Waldorf=Astoria, the UN, and Rock Center) with more reasonable rates for lengthy stays.

At this early hour, the lobby was practically empty, save one distracted clerk who barely looked up from his desk as I rushed the elevator and ascended ten floors. Racing down the hall, I found the shellacked slab of wood marked 1015, lifted my knuckles, and—

The door jerked open so fast I nearly pounded Madame's forehead.

"Clare! Thank goodness . . ."

It was just after 7 AM, the sun was barely up, yet my former mother-in-law was already smartly shining; her silver-white hair smoothed into a glossy pageboy; her high cheekbones lightly brushed the pale terra-cotta of Village flower pots. Even the hint of lavender on her eyelids perfectly matched the orchids printed on her silk, kimono-style robe, making her vivid blue irises appear their own mercurial shade of violet.

Clearly, this "matter of life and death" (whatever it was) had failed to rattle her. But I wasn't surprised.

"Survive everything," she once told me, "and do it with style."

The woman's fashionable aplomb was more than the product of a Parisian upbringing—or even the gently wrinkled chic of older New York ladies. All her life, Blanche Dreyfus had weathered countless personal storms, not the least of which was her family's escape from Nazi-occupied Paris. The harrowing flight had robbed the little girl of mother and sister, but she'd soldiered on.

Coming of age in New York, she found her bliss in the arms of Antonio Allegro, whose family had owned the Blend for a half century. Then Antonio died, tragically young, and Madame was left utterly alone with a boy to raise and a business to run (a clue to why she'd always treated the Blend's bohemian staff, and its motley bunch of customers, as family).

Later in life, she found a new mate in the wealthy French

importer Pierre Dubois. She lost him, too, but not her sturdy resilience—or her steadfast support of my beloved Village Blend, one of the oldest-remaining family-owned businesses in Greenwich Village.

For that, and many other reasons (especially her indefatigable support of my daughter), I loved her. Like the struggling actors, painters, playwrights, and musicians whom this woman had propped up or rescued over the years, I'd do almost anything for her, too, which was why I tried very hard not to be annoyed by her cryptic summoning.

"Alicia's inside," she told me. Stepping into the quiet hotel hallway, she pulled her room's door closed and leaned against it. "I thought it would be best if she stayed with me."

"This is about *Alicia*?"

"Yes."

"But this isn't her room?"

"No. This is my room. Alicia's room is down the hall. I didn't want her returning to it."

"Why not?"

"Alicia should tell you—in her own words."

I reached for the door handle.

"Wait, dear. I'll lead the way. She may need an interpreter."

"A what?"

"An interpreter. She's very upset."

"About?"

Madame took a deep breath, let it out. "She's innocent. Let me make that abundantly clear. Alicia simply is not capable of . . ." She closed her eyes, shook her silver pageboy.

"Of?"

"Murder," she whispered.

"Murder?"

Madame's eyes reopened and she grabbed my arm. "Let's take this inside, shall we?"

I nodded. (Finally, my curiosity trumped my annoyance.)

The room was standard-issue modern shoe box: Lilliputian bathroom off a truncated entrance hallway, double bed, dresser, flimsy desk, and an armoire holding a television. The color scheme was aquamarine, the kind of tranquil island shade that a Manhattan designer selects to help guests feel "cool and calm" (especially after they get a look at their bill—and the whopping hotel-room occupancy tax).

"Alicia?" Madame called in a soft singsong, as if addressing a nervous child (or excitable lunatic).

Draped in a loosely tied terry robe, Alicia's petite form was perched on the edge of the bed, facing a limited view (in more ways than one). The window was large, but only ten floors above Manhattan concrete it didn't frame much beyond the reflective glass of a modern office building.

"Clare is here," Madame crooned.

"Clare?" Alicia burbled. She turned, dabbed her eyes. "Thank g-goodness you've arrived. Come, my friend, sit down . . ."

My friend? I stiffened.

Over the past six weeks, this woman had been civil to me but far from warm—and she'd never, ever addressed me as *friend*. Before this moment, her treatment of me, a lowly shop manager (in her eyes), could best be described as mild condescension.

"Sit beside me, Clare, right here . . ."

Alicia patted the mattress. I ignored her direction and instead pulled over an armchair and positioned the seat opposite her—the better to see (and read) her face.

Although Madame claimed this woman was an old friend, even she wasn't sure of Alicia's age. (Fifties? Early sixties? I wasn't sure, either.) "Tasteful" plastic surgery was apparently involved, but whatever the contributing factors, Alicia Bower cultivated the sort of highly polished "urban executive" look that Esther, my most acerbic barista, referred to as *severely attractive*.

Favoring dark pin-striped suits, she typically wore her cocoa-colored hair in an angular flapper cut. Her flawless skin, pale enough for the undead to covet, appeared all the more milky with fresh-blood lipstick (vampiric overkill, if you asked me, but then I seldom wore any lipstick, so who was I to judge?).

A world traveler, Alicia lately resided in London, but I'd seen her type countless times in Manhattan. Her hyperpolish came off as intimidating, and she very well meant it to be.

On this particular morning, however, the soufflé had fallen.

Dried tears mottled sunken cheeks; her Dresden doll complexion had gone from cappuccino cream to sickbed blanched; and her usually perfect-as-plastic coiffure looked like a tangled crow's nest. What shocked me the most was her mental condition. Shaken and fragile, she had all the composure of a trapped chinchilla.

"Tell me, Clare . . ." She leaned closer, markedly widened her glistening eyes (to appear innocent?). "Madame mentioned you have close friends on the police force?"

I glanced at Madame. *You're kidding, right?*

Anyone who ran a business in Manhattan knew the entire town ran on favors. But no amount of *tucking in* an NYPD lieutenant (even a decorated leader of a task force) was going to get a suspect off a murder rap—and my former mother-in-law should have known that.

"Clare can *advise* us," Madame quickly interjected. "That's what I meant, dear."

"Well, before I can do any advising," I said, "I need to know exactly what we're dealing with. What in the world happened?"

"Tell Clare," Madame prompted.

"But that's the problem, isn't it!" Alicia blurted then her lower lip began to quiver. "I don't *know* what happened! That's the reason I need Clare's help!" With a mournful wail, she ripped a succession of tissues out of the box by her side and buried her face in the paper pillow.

I turned to Madame. *Okay, Ms. Interpreter—interpret!*

"The pertinent events began last night," Madame explained. "After our little brainstorming dinner . . ."

I remembered the meal well enough. Three of us, down-stairs, enjoying coq au vin and pot-au-feu in a little brasserie attached to the hotel. After my tarte tatin, I took off, leaving the two old friends chatting over French pressed Sumatra.

"Earlier in the day, Alicia had mentioned the brasserie's breakfasts were heavenly," Madame said. "Fresh-baked crois-sants, ginger-peach marmalade—"

"Strawberry-lavender jam and p-persimmon preserves," Alicia added. "J-just divine."

Madame nodded. "So I brought along a few things for an overnight stay and checked in. We hugged good night and Alicia went back to her room. Then she checked her mes-sages and found a business acquaintance had left her a re-quest for a meeting . . ."

"A business acquaintance," I repeated into the lengthen-ing silence. "A man? A woman?"

Alicia lifted her head. She burbled something. I looked to Madame.

"A man," she said flatly.

I turned back to Alicia. "So this man . . . he tried to mur-der you?"

"No!" She shook her head, began to sob. "He came up to my room and . . . well, he was quite attractive, you know? And we'd been flirting for a few weeks. Naturally, two adults, you know . . . we started to fool around . . . but I had s-so much wine at dinner, I m-must have j-just . . . *burble, burble . . .*"

I looked to Madame. "She must have?"

"Passed out."

"Uh-huh," I said. "And then what happened?"

Alicia threw up her hands. "That's just it! I don't *know* what happened! Something *must* have happened. But I slept through it!" She wailed again and buried her face back into the Kleenex cloud.

Madame patted Alicia's shoulder. "Calm yourself, dear, really . . . you must try. Your hotel room was dark when you woke, isn't that right?"

Alicia nodded, composing herself. "Dark, yes. The sun was up, but the curtains were drawn. I turned in the bed. Dennis was beside me. I reached out for him, and his skin felt so cold. And then I felt something sticky. I turned on the bedside lamp and then I saw . . ."

Her voice trailed off and Niagara Falls turned on.

Okay, that's it. Between Alicia's unremitting tears and this room's aquatic color scheme, I was beginning to get that drowning feeling.

Standing up, I faced Madame. "What's her room number?"

She handed me a key card. "Five doors down." She lowered her voice. "I saw the corpse myself. The situation appears quite serious for my friend here. You let me know what you think."

Ⓣhree

∿∿∿∿∿∿∿∿∿∿∿∿∿∿∿∿∿∿

Ⓟlaying people was easy, so astoundingly easy. Just tell them a story—the right kind of story, a story they want to hear. They'll swallow it whole and ask for seconds . . .

Five years ago, her suicide had been a rebirth—a new life with new people, new work, and a new identity. But she'd become more than a newborn marionette. Now she was the puppeteer, carefully pulling their strings, ultimately controlling the stage.

She glanced out the window, welcomed the strengthening light of the morning sun. Giggles bubbled up, as they often did, and she bit her cheek to quell them. Five years ago, on that railroad bridge, she'd anticipated sacrifice, challenge, pain. What she hadn't expected was the giddiness. Or the satisfaction.

Such sweet satisfaction!

She had never guessed what astonishing powers this new life would bring: the power to lie and manipulate; the power to be invisible and invincible; the power to dream, to plan, and finally to execute . . .

Ⓘ stepped out of Madame's room, into the carpeted corridor. Far down the hall I noticed a housekeeping cart, caught a glimpse of a slender woman with a dirty blond ponytail. Clad in the powder blue uniform of a hotel maid, she used a key card around her neck to slip into one of the guest rooms.

Other than her, the floor was deserted and deadly quiet. I moved along, passing complimentary newspapers, a half-eaten breakfast tray.

Five doors down, I halted. The metal handle looked clean (no blood, thank goodness). I pulled my henley's sleeve over the fingertips of my right hand. With my left, I dunked Alicia's keycard into the electronic slot. When the red light went green, I depressed the handle.

The door swung open easily. I took a step forward and shut it behind me.

Alicia had described waking up in a dark room and turning on a lamp, and there was indeed a dim light glowing somewhere inside.

From my position at the door, I couldn't see the bed, but I could see part of the window across the room. The heavy curtains were tightly closed, which only heightened the feeling of claustrophobic gloom.

In contrast, the air was sweet. A cloying scent seemed oddly familiar, yet I couldn't peg it. To my right, the bathroom door was half open, and I assumed the aroma came from a scented hair or beauty product.

I took a step along the short entrance hall and saw the edge of the bed. The coverlet and blanket were bunched up at the bottom. Another step revealed a naked pair of large Caucasian male feet. One more step showed hairy legs and finally—

Oh God.

The sight of blood sent me backward. The white sheets were saturated with it, dark red and appearing even darker in the dimly lit space. Dried now, the flow originated from the dead man. He was young (younger than Alicia, anyway) with a square-jawed cover-model face, a thick head of brown hair, and very long sideburns. His physique was long, too, and well muscled with weightlifter cuts and six-pack abs. His torso appeared shaved—all the better to show off his body-sculpting labors.

Unfortunately, Mr. Universe had performed his last rep. The twelve-inch carving knife protruding from his chest had seen to that.

I took a deep breath and swallowed down a bit of bile—along with the primal urge to flee.

"The man's no longer alive," I whispered to myself, trying to stay steady. "That's clear enough . . ."

His chest wasn't moving, and his complexion carried that "gray-white pallor of death" as Mike referred to it after one of his countless crime scene visits.

A medical examiner would do an autopsy before ruling on the time of death, but even in the dimly lit room, I could see his face, neck, and hands showed no signs of rigor mortis—the first parts of the body to register that morbid stiffness (according to Mike). Neither did they show any defensive wounds, which suggested to me that this man was killed in his sleep, probably within the last few hours. And *that*, among other things (*many* other things), would make Alicia a prime "person of interest" to the NYPD.

Of course, I didn't dare touch a thing, especially the body. I didn't move any farther into the room, either, but I did take a look around.

Alicia's laptop sat closed on the desk, a stack of files beside it. Her leather briefcase rested on the floor. A man's pants and suit jacket had been thrown over the back of a chair. The suit was a fine dark gray, expensive material that draped beautifully.

On the carpet near the base of the bed, Alicia's polished burgundy pumps were cuddled up to a large pair of scuffed leather loafers. On the bedside table, two empty martini glasses sat next to a vase of severely wilting flowers.

With a start, I heard sudden music—Mimì's tinny aria from *La bohème*. I pulled out my cell.

"Are you in?" Madame asked.

"Yes. I'm looking at the body right now."

"What do you think?"

"This is beyond bad."

"That's why I called you, dear. And an attorney. He's on his way."

"I'm coming back to your room to talk."

"Fine."

With a sigh I closed my phone. There was nothing more to do here, except say a silent prayer for the soul of this poor man—and Alicia Bower. Whatever she'd done (or hadn't done), a truckload of trouble was rolling her way.

Fearful of contaminating evidence, I carefully backed out of the room, then stopped. Remembering that maid at the end of the hall, I slipped my sleeve back over my hand and hung the *Do Not Disturb* sign on the outside handle.

I found my employer in her own room, pacing its stunted entryway. Alicia was now lying on the bed (in a fetal position), still facing the window, quietly sobbing.

I waved Madame into the bathroom and shut the door.

"Who is that man?" (Who *was* that man would have been more accurate, but she got my drift.)

"His name is Dennis St. Julian," she whispered. "He's a wholesale buyer in town for the ICE."

"The IC—?"

"The International Confectioners' Expo. It just kicked off at the Javits Convention Center. That's why Patrice Stone scheduled the Mocha Magic Coffee launch party for this evening—"

"Wait. Back up. Who's Patrice Stone? You never mentioned her before."

"Patrice is the right-hand girl to Aphrodite."

Madame wasn't actually referring to the Greek goddess. Alicia's boss was an enigmatic businesswoman known only by the name Aphrodite. Just a few years ago, she'd started a Web site called Aphrodite's Village Online.

The site began humbly enough as a chatty, informative little online catalog carrying products for women, focusing primarily on those interested in enhancing or improving their love lives and relationships.

Aphrodite found investors, added content, and ratcheted up the PR. Mentions in major newspapers, on television talk shows, and two Hollywood feature films catapulted the little product site into one of the most popular communities for women on the World Wide Web.

The site became so big that Aphrodite divided it into "temples," each one controlled by a different so-called Sister of Aphrodite. Much like the section heads of a magazine, each "Sister" was in charge of a different area of expertise: Health and Fitness, Travel and Leisure, Arts and Entertainment, Love and Relationships, and so on.

Alicia's temple of expertise was Food and Spirits, which was why her Mocha Magic Coffee was being given an international launch by Aphrodite. The woman and her company were essentially partners in the deal and cut in for a hefty share of profits, as well.

"Because of the ICE trade show," Madame continued, "a number of wholesale buyers are in town this week, looking for new products, and every last one of them has been invited to the Rock's Loft & Garden tonight to sample Alicia's Mocha Magic—and hopefully place orders."

"Okay. But that doesn't tell me why Candy Man had a date with a carving knife in Alicia's room. How long has she known this guy?"

"At the most, three weeks. He approached her in a downtown bar and they hit it off. I met the man myself last week, very briefly. He said he was originally from Long Island but based somewhere in the Midwest for the past few years—Missouri, I believe—but he travels quite a bit on business. He said he was ready to place a very large order for Alicia's new product."

"Why would he claim that when he hasn't even tried it?" I considered those empty martini glasses, sitting next to the vase of wilting flowers. "Has Alicia been using her aphrodisiac on him? Did she give him some last night?"

Madame frowned. "What difference would that make?"

"The man was stabbed. Through the heart. And appeared not to have moved. I think he was drugged."

"What does that have to do with who murdered him?"

"When the police see that crime scene, they'll *know* who murdered him!"

"*Shhhhh* . . . I told you. Alicia is not capable of murder. She did not do it."

"Okay, but you're not suggesting that I help you cover this up, are you? You know we have to call the police, right?"

"Yes, I understand." Madame exhaled. "You don't know Alicia like I do. The history we have."

"What history is that? I've asked you. But you haven't yet enlightened me."

Madame shook her head, studied the bathroom floor. For almost a minute she seemed lost in thought—or memories.

"Madame?"

"She worked as my barista for about six months."

"When?"

"A long time ago. Before you and Matt were married."

"Why didn't you ever mention her before? And why do you feel you owe her so much?"

"It's not something that I ever intended to share. And I . . . well, I don't wish to here and now." She lifted her gaze. Her blue-violet eyes were actually damp. "The counselor is on his way. In the meantime, won't you please help us, Clare? Tell the detectives that Alicia would never do a thing like this."

Oh man.

I didn't argue with her anymore. I just couldn't. Reaching into my jeans pocket, I gripped my mobile phone.

Four

Once I brought up my cell's address book, I began toggling through names—

Joy Allegro—my daughter. No. (Obviously.)

Mike Quinn—No. Not only was the man exhausted, he was no longer a precinct detective. The only thing he could do was advise me on who to call at the One Seven, and I already knew that.

I moved past my ex-husband, Matt, who'd been touring coffee farms in Indonesia, which put him out of cell phone range for weeks (as usual). I swept by my baristas—Tucker, Esther, Gardner, Dante, Vickie, and Nancy—blew by more names (acquaintances and suppliers). Finally, I came to the entry I needed and pressed the auto-dial.

"Lori Soles."

"Good morning, Detective."

"Clare Cosi, what are you doing calling me? Aren't you right upstairs?"

"You're sitting in my coffeehouse now, correct?"

"First cup of the day." She took a loud sip to make her point.

"I have a situation . . ."

Lori Soles and her partner, Sue Ellen Bass (together known around the NYPD as "the Fish Squad"), had worked out of the nearby Sixth Precinct for years. Both had become addicted to my Americanos, and both still stopped by for their fix every morning before heading north to work at the Seventeenth, their newly assigned precinct house in Midtown.

Soles listened to my brief description of the homicide and thanked me.

"We just had a court appearance rescheduled," she said, "and this sounds like it's worth an early start. Sue Ellen and I will call it in. You know the drill?"

(For a variety of reasons, Soles and Bass were under the impression I possessed a private investigator's license. Not even Mike Quinn had set them straight on that, and considering the situation, I didn't see it as a disadvantage.)

"I'll be seeing uniforms here first to secure the scene, right?"

"Right," said Lori. "Are you with the body now?"

"No, I'm in another room at the hotel."

"Well, smarten up, Cosi. Go seal the room."

"It's locked. And I have a *Do Not Disturb* sign on the handle."

"So what? Housekeeping has a pass key. You can't take the chance they'll honor a *Do Not Disturb* sign. Go babysit that DOA till we get there."

"No problem, detective. Thank you."

I hung up, reassured Madame, and hurried back to the crime scene before that poor maid with the dirty blond ponytail walked in to find more than used towels in the bathroom and no tip on the dresser. As I neared Alicia's door, however, my steps slowed. Just ten minutes prior, I'd made absolutely sure that Alicia's room door had locked behind me. Now it stood ajar.

Okay, this makes no sense.

A member of the hotel staff might have entered and left,

but wouldn't Madame and I have heard some kind of reaction? A scream? A shout? A frantic cry to call 911?

Taking a deep breath, I used the sleeve-covered elbow of my arm to push the door open a wee bit more.

I peered inside the dead man's room. I didn't see anyone or sense any movement. The place was quieter than a tomb, and if someone were inside, they certainly would have been making noise at the sight of a bloody corpse.

Despite the bright morning sun outside, the room was still gloomy, the heavy curtains drawn. A noise in the hallway—probably someone grabbing their complimentary newspaper—sent me hurrying all the way inside. I shut the door and stepped forward to check on my dead Candy Man.

Only there was no Candy Man. That's right. No corpse. No knife. No blood. The bed had been stripped down to the quilted mattress. The bloody sheets, the bunched-up blanket, and the rest of the covers were gone.

Four down pillows lay on the sea-green carpet like puffy white mushrooms. Their cases were gone, and so were the empty martini glasses sitting next to the vase of wilting flowers. Even that strange, cloyingly sweet scent had vanished. It was as if the whole scene had been erased—or hadn't happened in the first place.

I blinked, feeling slightly numb.

Knock! Knock! Knock!

The staccato raps gave me a start. They were so forceful I assumed the uniformed officers had arrived. No such luck. When I opened the door, I found a young woman towering over me. Her hazel-green eyes were slightly almond in shape. They widened at the sight of me, then narrowed down to slits.

"Who are you?" she said. "You're not supposed to be here."

"Who am I?" I so cleverly shot back. "Who are you?"

She was young, about my daughter's age (early twenties), her slender form coltish, her patrician face long and partially obscured by a fall of glossy, honey-colored hair spilling over one shoulder. Its golden color appeared even more striking against the dark backdrop of her charcoal pantsuit and shiny black raincoat.

We stared at each other a moment.

"Do you have the wrong room?" I asked.

She checked the number on the door and returned her sharp gaze to me. "Who *are* you?"

"My name is Clare Cosi. Your turn."

Instead of replying, Blondie brushed by me, entered the room, and stopped. For a few long seconds, she gawked at the vacant bed, her manicured hand moving to cover her gaping jaw.

"Where is he?" she whispered. "What happened?"

"Just what did you expect to find here? Did you know—"

"You!" She turned on me with one pointy French tip. "You're not supposed to be here!"

"You said that already."

In the hall another door opened and closed.

Blondie froze, listened.

"This is a crime scene," I said calmly. "The police are on their way. So if you don't want to talk to me, you can talk to them, all right?"

I thought that might encourage her to answer my questions—or at least prompt her to have an actual conversation. Instead, she grimaced and fled, elbowing past me so violently I nearly kissed the floor.

"Hey!" I shouted, regaining my balance. "Come back here!"

Of course she didn't. Nobody ever does.

FIVE

꩜꩜꩜꩜꩜꩜꩜꩜꩜꩜꩜꩜꩜꩜꩜꩜꩜꩜

I rushed out of the room, certain I could catch her at the elevator. But the coltish blonde was galloping in the opposite direction, the end of her patent leather raincoat fluttering like Black Beauty's tail.

"Stop!" I shouted.

"Clare? What's happening?"

I turned to find Madame standing in the corridor.

"Guard Alicia's room!" I shouted over my shoulder. "Tell the police where I'm going! Tell them she might be dangerous!"

"Where *are* you going?"

"I'm chasing that blonde in black!"

"Blonde in black!" Madame called. "What blonde in black?"

Looking ahead, I realized the woman had already turned a corner. I picked up speed. She was wearing stilettos. I was in low-heeled boots. It seemed inevitable I'd catch her. What I would do *after* I caught her, I'd have to improvise. (Tripping came to mind. Also holding on and yelling.)

One thing I was certain of: My simple mention of the

police had rattled that woman. She knew something about the butchered Candy Man, most likely something incriminating, and I wasn't letting a source like that get away.

As soon as I rounded the bend in the hall, I spotted the lighted *Exit* sign thirty feet ahead. After Blondie dove through it, I picked up speed, dodged that housekeeping cart, and caught the steel fire door just before it clicked shut.

On the stairwell landing, I stopped, held my laboring breaths.

Footsteps echoed below me.

I took off again, heading down. This was a service staircase, and I assumed it would lead to a kitchen, a store room, or some kind of back alley door at street level. As fast as I could, I continued descending. When I hit the fourth-floor landing, I heard a stumbling sound below, followed by a hissed curse.

Got you!

At street level, I tried the exterior door, but it was firmly locked. That's when I heard a new noise below me—a door opening and closing!

I hurried down two more flights, found an interior door marked *Staff Only.* Pushing through, I saw nothing but a green cinderblock wall, but the hot, dry air washing over me told me where I was—the hotel's laundry.

I turned sharply and raced down a long concrete ramp. The stinging stench of bleach and soap grew stronger; the whir of machinery louder. When I finally hit the bare concrete floor, I faced a wall of giant washers and spinning dryers.

Despite the glaring fluorescent lights, much of the room was shrouded by mobile ceiling racks. Acres of dry-cleaned clothes hung like the vines and fruit of a plastic-covered rain forest.

A half-dozen workers were busy at the far end of this huge basement. Much closer, a slender woman stood beside a massive laundry bin on wheels. Her back was to me, but I could see the blue housekeeping uniform and dirty blond ponytail. This was the same maid I'd seen on the tenth floor!

Encouraged that she might have seen the woman in black or noticed what had happened with the corpse in Alicia's room, I approached her. I doubted she could hear me coming with the noise of the washers and dryers. I didn't want to startle her. So I reached out and gently touched her shoulder.

She whirled to face me, and that's when I realized this wasn't a *she* at all, but a scrawny skeleton of a man with watery blue eyes, a yellow-toothed snarl, and enough chin stubble to cover a saguaro cactus. Around his neck was a long nylon rope with a key card attached.

Boy, does this guy look wrong. "You work here?" I yelled over the noise.

Immediately, he swung his fist, but I was already moving back from surprise, and his roundhouse just missed connecting with my left temple.

Before I could bolt, he brought his left into action—and there was more than a fist this time. A large, white object sailed toward my head. I dodged enough for the thing to wrap around one of the support poles for the dry-cleaning racks. The pole wavered, the rack trembled, and the dry cleaning swayed as the white thing burst open, scattering enough watches, rings, cash, iPhones, and gold jewelry to fill a Saudi prince's birthday piñata.

That's when I realized: the white thing was a pillow case; the booty inside was stolen; and the man in a maid's uniform was a hotel burglar. Somewhere in my chase, I had lost the Blonde in Black and ended up following this creep!

The burglar cursed. I turned to run, but after three steps the man body-slammed me into that gigantic canvas laundry bin. The brakes must have been on because the bin's wheels didn't budge. Before I could turn and fight, he grabbed my legs and pitched me into it. I tumbled down, hitting the wooden base with a solid clunk.

For a second, I saw little stars dance. As my vision cleared, I rolled over and found myself staring up at two aluminum doors in the ceiling—just as they swung open.

Oh crap.

Soiled laundry tumbled out of the chute, and an avalanche of damp towels, rumpled blankets, and wrinkled sheets came down on me. *That jerk pressed the release button!*

Furious, I tried to stand, but the crushing mass pushed me back to my knees. My arms windmilled, batting blankets aside, but the torrent of wool, silk, and cotton was too much. I was wrestling a textile octopus with a hundred tangling tentacles!

The whirring washers and dryers became muted, and my world grew decidedly smelly. Still, bad air was better than none. As the dark, suffocating pile grew heavier, I imagined an ignominious epitaph: *Beloved mother and coffeehouse manager smothered under a shroud of soiled bedclothes.*

Oh, hell no!

Forcing my muscles into locomotion, I dug and dug, struggling against the mass like a swimmer pushing through black quicksand. I didn't even know if I was making progress until I smashed my finger against the bin's canvas wall.

"Son of a—!"

Hand stinging, I managed to trace the rough cloth to the top of the bin and grasp the edge. Using one, fast-weakening arm, I pulled myself up. I knew I was close to breaking out when the noise from the machines grew louder. Finally, my head emerged, and I was out of the underworld, although my face was still covered with a used hand towel. (*Ugh.* I could still smell the shaving cream.)

Before I could swipe aside the white blind, I felt strong fingers wrap around my right wrist. Another hand gripped my left arm. I struggled, thinking the creep was back to finish me off, until the damp cloth fell away and I found myself staring into the faces of two young male police officers—one Caucasian, the other Hispanic.

The cops lifted me out of the laundry bin, set me down on shaky legs. As I sucked in gulps of bleach-tainted air, I noticed two more uniformed officers standing over the burglar.

The thief was on his knees, still wearing the maid's getup.

His hands were cuffed behind his back, his long, dirty blond hair released from its ponytail and dangling around his face.

"Are you okay, ma'am?" the Hispanic officer asked. His name tag read *Suarez*. "The elderly lady upstairs sent us after you. Looks like we got here just in time. I saw that perp assault you, toss you in."

"I'm okay," I said, wondering if he could hear my little croak over the noise of the washers and dryers. "Thanks for the help."

A big African-American officer, swinging a long nylon rope with a keycard attached, stood beside the prisoner. I remembered seeing that thing hanging around the burglar's neck. The big cop noticed me staring and flashed me a thumbs-up.

I blinked, still trying to get my bearings when I noticed the Caucasian officer talking on his radio. His name tag read *Grimes*. Suddenly, he turned to me, yelling over the noisy machines.

"Are you Clare Cosi?"

"Yes!" I told him, too loudly.

"I'm happy to hear that," Grimes said, looking relieved. "Because we've got a pair of seriously annoyed detectives waiting for you upstairs!"

"Okay, I'll go right up," I said. But then I stopped to consider that murky underworld of towels, sheets, bedding, and blankets from which I'd been resurrected.

"Ma'am? Is there something wrong?"

"Officer," I said, "would you look into something for me?"

"What?"

"Dirty laundry."

Six

~~~~~~

BACK on the tenth floor, I found Detectives Lori Soles and Sue Ellen Bass milling around the crime scene room as if it were the observation deck of the Empire State Building. The window curtains were fully open now, the morning sun streaming in.

"Why isn't this room sealed?" I demanded.

Detective Bass folded her arms and threw a withering glance at her partner. "Excitable, isn't she?"

Both women were dressed in beige slacks, white blouses, and sporty blazers—Lori's milk chocolate, Sue Ellen's bittersweet. They were acting true to form, too. If ever the Fish Squad pulled the old good-cop/bad-cop routine on a suspect, I had no doubt which one would play the heavy.

Right now Lori was shaking her short, yellow curls like a six-foot Raphaelite cherub while Sue Ellen's dark ponytail appeared to be lashed tight enough to qualify her as a model for Munch's *Scream*.

"Take it easy, Sue," Lori told her partner, then turned to me. "When we arrived, Mrs. Dubois admitted us. There's obviously no DOA here."

"But there was. Didn't she tell you that?"

"No," Lori said, "as a matter of fact, she didn't."

I glanced around. "Where is Mrs. Dubois?"

"She went back to her hotel room. A lawyer arrived to consult with her friend, and they're having a private conversation."

"Well, take my word for it," I said. "This is a crime scene."

Sue Ellen waved an arm. "Does this *look* like a crime scene to you?"

I took a breath, let it out. "Listen, I saw the body and so did Mrs. Dubois. What exactly did she tell you?"

"What she told us," Sue Ellen said, "was that she suspected there was some misunderstanding."

I blinked, shocked at Madame's equivocating. "There's no misunderstanding. I know what I saw—"

Sue Ellen smirked. "So you know the difference between the terms DOA and MIA?"

"My DOA *is* MIA—and I have no idea where he went!"

"Maybe he got up and walked away."

"That would make him a *zombie*."

"Not unheard of in this town, Cosi."

"Be serious."

"I am. You ever work Midtown graveyard? Try the Port Authority Bus Terminal at three AM—"

While Sue Ellen and I continued to battle (what passed for) wits, Officer Suarez appeared in the doorway and motioned Lori Soles into a huddle. When they broke, she was all smiles.

"We'll have to cut the Coffee Lady here some slack," Lori told her partner. "She just helped nab the Key Card Burglar! They're putting him in a sector car now."

Sue Ellen stared. "Pull the other one."

"No, it's true. The uniforms responded to our call. So it's our collar."

Sue Ellen's expression went dark for a second, but then a grin broke wide. "Nice going, Coffee Lady!" Her big hand slapped my back so hard I felt my teeth rattle.

Suarez nodded. "You two detectives are going to have some day. The whole city's been waiting for this case to break."

"Yeah," Sue said, "the brass'll be out for this one."

"Hold on!" I said. "The Credit Card Burglar is not why I called you two here!"

"Key Card," Lori corrected. "Don't you know about this guy? He's part of a ring that's been ripping off rooms all over Midtown—"

"But—"

"Your loo had a theory on the case, right?" Suarez asked.

Lori nodded. "With no sign of forced entry, our lieutenant figured the perp was bribing staff members at different hotels. The staffers would sweep through rooms with pass keys, picking up small, expensive items but not taking any risk of holding them or stashing them in their lockers—"

"Smart," Suarez said.

"Excuse me," I said.

"Instead," Lori went on, "they'd leave the stolen goods in one empty room where this guy would pick them up and walk them out. With this perp finally in custody, we should be able to take the entire ring down."

Sue Ellen nodded, dark ponytail swinging. "You bet."

"Hello! What about the dead man? There was a corpse in this room!"

Suarez gawked at me, along with the two Amazon detectives.

"Okay, Cosi," Sue Ellen said, hands on hips. "Produce the body."

I scowled up at the woman, ready to retort when Lori jumped in. "Sorry, Cosi. My partner's right." She gestured to the room and slowly shook her curly blond head. "There is no evidence that anything happened here."

Once again, Sue Ellen smirked. "Maybe the burglar stole the body."

"I saw what that burglar stole," I shot back. "A giant pillowcase full of it. And nobody runs down ten flights with two hundred pounds of dead weight on his back. Can't you canvass the floor, start knocking on room doors?"

Lori put her hand on my shoulder. Her big blue eyes went wide, sympathetic. "Calm down. We'll be canvassing guest rooms as a matter of course because of the burglary—and we're going to need your statement on what happened in the basement between you and the perp. Can you do a lineup for us?"

I held my head. "How long will that take?"

"Maybe two hours."

"Fine," I said, "whatever you need, but listen to this statement, okay? I saw a man's body in here. He had a carving knife in his chest, and there was blood all over the bed. A blond woman in a black raincoat came to the door. When I mentioned the police were coming, she ran. I chased her. She must have gone up the stairs instead of down—and I ended up chasing the burglar instead. I'm certain she'll have some answers if we can find her. She may even be an accomplice."

"Accomplice to what?" Sue Ellen asked. "The burglaries?"

"The murder!"

I threw up my hands. Something rotten had gone down here, and I was starting to formulate a theory. Alicia's polished pumps were still sitting on the carpet, but the man's scuffed-up loafers were gone, along with his clothes. The fact that the martini glasses were gone, too, made me look at that vase of wilting flowers in a whole new light.

I moved to the vase, picked up the flowers, and sniffed. "These stems smell like alcohol!"

Lori frowned. "Are you feeling okay, Cosi? You want to sit down?"

"There were two empty martini glasses on this nightstand," I told them as calmly, clearly, and *sanely* as I could. "Someone removed them, along with the body and the bloody sheets. But before that happened, someone else must have dumped alcohol into this vase. Why?"

Sue Ellen glanced at her partner. "Maybe they wanted their drink shaken, not stirred."

"Maybe the drink was drugged," I said.

"I didn't *want* the drink . . ." The voice was loud and cuttingly clear. Alicia Bower was back.

All of us turned to see her striding into the room, head high. Her loose terry robe was now tightly wrapped and firmly knotted. Her tangled short hair was combed smooth. Her face was washed clean of tear streaks; her sickly complexion dusted with enough peach blush to make a zombie look fit.

"Dennis St. Julian and I were business acquaintances," she explained with assiduous crispness (not one syllable burbled). I noticed her slight British accent had rejoined us, too.

"He rang me. I invited him up to my room. He brought mocha martinis from the hotel bar. I'd already had plenty of wine at dinner. Unfortunately, he insisted I drink it. I didn't wish to argue. Instead, when he began to disrobe, I simply dumped most of it into *that* vase—"

She flung out her arm and held it there, pointing to the end table in the sort of exaggerated pose I hadn't seen since I stopped watching daytime drama.

Lori Soles looked briefly at me then studied Alicia. "Was this Dennis St. Julian alive when you last saw him?"

"I woke up in a dark room," Alicia replied, slowly lowering her arm. "I was disoriented. I'm not sure what I saw . . ."

I noticed Madame had drifted into the room. Just behind her stood an older gentleman, briefcase in hand, a scowl on his face. This, I assumed, was the lawyer Madame had called, and he didn't appear happy with Alicia's making statements to the NYPD. What lawyer would be? But then, I realized, what choice did he have?

Clearly, Alicia Bower's inner executive had reemerged, most likely the instant she heard about Dennis's body disappearing (along with all the evidence), and she'd decided to "handle" the police herself.

When Alicia fell silent, Lori glanced at me again, pointedly this time.

I was dying to speak up—with questions, accusations,

critiques of Alicia's acting ability—but Madame's eyes were now mutely pleading for me to hold my tongue.

Fine, I thought, *I'll play along. But what the heck happened to the body? Not to mention the man's clothes, the martini glasses, and the bloody bedding?*

The answer came without my having to ask. Grimes, the officer from the basement, rushed into the room, slightly breathless, carrying a bundle of white sheets saturated with dried pools of burgundy.

"The bloody sheets!" I cried. "You found them!"

"In the laundry bin," Grimes said with a nod. "Just like you thought, ma'am. Only I don't think this is blood . . ."

"What?" I crossed to him, the detectives on my heels.

When I'd first glimpsed these sheets, it was at a distance, in a dimly lit room. Now the curtains were open, shedding light in more ways than one.

"You're right . . ." I told Grimes.

The stains felt sticky and smelled sweet. I pulled a swatch of the material up to my nose. The cloying candylike scent was the same aroma I'd noticed when I first walked into the room.

Finally, I recognized the stuff. I'd just used it in my own kitchen!

"This is corn syrup."

"Corn syrup?" Lori and Sue Ellen were now flanking me, handling the sheets for themselves.

"Are you sure?" Lori asked.

"I just used it last night on my chocolate-glazed hazelnut bars. Corn syrup is what gives the chocolate glaze the right consistency for drizzling."

"But corn syrup is clear, isn't it?" Sue Ellen countered. "This stuff is red."

"Because this is flour, corn syrup, and food coloring," I said, touching and smelling it more aggressively, "the recipe for fake blood!"

"And you know that how?"

"You've never heard of the Village Halloween parade? I

run a coffeehouse on Hudson Street! My assistant manager is an actor *and* I'm a mother. . . ." Joy's vampire phase was only eclipsed (pun intended) by a brief obsession with zombies.

"Okay," Sue Ellen said, turning to Alicia. "So that's it? The whole murder scene Ms. Cosi saw here was faked?"

"A prank?" Lori pressed, her big blue eyes carefully watching Alicia. Sue Ellen was watching, too.

I joined them.

With all of our gazes trained on Alicia, she appeared to be fighting for composure. I reconsidered the tale of Dennis St. Julian, the inconsistencies, not to mention the coltish blonde who came pounding on the door, acted authentically stunned at not finding him in bed, then bolted at the mention of the police.

"Alicia," I finally said, "please tell these detectives the truth. You thought the man in your room was murdered. You were frantic, and someone wanted to put you in that state. This was much more than a prank."

I caught her wince, but she quickly recovered, shaking her head. "This was all just a *misunderstanding*."

That word again! I faced Lori and Sue. "The timing alone is alarming. Tonight is an important launch party for Ms. Bower. A new product of hers is about to be presented to the press and an international group of wholesale buyers. I think someone was setting her up. I think someone—"

"Clare, please." Madame stepped forward, put a hand on my shoulder.

I knew she was unhappy with the direction of this conversation. The Village Blend was deeply aligned with Alicia's deal, and Madame, for whatever reasons, never appeared to trust the police.

But I did. Something criminal had gone down here—or was just about to—and I thought these detectives should be informed of it. When I turned to tell Madame this, however, she put her finger to her lips.

"À cheval donné on ne regarde pas les dents!"

I sighed, stopped talking.

Lori frowned at me, drawing her own conclusion from my limited facts, and moved closer to Alicia. "Have you received any mysterious phone calls or messages, Ms. Bower? Any threats? Has anyone made demands?"

"Of course not," Alicia replied, folding her arms.

"And you'd report them if someone did?" Sue Ellen asked, her tone dubious.

"Most certainly!" Alicia said, smoothing her robe before recrossing her arms, even more tightly this time.

"Do you want to file a report?" Lori asked.

Alicia waved the woman off. "Please . . . I don't have time for that. As Clare explained—against my wishes, I might add—I have a product launch to attend to. A year of work is at stake. Whatever . . . silliness happened here, we should all simply forget it ever happened."

Lori Soles shrugged. "All right, Ms. Bower. If you don't want to file a report, then our hands are tied."

Alicia forced a smile. "I thank you both for coming, and I'm so sorry that Clare put you to any trouble." She sent a pointed look my way.

Before I could retort (or lunge), Lori jumped between us: "It's our job to investigate. Here's my phone number . . ." She handed Alicia a business card. "Call me anytime, day or night, if anyone does attempt to threaten you or shake you down, okay?"

Madame touched Alicia's arm. "Let's go back to my suite, dear. We can order room service. You have a long day ahead, and you'll need fortification."

Alicia approached me before following Madame and the gentleman lawyer out the door. "No hard feelings, Clare. I realize you were *just* trying to help."

"I would still like to know—"

"I'll see you tonight at the launch party!" She waved as she whirled. "We'll talk more there!"

Sue Ellen waited for the women to leave before turning to me. "Well, Clare, all I can say is, *we're* very glad you called us."

"The Key Card Burglar. I know."

"No," Sue Ellen said, surprising me. "I agree with your concerns. Your client is definitely a target."

"My client?"

"Ms. Bower."

"Actually, I work for the other woman."

"Well, keep an eye on both of them," Sue Ellen warned.

"What do you think happened here?" I asked.

Lori and Sue Ellen exchanged looks. "We shouldn't speculate without more facts," Lori said. "But we can submit the contents of that vase for a toxicology test—just in case Ms. Bower does end up being shaken down."

"Thank you, Detectives. Thank you both for everything."

"No," Lori said, "you're the one we'll be thanking—and publicly. Are you ready to go down to the One Seven now? Do that lineup?"

"Sure."

As Lori instructed Suarez to treat the vase and its contents as evidence, Sue tapped me on the shoulder.

"One more question, Cosi."

"What's that?"

"I barely passed high school French. I can ask your name and order snails, but that's about it. What did Mrs. Dubois say to you?"

"*À cheval donné on ne regarde pas les dents,*" I repeated with a sigh. "I'm far from fluent, either, Detective. But she's said it often enough. And her son practically lives by it."

"And it means?"

"Loose translation: 'Don't look a gift horse in the mouth.'"

I didn't tell Detective Bass, but the grandmother who raised me also had a favorite saying—only she said it in Italian: *Vedo le tazze e senza café.* Loose translation: "I see the cups, but there's no coffee."

Well, I saw the cups, *and* I smelled something brewing. This morning's charge of murder may have vanished, but trouble was almost certainly heading Alicia Bower's way, and that meant my way, too.

Seven

THREE hours later, I was back in my coffeehouse, mainlining the tranquillity of an Athenian temple. The sun god was smiling through our spotless French doors, gentle flames danced in the exposed brick hearth, and caffeinated customers were quietly bowing over books, notepads, and laptops.

Our morning "crush" wasn't quite finished. Our tables were still crowded, but no ugly jam-ups were evident in the queue.

I have no idea what Wharton professors teach their aspiring administrators, but in my humble experience managing a business had plenty in common with raising a child. Case in point, one of my first shining moments of motherly pride was hearing my daughter's preschool teacher declare, "Joy is a joy!"

So, okay, my girl hasn't worn Hello Kitty underwear for two decades, but you just know you're doing something right as a mommy when your child behaves without your direct supervision; and you know you're doing something right as a manager when your shop runs like a high-performance sports car without your shouting when to change gears.

Esther Best was now actively engaged behind the espresso machine. Nancy Kelly looked confident at the register. Neither sight surprised me—Esther was on the schedule, and I'd called in Nancy.

What did surprise me was the sight of the six-two floppy-haired actor chatting with customers from behind my counter.

"Tuck, what are you doing here?" He wasn't scheduled to work until this evening. "Did you misread the schedule?"

"No," he said. "I called in to ask for a favor, but Nancy picked up and told me that you had a personal emergency, so I came on down to help out."

I squeezed Tucker's arm. "Thank you."

If our Blend crew was a family, then Louisiana-bred Tucker Burton was the responsible older brother. An actor-playwright and occasional cabaret director, he had an easygoing southern charm and showman's wit that made him as popular with our customers as the near-perfect God shots he pulled.

"Whatever your favor is," I told him, "consider it granted."

"Really?" he said. "I know we're short-staffed right now, but I need someone to take my shift next Friday."

"I'll work it myself."

"Oh, you're a peach!"

"More of a pear with these hips, but you're welcome. What's the occasion? Starting rehearsals for something new?"

"I have a hot date!" He beamed. "Punch has tickets to the Met and a friend in the chorus of *Cavalleria rusticana*."

"*Rustic Chivalry*," I translated. "Isn't that the opera Coppola used in—"

"*Godfather 3*. Indeed, it is."

"So if Talia Shire sits down next to you with a box of cannoli, you should—"

"Just say no. Very funny. But, really, Clare, given the smorgasbord of slayings in this town, there are worse ways to go than eating poisoned mascarpone while listening to a cute tenor sing 'Hail to the Bubbling Wine.'"

Tuck was right. There were worse ways to go—like a carving knife jammed into your chest while you slept off an aphrodisiac. *But where there's fake blood, there must be a fake knife, right?*

During my three hours at the Seventeenth, the Fish Squad let me know that nothing was discovered during the canvas of the Topaz guest rooms. No dead bodies, anyway. They'd found victims of the burglaries galore, which made their case. Personally, I continued to pray no corpse would turn up in the hotel Dumpsters.

"Excuse me, Tuck, you're keeping me from my art," Esther said, sidling around his lanky form.

Esther's hips were twice the size of mine, and her latte-arts skills nearly as lean and mean. With an effortless flick of her wrist, she poured a thin stream of textured milk out of a small silver steaming pitcher. As if by enchantment, a cloud-colored phoenix floated up from just beneath the backdrop of chocolate-kissed espresso shots.

After proudly sliding the hot café mocha to a young, pierced sous-chef from a nearby bistro, Esther acknowledged my presence with a nod.

"Good *almost* afternoon, boss," she said. "I understand an officer of the law is on the premises. I hope he doesn't distract you too much. We *do* have that party to cater tonight."

If Tuck was the Blend's dependable older brother, then Esther was its challenging middle child. With a figure as full as the old *Ziegfeld Follies* hotties, and wild dark hair either sculpted into a retro half beehive or ironed as straight as Vampyra (which she attractively librarian-bunned for barista work), she ruled the neighborhood as a local urban poetess and Goth icon.

She was also my best latte artist and a reliable draw for two distinct fan bases. The slam poets came to see her throughout the day, many of them NYU students, where she worked as a TA while completing her graduate degree (don't ask in what—she'd changed it two times already). After sunset, the rappers dropped by, many of them also rabid followers of her Russian boyfriend, Boris—a baker's assistant-cum-minor rap recording artist. (The happy couple had met at a slam poetry throwdown in Brooklyn.)

All of these friends and admirers tended to hang around the Blend for hours. Fortunately, they downed lots and lots of caffeinated drinks.

"Is everything okay, Ms. Cosi?" It was Nancy Kelly asking. Seeing me behind the counter, her young brow crinkled. "You sounded kinda frazzled on the phone this morning."

"Yes," I said, "I had to deal with . . . a situation. Thanks for coming in on such short notice."

"Holy smokin' rockets, Ms. Cosi, no problem! I was already up and rarin' to go anyhow!"

I smiled. Nancy was the newest addition to the Blend family. At close to her age, I'd moved to New York City with an equally effervescent outlook (most young people did). It took a year or so before the city's pinpricks collapsed most of their bubbliness.

The crowds, crime, and insidious corruption inevitably boiled down fizzy new excitement into firm guardedness. A few years more and any remaining youthful optimism was usually cooked into hard-crack cynicism. In my experience, though, the transplants who thrived in this town found a way to hold on to that inner Nancy. (At least that's what I tried to do.)

"Well, I appreciate the fact that you're an early riser," I told her. "I guess you weren't kidding when you said you rose with the chickens."

"Roosters, actually," Nancy said, then pursed her lips in a lemony frown. "You know it's those *males* who make all the dang noise."

"How now?" Esther sang, pushing up her black-framed glasses. "Is that a thinly veiled man bash I hear?"

"I guess."

"Does that mean your first night of New York clubbing didn't go so well?"

Nancy blew air out of her ruddy cheeks. Like me, she wasn't cover-model material, more sturdy than willowy, but she had the trustworthy complexion of a Vermeer Dutch housewife and the kind of generous curves that magnetized roving male eyes. Her baby-fine wheat-colored hair went well past her shoulders. At work she kept it secured in braids.

"I did meet a guy last night," she confessed. "But . . ."

After a lengthy pause, Esther planted a fist on her bountiful hip. "Hello! *But*s in stories are frequently followed by the best part, so please do dish, Ms. Kelly. I assume this guy was somewhat hot, right?"

"Smokin'!" Nancy's head bobbed. "I thought things were going great, too. Really great—until I asked him where he lived."

"You're kidding?" Esther said. "How bad could it be? South Bronx? Newark? That big metal trash bin in the alley behind Whole Foods?"

"The dude told me he lived in 'Alphabet City,' " Nancy explained, using her fingers to make little air quotes.

"Alphabet City." Esther nodded. "So?"

"Well, geez! I may be a newbie to this big ol' town, but I'm not *that* naive!"

Esther and I exchanged glances. *Okay, we're both confused.*

"Nance," I said, "what exactly do you mean by that?"

"I mean I got the hint! When a guy makes up a stupid, phony address, he's telling you to get lost. I felt like calling him out: asking him if 'Alphabet City' was near 'Conjunction Junction' or if Big Bird lived next door. But I didn't waste my breath, just picked myself up and left him cold in that chill-out room."

Esther made a moaning sound.

"What?" Nancy asked.

"That boy you met . . ." I said as gently as I could. "He wasn't channeling *Sesame Street*. There are avenues named A, B, C, and D on the Lower East Side of Manhattan. It's what New Yorkers call Alphabet City." (I left out the air quotes.)

The stricken look in Nancy's puppy dog eyes made my

heart ache. But then she bucked up and gamely waved a hand.

"Oh well. He wasn't all that hot, anyway. And he kept on showing off his stupid watch to me, bragging how much it cost. There are much nicer and hotter guys around. Like . . ."

Nancy's voice trailed off again, but I knew what she was thinking. In the four weeks she'd been with us, Nance had developed a fairly obvious crush on Dante Silva, another of my baristas. With self-designed tattoos on ropey arms, a shaved head, and the authentically sensitive soul of a true artist, Dante was what Tuck called a "coed magnet," which actually didn't hurt our bottom line. In addition to being an aspiring artist, Dante was also a very talented barista who learned the skill in his family's Quindicott, Rhode Island, pizza business.

Dante was either unaware of Nancy's feelings, or he was very good at pretending not to notice. The whole thing worried me as a manager. Frankly, I did what I could to schedule them on different shifts, although that wasn't always possible.

It was Esther who finally took Nancy aside and tried to talk some sense into the girl (something I wish someone had done for me at her age, during my long, hot, far-too-steamy summer in Italy with Matteo Allegro).

"There's a serious line of admirers waiting for Dante's attention," Esther had warned, "and right in front you'll find Kiki and Bahni, his two roommates."

"Which girl is Dante hooked up with?" Nancy asked upon hearing this news.

"Both, we think," Esther replied. "But none of us have actually asked. In New York it's sometimes better to adopt the 'don't ask, don't tell' policy."

"Boss, could you come here for a minute?" Tuck suddenly called.

He'd been chatting with an older customer at the end of the espresso bar. I'd noticed the man when I first came in, probably because the silver-haired stranger had claimed Mike Quinn's favorite barstool.

Mike told me he preferred the seat because with one quick half turn, his back was protected by the wall, and he had a view of the entire coffeehouse, including the spiral staircase to the second floor, and the front door. (Such was the fiction of a coffee "break" for an officer of the NYPD.)

I got the same hypervigilant vibe from this older man.

"What's up, Tuck?"

"This is Mr. . . . . Sorry, I didn't catch your name?"

"Bob," the man said.

Even sitting down, he impressed me as tall with a highly sketchable profile: prominent nose, jutting jaw, and the sort of interesting crevices that begged further exploration. He seemed solidly built for his age (late sixties, seventies maybe?). His eyes were bluish gray, an autumn sky before a storm, with unruly white brows suggesting the wisdom of Socrates.

I would have warmed to him immediately apart from two things: his scrutiny for one. That stormy gaze was boring into me like a TSA agent with an itchy Taser finger.

The bone-colored scar was my other concern—the jagged line mapped a path from his left ear, across part of his cheek, disappearing somewhere under his chin. While some kind of accident might have caused the faded wound, I couldn't help flashing on my childhood in western Pennsylvania, where I'd worked in my *nonna's* little grocery.

Behind a thick curtain in back of the store, my pop ran a quiet bookie operation. Clients were mostly neighborhood people, factory workers, and little old men. But every so often, a thuglike character moved through our aisles, sporting a scar similar to this man's—the cause, invariably, was not from a factory mishap or motorcycle accident but the business end of a switchblade in some barroom scuffle.

"Your Americano is excellent," Bob declared.

The man's lined face shed decades when he smiled. He looked far less intimidating, too.

"Thanks," I replied, happy he'd noticed. (Few people realized how tricky the drink was to get right.)

"It's the best I've tasted in over twenty-five years."

Now I was smiling. "We try to put love into every cup."

"I'm glad to hear that's still the case."

Still the case? I glanced at Tuck.

"Bob has a few questions about the Blend. I thought you should answer."

I extended my hand. "It's nice to meet you. My name is Clare."

"Clare," he said in a gruff tenor. "I've always loved that name. I had a sister named Clare . . ."

His accent was stronger now, Brooklyn—but not Yuppie Brooklyn where Manhattanites flocked to buy artisan pickles and microbrewed beers. Working-stiff Brooklyn, areas like Coney Island and Bensonhurst. On the other hand, his camel hair jacket, finely woven shirt, and high-end watch implied an address other than those immigrant-packed 'hoods.

"I haven't been here for twenty years or more," he said, "but I remember this place well. I was wondering if it's still a family-owned business."

"The Allegro family still owns the Blend, and if I can help it, someone from the family always will."

His eyes sparkled. "I take it you're a member of the family?"

Was. Past tense. By marriage. I could have said as much, but the man's continued scrutiny was making me uncomfortable.

"Did you know Antonio?" I asked. "Or Madame?"

"Madame?"

"Madame Blanche Dreyfus Allegro Dubois," I said.

The sparkle faded, the lines returned. "So, she's married again."

"Widowed, for a second time, I'm sorry to say." I leaned closer. "Listen, I'm sure Mrs. Dubois would love to speak with you. Why don't you tell me your last name. Bob—"

"Clare!" Tuck was calling me again. I hadn't noticed he'd stepped away. "Sorry, but our Chocolate Nun is on the phone. She has a delivery issue."

"Excuse me," I told Bob.

"Chocolate Nun" was the nickname for Gudrun Voss, the young proprietress of Voss Chocolate. *New York* magazine gave her the moniker in a piece it had done a few months back. While "chef's whites" were traditional, Gudrun's daily uniform consisted of a black chef's jacket and chocolate-colored Kabuki pants. The black garb combined with her austere personality and zealous focus on bean-to-bar quality had inspired the reporter to come up with the Homeric epithet.

I'd never met the "Chocolate Nun" face-to-face and still didn't know much about her. Even the magazine piece included little about Gudrun Voss's background, focusing instead on her Williamsburg factory as part of Brooklyn's artisanal food movement.

Picking up the phone, I was relieved to hear Gudrun had no problem getting the pastries and chocolates to the party tonight. All she needed from me was the direct phone number of the catering kitchen at the Rock Center event space.

By the time I finished the conversation, I was even more curious about Bob's questions. But when I moved back to the counter, Mike's favorite barstool was empty, the elderly stranger gone.

I checked my watch. It was time for me to go, too. I needed to shower and change. Even more pressing was that important meeting Mike had mentioned at the break of dawn. I'd promised to caffeinate him up for it.

Moving to my espresso machine, I went to work.

EIGHT

~~~~~~

GIVEN the events of my morning, I couldn't wait to see a male body lying on sheets that were *not* covered in fake blood. When I walked into my bedroom, however, I found the four-poster empty.

Like silver-haired Bob downstairs, Mike Quinn had gone missing. His clothes and shoes were still here. So was his weapon. I could see it peeking out of his shoulder holster, which was still hanging from the back of Madame's Duncan Phyfe chair.

"Mike?" I called, stepping into the hallway.

Before I could tap on the bathroom door, it swung open. The man himself filled the frame. His hair was damp and slicked back, his skin shimmering with shower dew. Around his hips, he'd tucked one of my fluffy white bath towels.

Forcing my attention away from the glistening slab of naked cop, I focused instead on King Kong (what my staff called the largest cup we stocked).

"Here you go," I said, lifting the twenty-ounce behemoth. "The Blend's Depth Charge for your eye-opening pleasure."

The King Kong DC was a triple espresso poured into a giant Breakfast Blend—essentially a java boilermaker. It was also the highest-caffeinated drink we served. A café in Brooklyn actually slung a ten-shot espresso they called the *dieci* ("ten" in Italian). The café's customers dubbed it "porn in a cup," but I refused to carry a similar monstrosity.

Back in art school, one of my professors had impressed me with his love of ancient Greece, whose citizens had inscribed *Nothing in Excess* on their great shrine of Delphi. Certainly Athenians would have *poo-pooed* the *dieci*. But my objection had less to do with a philosophy of moderation than a base-line of quality: by the time the fifth double was pulled for the beverage, the espresso's *crema* and texture were completely destroyed.

So, okay, our super-large speedball wasn't the sort of drink coffee connoisseurs ordered, either. Consumers of it veered toward the bleary-eyed NYU law student, night-shift beat cop, and overworked RN—but we had our standards.

Mike set down the razor he was holding and knocked back almost half of the twenty-ouncer (a feat in itself).

"Your hazelnut bars are on the kitchen counter," I said, thinking how sexy his hair looked wet. Probably because it appeared darker, which seemed more dangerous. (Stupid? Yes. But who can argue with libido?)

"Thanks," he said, and raised the giant cup. "This is outstanding."

I smiled. "I thought I'd find you in bed."

He arched an eyebrow. "Disappointed?"

"Yes. I am."

"Well, no cause for that. You found me didn't you?"

He leaned down. I backed up. "Sorry," I said, stiff-arming him. "As much as I'd like to, the morning I had was . . ." I shuddered, thinking of that laundry bin. "I need to clean up."

He laughed and tugged back the wet shower curtain. "Tub's free."

"Oh no. Not with you in here shaving."

"You don't trust me to control myself?"

I looked him over, sighed. "It's not you I'm worried about."

"Well, okay. Now we're talking."

"And that's *all* we're doing. You have an important meeting, and I have an endless day ahead."

I turned to leave. He caught my arm. "Stay. Keep me company." He threw me a sweet leer. "You can keep your clothes on."

"Gee, thanks."

"You're welcome . . ." He flipped on the hot water. I leaned against the doorjamb, watched him lather up.

The shaving kit was Mike's, of course. He kept personals here just as I kept things at his place.

"So . . ." Mike said, as he rinsed his razor. "What was that urgent call about?"

"Call?" The last thing I wanted to discuss. "Oh, nothing," I said, making *nothing* sound lighter than pink cotton candy. "No big deal. Not important."

Mike turned, met my eyes. "You're actually trying that with me?"

So much for playing a man who interviews perps for a living. I cleared my throat. "Madame and Alicia—they had a . . . problem." *There, that was true.*

"What problem? Clare, what exactly did you deal with this morning?"

"Deal with? Well, let's see . . ." *A disappearing dead body, a skeevy hotel burglar, two agitated detectives, and a wildly duplicitous business associate.*

"It really just boils down to advice. The women needed to speak with someone who had friends in the NYPD."

He stared. "Am I going to owe someone a major favor?"

"No. Actually, it's the other way around. Two gold badges now owe me one."

Soles and Bass had received so many handshakes and back pats at the Seventeenth you would have thought they'd brought in all ten of the FBI's most wanted instead of some two-bit hotel bagman.

"Okay." Mike appeared relieved—and intrigued. "You're going to fill me in on the details later, right?"

"Yes, of course, when you don't have a meeting with the first deputy commissioner to make." I tapped my watch and he went back to shaving. Then his gaze found mine in the mirror.

"I can't wait to hear who owes you this favor." His eyes were smiling.

"You seem in good spirits, considering what you told me this morning."

"That's because I was conflicted earlier this morning. Now I'm resigned."

"To what?"

"Resigning."

"Excuse me?"

"The way I figure it," he said, "the Fourteenth Floor already knows how this story is shaping up in the press—"

Mike was referring to the police commissioner's office, which was located on the fourteenth floor of One Police Plaza—a location he also called the "Puzzle Palace." (I always thought "Puzzle Palace" was what soldiers called the Pentagon. "They do," Mike once explained to me, "but when New York cops use it, they mean police headquarters, especially when NYPD administrators issue politically motivated directives that are a complete puzzle to the rank and file.")

"Just to be clear," I interrupted. "This news story you're talking about—it's that young artist, right? The one who killed himself yesterday by jumping into his own painted bull's-eye on a Brooklyn sidewalk?"

"Yes. My guess is . . . the commissioner's people have been monitoring incoming questions from the press. The angle could be bad."

"In what way?"

"The press could be gearing up to spin the NYPD as the big villain of the story."

"I don't understand. How can you be the villain?"

"My guys were the ones who handled the kid after his fiancée died of a drug overdose. Sully and Franco were the ones who nailed him down as a key witness against a Jersey drug dealer doing business in our jurisdiction, and they'll be the ones accused of mishandling the boy."

"Mishandling?"

"Pressuring, harassing, coercing—driving him to suicide."

As Mike dragged the razor across his cheek, I took a breath.

"They didn't, did they?" (I hated asking, but I had to know.)

Mike's body went rigid. "I went over everything, Clare, all night long. Every report, every statement, every phone call and follow-up. Franco and Sully did everything right. They called in Social Services for the kid, offered him witness protection—which he declined. They took his statement, left him their phone numbers, and moved along."

"But this morning you said there was something that concerned you about their interview."

"The kid's timeline, that's all. I needed firmer statements from him on the fiancée who OD'd—exactly when she'd taken the drugs he'd bought for her, how long he'd been making purchases, and more specifics as to how and where the purchases were made. He'd answered all of that on the initial interview, but his statements were too vague. I needed more to launch official surveillance and an undercover sting. At the time, right after the girlfriend's death, Franco and Sully simply didn't want to push the kid too hard."

"They did everything right," I quietly echoed.

"They did. So if the first deputy commish wants a head, he can have mine."

"What does that mean?"

"I'm volunteering to step down as head of the squad."

"Mike, no! You love your job."

"I'm not passing the buck, Clare. I can't live with that."

"Can you live with a demotion? A public censure?"

"It won't be public. We did everything right, and the Fourteenth Floor isn't stupid enough to open us up for a raft of civil suits, although that usually happens anyway. This is internal stuff I'm talking about. I'll still be on the force. I'll just be reassigned to precinct work, probably Siberia. Some outer borough desk—"

"I can't believe your captain would let that happen!"

Mike's laugh was sharp. "My captain was the one who told me to take this meeting solo. He expects me to offer up one of my crew to the political gods. That's why I came in here so wrecked. But then I slept on it, and when I woke up, I had my answer. I don't have to sacrifice anybody's career but my own."

"Mike, no—"

"That's it. My decision's made."

I wanted to talk him out of it, but I couldn't think how. Then my pocket started ringing. "Listen, there must be another way—"

"Answer your phone, Clare." He gently squeezed my shoulder. "I'll see you at the party tonight. I've got to get going."

As he moved toward the bedroom, I pulled out my cell, checked the screen to see who was calling—although I really didn't need to, the *La bohème* ringtone was signal enough.

I had so many questions (not to mention unbridled *rants*) for my former mother-in-law, I didn't know where to start. I took a breath, let the call go to voice mail, and stepped into the bathroom.

A long, hot shower, that's where I start.

Nine

PLANNING *was overrated. She knew that now. The goal itself was paramount.*

"Unexpected hurdles may spring up tonight," she whispered to the image in the bathroom mirror, "but you must remain calm, evaluate quickly, counter with flexibility . . ."

Her first execution had taught her that.

She'd written out everything three years before—details worthy of a textbook flowchart. The result was a rough job at best. Stealing that van, for instance, had been harder than she thought, then pacing the judge's SUV, lining up the accident . . . so much had been trickier than she'd anticipated. Luckily, on winter nights, most of the roads around the country club of Bay Creek Village were dark and empty.

With the "fatal crash" coming down as little more than a fender bender, improvisation became the order of the day. Idling the engine on the stolen van, she waited for just the right moment. When the judge stumbled out of her banged-up vehicle, down went the gas pedal!

The morning news called it an accident, "a terrible, tragic, hit-and-run . . ."

Boo-hoo *for the judge's husband and family—the same family that cared not a whit about the fate of her own!*

By the next day, the idiot box was spinning the story another way: "Police are investigating the suspicious hit-and-run that killed longtime Long Island judge . . ."

"The authorities," *she was continually told, were* "actively looking" *for the driver.* "Was it a tragic accident?" *the anchor posited.* "Or a premeditated act of vengeance?"

Day after day, it went on. She'd been sick in the bathroom for most of it. The police were going to find her! She was sure of it. They would drag her to prison like her poor mother!

But no one came for her. No one. And the relief was transcendent . . .

She waited after that—an entire year. Then she struck again, her very own act two. The second kill had been as problematic as the first, but she'd succeeded.

Once more, subsequent news reports seemed unfair, relentless, at times even ridiculous, but there was no getting sick in the bathroom. For some reason, she found the second evacuation much easier to swallow.

No one came for her, of course, and she felt even freer to do as she pleased. Still, she wasn't stupid. She went back to waiting, this time even more than a year . . .

And now the waiting was over.

The world was her stage again, her theater for new trials. "Tonight," *she confided to the mirror.* "Tonight begins act three . . ."

ten

~~~~~~

"**I** can't believe you slapped me!"

Esther glared at Tucker, shaking her reddening hand, though she managed to hold on to the cookie she'd purloined from his silver tray.

"If you touch *another* Cappuccino Kiss," Tuck warned, "I'll whack your fingers again."

"There's no *another*. That was my first."

My two senior baristas had been bickering since we got here. Happily, there were no witnesses. Arriving guests were immediately ushered into the rooftop Garden while we set up inside.

And where was *inside*, exactly? The seventh floor of a sky-scraper in the legendary Rockefeller Center, a sprawling complex in midtown Manhattan, home of the GE Building and NBC television.

I had to admit, Alicia chose an impressive address to launch her new product. Crowning this art deco tower was "the Top of the Rock," a multistory observation deck, some-what lesser known than the Empire State Building but with equally breathtaking panoramas. Down here on the seventh floor, the Loft & Garden served as a popular space for society weddings and corporate parties. On the east end of this glorified rectangle sat the open-air Garden. It boasted a fountain and reflecting pool. At the west end was the Loft interior with floor-to-ceiling windows and space enough for a reception of two hundred.

As twilight deepened into darkness, the tall windows treated us to views of Radio City's neon marquee and the fairylike lights of Rock Plaza's courtyard, where a bronze-cast statue of Prometheus attempted to offer the gift of fire to oblivious tourists strolling below.

From what I remembered of the Greek myth, in repayment for Prometheus's heroic act of bequeathing fire to humankind, Zeus ordered him chained to a rock where an eagle visited him daily to dine on his liver.

No good deed goes unpunished sprang to mind. Mike occasionally muttered the aphorism in reference to police work.

Today I knew why.

Mike's visit to the NYPD's version of Mount Olympus was certainly over by now, but he had yet to return my call. With every passing hour, I worried a little more. Sure, Mike sounded firm in his decision to protect Sully and Franco by resigning, but that was only in theory. In my experience, hard facts hit you in the face with a whole lot more impact than airy little theories.

So where was he now? I wondered. *Is he with his squad? Or in some pub across town? Did he seek out some shoulder (other than mine) to cry on?*

Punishment for good deeds, or at least good intentions, had me reconsidering my own morning. After my long, head-clearing shower, I'd returned Madame's call, absolutely insisting on straight talk. Thank goodness, she agreed. No more equivocating.

Like me and the Fish Squad, Madame believed Alicia had been targeted for some sort of nefarious scheme. She even volunteered to question the woman, but I'd specifically asked her to get Alicia here early so we three could hash things out. At this late hour, my calls went unreturned, and I had yet to see either lady.

I was beginning to feel like Prometheus's brother, Atlas, whose bronze likeness was power-lifting a weighty sphere on the other side of this complex. With my own worries heavy on my shoulders, I focused instead on that universally acknowledged painkiller . . . *chocolate*.

Like the Greeks and their theory of fire, the Aztecs thought of chocolate as a gift from a god, one who'd stolen the cocoa tree from paradise and delivered it to us mortals on the beam of a morning star.

I could see Esther appreciated her little bites of heaven as much as I did. Glancing back to my senior baristas, I noticed Tuck explaining why he'd slapped her hand.

"Sorry, but I was counting. That was your *third* kiss."

Esther's response: "Nah-*ahh*."

Hands on hips, Tucker faced her. "Did I just hear the Dark Princess of street poetry murmur the astoundingly jejune phrase 'nah-ahh'?"

Esther smirked. "When you fail to amuse, I'll disabuse. You don't inspire . . ." She snapped her fingers. "You tire."

"Hey, you two," I called, attempting to derail this hip-hop train before it fully left the station. "Tell me how this looks!"

I had just finished placing two hundred shot glasses filled with triple-chocolate *budini* on a miniature staircase of blue-hued ice. The chilly steps were a dramatic way of keeping the creamy Italian puddings fresh. They circled a frozen-water sculpture of Aphrodite—your basic, armless, Louvre Venus de Milo rendered as Giant Popsicle.

I'd recommended the *budino* to Alicia as an alternative to gelato, which never would have held under these circumstances. Of course, chocolate, sugar, eggs, and cream weren't its only ingredients. Like everything else we were serving, the treats were laced with Alicia's Mocha Magic Coffee "love" powder.

Tucker and Esther, who'd been filling silver trays with

goodies, now turned to offer their *oohs* and *aahs* at my frosty staircase of passion-inducing pudding shots. Then Esther went back to munching her stolen kiss and Tucker returned to fixing the chorus line of cookies she'd disturbed.

Their verbal sparring ceased, but Tuck couldn't stop himself from pointing two fingers at his own eyes before thrusting them at Esther.

"I'm watchin' you, girl," he said, playing up his Louisiana twang.

Esther pulled her serving glove free, pushed up her black-framed glasses, and stuck out her tongue. Then she snatched a piece of broken tiramisu bar from the "damaged goods" bowl and waved it in the air before popping it in her mouth.

"Chill, you two," I warned.

Esther faced me, mouth full. "I'm out," she garbled then swallowed. "What next?"

"More's coming." I pointed across the room to Nancy Kelly, who was wheeling a stainless steel bakery cart our way.

"Holy smokin' rockets!" she cried. "Those cute little ice steps are really something!"

"What's that?" Esther slid her dark frames down enough to peer at Nance over them. "You didn't have ice back in Yokelville?"

"We didn't have ice stairs, except maybe in the winter," Nancy replied honestly.

"Where *are* you from exactly?" Tuck asked.

"All over. I come from a lot of places."

"Where they get up with the chickens, apparently," Esther said.

"Roosters."

"Which implies Nancy actually kept chickens."

"Why should I tell you anything!" Nancy threw up her hands. "All you guys ever do is make fun of me."

"We're not making fun of you," Esther said. "We're alternately appalled and yet charmed by your bumpkin ways."

Tuck waved a gloved hand. "Don't sweat it, honey. All

newbies get tortured. When I first came to New York, my bayou accent earned me so much ribbing I tasted barbecue sauce."

"How did you get it to stop?"

"Simple, sweetie . . ." He snapped his fingers. "I stuck."

"To what?"

"To doing what I came here to do. When you stick around long enough, you become a New Yorker. It's inevitable—although you do have to hold on tight."

"To what?"

"Oh, I don't know. Your dreams, your soul, your sanity . . ."

"It's like that sign you read before you get on an amusement park roller coaster," Esther said. "Secure your belongings."

"You'll see," Tuck added, "unless you beat it for a kinder, gentler burg. Believe me, there are plenty—but none as exciting . . ."

I didn't say anything to counter Tuck and Esther, mostly because I agreed with them. New York was a glorious town filled with memorable thrills, but like any carnival coaster enduring the dips required gripping the bar with everything you had.

"Oh, wow!" Esther pointed to the tray I'd pulled from the bakery cart. "What do you call these?"

"*Gianduia*," I said. "It's a lovely brownie named after a hazelnut-chocolate invented a few hundred years ago in northern Italy. We also have a tray of *gianduia* fudge."

Esther blinked. "Za-*do*-ka? Like bazooka only with a *z* in front?"

Nancy shook her head. "It's Zudoku, almost like the game."

"No, no. It may start with a *g*," I explained, using the appropriate Italian arm gestures. "But you pronounce it zhahn-*doo*-yah."

Esther munched one of the chocolate triangles and rolled her eyes. "Ohmigod, it's so delicious, rich and chocolaty, moist and chewy, with the most perfect toasted hazelnut finish, but . . ."

"It's *gianduia*, Esther. How can there be a 'but'?"

"Listen, boss lady, trust someone whose grandfather turned the name Bestovasky into Best: this particular treat needs a reassessment of nomenclature."

"Excuse me?"

"The name should roll off the tongue, not tie it into knots." Esther took a second bite, stared off into space. "What do you think of Cocoa Hazelnut Bliss? Or . . . I've got it! Brownies Italiano!"

"I like that name!" Nancy cried. "Brownies Italiano sounds really cute."

I stared.

Esther folded her arms. "Okay, maybe not."

"Maybe Ms. Cosi's right," Nancy said. "The name kind of reminds me of Nanaimo bars. It's a weird name for a dessert, but nobody in Canada has a problem eating them!"

"Nano-*what* bars?" Esther said.

"Nun-EYE-mo," Nancy repeated. "They're a no-bake bar cookie, yummy stuff. They're a little like Ms. Cosi's tiramisu bars."

"Good call, Nancy," I said. "Nanaimo is exactly what inspired me to make a bar version of tiramisu."

Esther squinted at Nancy. "So now you're from Canada?"

Nancy shrugged. "Like I said, I'm from all over."

"I am *completamente finito*!" Tucker interrupted with a Fred Astaire soft-shoe shuffle.

One glance at his section of the display and I could see why he was celebrating. With a field of Cappuccino Kisses and Chocolate Espresso Saucers as his canvas, Tucker used the lighter-hued Hazelnut Latte Thumbprints to create a series of interlocking hearts across half of the samples bar tables.

"We're pushing an aphrodisiac, right?" Tuck said. "So I thought, let's go for it!"

I smiled. "Really amazing."

"Neato," Nancy chirped.

"Not bad," Esther said with a sniff.

"It's simple stagecraft," Tuck said. "Five years of HB Studio classes taught me to strut across a stage and dress one, too."

I checked my watch. Most of the guests would have arrived by now. The Garden presentations should be starting any minute.

"We have about thirty to forty minutes to finish our work," I warned.

"Well, the urns of water are hot. I can start the coffee brewing," Esther said, "or whatever a coffee powder does while *real* coffee is brewing."

"It's too soon," I said. "I want the beverages served as fresh as possible. I'll give you a five-minute warning on preparing the thermal carafes."

"Fine," Esther said. "Do you guys need help with anything else?"

I looked around. "The tiramisu bars are laid out. The *budini* are bu-done, and Tuck took care of the cookies. All that's left are the Ganache-Dipped Chocolate-Chip Cookie Dough Bites, the Mocha-Glazed Rum Macaroons, and the candies."

"My God, woman!" Esther exclaimed. "They're not just 'candies'! They're Voss chocolates! Mini masterpieces. Where are they? What did they send?"

"Calm down," I said. "They're right here."

The top half of the bakery cart held black, glossy boxes. Esther, Tucker, and I carried them to the serving trays and peeked inside.

"Petit Nibs!" Esther yipped.

"Baby chocolate bars with crunchy cocoa nibs," I explained to Tuck and Nancy. "The chocolate in these is seventy-two percent cocoa."

"Hearts of Darkness!"

"These are intense," I warned. "Eighty percent cocoa."

"Mocha-Mint Squares!"

"Flavored with white crème de menthe and our espresso."

"Caramel Latte Cups!"

"Quarter-sized cups of milk chocolate laced with Village Blend espresso and liberally drizzled with *fleur de sel* caramel."

"Chocolate-Dipped Cinnamon Sticks! Be still my heart!"

I smiled. They were one of my favorites, too. Placed on the tongue, the treat delivered a sensual, sensory experience of quality chocolate and spicy cinnamon—two ancient aphrodisiacs in themselves. Used to stir a cup of hot coffee, the melting chocolate became an instant stick of delectable mocha.

"Voss Chocolate, I love you!" Esther cried.

"One more box, Ms. Cosi." Nancy reached down to a lower shelf of the cart and brought up a black box with the letters *REF* written in white grease pencil.

When we opened it, all of us frowned. The Raspberry-Espresso Flowers inside were not glossy and smooth like the other chocolates. They were mottled with dull white streaks.

I shook my head. "What a shame."

"What happened to these chocolate flowers?" Tuck asked.

"Bloom," I replied.

"Is that a joke?"

I pointed to the milky lines. "*This* is either fat bloom or sugar bloom. Both look the same."

"So what's the difference?"

"Fat bloom happens when chocolate hasn't been properly tempered—"

"And tempering is?"

"Basically, a process of heating, cooling, and mixing chocolate—it's what pastry chefs do before they mold it—and when chocolate isn't tempered correctly, the fats don't properly emulsify. When the cocoa butter rises to the surface and sets, you get fat bloom. Sugar bloom looks the same, but it's caused by condensation from improper storage." I sighed. The deduction was easy enough. "Given Voss's expertise in tempering, I doubt this is fat bloom."

I turned to Nancy. "Why wasn't this box on the same shelf with the others?"

She pointed at the box. "Someone in the kitchen saw the *REF* label and thought it meant to refrigerate."

"So this box has been in the fridge for hours?"

Nancy nodded.

"That's a shame," I said. "But it makes sense."

"I don't understand," Nancy said. "Why would putting chocolate in the fridge cause this sugar-bloom stuff?"

"When you store chocolate in a cold, humid environment and then return it to a warm room, you sometimes get condensation on the surface. As the water evaporates, the sugar in the chocolate crystallizes. That's what causes the white streaks. It's perfectly safe to eat—but the texture and mouthfeel are ruined. We can't serve this." I handed it back to Nancy. "Set it aside, okay?"

"Too bad," Nancy said, frowning. "The flowers were cute, like little hex signs."

"Hex signs?" Esther said. "What's up with that? Are you a Wiccan?"

"Not hex like a witch. Hex *sign* like from Pennsylvania Dutch country. American folk art, you know? Those cute little designs on houses and barns. I use them in my quilting and embroidery."

"So now you lived in eastern PA?" Tuck asked.

Nancy shrugged again.

"Well, I hope nobody tells Voss Chocolate what happened." Esther shook her head. "They're perfectionists at Voss!"

Tucker covered his ears. "'Voss Chocolate. Voss Chocolate.' You sound like a corrupt audio file. If you love this stuff so much, why don't you get your rapper boyfriend to buy you a truckload of champagne truffles the next time you visit his man cave?"

"I know you're Manhattan-centric, Tuck, but Boris lives in Brighton Beach, Brooklyn, which is not Williamsburg, Brooklyn. It isn't even *close* to Williamsburg, and Williamsburg is where Voss Chocolate has its only retail store."

"Whatever."

"Anyway, Boris can barely pay the rent on his Brighton Beach walk-up," Esther said. "So ten-dollar chocolate bars from Hipster Haven are definitely out."

Before Tuck could reply, a familiar song began to play.

We exchanged glances. "Isn't that 'You Light Up My Life'?" I asked.

Tuck nodded. "That's the *third* time I've heard that thing since we got here. I'd swear it was a ringtone, but whose phone would have a song *that* sappy on it?" He shifted his gaze to Esther.

Her pale cheeks reddened. "Boris put it on there while I was sleeping, okay? He thought it would be funny to have this dopey tune play whenever he calls me, but obviously, it's just embarrassing."

Tuck stared at Esther. "Debby Boone?"

"He heard the song on the oldies station at the bakery and liked it. I guess they didn't allow schmaltz in the former Soviet Union, so he was never exposed to the disease that is Debby Boone."

"If it upsets you that much," Tuck said, "why don't you change the ringtone?"

She threw up her hands. "Because Boris used a password to lock it in!"

I touched Esther's arm. "Please tell your boyfriend that we're going to be very busy, very soon, okay? Make your plans, then turn off your phone and let the rest of your calls go to voice mail."

Esther whipped the cell out of her pocket, cooed her regrets to Boris, and clapped her hands. "So are we going to taste this java-love-potion stuff or what?"

I tensed. By now, I'd sampled a few spoonfuls of a *budino* and small bites of the pastries prepared by Voss. All were borderline orgasmic—in flavor but not so much in any other way. Frankly, the aphrodisiac part of the equation seemed rather tepid, which was what I'd feared all along (the claims were likely bogus).

I did feel a very slight tingling on my skin and a little

flushed, but that was it. Maybe I needed a bigger dose for a bigger reaction? Or maybe it didn't work without an object of affection. Unfortunately, mine had yet to arrive—even worse, after the day he had, I doubted he'd be in the mood to take our featured product out for a private test drive.

As a flavoring agent, however, Mocha Magic was a raving success, and that provided a modicum of relief to my Atlas-level worries. As for the instant powdered-coffee version of the thing, the verdict was still out, and I honestly wasn't feeling up to hearing it.

"To tell you the truth, I'm a little apprehensive about sampling it," I confessed to my crew.

"Well, naturally you are!" Nancy cried. "The last thing you want is to go all dizzy act, before the guests arrive!"

Tucker, Esther, and I turned to face the young woman.

"What?" Esther said.

"Dizzy act," Nancy said. "The stuff in these pastries is an herb from Africa, isn't it? That's what you've been saying all night. This stuff is supposed to make you *act dizzy*, right?"

Tucker took hold of Nancy's shoulders. "Sweetie, the word is not *Afro-dizzy-act*. It's *aphrodisiac*."

She frowned and folded her arms. "So what's it supposed to do then, if it doesn't make you act dizzy?"

"Oy," Esther said.

"Nancy!" I cut in (before Esther could say any more). "We're going to need more cups. Would you get them?"

"No problem!"

Esther held her head as Nancy dashed off. "That girl can't possibly be that naive. It has to be an act—a really dizzy one."

"She's just young," I said. "You were young once, too."

"I was *never* young."

(That I believed.) Just then, a cell phone went off again. This time it was mine.

"Oh, those bohemians," Tucker gushed. "I do love Puccini!"

I silenced the ringtone opera. "Madame," I said, picking up, "where are you?"

"In the corridor, dear, across from the elevator bank near the cloakroom."

I slipped off my apron, retucked my white blouse, and adjusted my black skirt.

"Finish laying out all the choco-booty, okay?" I told my crew before pushing through the Loft's closed doors. "I'm checking on the guests in the Garden." *And a former mother-in-law who owes me some answers.*

Eleven

∿∿∿∿∿∿∿∿∿∿∿∿∿∿∿∿∿∿∿∿∿

"**Clare!** Here, dear!" A voice called as I moved into the long corridor.

Resplendent in a shimmering pearl sheath silk-screened with Monet's lilies, Madame stepped out from between a pair of faux-marble columns and waved me over.

Like me, she'd swept her hair into a neat French twist for the party. But her blue-violet eyes, lightly accented with periwinkle pencil, held a stressed expression that belied the put-together package.

We embraced, first thing, and I was relieved to feel the tight hug. Things hadn't been right between us since Alicia Bower entered our lives.

"Did you come alone?" I asked.

"Otto escorted me." She tilted her head. "I sent him out to the Garden."

I glanced down the corridor and through the closed glass double doors, but I couldn't see her current beau. The twinkling Garden was too crowded.

"What happened to your promise to bring Alicia here early, so we could hash everything out?"

"She stood me up! Otto and I waited in the Topaz bar for over an hour. When I called her, she apologized, but said she just didn't have time to meet and talk before the launch."

"You mean she's not here *yet*?"

"Oh, she's here. Out there somewhere." Madame fluttered her fingers toward the Garden doors. "She slipped by us at the hotel. Clearly, she's avoiding me."

"You mean *me*." (I'd been patient up to now. But this development was the last straw.) "My crew and I have been setting up in the Loft space for the last two hours. After Alicia drove me crazy micromanaging every minute detail of this launch, she suddenly has no interest in even glancing at our display? What does that tell you?"

"It tells me she's embarrassed."

"More like afraid."

"Of what?"

"Of me—and some hard questions about what went on this morning."

"Clare, you must allow me to apologize again for putting you in such an awkward position."

"It's all right. I told you on the phone, apology accepted."

"But you're still upset with me. Try to understand . . ." She waved me back into hiding between those faux marble columns, lowered her voice to a whisper. "With the blood pronounced fake and Dennis suddenly gone, the matter was no longer a criminal one. I had to side with Alicia. Involving the police any further would have risked bad publicity—and at the worst possible time for all of us."

"But don't you agree what happened this morning added up to much more than a *prank*?"

Madame nodded. "Yes. Now I do."

"Did you do any follow up with this Dennis St. Julian character?"

"We tried calling him. But his phone simply rang and rang. Not even any voice mail, which Alicia said he did have for the last few weeks."

"Probably a disposable cell," I said. "Something untraceable that he could quickly toss."

"Alicia did tell me that she welcomes your help tracking him down. If you can find out why he tried to scare her half to death, she would be most grateful. She's happy to pay you for your time."

"I'm far from a professional private investigator!"

"Please." Madame waved her hand. "What did Roman Brio call you? Shirley Holmes? He was right. As a mama snoop, you've done pretty well. And, as always, I am happy to be your Watson."

Oh brother. Here we go . . . "Alicia should *hire* someone. I'll ask Mike for a name—"

"Waste of time. Alicia was adamant. She doesn't wish to bring anyone else into this, especially a professional."

"Why not?"

"She fears her position with her company could be jeopardized if someone suspects a scandal brewing. And a hired investigator poking about asking questions is bound to raise *some* flag *some*where. Alicia would prefer to keep all of this as quiet as possible, within our little circle."

"But—"

"Legally, we're tied into this venture," Madame pointed out, "which means you're already publicly associated with Alicia. *You* can be a nosy Nellie without raising alarms. Simply make your queries sound innocent."

Like I have time for this!

"Clare . . ." She touched my shoulder. "I know you're not fond of Alicia. But won't you do it for me . . . for the Blend? Please?"

I massaged my forehead. "Did this Candy Man character give you a business card?"

"Yes!" Clearly excited to reprise her Watson role, Madame gleefully fished around her small evening bag. "Here you are."

"Kogo Sweets Inc.," I read. The logo wasn't embossed, and the white cardstock felt textureless and flimsy.

"The company is real," Madame said, watching me bend the card back and forth. "I looked it up after Mr. St. Julian introduced himself a few weeks ago."

"But if I place a call to Kogo Sweets' main office," I said, waving the cheap rectangle, "I doubt very much Dennis St. Julian will be a name they recognize."

"You think the card is fake?"

"I think the man is fake."

"Why?"

"Because he was ready to place a 'large order' for Alicia's product without even sampling it. Because his clothes were made of gorgeous, expensive material, but his loafers were old, worn, and scuffed up. Because he was built like a ready-made model for Michelangelo, that's why!"

"What does the man's build have to do with anything?"

"He claimed his job was tasting candy for a living, yet he had six-pack abs, muscle cuts, and a shaved chest?"

"You don't think he lifted weights to counteract all the candy sampling?"

"Serious bodybuilders are rigorous about their diets. They don't make their living as wholesale junk-food buyers. The candy buying was a spiel to get close to Alicia, I'm sure of it. Someone hired that guy."

"Who? And for what? This is the first product Alicia's ever pitched to the confectionary trade. Do you suppose this St. Julian character was after the Mocha Magic Coffee's secret ingredients?"

"I don't suppose Mr. St. Julian *was* Mr. St. Julian, and I say we keep our eyes and ears open tonight. If you see a dead guy rise again, let me know ASAP, okay?"

"You expect that man will have the nerve to show up here?"

"Yes. Possibly in disguise. For all I know, he may be in the Garden already." I glanced again at those glass double doors. "Just remember, whatever he wanted from Alicia, he failed to get this morning."

"And you think he's going to try again?"

"Or his partner will," I said.

"His what?"

"Don't you remember the reason I was buried in dirty laundry this morning? The blond woman in black I was chasing?"

"Oh yes! You know I never did see her. I took your word for it and sent those young police officers after you."

"Maybe I should sketch a picture of her for Alicia."

"Oh, good idea!"

"On the other hand, she might be . . ."

"What?"

I was too busy staring to finish my sentence. A slender woman in a sleek black pantsuit had exited the elevator and moved swiftly toward the glass doors, but she didn't push through them. She just stood there staring at something in her hand—a smartphone. She was text messaging.

Look! I mouthed, pointing to the blonde. The contrast of her long, glossy ponytail against the black backdrop of her silky suit material appeared just as striking as I remembered.

Madame's eyes widened. *Is that her?*

"Wait here," I whispered. If I had to fight the woman to hold her, I didn't want Madame catching any flying elbows. Quickly and quietly I moved across the faux-stone floor. Thank goodness, the woman appeared too distracted to notice me.

I gripped her upper arm, held tight.

"Who are you?" I demanded.

Slowly, the woman turned.

Twelve

~~~~~~~~~~~~~~~~~~~~~~~~~~~~~~~~~

"**Clare!**" Madame's heels clicked hastily across the floor. She touched my shoulder. "This is Patrice Stone."

The young woman regarded me. "Clare? Oh, you must be Clare Cosi!"

Madame eyeballed me with a silent question: *Is this the blonde you chased?*

I sent her a very subtle shake of my head. *No. Sorry, it's not.*

Oblivious to our exchange, Patrice beamed at us with a smile as bright as a Great Plains sunrise. Holding tight to the smartphone in her left hand, she extended her right.

"So nice to meet you! Alicia has been bragging about your mocha recipes all week. I can't wait to taste everything!"

Surprising me, she moved from a quick handshake to a big, warm hug. "Thank you for all you've been doing! And thank your staff for me, too."

Stepping back, Patrice swiped a long lock of corn-yellow hair away from her oval face. She wore almost no makeup— with her youthful skin and those prairie-sky eyes, she really didn't need to.

Madame cleared her throat. "Patrice works with Aphrodite."

"An understatement," Patrice said with a laugh. "When I was Aphrodite's personal assistant, I pretty much worked for all the Sisters—"

"Sisters?" I interrupted. "Oh, sorry, I forgot. That's what Aphrodite calls the heads of her sections—I mean *Temples*."

"That's right. You've got it! When you reach Sister level, you're also a kind of board member of the community."

"Board member?" I glanced at Madame. "You mean the Sisters actually share in the profits?"

"Oh yes. That's why everyone strives to become one. After four long years, I *finally* made it. I'm still training a new assistant to take over my old duties. Her name is Minthe. You'll meet her soon, I'm sure."

"Congratulations," I said, even more curious now. "Are there always a set number of Sisters, then? Or does it fluctuate?"

"Seven Sisters. That's what Aphrodite's worked out for her financials."

"Then the competition must be pretty fierce? I mean—to become a Sister?"

"Oh yes. To become one and *stay* one." She lowered her voice. "I was forced to cancel one of the Sisters' launches this afternoon." She paused. "It wasn't pleasant."

"I can imagine," I said.

"You know how it is. These ladies are super competitive."

Madame raised an eyebrow. I gave her a nod, thinking—

Just how competitive is "super competitive"? Enough to sabotage your competition with some kind of fake murder scheme?

With a jerk of her head, Madame directed me to continue grilling Patrice. She didn't have to.

"Now you've got me curious," I said, forcing a laugh to keep things light. "What exactly happens if a Sister has her launch canceled?"

Patrice hesitated.

Darn. I spooked her. I shot Madame a look. *Okay, Mrs. Watson, you're on . . .*

"You'll have to forgive Clare for all her questions," Madame said, waving her hand. "Alicia's been so busy, she hasn't explained much about your business. I have to admit, I'm still learning how it all functions."

"Oh, well . . . it's pretty simple, really: Each of the Seven Sisters has her own area on the Aphrodite Web site. And each is responsible for the traffic—"

"Traffic?" I asked, looking appropriately clueless.

Patrice nodded. "We track the number of visitors to our site in all sorts of ways."

"And you want as many visits as you can get, right?"

"Right. The more visits, the more we can charge for our advertising. Unfortunately, ad dollars fluctuate with seasonal traffic, so Aphrodite now expects each of the Sisters to submit a lucrative product idea designed to bring steady revenue to her Temple."

"I see. So each Sister's job depends on the success of her product?"

"In a word, *yes*. Aphrodite invests in each product. She becomes a full partner with every Sister, and she expects them to deliver a profitable payback." After a pause, Patrice shrugged. "I know it sounds harsh, but Aphrodite has worked very hard to build our site globally. There are plenty of talented editors, writers, and Web developers applying every day to work for us. Competition keeps all of us at the top of our game."

Game . . .

I gritted my teeth. I actually liked Patrice, but to me a business was not a game. In the best possible world, a business was a close-knit unit, working toward a common goal with colleagues. In *games*, there were always winners and losers—and, more often than not, cheaters.

"So," I said, "are you having a launch party this week?"

"Mine's done, thank goodness! We held it two weeks ago in California."

"What's your product, dear?" Madame inquired.

Patrice beamed. "Next season our brand-new *Love in the Afternoon* feature will debut. It's the very first, original Webisode series that's produced especially for the Aphrodite Village community. It's even based on an original e-book novel from my Arts and Entertainment Temple! It's daunting, but I'll soon be in charge of it all."

"That's fantastic, congratulations!" I said, and exchanged another quick glance with Madame. She appeared to be wondering the same thing I was. "What happened to the Sister whose job you took?"

Patrice shrugged. "She got married."

"Why would that matter?" I answered. "Aren't Sisters allowed to get married?"

"Of course, Sisters can get married!" Patrice laughed. "Selma's new husband is an independent software developer. He persuaded her to work with him. That's why she left."

Laughter from outside interrupted her, followed by applause.

"Looks like things are going well," Patrice said, pointing to the crowd.

The guests stood among a dozen ionic columns. The columns were faux marble, of course, like the two in the corridor. Composed mainly of fiberglass, they were lit from within and scattered around the Garden's hedges and potted plants. (As Tuck would say, it was great stagecraft.)

"Is that Aphrodite at the podium?" I asked.

A thirtyish woman in a maroon-red wrap dress was now speaking in front of the Garden's shallow reflecting pool. Rimless glasses gave her a serious look, though her light brown hair, worn loosely to her shoulders, implied a more casual, approachable style. Beautifully silhouetted by the illuminated spires, she easily held the attention of her listeners.

"That's Sherri Sellars," Patrice replied. "She's a media personality on the West Coast. She also does a weekly satellite radio show called the *Luv Doctor*."

"So Sherri Sellars is a Sister, too?"

Patrice nodded. "She governs our Love and Relationship Temple. Right now, Sherri is explaining the psychological benefits of a healthy sex life. Then she'll introduce Alicia, who will give the big pitch. I'm closing by going over the contents of their press packets and telling them how to order and who to contact."

She studied both of us. "You two should stop worrying! Alicia's got one of the most promising products, given the majority of our site's user profiles."

"Will Aphrodite speak tonight?" I asked. "I'd love to see her in action."

(I didn't think the woman would try to sabotage her own employee, but I did want a better handle on this bizarre shop with its Temples, Sisters, and cutthroat business philosophy.)

"I'm sorry, Clare. Aphrodite won't be speaking at any of the events. She doesn't even like to appear in public." Patrice lowered her voice again. "But she will make a showing at all the parties, including the one tonight. I'll try to introduce you when she arrives. But if things get crazy, you'll have another chance to see her. You're scheduled to cater the yacht party on Friday, right? And one other launch event. Sorry, I can't remember the dates now. Too many details to keep them all straight! That's why this baby's my lifeline—"

As she waved her smartphone, we heard a new burst of applause.

Just then, the Garden doors opened, and a young brunette poked her head through. Her chili-pepper red cat glasses, large for her delicate features, made her auburn-streaked pixie seem all the more adorable. Smiling, she tapped her wristwatch.

"Sherri's wrapping it up in five. Alicia's up, then you. Are you ready?"

"No problem, Daphne," Patrice replied. "I'll be right there."

When Daphne departed, Patrice took another deep breath and held it. "Almost time for my big moment. I still get butterflies when I speak in public. But when I'm about ready to faint, I remind myself that I'm not doing too badly for someone who was a pimply faced teenaged blogger ten years ago."

She activated the digital pad, and Patrice's nervousness seemed to evaporate with a glowing smile. "My fiancé sent me a message," she explained. "He said I should break a leg."

"Is he in the audience?"

"Actually, he's in Afghanistan. He'll be back in six months, three days, and nineteen hours."

"You have that memorized?"

"I have a countdown clock on my digital pad."

Eyes on the podium, Patrice rocked on her heels several times.

"Wish me luck," she said softly.

"Break a leg," I replied, then laid a firm hand on her arm. "One last question, if you don't mind?"

Patrice tensed. "What's that, Clare?"

I lowered my voice. "The Sister who had her launch canceled—she's out, right? Essentially fired off the board?"

Patrice tilted her head. "Why are you asking?'

"I, uh . . . I'll be making small talk with guests coming by the samples table, and I'd hate to put my foot in it with her. What's her name?"

"Maya Lansing. She's our Health and Fitness Sister. But you don't have to worry about saying the wrong thing."

"She's gone for good, then?'

"Well, not exactly. Aphrodite makes all the final decisions about who stays and who goes on her board. Sorry—but now I've really got to go!"

"Of course! Good luck!"

Patrice pushed at the heavy glass doors. As she stepped out, a moist gust flowed in, smelling of sea salt and rain. I frowned. Tonight's weather forecast had been iffy at best, but the threats in the air were impossible to dismiss.

Some kind of storm was headed our way.

THIRTEEN

~~~~~~

"So, what do you think?" Madame whispered.

I folded my arms. "Aphrodite may be in love with this Greece motif, but I'd say her corporate culture looks more like ancient Rome."

Madame sighed. "*I, Claudius* does come to mind."

"The motivation just got clearer."

"Do you think Patrice was involved with what happened to Alicia?"

"I doubt it. Patrice's cheerful 'out with the old' view is pretty typical for someone who's young, ambitious, and thinks she's immune to failure."

"Agreed. But what about the other Sisters?"

"We'll need to take a look at them, especially the woman who was all but fired today—the Health and Fitness Queen."

"Sister," Madame corrected.

Corporate jargon? I wondered. *Or a twisted convent?*

"Well, I'm happy to help." Madame tilted her head toward the Garden. "After Alicia's presentation, I'll find a moment to speak with her. I'd like to know whether she and Maya Lansing have any bad blood between them."

"Good idea. While you're at it, keep an eye out for the Candy Man, okay? Whatever he was attempting to pull on Alicia this morning, he failed, and he may just try something else tonight."

"The game is afoot!"

Ugh, I thought, *that word again . . .*

As my former mother-in-law pushed through the Garden doors, I turned to find an unnerving sight—a mountain of male flesh barreling toward me.

"Excuse me, ma'am. Are you Clare Cosi?"

Dressed in khaki pants and a blue sport coat—with a neck so large his collar gave his throat a muffin top—the guy was big enough to sub for half the Jets' defensive line. Whoever he was, I needed a moment to find my voice.

"I'm Clare."

"We have a situation."

"A situation?"

The mountain flashed an ID. He was some kind of director for building security.

"A gentleman is trying to gain admittance to this event. First he claimed he was a guest, but he didn't have an invitation. Then he said he was a member of your catering staff, but he didn't have a pass and his name wasn't on the approved list. We're detaining him downstairs—"

"What does this guy look like?"

The guard repeated my question into a headset and touched the Blue Tooth listening device in his ear.

"He's well built," the guard said, then paused to listen. "Muscular. Hair dark and longish . . . he has facial hair . . . a trimmed goatee . . . ."

I tensed. It had to be our Candy Man. Dennis St. Julian was a bodybuilder, and a fake beard and wig would help disguise him.

"Let's go!" I said.

When the doors closed on our elevator, I cleared my throat. "Listen. If this is the person I think it is, he could be real trouble."

With newly alert eyes, the Blue-Toothed Matterhorn passed on my warning in a low rumble.

"I don't know if he'll be violent," I said, "but better safe than sorry, right?"

Again the guard spoke into his headset. One of his meaty hands balled into a fist. By the time the elevator hit the ground floor, I was keyed up and ready for anything.

The guard walked me to a corner of the vast lobby. Five men in uniforms had formed a ring around their captive.

"Back off!" a deep voice boomed.

Oh crap.

I still couldn't see the man, but his two-syllable yell told me all I needed to know. This party crasher wasn't the Candy Man; it was my ex-husband.

"I've had just about enough pat downs in the last twenty-four hours!"

"What are you doing here?!" I cried.

"Clare! Will you please tell these tin-plated fascists who I am!"

"It's okay!" I assured the guards. "I know this guy. I'll sign him in . . ."

"This guy," of course, was Matteo Allegro, the very same man who'd enticed me, with honey-drenched figs and a dazzling smile, into the room of his *penzione* more than two decades ago. At the time, Matt was barely older than my nineteen years and no better educated. In the language of love, however, the boy was a polysyllabic genius (the figs had been just as hard to resist).

With my unexpected pregnancy, Matt proposed marriage. It didn't last. The primary reason: his nonstop use of linguistic talents—too many languages with too many women, about whom he didn't give a fig. I might have forgiven him if it weren't for the coffee-buying trips to Columbia, where recreational cocaine use slowly transformed my dream boy into a newlywed nightmare.

By now, our relationship had improved a great deal. Matt had kicked his bad habit (the drugs, not the women), and with my return to his mother's coffeehouse, he and I became partners again—in the coffee business, that is, and in the business of parenting our daughter.

When Rock Center security finally backed off, I exhaled with relief. So did Matt. (One guard had a Taser all ready to go.)

"What are you doing here?" I asked again.

"I had a connection out of Paris," Matt said. "Went straight from JFK to the Blend, where I heard about this little shindig from Dante and Gardner."

"They're holding down the fort for me at the coffeehouse. Tucker, Esther, and Nancy are upstairs."

"Who's Nancy?"

"My newest barista. She just stared a few weeks ago."

"Well, Dante told me this thing you're doing tonight is something major."

"It is."

Matt swept back his dark hair, much longer now, and a marked contrast from his usual closely trimmed Caesar. He'd grown a goatee, too.

My ex-husband had always struck me as a pirate, but now he more resembled one of the Musketeers. Aramis came to mind, dashing as all get-out but *way* too popular with the ladies.

Even now, with fatigue circles under his eyes, Matt was turning the heads of random females passing by. (No surprise.) His black sport coat was cut to hug his buff torso; his latte-cream button-down contrasted attractively with his tan—not the spray-on kind but a deep, natural glow from the kiss of an African sun. Even his jeans were fashionably scuffed, though in Matt's case the wear and tear didn't come from some urban house of design; it was earned via treks around the world's coffee belt as he hunted the highest-quality arabica for the Blend and his other global clients.

"This is supposed to be a private party," I informed him. "Invitation only. What did you think you were going to do? Charm your way past teenage usherettes?"

Matt folded his arms, suddenly looking pleased with himself. "I told them I had to make a delivery. A last-minute addition to your catering staff."

"You mean you?"

"No. Not me, Clare. You know I don't cater—"

"No, generally you're the one catered to."

"Very funny." Matt jerked his thumb over his shoulder. "Your new assistant is in the ladies' room, freshening up."

"Oh God." My throat was closing up already. "You don't mean Breanne?" *(The second Mrs. Matteo Allegro and I didn't much get along.)*

"Relax. Breanne's uptown. Like I said, I had a connection in Paris so—"

"Oh God! You saw Joy?"

"Better than that."

"You mean—"

"Yup," Matt said with a nod.

"Hey, Mom, I'm home," a voice called from across the lobby.

"Joy!"

A moment later, my daughter and I were wrapping our arms around each other in a hug I wanted never to end.

Fourteen

AFTER signing in my daughter with building security, our little reunited family moved to the elevator bank. The spring in Joy's step fortified me, and I noticed her dark brown hair was much longer than I remembered.

Like father, like daughter, I thought, and not for the first time.

Over the years, Joy had picked up a few habits from Matt. The very worst of which (some drug use in nightclubs) I continually prayed would remain far behind us. Joy's height was her dad's, too, but her heart-shaped face and big emerald eyes were totally Cosi. What cheered me most of all was seeing the meat back on her bones.

Before she'd gone to France, a horrific ordeal had sunk Joy's spirits along with her appetite. She'd lost enough weight to worry me. But now her figure was back to displaying its natural curves, the kind that seldom wanted for male attention.

"So tell me?" I fished, "what's the boyfriend news? Another adorable French cook in your brigade?"

"Not even close!" Joy replied so quickly and lightly I

flashed back on my own attempt to snowball Mike earlier in the day.

I folded my arms, shot her the maternal X-ray.

"It's true, Mom! I've been *way* too busy at work."

"Then how did you get away?"

She waved her hand—a gesture identical to Matt's mother. It was so adult, so self-assured, I blanked for a moment, wondering how that could be. She was just five years old, wasn't she? Helping me frost her grandma's birthday cake. Or eleven, crying over some jerk of a neighbor boy who'd made fun of her. Fourteen, laughing as we tested a new recipe in our Jersey kitchen. Sixteen, alone at the stove, excitedly cooking a Julia Child feast for one of Matt's visits. How could she possibly be in her twenties now? All grown up and living in Paris?

". . . and next week Monsieur Boucher's youngest sister is getting married. It's a huge deal for their family. They rented a neo-Gothic castle in the Loire Valley, and since half his restaurant staff is related, he just threw up his hands and closed us down for a week."

In the pause that followed, I stared at my daughter, willing my mind to catch up to the incomprehensible passage of time. "Boucher's sister is getting married," I repeated. "Well . . . I'm surprised you weren't invited."

"Oh, I was. But then Dad showed up and offered to buy me a ticket home." She grinned. "How could I say no?"

My mind sharpened fast. Something about Joy's tone sounded off. "I hope Monsieur Boucher wasn't offended about your missing his sister's wedding. What did you tell him?"

"*Mon père et ma mère me manquent!*"

My father and mother miss me. "Oh, honey, we do . . ."

As I hugged her again, I noticed Matt staring.

"No boyfriend?" he said. "Really?

"Oh, Dad, the French guys I've met are okay, but none of them are worth hooking up with, you know?"

I stiffened. So did Matt. He was thinking the same thing

I was, but neither of us had the stomach to ask. I certainly wasn't going to bring up the dreaded *Franco* question, certainly not in front of Matt. Then my daughter turned the tables on me.

"So, Mom, when are we going to hear wedding bells for you and Mike?"

I blinked and stared. Joy's question surprised me so much I wasn't sure what to say. Thank goodness the elevator car *binged* its arrival. As we boarded, I was sure Matt would change the subject.

He didn't.

"Come on, Mom—" Joy was grinning now. "Don't go all quiet on me. I know you and Mike love each other."

"We do," I finally said. "And we may consider matrimony in the future. But right now things just aren't settled enough in our lives."

"That's no excuse! Look at Dad. His life is crazy, but he married Breanne."

Matt coughed—I'm pretty sure to hide a laugh. As I shifted from foot to foot, I could see he was smirking.

"What's so funny?" I said.

"The day has finally come when our daughter thinks I'm a good role model for you."

"Oh, please."

"Come on, you guys," Joy said, "don't fight."

"We're not fighting," I said. "But you should understand that Mike and I don't view marriage the same way your father and his new wife do. They don't have . . ." I was about to say a sacred union, but I knew it would come off badly.

"What?" Joy said. "They don't have a traditional marriage? I'm not a kid anymore, Mom. We can certainly talk about these things."

I didn't reply. For one thing, this wasn't the time or place. So I just gritted my teeth and checked our progress. *Man, this was one slow elevator!*

Bing, went the bell. *Finally!*

"Here we are!"

Leading the way down the corridor, I checked over my shoulder. The Garden was still full of guests, but it wouldn't be for long. We had fifteen minutes before service, even less if the weather turned. Recalling that smell of dampness in the outside air, I pushed quickly through the Loft's doors and waved Joy and Matt inside.

TUCKER and Esther yipped when they saw Joy. Hugs followed, and I introduced Nancy Kelly. Then Joy touched my arm.

"Dad wasn't kidding. I'd like to help out tonight."

Pleased as punch, I held myself back from hugging her yet again. Instead, I pulled out one of our pressed black aprons. As Joy stowed her red hooded jacket and tied on the Blend's version of formalwear, Esther suggested we taste test the coffee before the guests poured in.

I eagerly gave her the thumbs-up, surprised at how different I felt about the whole thing now that Joy and Matt were with me.

Mike Quinn was right, I realized at last. *You're fully on board with this thing. If it goes bad, you'll figure out the next step. You always do. . . .*

"All right," I said when the carafe was ready. "Let's try it!"

Esther poured four-ounce samples all around.

I put the paper cup under my nose. The aroma was an earthy combination of roasted coffee and dark chocolate. *Good so far.* I sipped, thinking everything was going to be okay, until Matt cried out—

"You're serving *instant* coffee! Clare, have you gone mad?!"

Tucker, Esther, and Nancy froze.

I narrowed my gaze. "What?"

"You heard me!"

"You mean to tell me that you don't know what this party is all about?"

Matt folded his arms.

"This is a product launch, Matt. Alicia Bower is introducing her brand-new beverage to the world, a mix of Village Blend beans, Voss chocolate, and natural herbs. It's a powder called Mocha Magic Coffee."

"Dear God . . ." Matt held his head. "My meticulously sourced beans are going into an instant coffee *powder*?"

"Oh, Mr. Boss?" Esther raised a finger. "Point of information. Mocha Magic is also a natural aphrodisiac." She fanned herself. "And the stuff is starting to work. Hey, anybody remember Edmund Spenser? Maybe you should rename this stuff Bower of Bliss!"

"The Faerie Queene!" Tucker gushed, raising his sample high. "Okay, Esther, now you're talking my kind of poetry!"

Joy sniffed her sample, rolled the hot liquid around on her tongue, and swallowed. "Not bad for an instant, Mom. Better than a lot of premium brands I've tasted." She smiled with daughterly encouragement. "And since chocolate and coffee are natural aphrodisiacs, anyway, I think this is a great idea for a product!"

"Thanks, honey. What about the rest of you? What do you think of the taste?"

"Quaffable," Esther said. "For a powder it's not swill."

"Oh, it's better than that," Tuck said. "It's much nicer than most espresso powders I've tried."

Esther shrugged. "Why worry about the taste, anyway? People won't be drinking it for that, right?"

"But it should taste good," I said.

"Luckily I have a late-night date!" Tuck drained his cup and went for a second.

"Clare, please . . ." Matt said. "For the love of all that is holy, give me some answers. Why didn't you consult with me about this insane venture?"

"Matt, what is the matter with you? Your mother said she wrote you a long e-mail explaining everything. She said you were on board!"

"My mother sent me an e-mail, Clare, about a deal she made to sell our beans to a boutique chocolatier. She conveniently left out the rest of the story!"

Oh God. "She never mentioned Alicia Bower?"

"No."

"Are you sure? Try to remember. Alicia is supposed to be a very dear friend of your mothers."

"Then why is this the first time I've heard the woman's name?"

"Your mother said Alicia used to be a barista at the Blend, once upon a time. You must remember her."

"Sorry. The only barista my mother ever referred to as her 'very dear friend' was the one I married."

Now I wanted to hold my head. Just this morning, Madame appeared ready to cover up a murder for Alicia Bower—a friend so important that her own son had never heard of her? What in the world was happening?

"I'm going to have a talk with my mother right now," Matt promised. "And then I'm confronting this Bower woman—"

"No, you're not." I gripped my ex's muscular forearm *hard.* "This is not the place for a mother-son showdown."

"So my mother is here?"

"She's in the Garden with the other guests. And she'll be incredibly thrilled to see her granddaughter. So please do not upset her."

"Fine. I'll *postpone* my talk until tomorrow," Matt said, gritting his teeth.

With almost two hundred VIP guests about to swamp us, I decided the same thing. I wanted to bring my ex up to speed on every bizarre aspect of this unfortunate deal, but tales of a fake murder and the very real threat of some kind of saboteur weren't likely to help Matteo Allegro find his center.

"Just keep your cool," I said. "And so you know, Mike's going to be here, too. Please be nice."

"Why? Is Dudley Do-Right going to make a bust? Investigate the herbal supplements in this powdered crap, maybe?"

Joy giggled. I sighed.

"This isn't a closed, little gathering, you know. We have international buyers and press here tonight."

"Press? What for?"

"Aphrodite's Village is launching this product. They're in charge of the PR, not me."

When Matt pushed with more questions, I explained it all—the site, the traffic, the competition, the odd associations with ancient Greece.

"Seven Sisters?" he echoed. "Temples? My God, Clare, it sounds like a cult!"

"A lot of industries use jargon, Matt. Cult or not, they're a global success story, and they're still growing."

While we were talking, I noticed the slightest streaking of rain across the Loft's wall of windows. I also noticed Joy talking to Esther, who'd brought out our broken goodies bowl.

"You should sample this spread, Dad!" Joy shoved the bowl under Matt's nose. "They're delicious. Esther said they're made from Mom's recipes."

Matt picked up a piece of Cappuccino Kiss. He sniffed the treat, his expression dubious.

"Come on, Dad! Don't be such a unit!"

"It's good," Matt conceded after finally taking a bite, "but it could be because I'm famished."

"Voss chocolate is primo," Joy assured him. "Higher cocoa content, no husks, just the nibs. They really know their stuff."

Matt reached for another damaged cookie. "Okay, this is good," he conceded.

As he snatched a third, the *pitter-pat* of precipitation turned into heavy *plinks* and *plunks*. Soon the windows were awash with an outright downpour. Within seconds, we heard the stampede. Guests abandoned the outside Garden and burst through the Loft's doors. Mad for mocha, they rushed our samples bar.

"Brace yourselves, team. Here we go!"

* * *

FOR the next thirty minutes, Esther, Nancy, and Joy wended their way through the crowd, doling out cups of Mocha Magic. I manned the samples table with Tuck, who dolefully watched the barbarian horde tear apart his culinary construction, one tasty goodie at a time.

Upon seeing her only grandchild, Madame opened her arms and cried (literally). The two drifted off alone, eager to catch up. A short time later, when I saw Joy again, she had an odd look on her face.

"What's the matter?" I asked.

"Grandma says you should come into the hallway. She's hiding by the cloakroom."

"Why is she hiding?"

"She's spying on a couple of women. She says you need to hear what they're talking about."

"What women?"

"Grandma says one of them is Alicia Bower and the other is . . . well, I don't know who she is, but she's not wearing clothes."

"What did you say?"

"She's not wearing—"

"She's *naked*?"

"Not exactly. She's just not . . . You know what, Mom? It's hard to explain. I think you should see for yourself."

"You know what? So do I."

FIFTEEN

∞∞∞∞∞∞∞∞∞∞∞∞∞∞

I found Madame, just as Joy promised, hiding in the corridor between our favorite pair of faux-marble columns.

". . . and the last thing you're going to do," Alicia Bower's voice warned from somewhere nearby, "is enter this party dressed like *that*."

"Who is Alicia arguing with?" I whispered in Madame's ear.

She put a finger to her lips. "Maya Lansing. The Sister who had her launch canceled."

Stepping closer, I saw Alicia Bower standing just inside the cloakroom. Still wearing her dripping trench, she seemed oblivious to the small puddles forming at her feet. Her attention was riveted on the woman going toe to toe with her.

Honed and toned, the Health and Fitness diva looked like a Latina Annie Lennox with a body so sculpted she could have been carved from seamless marble. Given Maya Lansing's cocoa-brown complexion (compared to Alicia's chalky-vanilla coloring) and her spiky platinum hair (to Alicia's dark flapper cut), the two might have been photo negatives of each other if it weren't for their vast differences in build.

Ounce for ounce, the whole thing struck me as a real David and Goliath showdown, a single-shot espresso versus King Kong Depth Charge—especially with the six-inch Lady Gaga heel-less platforms on Maya's toes.

In the first few seconds, I couldn't see why Alicia objected to Maya's outfit. Okay, the skirt was daring—a swath of black silk slit all the way up both sides to show off the woman's long, muscular legs. But the form-fitting bodice of Chantilly lace appeared conservative enough with its high neckline. Even the sleeves were long, covering part of her hands.

Then it hit me with a silent gasp. The skirt wasn't the issue. Everything above it was: the bodice, the neckline, even the sleeves of "Chantilly lace" were no more than a trompe l'oeil of elaborately applied body paint!

"Very daring," Madame whispered, almost admiringly. "Reminds me of Josephine Baker in *Princess Tam-Tam*."

"Who?"

"The Gaga of the thirties, dear. When I was a little girl in Paris, her half-nude dance was all the rage." Madame gave a little shake.

"Okay," I said. "Other than the *Tam-Tam* dance, what did I miss?"

"Now let's see . . ." Madame began. "Alicia ran out to the Garden for some reason. When she came back in, she saw Maya coming off the elevator with an escort and demanded they have a word in private."

Maya came in with an escort. I glanced around. "Where's the escort?"

"She sent him into the party."

"Did you get a good look at him?"

"No, just a glimpse from the back—a dark suit with some sort of naval cap on his head."

"Naval? Like the U.S. Navy?"

"I didn't see. There were other late arrivals in the elevator, and he disappeared in the crowd."

I filed that away. "What happened next?"

"Maya turned on Alicia, accusing her of undermining her product launch. Alicia retorted that Maya's diet shakes and fat-burning pills were twenty years out of date for the market and Aphrodite agreed. Then Maya accused Alicia of not knowing what she was talking about because Maya was the one who'd built a worldwide fitness following on the curve of her oh-so-perfect butt—"

"Leave now, Maya!" Alicia's voice was suddenly louder. "You should not be here."

"I'm on the guest list, and I intend to show my support for my fellow Sister."

"Don't even try that crap with me. You wore that ridiculous getup to ruin my launch and embarrass us all. You're pathetic!"

"Not even close," Maya replied with surprising calm. "And I'll tell you who's pathetic and why . . ." She fired off a series of missteps Alicia supposedly made while bringing her Mocha Magic to market, and the biggest problem, in Maya's view, was the "chosen spokeswoman for the product."

"I don't understand you," Alicia said.

"Just answer me one question," Maya demanded. "What is this Mocha Magic Coffee powder, anyway?"

The question appeared to rattle Alicia. Her vampiric pallor faded to specter white. "What do you mean?"

"It's not a food or wine. It's not a spice," Maya challenged. "Your sex juice is the kind of *lifestyle* product that belongs in *my* Health and Fitness temple."

"Are you mad? Mocha Magic is my creation!"

"You came up with the stuff, and that's great. But who would do a better job of *selling* your product for the enrichment of Aphrodite and our entire community? Me"—Maya ran her French-tipped fingers along her body as if she were displaying the grand prize on *The Price Is Right*—"or a shriveled old harpy like you?"

"I'd like to strangle you with my bare hands!"

"Go for it."

Body stiffening with rage, Alicia appeared ready to lunge

at Maya when I interrupted them. I hadn't meant to. One of my shoulders was flush against the fiberglass column, and I'd leaned forward enough to tip the thing over.

Ka-BOOM!

Woops. The column looked solid, but marble it wasn't. (I could almost hear Tucker's voice: *Stagecraft, Clare, stagecraft!*) The pillar hit the floor, then bounced and rolled, thundering along the mock stone until it reached the end of its electric cord. That's when the fluorescent light inside exploded with an oh-so-subtle flash.

In the silence that followed, Madame sighed. "It appears the jig is up."

Alicia and Maya were now gawking at us.

"Clare?" Alicia rasped. "Madame Dubois?"

"Friends of yours, Bower?" Maya snapped. "I can mess them up, too—starting with the little waitress." She strode toward me, Gaga platforms clomping like Frankenstein foot-wear.

Wonderful. I hadn't been in a real girl-fight for ages. *Too late now.* Like Tucker tried to warn Nancy, this was one exciting town, but when the coaster went south, it was time to hold on.

Standing my ground, I balled my hands and sent Maya the hardest stare in my arsenal. Yeah, she was bigger, but I was more balanced, and in my experience, with just the right push all giants fell.

Suddenly, the fitness queen halted. Noting the look in my eyes, she put French tips to slim hips, then altered her target.

"Who's the old bag?"

"Be careful, my dear," Madame replied with rapier charm. "When it comes to bags, vintage purses have great value. Shoddier things are bound for the trash."

"Why, you old—"

Maya stepped forward, but so did I, right in front of Madame. "Leave her out of this or I'll hurt you."

"Ladies! That's quite enough!"

I turned my head to find Patrice Stone hustling toward

us, shoes purposefully snapping. Trailing close behind were two women in their twenties with pixie haircuts. Like dutiful acolytes, they hung on Patrice's heels, then stopped and stepped back the moment Patrice grabbed Maya's arm and swung her around.

"What are you trying to pull?"

"I just came to show my support." Maya's tone was innocent, yet her gaze was icier than my *budini* staircase. "Has Aphrodite read my memo yet? Seen my demo analysis? Any decision?"

"This is hardly the time—"

"This is the perfect time," Maya insisted. "Right before I make my entrance and steal the show. Do we have a deal?"

Patrice's jaw was tight. "Aphrodite thinks an infomercial is a good idea, and she actually believes you would be a lucrative spokesperson for the Mocha Magic Coffee."

"Aphrodite rules!" Maya's expression went from anxious to triumphant.

"What?" Alicia cried. "Are your *both* crazy! There is no way this steroid-shilling witch is going to represent my product, or cut into my profits!"

"I'm not finished!" Patrice added, turning quickly to Alicia. "I am totally against Maya's proposal for a number of reasons."

Maya tossed her spiky head. "But you're not in charge, Patrice. Not yet, anyway. Aphrodite is."

"Maybe so," Patrice said, "but our boss changes her mind like the wind changes direction. Tomorrow she'll have forgotten your memo, and nobody is going to remind her. Least of all me."

"She may act flighty and eccentric, but you and I both know Aphrodite manipulates us into competing. She wants us to tear each other to pieces, trying to outdo each other. The harder we go at it, the wealthier she gets." Maya's frown flipped into a cajoling smile. "Come on, Patrice, we can work together on this. Alicia's product, my salesmanship—we can *all* become rich!"

But Patrice shook her head. "Listen to me: I've been Aphrodite's right hand for a long time now. What I say carries enough weight to make a difference to her, and you aren't getting near the Mocha Magic."

"Yes!" Alicia clapped her hands. "Oh, thank you, Patrice!"

"Now, Maya, I think you'd better go."

"Oh, I'll go. I'll go right into that launch party and prove to you and Aphrodite that I can sell more of that stupid sex potion than ten Alicia Bowers."

Maya whirled, with astounding grace (given her extreme footwear), and strode down the hall like a platinum-plumed peacock.

I hated to admit it, but Aphrodite wasn't wrong. Maya's poise, stature, and attention-grabbing presence were impossible to deny, which meant her power to sell would be, too. But the woman was obviously hard-to-handle trouble, and that could spell disaster for any growing corporation. As she vanished into the party, Patrice tried to calm Alicia.

"She's being ridiculous. Just try to ignore her."

"You *could* have taken her off the guest list!"

"Maya is still a Sister, Alicia, at least for now."

"But she'll ruin everything! Tomorrow Maya's going to be the story, not my product—"

"Hey, don't forget, we have a publicity machine of our own," Patrice reminded her. "I'll make sure any captions under photos of Maya mention Mocha Magic Coffee."

If that was supposed to calm Alicia, it failed to. She looked ready to cry, then kill. But Patrice was finished discussing the matter. She turned to Madame.

"I'm sorry you had to see that."

"I'm not!" The speaker's voice sounded amused. It came from one of the two young acolytes who'd rushed here with Patrice. I'd almost forgotten about the girls.

On first glance, they looked related. Both were average height (giving them several inches on me). Both were brunettes with identical Audrey Hepburn–esque pixie cuts, boldly painted with port wine highlights. Even their dresses were similar, with girlish cap sleeves and sixties-style kaleidoscopic prints. The way the two glanced at each other, they appeared tight. Both had delicate features, but one of the girls was Caucasian, the other Chinese.

"You're Daphne, aren't you?" I said, meeting the pretty, leaf-green eyes of the Caucasian girl.

"Yes." She extended her hand. "Daphne Krupa."

This was the same young woman who'd come out of the Garden earlier to fetch Patrice for her presentation. Her chili-pepper red cat glasses, which matched her opaque stockings, were off her nose now and hooked onto her dress's square neckline.

I introduced myself. "So you work for Patrice?"

"No," Patrice clarified. "For the past few years, Daphne's worked as the personal assistant of Sherri Sellars, who governs our Love and Relationship Temple."

"Our Luuuuuv Doc," Daphne sang, then grinned. "That's Sherri's call sign on LA radio."

"Nice to meet you, Daphne," I said, and introduced Madame.

"Nice to meet you both, too. Just don't call me *Daffy*, okay?" she said with a laugh.

"*This* is my new assistant." Patrice gestured to the second girl. Her face was round and smooth, her eyes chocolate-covered almonds, her lips slick with a pretty gloss that matched her sheer, plum stockings. She extended her hand. The shake was surprisingly firm.

"Susan Chu," the girl said.

"And don't call her *Sue*," Daphne warned.

Susan rolled her eyes. "Sue Chu sounds ridiculous, don't you agree?"

"Sue-Chu! *Gesundheit!*" The two young women chanted it together, like it was a very old joke.

"Both names sound pretty to me," I said.

Susan smiled. "Daphne and I are the glorified gofers for all of Aphrodite's Sisters this week. If you have any problems, just ask us to help."

"That's very nice of you . . ."

"Well," Patrice said, "now that the show's over . . ."

"It *was* a show, wasn't it?" Daphne said, eyes sparkling. Clearly, she wanted to keep dishing.

Susan giggled. "When it comes to Maya, it's more than show. That woman is a twenty-four-seven three-ring circus."

"And Susan knows of what she speaks," Daphne added.

"Really," I said, "and why is that?"

Susan shrugged. "During my first year with our community, I worked for Maya."

"Yeah, and Maya made Susan *work out* with her, too, didn't she?" Daphne teased.

Susan gave a mock shudder. "Let's not relive the horror . . ."

Madame touched my arm. *The escort,* she whispered in my ear.

Oh yes! "Would either of you happen to know anything about Maya's escort tonight?"

Susan made a face. "You mean the captain?"

"Captain?" I said. "He's a military man?"

Daphne and Susan laughed. "Oh, funny! . . . No, no! . . . Wow, not even close!"

"Herbie Lansing is an independent film producer," Patrice levelly informed us.

"That silly cap is for show," Susan explained. "He belongs to a sailing club on Long Island and swans around pretending he's a yachtsman to impress potential clients and investors, but really all he owns is a little Chris-Craft—"

"Okay!" Patrice sent a pointed glance toward the two young women. *Enough dirty laundry in public.* "Let's all get back to the party . . ." She looked ready to say something more, but as she reached into the tiny pouch on her belt, her face froze in horror. "Ohmigod!"

"What's wrong?" I asked. "Are you in some kind of pain?"

"I lost my smartphone!"

Automatically, we all looked on the ground, but there was no sign of it.

Patrice groaned. "I remember setting it down on the Garden podium. But the rain started before I finished my speech, and I got caught up in herding everyone inside. It must still be out there!"

"Won't your device be ruined?" Madame asked.

"No, the podium has a shelf. It should be perfectly dry under there, but I've got to find it. My whole life is in that thing!"

"I'll get it," Susan offered.

"No, it's my fault," Patrice insisted. "You all go back to the party."

Alicia touched her arm. "Do you have a trench?"

"No." Patrice shook her head. "I didn't think we'd get rain."

"Take my Burberry. It has a hood." Alicia handed over the still-damp coat. "Do you want an umbrella, too? There are several from guests in the cloakroom stand."

"The wind's blowing too hard," Patrice said. "And there's a canopy over the stage area."

"Just be careful out there—the floor is slippery." Alicia turned to us. "If you'll all excuse me, I need a moment to freshen up."

As Alicia made a beeline toward the ladies lounge, Patrice slipped on the pearl-gray trench, hurried to the Garden's doors, and flipped up the hood. The dark rectangle of glass served as a stark backdrop for her light-colored figure—the perfect subject for a pen-and-ink. Maybe that's why I stared at her image so long, or maybe on some level I felt a premonition.

Patrice cracked the door and a chilly gust swept down the corridor. The damp air swirled around my stocking-covered legs, sending shivers through me as she stepped outside.

The wind was still strong, but the steady rain was easing, its tattoo decelerating with a promise that waiting it out would be worth it. Beneath the narrow awning, Patrice lingered, watching drops turn to drizzle.

"Clare?" Madame called. "Are you coming?"

"Yes."

Turning to go, I stole one last glimpse of the desolate image: Patrice Stone, arms folded, waiting for the wind to die.

Sixteen

~~~~~~~~~~~~~~~~~~~~~~~~~~~

As we moved back inside the crowded party room, Daphne and Susan drifted away, and I leaned toward Madame. "We need to find Maya Lansing's husband."

"Captain Herbie? Why, dear?"

"Because . . . the fake corpse we saw covered in fake blood this morning was a bodybuilder, and Maya is a fitness queen. There might be a connection. Alicia actually called her a 'steroid-shilling witch.'"

"Coincidence?"

"Mike says in police work there are no coincidences. This isn't exactly a criminal investigation, but . . ." I met Madame's gaze.

Her silver-gray brows knitted. "You think Maya really put her own husband up to seducing Alicia?"

"It's outrageous, I grant you, but Maya strikes me as the kind of woman who banks on outrage."

"But why bring the Candy Man here? How could it help her? What would it accomplish?"

"For one thing, it would rattle Alicia, goad her into causing a scene while Maya can stand back and look poised and together."

"Oh yes, I see. That would be disastrous—and diabolical."

We found Maya easily enough. She was holding court near the tall windows, her stunning body dramatically backlit by New York's cityscape. On the edge of the knot that had formed around her, I spotted my ex-husband. (Not a surprise. Next to coffee beans, half-naked women were Matt's favorite stimulant.)

Every few seconds he stole a glance at the daringly undressed fitness diva. The photojournalists weren't nearly as coy. Snapping pictures, they openly admired her display right along with the wholesale buyers, some of whom actually took personal cell phone shots.

"That Maya is one clever operator," Madame whispered.

I wasn't going to argue. Her topless stunt, plus a room of mostly male buyers, plus samples of our new aphrodisiac would add up to a stunning success for her attention grab—unless we could stop it. Unfortunately, as Madame and I crept closer, our hopes sunk. "Captain" Herbie Lansing was nowhere to be found.

"Dead end," Madame whispered.

"Not funny."

"Sorry, dear."

"Listen, Maya's husband is here somewhere. Maybe he stepped out to the restroom. Just keep an eye out for a cheesy yachtsman's cap."

Suddenly, Madame's eyes lit up. She pointed.

"You see Herbie?" (I assumed.) "Where?"

"Not Herbie. Someone else. Someone I know you've been looking for . . ."

Turning, I finally saw him: Detective Michael Quinn. He stood near the samples table, talking with my daughter, his broad-shouldered form draped in the blue serge suit that I'd helped him pick out a few months ago. Expertly altered by an NYPD-friendly tailor, the coat was nipped and tucked to curve with his athletic physique while giving away no sign of his weapon (in Mike's case, the gun and shoulder holster he wore like a third arm). As he turned, I noticed his tie, silver and blue silk—the one I'd helped his young son and daughter select for a special Christmas present.

Whatever Joy was discussing with Mike appeared to amuse him immensely. His lighthearted mood surprised me. Could he really be over his resignation so fast? Or was laughing with my daughter just a polite act?

"Go visit with your man," Madame said. "I'll keep an eye out for Captain Herbie."

"Captain Herbie?" It actually took me a second to refocus, but refocus I did. Leaning close, I left Madame with a piece of advice: "When Alicia gets back here, warn her—in no uncertain terms—what could be coming her way."

"Oh, I will. Don't you worry, but . . ."

"But what?"

"If Maya's husband does turn out to be Alicia's Candy Man, what next?"

"Tell Alicia she should use the situation to her advantage. She needs to stay calm and composed. She should pull Maya aside and demand she leave the party right now and drop all attempts to cut herself in on the profits of Alicia's product or else."

"Or else what?"

"Or else Alicia will file charges." When Madame tilted her head in confusion, I reminded her: "You know that martini the Candy Man pushed on Alicia last night?"

"The drink he brought to her hotel room?"

I nodded. "Alicia was smart. She pretended to drink the stuff but poured most of it into the flower vase. Then those two martini glasses vanished the very same time that Dennis did, and I got suspicious. I convinced Detectives Soles and Bass to have the alcohol in the vase tested for drugs. If they find any, the Candy Man can be charged with a felony, and if Maya put him up to it, then she's culpable . . ."

I stopped talking when I saw Madame was no longer paying attention to me. "What are you looking at?"

Lifting her chin, she smiled. "Good evening, Detective Quinn."

"Good evening, Madame Dubois. Mind if I borrow your manager?"

Her violet eyes sparkled. "I think she'd be disappointed if you didn't."

A moment later, Mike's breath was hot at my ear. "Somewhere private where we can talk?"

I swallowed, surprised at the voltage just one of Mike's whispers could send through my system.

"Follow me," I said, taking his hand.

The kitchen was dimly lit and empty, the constant whir of large refrigerators the only sound. As I turned to face him, he deftly slid an arm around my waist and yanked me close.

"Whoa, slow down!" I said, flattening my palms against his chest. "What's gotten into you?"

"Five shots of that Mocha Magic stuff . . . Or maybe it was six."

"Six shots!"

"Esther fixed me up." Mike's hands slipped up and down my back, then over my backside.

"Seems to me, she fixed *me* up!"

"Not her fault," Mike said. "I told her I needed a major caffeine hit, and she said there were more than enough samples to go around."

"Believe me, Esther loves to play imp."

"You wanted us to test this stuff, didn't you?" Mike's reply was somewhat garbled. His lips were too busy tasting my neck, my jaw, my earlobe.

"Hey, I've been worrying about you for hours," I said, squirming in his grip. "I want to know what happened today. You seem pretty darn happy for a guy who just resigned from a job he lives for."

"I didn't resign."

"You reconsidered?"

"I reassessed."

"What does that mean?"

"It means my paranoid assumptions were flat-out wrong. The first deputy commissioner wasn't hunting for a head. He knew about our case coming apart with that poor kid's suicide, but he said he understood. He'd had his own share of jobs gone wrong. He seems like a good guy—Larry Hawke is his name."

"Hawke?"

"He's a real old-timer. Hero cop, decorated while still in uniform . . ." Mike smiled down at me. "See? No more worries."

"But—"

My reply melted away in a kiss so electric it could have been licensed as a stun gun. Fighting to keep my head, I broke off, pulled away . . .

"Take it easy, okay? Anyone could come through that kitchen door at anytime." I exhaled. "Alicia claimed this stuff was potent. It looks like she was right."

Mike laughed. "I haven't enjoyed herbs and spices this much since I was in uniform, splitting a bucket at KFC. I ever tell you that?"

"No."

"My partner liked the wings. I was a breast and leg man."

I removed his roving hand from my thigh. "What were you and Joy laughing about, by the way?"

"You don't know?" Mike said in a tone that implied I should.

"No. I don't know. What?"

"I'll tell you about it later."

"Well, I hope you weren't telling her what happened with me this morning. I take it you heard about the Topaz bagman by now? Cop gossip. Or maybe the Fish Squad filled you in—"

"Oh, I heard. You're the talk of the PD today, Cosi. Let's just say I got a lot of pats on the back, along with plenty of ribbing, mostly guys asking why my girlfriend didn't phone me for the collar."

"It wasn't your jurisdiction."

"My jurisdiction? I see. Well, how about we *find* my jurisdiction . . ."

Mike grabbed my wrist and tugged.

"Hey! Where are we going?"

He didn't reply. Like a caveman in a mating frenzy, the man simply pulled me toward the kitchen's glass double doors, a service exit that allowed the catering staff to reach the Garden.

Against my better judgment (although not my hormones) I willingly followed. The rain was still coming down, but an awning extending out from the doorway kept us relatively dry.

This part of the roof had the feel of a balcony or (given the downpour) a narrow section of Noah's deck. A corner of the building cut us off from the bulk of the event area. Far to my right, I could barely make out a sliver of the lighted Garden—like catching part of an ark's bow from the vessel's port side. Yet in front of us we had the same billion dollar view, a virtual sea of city lights.

At only seven stories north of Fifth, we floated just above the Midtown streets. Glistening towers of glass and stone rose up around us like dramatically lit stalagmites. Across the avenue, the Gothic steeples of St. Patrick's Cathedral loomed whitely in the night like twin spires of a delicately carved ice palace.

Mike kept us under the overhang, just a few steps away from the kitchen doors still veiled by shadows. He swung me around and pressed my back to the wall. The surface was cold, but his caressing hands felt warm against my chilled skin.

"I still don't understand," I whispered as his lips began to nibble. "Why did this deputy commissioner Hawke make such a big deal about calling you in?"

"He wanted all the paperwork on the Brooklyn suicide

and the Jersey drug dealer the kid had been buying from. He's turning everything over to the Feds. In the meantime, he had another case for me. An important one."

"What case?"

"A cold case. He said I was in a unique position to handle it."

"Why?"

"I'll tell you about it—later."

"You're putting me off?"

"Only for a little while. The truth is, I'm going to need you."

"Seriously?"

"Seriously. This cold case puts you in a prime position to help me. And speaking of prime positions . . ."

Mike's body pressed into me.

"We shouldn't be doing this—" I lamely rasped, until his kiss convinced me otherwise.

For a time we were content, wrapped in a cocoon of bliss, our mouths sealed, the magical lights of Rockefeller Plaza shimmering through the soft rain. Then something far less ethereal kicked in.

My skin began to tingle and my heart rate picked up. A rush of adrenaline seemed to heighten every touch, every kiss. Was Mocha Magic really this potent? I'd only sampled a little yet I felt genuinely breathless, slightly dizzy. Clearly, Mike did, too. When his big hands began roughly tugging up my skirt, I knew he'd lost his head.

"Mike, no!" I pushed hard at his chest, smoothed my skirt back down. "Not here."

"Where, then," he whispered, breath searing my ear. "Your place? Later?"

"Actually, no."

He tensed.

"Joy's come home unexpectedly. She'll be staying with me."

"How about after Joy goes to sleep?"

I shook my head.

"Come to my place, then."

"I'll try."

"Better do more than try, Cosi . . ."

Mike's primal need for fleshly delights reasserted itself. Once again, I felt his hands shortening my hemline. This time I didn't stop him. My own unbearable need for release had finally short-circuited every synapse of my better judgment.

Thank heaven for the *urgent* ringtone of his cell, which put the brakes on his out-of-control libido (and mine). Mike cursed softly as he answered the cell call with one hand, kept tight hold of me with the other.

"Yeah, Sully."

Mike listened, his face growing impatient. "And this has to be done now and not later?"

Within a minute, the conversation was over. As he put away his phone, I readjusted (and rebuttoned), which took a good minute.

"It seems a certain member of the NYPD requires my attention," he said, clearly annoyed. (Those little veins at his temples were more accurate readers of his mood than a standard polygraph test.)

"Hey, look on the bright side," I said, "this morning you thought you were out of a job."

"I also thought I'd be spending the evening with you."

"The evening's not over yet," I whispered.

"You really understand?"

I smiled, leaned close, and kissed him deeply. "I know you, Michael Ryan Francis Quinn. When duty calls, you go . . ." Then, taking his hand, I led him out of the Garden and back into the light.

Seventeen

~~~~~~

At the elevator bank, I gave Mike's hand a final squeeze. By now, the gathering was breaking up, and the cars to the lobby were crowded. Just before the doors shut, Mike sandwiched himself between a pair of jovial middle-aged confectionary executives, asking directions to the Carnegie Deli.

Before returning to the party, I used the glass on the rain-streaked Garden doors as a mirror to check my state. As I turned my wrecked French twist into a simple ponytail, I spied another reflection in the glass.

A young woman in a red jacket moved toward the elevator bank with a new group of departing guests. Despite her hood being up, I recognized my daughter immediately.

Now where is Little Red Riding Hood going? I wondered. If I were a *suspicious* parent, I *might* conclude she was up to something.

The moment I confronted Joy, she turned doe-eyed. "Oh, hi, Mom!" she chirped, way too energetically. "I was looking all over for you!"

"Well, you found me. Where are you sneaking off to?"

"I'm not *sneaking*. How funny!" Joy laughed (in a pitch too high) and gave me a one-armed hug. When the elevator car binged, she pecked my cheek and ducked inside. Only then did I spot the glossy black box tucked under her jacket—the one marked in white grease pencil with the letters *REF.*

"I'm just meeting a friend!" she sang while jamming the lobby button over and over. "Going to catch up while I'm in town . . ."

"What friend?" I asked.

"I'll tell you in the morning. I have the key to the duplex. Don't wait up—"

The sliding doors cut off any further discussion.

Okay, so my daughter was an adult and she had plenty of close friends in the city. But the stealthy way she was attempting to depart, along with that box of Raspberry-Espresso Flowers, set off alarms in my head.

I hurried back to the party to question Matt.

By now, the Loft space was half empty. The final, lingering guests had clustered themselves into two tight knots on opposite ends of the room. The larger group was exclusively male—all of them buyers, circling Maya Lansing.

I didn't see Matt, but it did dawn on me that Maya was *still* here. Clearly, no showdown had taken place between her and Alicia. Almost immediately, I saw why. The elusive Captain Herbie was now glued to Maya's side.

Given the fitness queen's oh-so-perfect butt, I was more than a little surprised to find her husband a stout, middle-aged regular guy. He was cute enough—a teddy bear with a yachtsman's cap, but he was obviously no bodybuilder, which meant the identity of "Dennis St. Julian" and the purpose of his fake murder this morning remained a mystery.

The second group in the half-empty room was mostly female. Among them were Madame and Alicia Bower, along with those two twenty-something acolytes I'd met—Susan Chu and Daphne Krupa. I also recognized Sherri Sellars, the Love and Relationship Sister. They'd gathered so thickly around a central figure I suspected it must be the one and only Aphrodite.

Putting off my desire to meet the World Wide Web's goddess of love, I focused instead on the pursuit of motherly truth. I found Esther Best at the samples table, merging what was left of the pastries into tidy new displays.

"Where's Matt?" I demanded.

"Gone," she said. "He left shortly after you disappeared."

"I see." Folding my arms, I considered the bait. "So tell me, Esther, are we completely out of Voss chocolates?"

"Nearly," she replied, clearing away an empty tray. "We still have some Hearts of Darkness and Petit Nibs, but everything else is *nom*-ed."

I pretended to weigh her assessment. "You know what? Let's put out that box of Raspberry-Espresso Flowers, after all. They may have sugar bloom, but I'm sure they're delicious and the remaining guests might enjoy them."

"Uhm . . ." Esther froze. "Sorry, boss, I think most of those are gone."

"Gone? How can that possibly be?" I stared. *Hard.*

She threw up her hands. "I put half the box aside to share with Boris, okay? Joy saw me and asked for the rest. She wanted some cupid helper, too. Where's the harm? They were just sitting there, going to waste!"

Cupid helper? I closed my eyes. "Esther, *who* is Joy meeting tonight?"

"I'm not supposed to say."

Hands on hips, I tapped one foot in a managerial countdown. "Unless you want nothing but opening shifts for the next *five* months, you better—"

"Okay, okay! If you're going to use Gestapo tactics!"

"*Who?*"

"I'll tell you. Just don't let Mr. Boss find out. Joy already knows how her dad feels about this dude, and if he—"

Oh no. "Not Franco!"

"Oh yes. The General, aka Sergeant Rambo, aka Mr. Magic Hands, aka—"

"Stop. Please!" *Could this day get any worse?* "She told me their little fling was over!"

"Naw," Esther replied. "The whole 'moving on' thing was just something she said to humor you and Matt."

"There'll be no 'humoring' Matt if he gets wind of this."

"Well, I'm not about to tell him."

"Good," I said, and quickly collared Tucker.

"What now?" he asked.

"Don't try to play me," I said. "You heard every word."

"I hate to be the bearer of obvious news," Tuck said, "but Joy's *really* into Franco. The guy's funny, streetwise, has washboard abs, and kept in touch with her all these months. Plus he carries a badge and a gun—useful little perks in all five of our boroughs. Face it, Matt's going to find out."

"But he doesn't have to find out this trip." *Or this year,* I silently added. "Matt's already in a state over the Mocha Magic powder. If he hears his own daughter took a box of *cupid helper* to Emmanuel Franco, he'll blow an artery. And the last thing I need this week is a trip to the ER!"

"Don't sweat it," Tuck replied. "I wouldn't want to drop the news about Franco on any daughter's daddy—especially not Matteo Allegro."

"Thank you," I said, glancing around. "Now let's get Nancy on board. Where is she?"

"Gone," Tuck said.

"Gone where?"

Tuck arched an eyebrow. "Before you disappeared with Mr. Blue Suit, Nancy declared she was feeling faint."

"*Woozy* was the word she used," Esther said.

"Is she okay now?" I asked, worried.

"She spent a little time in the bathroom," Esther said. "When she came out, I sent her home in a cab. We don't need a barista keeling over in the middle of service. Not good for public relations."

I frowned. "Did she have a fever? Chills?"

"Nope." Esther smirked. "In fact, now that I think about it, the whole thing might have been a 'dizzy act.'"

"What does that mean?"

"Well, she sampled quite a few of our aphrodisiac-laced goodies. Maybe she faked being ill so she could go back to the Blend to try hooking up with Dante. She's pretty excited about some special tattoo he's supposedly creating for her."

The fact that Dante was designing a "special tattoo" for Nancy was news to me. Either Dante was humoring her, or Nancy had finally figured out a way to get the artistic attention of her boy-crush.

Before I could speculate which it was, Alicia tapped my shoulder.

"Excuse me, Clare, I have a question . . ."

"Alicia? What is it?"

"Have you seen Patrice Stone? I ran out of business cards. I have more in my coat pocket, but I can't find my Burberry—the trench I lent her? Patrice needs to tell me where she tossed it . . ."

"It's not in the cloakroom?"

"No."

Susan Chu drifted over. "Daphne and I were looking for Patrice a little while ago, but we couldn't find her. I mean, this isn't that big a place so where did she go, right?"

My daughter, my ex-husband, and my newbie barista were gone, and now Patrice was missing . . . *Great*.

"Let's pan out," I said. "Susan and Daphne, check the ladies' room—all the stalls . . ."

With a nod, they dashed off.

"I'll go speak with Aphrodite," Alicia said. "Perhaps she sent Patrice on some errand and didn't tell anyone . . ."

After they were gone I thought back to the last time I saw Patrice Stone, it was right before she slipped into Alicia's hooded raincoat and dashed outside to retrieve her missing smartphone.

"Keep an eye on things," I told Esther.

"Sure, boss. Where are—"

I hurried across the half-empty party room, down the corridor, past the elevator bank, and pushed through the doors that led to the rooftop Garden. The air felt chillier, but the storm was letting up fast, the steady rain dissolving into drizzle. Rippling puddles still covered the Garden's stone floor, acting as mirrors for the illuminated columns above them. The most brilliant light, however, radiated from St. Patrick's white spires, gleaming across Fifth Avenue. The bells inside those twin steeples began to chime the hour. The sad, haunting sound rang across the concrete chasm and echoed through my bones.

Ignoring the few droplets of rain that pelted my skin, I dodged the puddles at my feet and headed for the podium. The little canopy over the raised stage had failed to protect a thing. Every surface was completely rain swept. I carefully climbed the few slippery steps and looked around the podium, searching for any sign of Patrice or her missing smartphone. Finally, I turned to face the rear of the stage and the reflecting pool behind it.

That's when I saw her. Sprawled facedown in the blue water was a human figure. The brightly lit pool framed the woman's silhouette. Around her battered head, a blood-flecked cloud mingled with locks of golden hair to form a scarlet halo.

I stumbled back down the stairs, nearly slipping off. When I reached the pavement, I hurried to the pool's edge, dropped to my knees, and seized Patrice with both hands.

As I heaved her toward me, Alicia's pearl-gray trench billowed on the surface like angels' wings. The pool sloshed over, soaking my skirt and legs. The body was heavy and limp. It took all of my strength just to drag her out of the water and roll her onto her back.

Her flesh appeared gray-white. The terrible wound on her forehead had drained to a pinkish hue. Her prairie-sky eyes were half-open and unfocused, her limbs already stiffening in the icy air.

I didn't check for respiration or a pulse. With the dying chimes of the cathedral's bells, the horrific truth was plainly evident. Poor Patrice Stone was stone-cold dead.

Eighteen

~~~~~~

Dripping wet from the reflecting pool and fighting back tears, I returned to the hallway and the elevators. The party continued, the remaining revelers oblivious. I was numb during the ride downstairs, and by the time I reached the security station I was shivering uncontrollably, my wet ponytail plastered to my back.

I found "Matterhorn," the security director with the muffin top neck, and stammered that I'd discovered a dead woman in the Garden. He mobilized his force, ordering them to seal off the area and lock down the elevator bank.

Despite the flurry of activity, Kevin (his real name) sat me down in a folding chair, took off his own giant blue sport coat and wrapped it around me, insisting I wait right there with him for the NYPD to arrive.

Within minutes, the night air was filled with sirens, the streets with flashing lights. Uniformed officers swarmed the art deco lobby, followed soon after by plain-clothed detectives, enough to number an entire squad. Many of them looked familiar to me since I'd seen them that morning at the One Seven.

Among the sea of suits were two of my favorite customers: Detectives Lori Soles and Sue Ellen Bass. Both were still wearing their chocolate blazers and beige slacks. Sue Ellen's dark hair was down now, but she was still keyed up. The pair noticed me but didn't approach. Instead, they fell into a huddle with Kevin and a man in a trench with prematurely gray hair who was most likely the squad's senior officer. They glanced at me several times, but then the huddle broke and the Fish Squad flanked me.

Lori Soles crouched down. "How are you doing, Cosi?" she asked. Her short blond curls were frizzy from the rain; her blue eyes big and unblinking. "You okay?"

"I'm okay."

She asked me to recount how I found the body. I did. Finally, Sue Ellen broke in with a question.

"Do you feel up to returning to the crime scene?"

"Of course." I nodded. "I want to help."

I tried to give the sport coat back to Kevin, but he insisted I keep it around me to stay warm and ward off any shock. I thanked him again and followed Soles and Bass to the elevator.

In the Garden the rain had stopped completely, even the mist had cleared, yet there was still silent lightning—multiple flashes from police cameras photographing every angle of the crime scene. We circled the stage and halted a dozen yards away from the reflecting pool, now surrounded by so many officers wearing CSU jackets I could hardly see the doctor who knelt at Patrice's side. The occasional blast of wind or blare of car horns echoed up from the street below, but I clearly heard the grim words from one of the city's thirty-two medical examiners pronouncing her dead.

Sue Ellen tied back her hair, and Lori stood quietly watching while members of the Crime Scene Unit knelt on the cold, wet stones and methodically stripped away Patrice's clothing. They carefully searched each piece before placing it in its own plastic evidence bag. Meanwhile, the medical examiner handled the corpse with latex gloves, checking for hidden wounds, defensive marks, any evidence of foul play.

During this grisly search, I caught a glimpse of Patrice's unfocused eyes and looked away. Gazing instead at the gleaming spires of St. Patrick's Cathedral, I recalled the dying bells and recited a silent prayer.

One member of the CSU stepped out of the crowd and called for the lead detectives. He was clutching an evidence bag in his hand, but I couldn't see what was in it.

"Wait here," Lori said as she and Sue Ellen consulted with the man. Then Sue Ellen placed a quick call. After a few minutes, the detectives flanked me again.

"Her name is Patrice Stone," I told them.

Lori must have thought I was rattled. She put a hand on my shoulder. "We know the woman's name," she said very slowly and carefully. "You told us already."

"I know I did. I just wanted to make sure you didn't get confused. I saw them going through her pockets, and I know there are business cards in there belonging to another woman, Alicia Bower. Patrice borrowed Alicia's trench. Did I mention that?"

"No." Lori paused. "Alicia Bower? Isn't that the same woman who was involved in that fake murder scene this morning at the Topaz?"

I nodded. The detectives exchanged glances.

"Listen up, Cosi," Sue Ellen said. "Crime Scene didn't find any business cards. All the pockets were empty, except for the breast pocket of the raincoat."

She displayed the evidence bag. Inside was a sheet of paper with a single word printed on it.

"LAETA," I read.

"Does it mean anything to you?" Lori asked.

I shook my head. "Looks Latin to me . . ."

"We think it's Latin, too. We've got detectives backing us up at the One Seven. They'll compile a list of possible meanings."

"Laeta might be a last name," Sue Ellen said. "You know anyone with that name?"

"No, I don't. Alicia might. It's her coat."

Lips pinched, Sue Ellen nodded and returned the evidence bag to the CSU officer.

"Don't sweat it," Lori said. "We'll follow up with the usual twenty-thousand questions. Something will turn up . . ."

"What do you two think happened here?" I asked.

Lori faced the scene, gestured as she spoke: "Ms. Stone could have climbed the podium in a hurry, slipped on the sopping wet surface, hit her head on the edge of the stage, tumbled unconscious into the pool, and drowned. CSU is on that stage right now, looking for blood splatters—tough after all the rain, but we have Luminol."

"Luminol?"

"A chemical cocktail that adheres to the iron in hemoglobin. The blood will show up even if most of it has been washed away."

"Of course, Ms. Stone might not have fallen by accident." Sue Ellen noted. "Someone could have struck her in the head and dumped her in the pool—"

"We'll know better when we get the results of the autopsy," Lori cut in.

"Aren't there hidden security cameras up here somewhere?" (I realized the possibility almost the moment I said it.)

"There are." Lori turned me around and pointed to a small box on the building's dark wall. "As you can see, one of them is aimed directly at the Garden entrance."

I couldn't believe how easy this was going to be. "Won't the camera reveal who came out those doors after Patrice? And if she was murdered, won't that be your evidence of the killer's identity?"

"Pretty easy, huh?" Lori nodded with a little smile. "We're waiting for a judge to grant a warrant to review the digital files. In the meantime, why don't you give us more background on Ms. Stone and this party . . ."

I filled them in on everything: the product launch, the guests, Patrice's job, the cutthroat company she worked for.

Then Lori's cell phone beeped and she answered. "Hello, Judge Harman, thank you for returning my call . . ." The conversation was a short one and ended with Lori smiling. "We have our warrant."

"Now what?" I asked, pulling Kevin's giant sport coat closer around me.

"First we meet up with the lawyer for the property management company. Then we'll review those images—"

"Take me with you."

Lori nodded. "We plan to. You were at the party, so we're hoping you can ID any guest or staff member who came through those doors."

We followed Kevin deep into a subbasement beneath Rockefeller Center. At an unmarked door, he pressed a buzzer. The door opened, and a man greeted us.

"I'm Ruben Salter."

The private attorney was a balding man, not much taller than my own five-foot-two frame. He wore a three-piece suit and glasses with frames as thin as piano wire. His mouth appeared locked in a permanent grimace, but his apparent professional indifference evaporated when Lori Soles shook his hand.

The attorney could not stop staring at the Amazonian detective with a cherub's blond curls, and it seemed to me his touch lingered longer than necessary. Even his rigid frown flatlined into what I assumed was his version of a corporate-lawyer smile.

Stepping back, Salter waved us into a series of windowless spaces. Behind a soundproof wall of glass, uniformed personnel monitored activities in and around the sprawling complex. Instead of leading us into that high-tech venue, we were ushered into a cramped room with concrete walls and unhappy green carpeting. A small fridge hummed in the corner, and a few ill-matched chairs were scattered about.

The only sign of advanced technology here was a small

desk with a wide-screen monitor and a keyboard with bells and whistles I didn't recognize. Kevin folded his massive frame onto a small chair (for him) and adjusted his position in front of the keyboard.

While Lori, Sue Ellen, Ruben Salter, and I pulled up chairs around him, Kevin cracked his big knuckles and opened a decidedly low-tech ring binder with a scuffed plastic cover.

"This is the master directory with the access codes for all the security cameras," he explained while flipping through the binder. He squinted at an entry page while typing in a series of numbers.

The monitor came alive with a split screen image. On the left, I recognized the double doors for the Garden's guests. On the right were those smaller, hidden service doors, the ones that led to the catering kitchen. A digital clock indicated this was real time.

"Let's start by rewinding an hour or so," Lori said, "to the moment when Cosi went outside and found the DOA."

Kevin placed his hand on the mouse ball. As he spun it, the on-screen image wavered with the eerie retreat of time.

"Bingo!" Sue Ellen declared, pointing at the screen.

Kevin magnified the image. My face became more blurry, but there was no mistaking my identity.

"Go back further," Lori said, excited now.

The split screen images wavered again. Speckles of rain hit the lens and vanished in the blink of an eye. A few times the picture shook from the wind buffeting the camera during the furious storm.

"Wait!" Lori cried. "Look at the other door, the one around the corner from the main entrance."

"Those are the service doors," Kevin said. "They lead to the kitchen."

"Two people came through there."

"I saw it, too," Kevin agreed.

He enlarged the image of a man and woman. Though their faces were partially obscured by shadow, their activity was clear enough. Lips locked, their bodies seemed to meld together in the darkness.

I watched with mounting dread as Kevin slowed down the playback speed. Finally, he froze the image to give us all the opportunity to study every embarrassing detail.

"What the—" Sue Ellen's eyes went wide. "Is that *you*, Cosi?"

ÑINETEEN

~~~~~~~~~~~~~~~~~~~~~~~~~~~~

"**T**HAT'S her, all right."

Lori Soles glanced at her partner, tried not to laugh. "But who's the lucky guy? I can't quite see his face. Do you think we have this mug's mug shot?"

"We do," Sue Ellen said, folding her arms. "From what I know, he's on quite a few Most Wanted lists. The ladies of the Gold Shield Bachelor's Watch for one."

"What's that?" Lori asked.

"A feisty little Yahoo! group I just discovered. Not sanctioned by the PD, you understand—"

Kevin loudly cleared his throat, zoomed past the image. "Let's move along, shall we?"

Face burning, I remained silent.

Kevin glanced back at me, held my eyes. "This camera recorded without a human monitor. In real time, you had your privacy."

"Thanks," I said, willing to take my licks. "But we're not in real time anymore."

"Sorry, Cosi," Lori said after a beat. "One of the drawbacks of any investigation: personal secrets get exposed."

"Nothing to be ashamed of," Sue Ellen added, slapping my back. "There are plenty of straight females on the job who wouldn't mind slipping away from a party with Quinn—"

"Oh, really?" I said, finding my spine. "And who would they be?"

"Ladies—" Lori said, then mouthed to her partner. "Let's not go there."

Sue Ellen twirled her finger at the monitor. "Rewind some more," she told Kevin, suddenly eager to refocus on work. "Patrice stepped outside between nine thirty and ten. I'm sure we'll spot our person of interest—"

"Person of interest?" Ruben Salter echoed. "I thought you were looking to track the deceased's movements."

"We're looking for a murderer," I said.

"Murderer!" Salter blurted so loudly we all tensed. He looked shocked a moment then seemed almost happy to hear it. "So this is a homicide investigation? Because I was led to believe this was about possible negligence."

"The case for murder has yet to be proven," Lori cautioned.

Kevin rewound to the moment Patrice came through the doors. My breathing stopped as he slowed the speed.

"Okay, here it is," I said. "Go forward, one minute at a time."

We watched as Patrice stood under the awning, waiting for the downpour to slow. Finally, she moved beyond the camera's eye. Within a minute, a mysterious figure followed her through the Garden doors.

This should have been our eureka moment. Unfortunately, it wasn't. The figure stalking Patrice was carrying a very large black umbrella—an umbrella that appeared to move with the person under it, strategically blocking the camera's view.

Sue Ellen cursed.

"Hold on," Lori said. "This person had to come back in again."

Kevin toggled the ball until he found the very same black

umbrella going back inside. Again, the person under it used the umbrella as a shield, carefully moving it to avoid being seen.

"The ID's blown coming and going!"

"It looks like this person knew the camera was there," I said.

Ruben Salter was more devastated than any of us. "All these cameras and a murderer gets away? How is it possible? Kevin, do we have any other footage of the Garden?" He lowered his voice. "The hidden lenses?"

Kevin checked his log, began punching the board. "I'm getting us rotating shots from two angles. I'm putting them up."

We studied every image, but there was nothing showing the small canopied stage and podium area in the sprawling rooftop Garden at the exact time of Patrice's death. Nothing gave us a glimpse of the killer—or even Patrice—in the brief seconds it took to move from the door to the crime scene.

"How long was that person in the Garden with Patrice?" I asked.

Lori glanced at her notebook. "From the time clock: between nine and ten minutes."

"More than enough time to commit murder," I said.

"*If* this is a homicide," Lori cautioned. "It could be man-slaughter. Or something else."

"Ten minutes out there, right after the victim," Sue Ellen declared. "Golf umbrella moved enough so we can't make who it is? This looks wrong and you know it."

"Kevin, would you go back and hold on that umbrella?" Lori asked. When he did, we all studied the frozen image.

"Look there," I said. "Is that something printed on it?"

The letters were blurry. Kevin tried to magnify them, but they became even more pixilated.

"Two *M*s?" Lori said. "M&Ms? Do they sell umbrellas at the M&M store in Times Square?"

"They're *N*s," I said. "Double *N*s—like a corporate or store logo."

"Might be a club," Sue Ellen said. "Neo Nirvana on the Lower East Side. Or Night Nosh, that new twenty-four-hour retro diner on Eighth."

"What about the National Network?" Mr. Salter suggested. "It's an online bank that focuses on secure Internet transactions."

"I like the bank angle," Lori said, scribbling in her notebook. "Banks are always giving away freebies. Umbrellas are a popular item to push their logo." She swung around to face the lawyer. "Good call, Mr. Salter."

Ruben beamed.

We reviewed the elevator cars to and from the Loft, but no one turned up with an umbrella during the appropriate times, and the few umbrellas we saw weren't black.

"Let's try the lobby cams," Sue Ellen suggested.

"We can't." Lori said. "We'd be exceeding the parameters of Judge Harman's search warrant." She locked eyes with Mr. Salter. "It's a shame, but . . ." She shook her head, appearing crestfallen. "We're only permitted to view the Loft & Garden, and the elevators to and from."

"Oh my. That won't do. I'm giving you permission right now, Detective Soles. We've got to find this killer before he takes it on the lamb! Kevin, do what these ladies tell you."

"Yes, sir."

For the next thirty minutes, we studied images from the lobby cams. We found a sea of people, but no one with a large black umbrella in hand.

"The killer must have taken the stairs to another floor, or tossed the umbrella and slipped back into the party," Sue Ellen speculated.

I noticed Lori staring at me. "Well, Cosi? You had a front-row seat for it all. Do you have a theory?"

I took a breath, considered the consequences of what I was about to say, then said it anyway. "Alicia Bower had a lot to lose tonight. You should question her. Another woman, Maya Lansing, the company's fitness guru, should be questioned, as well, along with her husband, Herbie Lansing . . ."

I did my best to explain the motives then added: "Maybe Patrice argued with Alicia or Herbie. Maybe it was a simple fight that went too far, a shove on a slippery stage. Maybe nobody meant for her to die . . ."

Lori and Sue Ellen took notes, asked more questions. Finally, we all stood up.

"I'll have these recordings copied, Detective Soles," Ruben Salter said. "You might find more clues with time to review them more carefully. Perhaps you'll see the killer bringing the umbrella into the party."

"Bringing the umbrella in won't prove anything," I pointed out. "Anyone could have grabbed an umbrella out of the cloakroom—"

"Thank you so very much, Mr. Salter," Lori quickly cut in. "I appreciate everything you've done to help us here."

"You're quite welcome, Detective. Please take my card. Call me if you need more help with this case, or if you need a lawyer, or for anything. Anything at all."

Mr. Salter watched us until we reached the end of the corridor and filed into the elevator.

"Lori's got a boyfriend," Sue Ellen quietly sang after the doors closed.

"I got us the access to the lobby cams, didn't I?" Lori smiled.

Sue Ellen snorted. "You little tramp! You did it again. What would the other Officer Soles say if he knew about your doe-eyed act? You know, the sergeant you married?"

"Who do you think suggested it?"

FORTY-FIVE minutes later, the corpses were piled high at the NYPD's temporary command post inside Rock Center's lobby. Dozens of dead umbrellas—wet, torn, and twisted by the wind, abandoned on sidewalks or stuffed in trash bins— were heaped like cordwood at a bonfire. All had been collected within a five-block radius around the complex, in a search that involved more than a dozen officers.

Unfortunately, the black umbrella with the NN logo was not among the casualties. Now I waited by the mutilated parasols while Lori and Sue Ellen received a final report from their superior.

"A detective located Patrice Stone's smartphone," Lori told me when the huddle ended. "It was dashed to pieces on Fifth, right below the Garden. I assume it was tossed over the side by the killer."

As we walked to the elevator, I remembered the count-down clock Patrice had set up on that phone, a digital monument tracking the months, days, hours, and minutes before the man she loved returned from duty in Afghanistan. Now that reunion would never take place. If her soldier came home at all, it would be for his fiancée's funeral.

"The pieces have been collected and bagged," Lori continued. "We'll check for prints and get the exact time the phone was destroyed from its chip, but the junk's been lying in the street for hours, so . . ."

Her voice trailed off when she noticed my eyes. I'd felt the tears welling but couldn't stop the flow.

"Sorry, Cosi. When bad guys win, I know it's hard to take. But that's the world we live in. Answers never come easy, and you can't expect miracles."

Twenty

~~~~~~

As we moved toward the elevator bank, things got hazy. I swiped at my cheeks, but residual tears fractured my vision.

Famous art deco murals adorned this grand lobby. Colossal human forms cavorted along the walls and sprawled up onto the ceiling. Now those sepia-toned images swirled into muddy chaos.

Chaos churned inside me, too.

Only seven or eight years separated Patrice from my Joy. I pictured Patrice's mother hearing the news of her pointless death, and my sadness spun into outrage. I saw Patrice's fiancé, getting the awful word in Afghanistan, and my outrage whirled into fury. Disturbed, I looked up, but the Titan-like portraits only made my existence feel more diminished.

Answers never come easy, and you can't expect miracles . . .

But I did expect miracles. I expected them because I saw them every day. My daughter was a miracle; Mike was a miracle; love was a miracle; and so was life itself. Patrice's earthly existence may have been extinguished tonight, but that had more to do with hell than heaven, and I had no problem calling on a higher power to help me find justice for her.

At the elevator bank, my gaze drifted north again, over the heads of the detectives. In one of the lobby's murals, five muscular men kicked a small globe around as if playing a game of soccer. Each of these giants represented a different race of mankind. Each appeared bent on winning control of that kicked-around world.

The masterpiece was dynamic, bold, commanding attention. The detectives didn't even glance at it.

"Matisse was right," I murmured.

"What's that?" Sue Ellen asked.

I gestured to Sert's famous *Contest*. "While John Rockefeller was building this complex, he tried to hire Matisse to paint a mural for his lobby."

Lori and Sue Ellen finally looked at the work.

"That's Matisse?" Lori asked.

"No. That's José María Sert, a Spanish artist. Matisse turned down the commission."

Sue Ellen snorted. "Not enough money, right?"

"Money wasn't the issue. Matisse didn't think workers hustling to and from their offices would have the patience to see the qualities in his art."

"Uh-huh," Sue Ellen said, but her head was already down again, considering her leads.

In my own way, I was, too.

On our ride up, I thought about Matisse's rejection—and how it became Sert's opportunity. I considered the figures in his *Contest,* a group of competitors struggling against each other to obtain control of a world.

I could almost hear Mike's voice: *Just think of it in your terms, sweetheart. If someone commissioned you to paint a mural of tonight's competing players—suspects who had motive and opportunity—who would they be?*

Certainly, Alicia and Maya would be in the foreground. That pair had the strongest motives for wanting Patrice dead. Herbie Lansing I'd put right next to his wife, Maya.

The next figure wasn't as compelling a subject, but it was one I couldn't erase: the pixie-haired Susan Chu. As Patrice's assistant, Susan might advance with her boss's sudden demise. That wasn't a strong motivation, but it was cause enough for concern.

Sharing that background horizon would be the "Luv Doctor," Sherri Sellars. The radio psychologist had come here to help Alicia pitch Mocha Magic, but I couldn't help wondering if that was her only business tonight. Did Sherri secretly covet a piece of Alicia's product, just like Maya, the fitness queen? Would getting rid of Patrice advance that goal in some way?

Almost at the vanishing point (yet still in the picture), I saw Sherri's assistant, Daphne Krupa. "Don't Call Me Daffy" struck me as a young woman with intelligence, energy, and ambition—and with those chili-pepper red glasses and matching stockings, she was obviously vying for some kind of attention. Like her friend Susan, Daphne might score a major advance now that Patrice was out of the game.

Before the elevator doors swished wide again, I made my quick, final suggestions to Lori and Sue.

"Add Sherri Sellars, Susan Chu, and Daphne Krupa to your possible persons of interest. If Maya, Herbie, or Alicia don't pan out, take a look at those three. If nothing else, they're all good sources for victimology. Patrice's boss should provide some good background, too. She goes by the single name Aphrodite . . ."

The detectives nodded, made their notations, and I followed them along the corridor and into the Loft space. Several guests glanced our way as we entered. From their flinching gazes, I knew I looked a sight—torn stockings, matted hair, and Kevin's jumbo sports jacket wrapped around me like a Big Apple circus tent.

Not my best moment.

Lori touched my shoulder. "The names you gave us. Are they in this room?"

"Yes."

"Point them out."

I did, quietly describing each person.

"You know to stick around, right?" Sue Ellen said. "We may have more questions for you."

"Whatever I can do . . ."

While the Fish Squad drifted across the sea green floor, I noticed a dozen men in suits, standing stiff as Doric columns among the sagging clusters of remaining guests. These men were Lori and Sue's colleagues from the One Seven. They were still taking statements—and in their hands were familiar looking paper cups. I tensed at the sight. Sure enough, one glance at the samples bar confirmed my fear: a line of cops stood waiting for refills on Mocha Magic.

I hurried toward my baristas, waving my hands. "Stop serving!"

Esther glanced up from her French press pour. "What's your issue, boss lady?"

"You know what my 'issue' is. You're passing out aphrodisiacs to half the badges in Midtown!" I turned to Tucker. "I'm surprised at you."

He shrugged. "They're thirsty."

"No more cupid helper. The faucet is off as of now!"

I shooed away the refill line and helped my baristas break down the station. In the process, I broke down myself and knocked back two successive cups of Mocha Magic. Yes, okay, I was being a total hypocrite, but exhaustion was setting in, and I badly needed something warm and stimulating.

Unfortunately, as I started ingesting my third cup, the world began to look hazy again—and not from unshed tears. Beyond the Loft's wall of windows, the city's neon rainbow pixilated and spun. I gripped the samples table and closed my eyes . . .

Opening them again, I noticed a familiar figure in a blue serge suit stepping out from a cluster of bodies. A head taller than the other detectives, this broad-shouldered lieutenant drained his paper cup as he approached.

Mike? I rubbed my eyes. Was I imagining him?

"When did you get back?"

He didn't answer, simply took hold of my wrist and pulled me along. We retraced our steps to the catering kitchen. Honestly, I was relieved to go. After tonight's horrific events, I badly needed to talk things over.

At the kitchen door, Kevin the Matterhorn stood guard. This surprised me, but Mike gave the young man a quick nod. Kevin stepped aside, and we moved into the kitchen.

The space was deserted and dimly lit, giving us plenty of privacy to talk. Mike didn't appear interested in talking. Tossing away his empty cup, he headed for the exterior doors.

"Wait!" I said. "I don't want to go back out there!"

Like a soundless phantom, Mike continued pulling me—through the exit and onto the balcony-like strip that led to the rooftop Garden. Pivoting, he used his body to back me into a wing of the recessed doorway.

The storm may have ended, but its heavy air lingered, dropping damp, gray fog over everything. A gauzy curtain of mist hung between us and the city, turning skyscrapers into looming Titans. Dark and motionless, the giants hovered with more menace than the lobby's sepia-toned ceiling gods.

"They're watching," I whispered, pointing to the security camera. "We're not alone."

Mike didn't appear to care. His free hand flashed behind him and then I heard a click. I jerked to pull away but couldn't. Looking at my arm, I saw why—

"You handcuffed me?"

Mike shook his own cuffed wrist. "We're linked now."

What kind of game was this? "Unlock these! Let me go!"

"You're not going anywhere, Cosi."

"The hell I'm not!"

I moved to leave. He tugged me back. I tried again, but he was stronger. With a chuckle, he pulled my cuffed arm up around his neck. He grabbed my other wrist, placed it there, too. *Click-click!*

I tugged at my wrists, tried to pull them back from behind his neck. I couldn't. Mike had freed himself while locking my wrists together.

"How did you do that?"

"Magic," he said. "Now hold on." His big hands reached under my thighs and lifted me up, pressing my back to the hard stone wall—

"You're acting crazy, you know that? We can't do this!"

He obviously didn't agree. While his lips nuzzled my neck, he angled his lower body to brace me. With one arm, he held me close, freeing the other to tug up my skirt.

"Mike, slow down!"

Struggling against him, I raised my arms to gain some slack. My bonded wrists nearly cleared his head when he dropped me a few inches, locking me close again.

This is insane! "They're watching!" I cried.

"Forget them," he whispered. "Forget them all . . ."

Sealing our mouths, he used his tongue for another kind of persuasion. Soon my tension melted, my limbs relaxed.

"Say yes," he rasped.

The moment I nodded, the handcuffs unlocked, clothes were shoved aside, and finally, inexorably, he joined us. The city lights blurred as he moved, faster and faster. I felt breathless, feverish. Beads of sweat formed on my limbs and forehead. I closed my eyes, letting his body blot out everything until my need for release made me dizzy. At last, he was crying out and so was I . . .

When I opened my eyes, I found myself standing, my clothes back in place and Mike on the ground. He was propped against the building's wall, his long legs stretched out in front of him. I was still handcuffed, although not to myself. We were back to one cuff on me, the other on Mike.

"Hey!" I called, nudging him.

He snored lightly.

"You're sleeping?" I shook him, but he failed to stir, and that's when I heard it—a small, wild voice.

"Clare!"

I stilled. Traffic sounds drifted up from the avenue but no voices. I leaned out of the recessed doorway, peered down the long balcony. Against my cheek, the night mist felt sticky, like sky nectar.

"I'm in the Garden! Help me!"

I bent over Mike, shook him more violently. "Wake up!"

His eyes half opened. "Can't a guy catch some z's?"

I rifled through his pockets. Finally, I found it—the handcuff key! Working quickly, I freed myself, then moved toward the voice.

"Hurry! Please, hurry!"

I flew through the mist, but the Garden was gone; some unearthly cloud had swallowed it whole.

"Clare!"

With every yard, the gray soup grew denser. I nearly gave up—until a light appeared and then another. Like gas lamps along a foggy street, the faux Greek columns illuminated small pools of rooftop. From one to the next I moved, shadowy outlines jumping out at me, ghosts of potted plants, specterlike folding chairs.

But where are the police?

I saw no uniforms or nylon jackets; no notebooks, cameras, or latex gloves. Only the puddles were left, like liquid mirrors, reflecting my moving legs as they hurried along until a flash of red stopped me—my daughter, dashing by in her red hooded jacket.

"Joy!" I called, but she vanished in the fog.

"Help me! Please!"

The rain-swept platform stood before me, its white canopy fluttering. I searched the stage. Empty.

"Here I am!"

In the Garden pool, I found her—Patrice Stone, alive! Her prairie-sky eyes were blinking, her mouth moving.

"Help me! Please!"

I saw no blood in the water, no terrible wound. Her skin no longer appeared gray or pasty but radiant as an angel, warm as a sun. Locks of golden hair floated like a halo around her head. With her expression so lovely and serene she didn't appear to need help at all.

But she's underwater! She must be drowning!

I lunged to the pool's edge, seized both her hands, and heaved. She felt heavy as a block of marble. With all my strength, I yanked again then abruptly the force was reversed. A jolt came and then a shock. I was no longer pulling her out. She was pulling me in!

The pool roiled with our tug-of-war. Water sloshed over the side, soaking my skirt and legs. I battled like a madwoman, strained every muscle, but her strength was unreal. Now I was in the water, suddenly cold. My hands felt like ice, and then Patrice turned to ice, *actual* ice.

I thrashed and fought, aware her features were transforming. Soft curves resculpted themselves into hard angles until Patrice was no longer Patrice. She'd become the Venus de Milo, carved from frozen water, like the centerpiece of my *budino* staircase—except this Venus had arms, glacial arms, and they locked around me.

Reclining in her pool, the icy beauty hugged me tight. Then we sank together toward her underworld, the shallow water bottomless. I gasped for air, I choked and coughed. An umbrella opened over me. Black as death it floated, down, down, down . . .

As freezing fluid filled my lungs, I closed my eyes and screamed.

Twenty-one

~~~~~~~~~~~~~~~~~~

"**Clare?** Are you okay?"

I opened my eyes.

Mike was bending over me, his hand on my shoulder. I took a breath, felt the certainty of air in my lungs, the sweetness of a pillow behind my head. My clothes were no longer damp. My thin blouse and torn stockings were gone, replaced with a faded Steelers jersey and fleecy sweatpants.

Propping myself up, I found my duplex living room softy lit, flames crackling in the hearth. Firelight flickered across the polished surfaces of Madame's antiques, bringing me back over twenty years to those nights when Matt's mother sat up with me, soothing away my expectant-mother anxieties with cups of Belgian chocolate melted into hot milk and plates of buttery praline *sablés*.

Despite the cozy externals, my heart was still hammering.

"What time is it?" I checked my wristwatch—2:55 AM.

Mike, still in his blue suit, sat on the edge of the sofa, concern creasing his features. "You were crying for help. Did you have a bad dream?"

A *dream*, I thought. *Of course.* Clearly, I'd been dreaming.

What wasn't so clear was when it started. Maybe my head was too fuzzy from sleep, but I couldn't discern where my real memories ended and my nightmare began.

I glanced at Mike, about to ask what (if anything) had happened between us on that Rock Center rooftop when—

"Mom?"

My daughter's voice. Excited, I sat farther up, searched the room to find her standing in the shadows, still wearing her red hooded jacket. I swung my legs to the floor, patted the cushion next to me.

"Sit!"

Joy stripped off her jacket and sat down. I put my arms around her and hugged her tight.

"Why did you run off like that?"

"I'm sorry, Mom. I just . . . all of a sudden . . . I really needed to see Manny."

Manny? I blanked for a second, forgetting Manny was short for Emmanuel, as in Sergeant Emmanuel Franco, the young detective on Mike's squad who'd once arrested me and Joy's father. (But that was another story.)

By now, I'd forgiven the guy. My ex-husband had not. In fact, a short time ago, Matt stupidly forbade Joy to get involved with the cocky cop, which (knowing my daughter) made the prospect all the more enticing.

"I know you're not a child anymore," I told her, "but I'm never going to stop worrying about you . . ."

Joy sighed, shook her head. She really did appear sorry. "I don't know what came over me . . ."

"It's okay. That Mocha Magic powder had us all acting a little"—I shot Mike a look—"out of character."

Mike arched an eyebrow. "At least you know the stuff works."

"Works?" I said. "I'm beginning to think the product needs an outsized warning label."

"Like what?" Joy said. "Do not take without your significant other present?"

Mike smiled. "Consuming alone may prove hazardous."

"Consuming while *driving* may prove hazardous!"

Joy laughed.

I didn't. "Is that what you and Franco were doing all night? Driving around eating aphrodisiac-laced chocolates?"

"We were driving and then"—Joy couldn't hide her amusement—"we weren't!"

Right, I thought. But it failed to explain Mike's involvement. I speared him. "So you tracked Joy down and gave her a lift home?"

"I tracked *Sergeant Franco* down," Mike corrected. "Police business." He'd clipped the words, unwilling to elaborate, at least in front of Joy.

"Don't be angry, Mom. I know I shouldn't have run out on you . . ." She playfully nudged me. "You know, a part of me was surprised I actually got away with it, considering what you used to pull on me in high school."

"Is that right?" Mike said, moving to stoke my dying fire. "And what was that?"

"Mom always knew when I was getting ready to sneak out. Always! I'd call my friends from my bedroom, make my plans, quiet as anything. Her door would be shut, her lights off, but just as I climbed out my window—she'd be in the yard waving me back inside with a flashlight! I couldn't figure out how she knew, but she always did. She used to tell me she was a little bit psychic."

"That's right, honey. I am. Just remember that. I always know when you're about to do something stupid—so don't."

"I really am sorry."

"It's okay. As it turned out, your leaving was for the best. Something happened at the party and . . . frankly, I'm glad you weren't there for it."

"What happened?"

"I'll tell you about it tomorrow."

"C'mon, Mom!"

I exchanged glances with Mike. "Someone had an accident, okay? No one you know. The police came. They had to do interviews, take IDs. It's good that you *and* your father were gone by then. As you know, your dad doesn't react well to authority—and you need to return to France very soon. The whole thing might have held you up."

"Oh, *merde*! You are *so* right! After what I went though with Chef Keitel's death, I absolutely hate dealing with the police!" Joy froze. Cringing slightly, she cast an apologetic expression Mike's way. "I mean except for you and Franco. I don't hate you guys."

"I know." Mike patted her shoulder. "Don't worry about it."

"Okay, honey, you've had a long day." I hugged Joy again. "The guest room bed is all ready for you."

"Thanks, Mom. I love you."

"I love you, too."

"Good night, Mike."

"Good night."

Joy gave him a hug, too. I was surprised how much it warmed my heart.

When she headed upstairs, Mike shrugged off his beautiful blue suit jacket, threw it over a chair. For the briefest moment, the sight of his shoulder holster and weapon actually startled me. It was easy to forget what kind of weight Quinn carried around with him all day, every day.

He sank down next to me, exhaling like a battered balloon. Leaning back, he stretched out his strong arm. I nestled into him, and for long minutes, we simply watched the fire snap and crackle, both of us too drained to talk. Finally, I wrapped my arms around him and squeezed.

"Thank you for bringing her home," I whispered.

"Glad to."

"You want to crash here again?"

"I thought you didn't want me to sleep over when Joy was here."

Mike was right. That was my rule. But sending him away seemed even more wrong.

"It's okay," I said. "I mean, it's pretty obvious Joy won't mind."

"All right, then, I will . . ." He paused. "Okay if we stay up a little longer?"

I'd been through this before with Mike whenever he came off duty late. If he went to bed now, he'd be staring at the ceiling for an hour.

"You're wired, right?" I said.

"I just need to unwind a little more."

"Good. Because I'd like to know what the heck happened between Sergeant Franco and my daughter."

"I figured you would."

"Then come into the kitchen. I'll fix you a snack."

Mike smiled. "Now who could say no to that?"

"So how did you do it?" Mike asked, folding his long body into one of my kitchen chairs.

"Do what?"

"Catch Joy in the act of vacating her bedroom via the window, past midnight, every single time she tried it?"

I smiled. "Trade secret of the Maternal Union."

"I see . . ." Sitting back, Mike began to roll up his starched white shirtsleeves. He did it to keep his cuffs clean, but the gesture always reassured me.

Quinn was the most trustworthy man I knew—the most dependable, patient, and steady—but all that control came with a caveat. He was also the most guarded. For years, I was forced to guess what he was thinking—until he rolled up those sleeves. Then, at least, I knew he could get comfortable in my kitchen.

"You can trust me, you know," he said.

"I know . . ." Bending down, I poked my head in the fridge, began pulling out ingredients. "But I like the idea of having valuable information to barter with."

Mike eyed my backside. "Sweetheart, you can barter with me in that position all night."

"Don't get fresh, Detective."

"Fresh is the last thing I am right now."

"Which is why coffee is on our midnight menu . . ."

Caffeine and I were such old friends, drinking coffee late seldom kept me up. In fact, a hot cuppa joe relaxed me like most people's cocoa, so I reached for my French press.

The bean choice was easy enough. Matt had sourced some amazing new cherries from Rwanda and Sumatra. During my last roasting, I'd paired them with an old favorite from Costa Rica. The new blend I'd created produced a rich, enticing brew with notes of brown sugar, chocolate, and spices. The blend was so new, I hadn't yet thought of a name for it . . .

"And is there going to be food on our menu?" Mike inquired.

"But of course. Croque monsieurs with coffee Welsh rarebit."

"In English?"

"The croque monsieur is just a French bistro version of a grilled ham and cheese—thin slices of ham, Dijon mustard, and melted cheese on buttered and grilled bread. The coffee cheese is my own little spin on it."

"And what exactly is coffee cheese?"

"Watch and learn, grasshopper . . ."

I cut four thick slices from a rustic French loaf and buttered them. On two of the slices, I laid out my beautiful Black Forest ham and caressed it with Dijon. Next I began making the coffee cheese.

"You're kidding," Mike said, watching me. "Where in the world did you come up with this one?"

"College . . ."

My short answer. The truth was, during my two years of fine arts education—before I'd spent a summer studying in Italy, met Matt Allegro, and became pregnant with Joy—I kept two small appliances in my dorm room: a toaster and an electric kettle. With the kettle I conjured countless pots of French-pressed bliss. With the toaster, I created tasty snacks, slathering toasted bread with everything from compound butter, fruit preserves, and Nutella to freshly made deli salads. Then one day, I had a craving for a grilled cheese. I tried using the microwave in the community room, but the results failed to inspire.

Well, I thought, *some people make Welsh rarebit with beer. Why not try coffee?*

The recipe I came up with was ridiculously easy—in other words, perfect for an eighteen-year-old dorm rat. I half filled a coffee mug with shredded cheese. Tonight was a combo of mild cheddar and Gruyère, but over the years I'd used almost every semisoft variety: Colby, Monterey jack, provolone, Gouda, mozzarella, cellophane-wrapped American, you name it.

When my freshly brewed coffee was good and hot, I poured it over the cheese in the mug. Mike couldn't quite believe what he was seeing. His eyebrows practically fused together with naked skepticism.

"Oh, ye of little coffee faith," I scolded. "As I recall, you were just as squeamish about trying your first café latte."

"True."

"And now they're your favorite."

"I don't know—that giant Depth Charge you made me today practically let me see into the future."

"Well, don't tell Esther. She'll insist we rename it Nectar of Delphi."

For about fifteen seconds, I stirred the mug's contents then poured off the greasy coffee, carefully holding back the gooey ball of spreadable goodness. What I had left in the mug was a unique delicacy—melted cheese with a meatier, more complex *umami* flavor, like a Welsh rarebit.

Finishing our croques monsieurs, I covered the two remaining slices of bread with my melted coffee cheese, slapped the ham sandwiches together, and slipped them into a hot skillet of bubbling melted butter.

After frying them on both sides—getting that chewy, crusty, rustic French bread to turn a golden toasty brown—I slid the sandwiches onto separate plates, cut them on the bias, and presented one to the skeptical cop at my table.

Mike took a tentative bite and closed his eyes. "Oh man . . ." He took a few more bites, made a guttural kind of man-in-ecstasy noise, and inhaled the rest.

I finished off my own sandwich. As I licked my fingers, I noticed Mike casting a sheepish glance my way. "What's wrong?"

"Can I have another?"

I laughed. "Didn't I tell you it was good?"

"You did—I should have trusted you."

"I guess that admission earns you another, but it'll cost you . . ."

He brightened. "Personal favors? I'm up for that."

"Rain check," I said. "Tonight I just want information."

"Franco and Joy?"

I nodded. "I'll start cooking and you start talking . . ."

Twenty-two

~~~~~~

"You remember why I had to leave the party, don't you?" Mike began.

"An urgent phone call," I said, prepping the man's second sandwich. "A 'certain member' of the NYPD required your attention."

"Well, that 'certain member' was Franco. Sergeant Sullivan wanted to warn me about him."

"*Warn* is not a happy word."

"When Franco found out about my handing his and Sully's case over to the Feds, he blew a gasket. Sully stressed the decision wasn't mine; it was Hawke's—the first deputy commissioner."

"I remember who Hawke is."

"Well, Franco didn't care. He went off half-cocked, anyway."

I slipped the croque monsieurs into the bubbling butter. "What does that mean exactly?"

"It means he went rogue."

"In English."

"He went after the Jersey dealer himself, beyond our jurisdiction and counter to his superior's decision, which is grounds for reprimand—or even termination. Given the situation, I understood his feelings. Sully is just as emotional about the case, but he's not as young and hotheaded as Franco. So he called me, and we took off to track Franco down and stop him before he did something actionable."

"I need a little more here . . ." I slid Mike's finished sandwich from the pan to his plate.

"So do I. Give me a sec—" He crunched into his croque monsieur, chewed, swallowed, and sighed with satisfaction. "Okay," he mumbled around another buttery bite. "What don't you get?"

I refilled Mike's cup and my own, then sat down opposite. "I don't get why Franco blew his top. What's the difference who puts this drug dealer behind bars?"

"That's just it. Putting him behind bars is the issue. This dealer has no previous record. If he's smart, he'll cut a deal with the Feds and do little to no time."

"But he's responsible for at least two deaths, isn't he? The girl who overdosed on his drugs and the artist boyfriend who killed himself over buying them for her."

"The Feds won't see it that way. In the bigger picture, this dealer is small time. If he offers good intel on perps higher up the supply chain, they'll use him as an informant." Mike finished off his sandwich, sat back.

"And you're okay with that?"

He folded his arms. "No, I am not 'okay' with that, but my feelings are not the law. When you're on the job, you have to pick your battles. Earlier today, I picked mine. I was willing to go down for my squad. Franco seems willing to go down over this lowlife drug dealer."

"Why?"

"Because he feels responsible for that kid's suicide. He thinks he should have seen the signs."

"Okay, so Franco's having problems with cop guilt. How does 'going rogue' help? What did Franco do exactly?"

"He sat on the dealer."

I blinked, flashing for a second on those hulks from *WrestleMania.* "Literally?"

Mike's grim expression finally broke. "No, not literally. Although Franco's not above a move like that—" He reached for his coffee mug. "What my young sergeant did was conduct his own private stakeout. He took a little drive across the river to see this perp, and it turned into a very long drive. We tracked him for hours from his radio's GPS."

"Wait a second. Are you telling me your sergeant took *my daughter* on a stakeout of a drug dealer?"

"Calm down. Nothing happened. Absolutely nothing."

"What in the world was Franco thinking?"

"It wasn't his idea. Apparently, Joy called him before he got to the Lincoln Tunnel. He picked her up, they parked by the river, and he explained that he was heading to Jersey on a stakeout. He was about to drive her home, but she insisted on going with him."

"What in the world was *she* thinking?"

"They weren't thinking, neither of them . . . As I understand it, Clare, your chocolates were involved."

I massaged my temples. "Half a box of Voss Raspberry-Espresso Flowers."

"Well, Sully and I tracked those flowers all over Jersey. Franco and Joy started off watching the scumbag's house, saw him drive away, tracked him to a nightclub, waited him out there. They hit a diner and finally followed him to a girlfriend's house. They were practically in Pennsylvania when we caught up with them. Never once did this dealer cross into Franco's jurisdiction so he never made a move."

"What move would that be?"

"A move to find cause . . . a new reason to arrest the guy."

"Okay, I get it. But you still haven't told me what happened between Joy and Franco while they were alone in that car?"

"I didn't ask."

I sighed. "She's really smitten, isn't she?"

"I think so."

"What about Franco? How does he feel about my daughter?"

"He's a hard case, Clare. I don't know."

I closed my eyes and saw Joy in a wedding gown; Franco in formalwear with matching black do-rag and motorcycle boots; Matt sweetly walking his little girl down the aisle—then lunging to strangle the groom.

"Try not to worry," Mike said. "Joy will be back working in Paris soon enough, right?"

An argument beyond lame. I'd made it myself two times already—to no avail. Joy had been drawn back to Franco like pig(headed) iron to an industrial magnet.

"Let's talk about something else," I said. "I don't need a new nightmare."

Mike studied me. "What was it about? You never said."

I took a breath, met his gaze. "You were on the road for hours, right? You never came back to Rock Center, did you? Never used your handcuffs on me?"

"Uh, that would be a no . . . not that it hasn't entered my fantasy life." Mike began to smile, until he saw my expression. "I was joking, Clare—for the most part, anyway. Are you telling me your bad dream was about me?"

"I had an erotic dream that turned bad. We made love. You sort of handcuffed me and seduced me into it . . ." Mike's eyebrows rose with fairly predictable male fascination. "Then I found the body all over again."

"Body?" His eyebrows fused. "*What* body?"

Before I could answer, Mike guessed: "That 'accident' you told Joy about—you were in the middle of it? Is that what you're telling me?"

I nodded and he softly cursed. "I heard the chatter on the police radio, knew there was an incident at Rock Center, but it's a big place, and I was sure you weren't involved. And do you know why? *Because I never got a call from you!*"

"Don't be angry."

"Why didn't you contact me?"

"I turned off my cell during service, and after I found

Patrice dead, the events just snowballed . . ." I did my best to quickly fill Mike in on the evening's festivities—witnessing Maya's threats, finding Patrice's body, working with Detectives Soles and Bass.

"So you think Patrice Stone was murdered?"

"I *know* she was murdered. Why else would the killer hide from a visible security camera under a giant black umbrella?"

"There could be a reason. A good defense attorney will find one—have no doubt. Did Soles and Bass make an arrest?"

"We couldn't get a clear ID from the camera, but they're gathering all the digital footage, having it analyzed frame by frame."

"You were at the party, Clare. Do you have a theory?"

I told Mike about Maya and Herbie and a few other possible suspects, including the suspect who worried me most: Alicia Bower.

"Alicia?" Mike frowned. "Isn't she your new business partner? The one who invented the Mocha Magic stuff?"

"She is."

"What about her worries you?"

"She's a headstrong business woman, yet I found her in a fetal position yesterday morning at her hotel . . ."

The whole fake knife in the chest Candy Man incident seemed like a week ago by now, but I did my best to bring Mike up to speed on it.

"Despite being the obvious target of a horrible prank, she refused to cooperate with the police. According to Madame, Alicia actually wanted to hire me to get some answers rather than bring a professional investigator into it."

Mike met my eyes. "Would you describe Alicia as mentally unstable?"

"I'd describe her as under extreme pressure—and extremely secretive. But then so is Madame when it comes to whatever past they shared."

Hearing that, Mike fell silent for a long minute, his expression moving from cop curious to obviously troubled. "So you're telling me Alicia is connected to Madame's past? But she's surfaced only lately?"

I nodded. "Madame says she owes Alicia a great deal. But she won't say why. And Alicia was supposedly a barista at the Blend, yet Matt doesn't remember her."

"I get the picture," Mike said. "And I'm sure Soles and Bass are already doing a background check on her . . . I'll talk to them tomorrow, try to find out if she has any kind of criminal record or history of mental problems—but there's something else you need to know . . ."

The grooves of tension in Mike's forehead made me stiffen. "Bad news?"

"The primary reason I went to the Fourteenth Floor today wasn't to turn Franco and Sully's case over to the Feds. That was incidental. First Deputy Commissioner Hawke was far more concerned about a cold case that's suddenly heating up. He said I was in a unique position to crack it for him."

"Unique position?"

"The case involved the Village Blend."

"My Blend?"

"Hawke learned about my ties to you, this place, and he asked me to investigate."

"This is the old case you mentioned on the rooftop? The one you said I could help you with?"

Mike nodded. "Your former mother-in-law was somehow involved. She was taken into custody for a short time during the height of it."

"She was arrested?"

"Yes."

"For what?"

"Refusing to answer questions before a grand jury."

"Questions about what?"

"The murder of a police officer."

I blinked, stared. "I don't believe it . . ."

Mike said nothing, just waited for me to absorb the shock.

Finally, I asked: "Was Alicia involved?"

"I don't know," he said quietly. "Hawke only gave me an oral briefing today. Sometime this week I'll be given access to the files and evidence. I'll let you know more after I review them."

"What am I supposed to do in the meantime?"

"What detectives do all the time, Cosi. Wait."

"Well, I'm not waiting in this kitchen." I drained my cup, grabbed his hand. "Come on . . ."

By the time we reached the master bedroom, I was more than ready for unconsciousness. My daughter was home safe, thanks to the man climbing under the covers next to me, so I snuggled up close and held on tight.

"Do me a favor," Mike murmured, stroking my hair.

"What?"

"Don't have any more bad dreams about me."

"Believe me, it wasn't my choice."

"You know, I've been dealing with crime scenes for a lot of years. You want some advice?"

"Absolutely."

"Try to think good thoughts before you drift off. Focus on a positive image."

"I'll try . . ."

Closing my eyes, I summoned the first moment I saw Joy today, looking so lovely and grown up in the grand lobby of Rock Center. I saw us hugging and felt my spirits lift. Next I brought back the image of Joy embracing Mike before she went off to bed. My heart soared even higher. Finally, I recalled my first glimpse of Mike at the party, all freshly shaved and smartly pressed in that blue serge suit, chuckling with Joy at the samples bar . . . which reminded me—

"What were you and Joy laughing about at the party?"

"Oh, that . . ." I could almost feel him smiling in the dark. "We were kidding around about her big question."

"Big question? What big question?"

"Come on, Clare . . ." He chuckled. "You don't have to play me."

"Mike, I swear. I have no idea what you're talking about."

"You didn't put Joy up to asking me when you and I are getting married?"

Oh good God! "No. I did not . . ." Tension flowed back into me. I took a breath, let it out. "She asked me that same question earlier today. I don't know why she suddenly cares so much."

"You don't? It's a pretty basic deduction, sweetheart. She loves you, and she wants to see you happy, settled . . ."

"And she might be thinking over that question for herself."

"It's certainly possible," Mike conceded. "So . . ."

"So?"

"So when are we getting married?"

I stiffened. "I don't want to talk about that, Mike. Not now. I'm too tired. Aren't you tired, too? Can't we just go to sleep?"

Mike fell silent for a long moment. I felt the tension in his body now. My reaction obviously threw him. But soon he relaxed, letting it go. "Good night, Clare," he finally whispered and softly kissed my head. "Sweet dreams . . ."

Twenty-three

~~~

THE calm after the storm. That's what I'd hoped for, and when I came downstairs the next morning, my expectations were seemingly met.

Outside the fog had passed; the cobalt sky was clear, and sunlight poured through the Blend's wall of spotless French doors, transforming our marble tabletops into luminous pools of gold. Everything seemed perfectly normal, except the shop's customers, most of whom were women—with green skin.

"Who killed the Witch of the East? Who? Who? Who?"

Either I was having another Mocha-induced nightmare or my Blend was hosting a coven of wannabe Wicked Witches. Okay, *two* covens, because a coven is only thirteen, and there were over two dozen witches, some wearing wigs and false noses, most with day-glow complexions more commonly seen on the Yellow Brick Road.

"Okay, Tucker, what's going on?"

"Good morning to you, too, boss."

I grabbed a stool at the espresso bar, motioned him closer. "There really *are* green women in here, right?"

"Don't worry, C.C., you're not hallucinating." He fluttered the back of his hand. "This is simply spillover from an open casting call at HB Studios."

"Glad to know I'm not crazy."

On the barstool next to me, a leanly muscled Latino man nudged me with a laugh. "Your customers are the ones who are crazy today. Crazy for a part in another ridiculous Broadway spectacle."

I greeted Punch—dancer-singer-actor and Tuck's current main squeeze. "Let me take a wild guess," I said. "It's not Stephen Sondheim."

The two silently shook their heads.

"Somebody's reviving *The Wiz*?" I tried.

"You'd think that, wouldn't you?" Punch said. "I mean, I wish!"

"You have to understand, these are post-postmodern times," Tucker said as if they'd been arguing about this subject. "One must either deconstruct the traditional or approach it with an innovative sequel."

"Innovative," Punch said, rolling his eyes. "Uh-huh."

"So what's the production?" I asked.

Punch smirked. *"Return to Munchkin Land."*

"It's a working title," Tuck noted.

"Who killed my sister? Who? Who? Who? Was it you, my pretty?"

Tuck slid an espresso in front of me. "Given the events of last night, *that* question's timely, you have to admit."

I blew out air and picked up the demitasse, not wanting to admit anything. But before I could take a sip, I felt a heavy hand on my shoulder.

"Clare, we need to talk . . . *now.*"

My ex-husband had spoken (and in such a lovely tone of voice). I could only assume he'd found out about Franco and Joy. I closed my eyes, not yet caffeinated enough for this discussion. As he plopped onto the empty stool on the other side of me, I knocked back the espresso so fast I barely tasted it.

Tuck gawked at me. (It was not my usual way of enjoying espresso.) I met his eyes. "Another one, please. ASAP."

"A *doppio* this time?"

I nodded.

Tuck glanced at Matt. "You want a double, too?"

With a grunt, my ex nodded his shaggy dark head. The length of his hair still threw me. Yesterday he had looked like a jet-lagged Musketeer. Today it was more like an Arabian pirate—a seriously hungover Arabian pirate. Twelve hours' worth of dark stubble had sprouted around his trimmed goatee and worry lines notched the skin flanking his rum-colored eyes.

"Whatever could be on your mind?" I asked as Tuck beat if for the back of the espresso machine. (He knew when to get out of the line of fire.)

"Breanne and I tried your Mocha Magic stuff last night," Matt said.

I cleared my throat, thanking heaven this was not about our daughter's brilliant decision to tail a known drug dealer with a rogue cop across half the state of New Jersey.

"So?" I croaked. "Did you like the herbal product?"

"That's precisely the issue, Clare. Your Mocha Magic is *not* herbal. You're pushing a *drug*!"

"Keep you voice down! What's your problem?"

"That damn Mocha Magic Coffee is my problem and yours, too. When I brought it home last night, Bree said it might make an interesting lifestyle piece in her magazine. So we talked about trying it together and . . ." He combed long fingers through his disheveled hair.

"And? What?"

"And, after two cups, we stopped talking."

"You made love?"

"That's a polite euphemism for what we did. We couldn't stop. Remember, I was already juiced from the party . . ." Matt sighed. "I guess it was my fault. I kind of swept Breanne off her feet."

"Wait a minute," I said. "You had great sex—with your *wife*—and that raises red flags in your head?"

"Listen to me. Your launch party pushed this as a drink mix of coffee, cocoa, and a few herbs. Well, I don't buy it. What exactly is in the stuff? Those individual packets don't list the ingredients."

"The ingredients are on the boxes—twelve packets to a box. They're also listed in the press kit. Wait! I have one behind the counter."

I ducked around the espresso bar for the envelope, spilled the contents on the marble top: a slick brochure, a contact sheet, and six single-serving packets. I scanned the brochure's ingredient list.

"Okay, here we go. There's *Panax ginseng*—"

"That's just ginseng grown in Asia," Matt said. "Why bother to stick the word *Panax* in there except as a cheap marketing ploy?"

"And *Pausinystalia yohimbe* extract—"

"Yohimbe!" Matt cried. "I smoked that crap back in high school. Everybody said it was a legal high. They were only half right."

"I'm waiting . . ."

"It was *legal*."

Punch snickered, and I realized he'd been eavesdropping.

"Okay," I said, still reading. "What about this: *yin yang huo*, otherwise known as horny goat weed."

"Excuse me?" Punch interrupted. "You're kidding with that one, aren't you?"

"No," I said. "In fact, there's a legend attached to it."

"Really?"

I handed over the brochure, and Punch began to read aloud: "Horny goat weed's aphrodisiac properties were first discovered when shepherds noticed their goats became amorous after they ate this herb . . ."

Tuck arrived with our double espressos. "Sounds like that legend about the origin of coffee."

"Which is?" Punch asked.

"Goats started frolicking around in an unusually spirited manner after chewing cherries on a coffee shrub. So the goat herder sampled them."

"Sampling coffee cherries would just wake you up," Punch pointed out. "What's a herder to do, all alone on a mountaintop, after trying horny goat weed?"

"Let's not go there," I said.

"Yes," Tuck said. "After all, in any given countryside, there's always a goat herder on the next hill!"

"*¡Ay ay! ¡Arriba!*"

While Punch and Tuck high-fived each other, Matt folded his arms. "Sorry to kill the fun, but no amount of *yin yang hooey* or ginseng can account for the effects Breanne and I felt last night."

"Wait," I said, trying not to panic. I grabbed the Mocha Magic brochure back from Punch. "There's *Passiflora* extract—that's passionflower—and damiana."

"Clare, you've had damiana before."

"I have?"

"Los Cabos, Mexico?" Matt said. "That week on the Baja Peninsula."

"Oh, right . . ." (Joy was three. She had stayed with Matt's mother while we took a little vacation—only there wasn't a lot of sightseeing beyond our waterfront bedroom, not after one trip to the bar.)

"They used damiana instead of triple sec in their margaritas," Matt reminded me. "You loved the taste. We must have sucked down a gallon."

"There you go! The bartender told us it was an aphrodisiac!"

Matt rubbed his jaw, but then shook his head. "Sorry, Clare, nice try, but damiana isn't that powerful, either. As I recall, before that trip, you and I hadn't seen each other for almost a month—we had a lot of catching up to do."

"True."

"Trust me, I've sampled every illicit narcotic known to man at least once, and this Mocha Magic contains a *drug*, not a collection of herbs."

"Maybe its Alicia's proprietary formula. She might have found a way to heighten the effects of those herbal ingredients. And you had a *lot* last night. Maybe you simply overdosed, and it came off more powerfully than it usually does. Maybe if she puts a warning on the label—"

"Why not just send a text message to the Food and Drug Administration?" He raised his voice an octave higher. "Oh, look at me, I appear harmless, but I'm really dangerous if you ingest too much of me, *and* I'm made with Village Blend coffee beans." His voice went down again. "Just imagine the lawsuits, 'cause I can."

"So what are you going to do? Send this Mocha Magic to a lab for testing?"

"Not me. You're the one who needs to have it tested. This stuff isn't a soil sample or a new hybrid—and you know my history with Bogotá Marching Powder. Why don't you get your boyfriend to do it? He sniffs out illegal narcotics for a living."

I chewed my lip. "I'll ask him."

"I can't believe this is such a surprise to you. I saw Dudley Do-Right at the party, sucking down cup after cup of this stuff. Didn't he say something when you two took this Mocha Magic for a test drive?"

"We didn't. Not exactly."

"Oh, really? Trouble in paradise?"

"No." I lowered my voice. "We were pretty turned on, both of us, but we were interrupted by . . ." What could I say? *A cop going rogue with your daughter? A woman bludgeoned to death and dumped in a Garden pool? An erotic dream turned nightmare?*

"By?"

"It's complicated."

"He's a narc, Clare. He should have noticed something."

"Mike Quinn always takes me at my word. I told him this stuff is purely herbal, and he believed me."

"Love is blind? You expect me to buy that?"

"Love is trusting. And Mike trusts me . . ." (I never realized just how much until this moment.)

"Well, here's the problem, Clare: you trusted my mother, and she trusted Alicia—but her product can sink us. You know we could lose the Blend over this?"

"Calm down, okay? Let's start with having the powder tested."

Matt gulped his *doppio*. "Damn. I *must* have OD'd last night. That stuff was crazy powerful—and, let me tell you, that half-nude woman at your party didn't help!"

"Her name is Maya Lansing . . ." I tapped my chin. "Matt, when exactly did you leave last night?"

"Early. Right after I grabbed the samples. Why?"

"Because something happened after you bolted."

I finally dropped the news bomb about Patrice Stone's death and the police investigation. I also told him about the rivalry among the Sisters of Aphrodite and the possibility that Alicia may have done the deed.

"So now our new business partner might be a *murderess?*" Matt cried.

"Keep your voice down. Maya Lansing is just as likely to be guilty here. She had the most to gain from Patrice's death."

Matt shook his hairy head. "That theory won't hold water. Maya never left that party, not once, not even to go to powder her . . . uh, nose. Believe me, I would have known, and so would every other man in that room."

"You're sure?"

"Absolutely."

I cradled my face in my hands. "Alicia can't be a murderer. This Mocha Magic can't be illegal. It will kill your mother."

"Want me to rub your shoulders?"

"No . . . Yes . . . No—wait! What about Maya's husband, Herbie Lansing? The guy with the yachtsman's cap?"

Matt nodded. "The captain? I nearly asked him why he left Tennille at home."

"Did he leave the party and come back? I'm pretty sure he did. But did you actually see it?"

Matt shrugged. "I wasn't staring at the chubby yachts-man—I was ogling his wife." He swatted the hair away from his eyes and drained his demitasse. "I've got to go. I'd love nothing better than to get a shave and a haircut, and then hit the sack. But that's not to be. I'm meeting Breanne for lunch."

"How long can it take to get a haircut?"

Matt shook his head. "Breanne loves the hair now. She said she liked me scruffy. Either that or the Mocha Magic scrambled her fashionista brain. Anyway, after last night, I'm sure she'll demand an encore performance right there in her office. So I'm going to the health club for a quick steam bath before I face the music."

Matt rose and snatched the powdered coffee packets from the countertop. Still clutching them, he shook his fist at me. "This stuff is a drug, Clare. I'm warning you," he said before cramming the packets into his pocket.

I folded my arms and glared.

"What?" he said.

"You just stuffed your pockets with it!"

"So? Using isn't selling. Big difference. One I'm sure Dudley will explain if you ask him *real nice*."

"Just go already."

Matt was about to face the door when I spied a familiar roughneck over his shoulder. Sergeant Emmanuel Franco had strolled in, espresso-dark leather jacket open, shaved scalp gleaming in the sunlight. His detective's gold shield dangled from a strap around his neck, but I suspected Franco wasn't here on NYPD business—and if Matt caught sight of him, there'd be hell to pay (and plenty of broken furniture).

"Wait!" I cried, seizing Matt's arms.

Annoyance registered. "What is it, Clare?"

Franco heard us, spotted Matt, and made a swift retreat.

"It's . . . It's your *hair*," I said. "Breanne might be right. It's very attractive long like that. Takes ten years off your face."

"Really? You think so?"

The coast was clear, so I released my grip. "Yes. I really think that's a good look for you."

"Thanks," Matt said, grinning now. "I'll drop by later," he added, then tossed me a wave before heading out the door.

Not even a minute passed before the Blend had a return customer. This time Detective Franco carefully scanned the coffeehouse before stepping over the threshold. When our eyes met, he sauntered toward me, flashing his cocksure grin.

TWENTY-FOUR

"**You!** Sit!" I tapped my index finger on the stool beside me. Franco's confident expression vanished.

"Detective," I said with motherly sternness, "I just saved you from a world of hurt. If my ex-husband knew you took his little girl on a dangerous stakeout—"

Franco blinked as he sank onto the barstool. "You got it wrong, Coffee Lady. Joy and I parked on a variety of suburban streets in *very nice* Jersey neighborhoods, ate fruity chocolate flowers, and talked."

I narrowed my gaze.

"Okay," he said, dropping his voice, "there was some lip-lock involved, but give us a break, we haven't seen each other in months."

"How could you take her on the stakeout of a criminal?"

"Joy was never in danger, okay. I wasn't going to do squat with her in the car. I just wanted to start getting a handle on this guy's routine. She's a grown woman, you know, and she wanted to come. I don't see the big deal. It's not like it was official."

"Not official? Don't you give me that dodgy crap! Mike

told me the whole story. You shouldn't be pursuing this dealer at all."

A shadow crossed Franco's face. "Listen, it's real simple. Some poor innocent schmuck of a wannabe artist kissed a Brooklyn sidewalk from ten stories up—partly because I couldn't see he needed bigger help than I threw his way. The scumbag responsible for his death and a beautiful young girl's overdose is going to *pay*. Just think of me as the cosmic collection agent. All I have to do is catch the SOB on *my* side of the Hudson." He folded his arms. "And when I'm done with him, the DEA is welcome to mop up what's left."

"I'm sure Mike warned you of the consequences if things go south on that plan."

"Hey, look, Lieutenant Quinn is the man. I have nothing but respect for my loo, but he can't tell me how to spend my free time, and I know what I'm doing." Franco met my eyes. "So truce, okay?"

I had plenty more to say, but I decided to save it for my daughter. This was a grown man with a deadly serious mission in his eyes, and making an enemy of a possible future son-in-law wasn't a brilliant move in any case.

I sighed. "How about a House Special? Double cream, double sugar?"

Franco's grim expression broke. "Aw, Coffee Lady, you remember?"

"That's what we do here, Manny."

I saw the line at the register. "I'll get it myself."

As I rose from the espresso bar, a young woman with green skin and a black fright wig sat down on the other side of Franco.

"Greeeeetings, my pretty!" she cackled.

"How'ya doin'?" Franco said with a calm little nod. (Now there was a New Yorker.)

To make Franco's joe, I used our Clover—essentially a cross between a single-serving French press and a high-tech vacuum pot. The handy little eleven-thousand-dollar machine allowed me to customize every cup by digitally calibrating everything from water temperature and pressure to brew time in order to coax the utmost flavor out of Matt's scrupulously sourced (and my roasted-with-love) beans.

As I ground those beans fresh, I noticed Tuck boning up on his director's skills while whipping up a slender actress's decaf ("why bother") latte with skim milk and sugar-free caramel.

"From what I understand," he told the young actress, "the witch role is pivotal to the entire show."

"Oh, come on," she replied. "The play's called *Return to Munchkin Land*, so the munchkins are going to be the real stars, right?"

"Actually, I got a peek at the script. It's really about a tragic love between the young Wicked Witch and a handsome munchkin. So you can see how the role of the Wicked Witch is actually the key to the whole story."

The woman's eyes lit up. "And I thought I was trying out for a small part."

"There are no small parts, honey, only small actors."

She frowned, pointed to her lime-green bodysuit. "Small actor might define me. These other girls went all out, with wigs and body paint, even fake noses and warts. Maybe I'm not showing enough commitment to the part."

"It's your voice, movement, and vulnerability that matters." Tuck completed her latte pour with a perfect little heart. "Show your warts emotionally, and you won't need fake ones on your face."

"Thanks for that. I'll do my best. I had no choice. That body paint is a bitch to get off, and I have this modeling gig at the Javits Convention Center later today. Those trade shows are pretty good jobs. Ever done them?"

"The Toy Show," Tuck said, handing her the drink. "I love it. One year I played a mad scientist for Creepy Crawly Critters—rewrote their sales pitch and everything. Where are you modeling?"

"The International Confectioners' Expo. The Nutrition

Nation booth hired me through my agency. They've got a pretty big setup this year—"

I spilled half of Franco's meticulously brewed coffee on our restored plank floor. "Excuse me," I interrupted, "who did you say you were modeling for?"

"Nutrition Nation," she said, a latte-milk moustache decorating her pretty upper lip.

I blinked. Adding it up was too easy: Nutrition Nation— NN—the letters on the big black golf umbrella carried by Patrice's killer. The company had a booth at the ICE show, where giveaways were part of doing business, and many of the ICE attendees were invited to last night's Mocha Magic party.

The actress glanced at her watch. "My audition! I'm up in ten minutes! I'd better go—"

"No!" Tuck said, raising a finger. "You're the Wicked Witch. You don't go . . . You fly."

"Got it," she said, flashing Tuck a thumbs-up.

"Break a leg," he called as she hit the door.

"If you need me, I'll be in my office," I told Tuck after brewing a new coffee for Franco—this one in a paper cup.

"What took you so long?" he asked.

"Everything takes longer when you're snooping."

"Excuse me?"

"I made your coffee to go, so let's go," I told him.

I headed to the Blend's second floor, where I had a small office and a computer. Franco followed me. As I slid behind my desk, he took the only other chair, throwing up his legs so he could cross his motorcycle boots on top of a stack of old invoices.

"So?" he said.

"So I'd tell you to make yourself comfortable but—"

"I always do."

"I can see that. Enjoy your coffee. I have to check something online, and then we'll talk."

I fired up my computer, typed *Nutrition Nation* into a search engine, and clicked on the corporate page. Scanning the site, I began to wonder what the heck NN was doing at the Confectioners' Exposition.

As far as I could tell, the company was shilling muscle-building powders, protein mixes, and enzyme shakes. *So where's the snack food?* I started to wonder whether the Wicked Witch had gotten her facts wrong when I spotted a link teasing a new line of products.

To be announced at the ICE show. Hmm . . .

The imagery for the ad was done with artsy flare: a black-and-white photo of a nude male photographed from the side. The muscular model's perfectly sculpted abdominal muscles were highlighted by stark light and deep shadows. I scanned up to the face, which looked awfully familiar, especially those long sideburns. A closer look and I was certain: This was Alicia's Candy Man, Dennis St. Julian!

"You're awfully quiet, Coffee Lady. What are you doing? Surfing for man-porn?"

"Kind of," I replied as I smacked the print command.

While the printer churned away, I phoned Detective Lori Soles to give her a head's up about Nutrition Nation. Unfortunately, all I got was her voice mail. I left a short "call me" message, reluctant to say more on a recording.

When I hung up, I discovered Franco also had been contemplating a photograph. The silver-framed snapshot on my desk had been taken more than a decade ago, when Matt and I were still married and Joy was around six.

My little girl had been dazzled by a young Olympic skater, whirling and leaping on an NBC morning show segment. The show was taped at Rockefeller Center, during those winter months when the courtyard was transformed into an outdoor ice skating rink.

Six-year-old Joy told her daddy she just *had* to twirl on that same skating rink as the Olympic girl. Before the day ended, Matteo Allegro was guiding shaky blades across ice for maybe the second time in his life.

When Franco caught me watching him, he set the framed photo back on my desk. "I guess Joy's always been into that

Hello Kitty stuff, huh?" He touched the little pink Hello Kitty brand hat and mitten set Joy wore that day. "Cute . . ."

The dreamy little smile on the man's face, the semiglazed look in his eyes—they told me all I needed to know. Franco knew about Hello Kitty. He *cared* about Hello Kitty. If I had any doubt before, I didn't any longer: Sergeant Emmanuel "Manny" Franco, street name "the General," was absolutely infatuated with my daughter.

Was I okay with that? *No.* But what could I do about it? And what did I really know about this young man, anyway?

Well, I thought, *here's my chance to find out . . .*

The printer finally disgorged the single sheet capture of the Candy Man's photo. I passed it to Franco and cleared my throat, focusing on the subject at hand, or at least in his hand—

"Do you think you could identify this model if you saw him in the flesh?"

Franco saw the image and winced. "What part of his flesh am I supposed to identify, 'cause there's a lot of it here? Maybe you should get a vice cop for this beefcake watch."

"You'll do. Let's grab a cab."

"Cab? To where? I came here to see—"

"My daughter, I know. But Joy went to brunch with friends from culinary school."

When Franco's face fell, I assured him she'd be back soon enough—and in the meantime, he could help me with a little backup (in case I actually *did* find Dennis St. Julian).

"So you want me to work on my one and only lunch hour?" Franco said.

"Don't think of it as work. It's the Confectioners' Exposition. There will be hundreds of vendors pushing sweet-tooth bliss with free samples at every booth."

"Samples? Of candy? And I'm going to do this because . . . ?"

"Because Dirty Harry never passes on a chance to dispense justice."

Franco snorted. I folded my arms and gave him a possible-future-mother-in-law stare. "You don't want me to tell Mike you're still going after that dealer, do you?"

He threw up his hands. "Fine. It will make my day to provide you with a little backup. But I want lunch first."

"I'll make you and Joy a nice home-cooked dinner tonight. Until then, gorge on chocolate. I plan to."

"Ugh," Franco rubbed his hard stomach. "I ate too much fancy candy last night. I need red meat."

Twenty-Five

"**Man,** is it warm in here," Franco said, tugging at the collar of his open shirt.

We were standing inside architect I. M. Pei's ascending "glass house" entryway to the Javits Convention Center on Manhattan's West Side. Unfortunately, on this pleasant spring afternoon the temperature in this sun-washed atrium was so high that "hothouse" would have been a more apt description.

Signs warned of "minor inconveniences" owing to the ongoing renovation, and the spotty air-conditioning in the lobby was definitely an inconvenience, especially since it provided Manny Franco with an excuse to gripe like a teenager.

"Just take off your leather jacket if you're uncomfortable," I said.

"Great idea, Coffee Lady, people tend to relax when they see the guy in front of them is armed."

"Sorry. I forgot about your shoulder holster."

"Well, people may need the police, but that doesn't translate to them liking us. A low profile means the jacket stays on."

"I understand. The only time I see Mike's shirtsleeves is in my—"

"Bedroom?" He waggled his eyebrows.

"Kitchen. Focus, Detective. We're at a foodie convention."

"Next!" A cashier waved us forward.

"Let me take care of this," Franco said, cutting in front of me with wallet in hand. Though his spirit was willing, the detective was floored by a case of sticker shock. He closed his cash flap and handed over his Visa card.

"I could go to a Jets game for what these tickets cost," Franco said as he gave me a badge pass.

"Look at it this way: the Jets usually lose, and you pay extra for snacks. Here you can stuff yourself with goodies for free."

"I'd rather have a plastic cup of beer and a pair of Nathan's foot-longs."

We passed through the doors into the first exhibition area, where hundreds of booths and thousands of attendees filled a quasi-industrial space as big as a space shuttle hangar. Like a foodie UN, this expo brought together a world of Candy Lands with colorful company banners dangling like national flags across the high ceiling. Exhibitors, large and small, were aligned in long rows displaying chocolates, pastries, and snacks galore.

Overwhelmed by the sheer number of booths, I leafed through the guidebook in search of some kind of map. "Okay, the Nutrition Nation booth is in aisle seventeen—"

"Answer me something."

"What?"

Franco leaned close. "You told me about the stunt at the hotel yesterday, about the guy with extreme sideburns and the blond chick in black. Was there anyone else involved?"

"No. Why? You have someone else in mind?"

"How about an older dude? Tall and lean, silver hair, sharp blue eyes. Smartly dressed with a bone-white scar on a ruddy face."

I shook my head again.

"Funny, because the guy I just described was hanging around outside the Blend when I got there this morning, and just now I saw him back here in the Javits lobby."

I whirled. "Where?"

"He's gone now. Back outside." Franco turned me back around. "Not interested in paying the admission, I guess."

"Do you think he was following me?"

"Well, he wasn't following me."

"There was an older man in the Blend yesterday," I said. "He called himself 'Bob,' said he was a former customer, and asked questions about Madame. Then he abruptly disappeared."

"Did he look like I described?"

"Was that scar nasty looking? Running down his cheek, over his chin, toward his throat?"

"That's him." Franco caught my alarm. "Take it easy, Clare."

"You don't understand. Mike told me he's looking into a cold case—one that involved the Village Blend and the murder of a police officer. So any 'former customer' around Scarface's age, who also happens to be stalking me, is going to make me plenty paranoid."

Franco scowled. "If that guy is shadowing you, he'll be lurking outside when we leave. I'll introduce myself—" He fingered the gold shield hanging around his neck. "Persuade him to tell me what he wants with you . . ."

"Yodel-AAY-eee-OOOH!"

The sudden Alpine cry made me jump, and I wasn't the only one. Given what we were discussing, Franco was so startled he reached into his jacket to touch the butt of his gun.

"Yodel-AYYY-eee-OHHH! Swiss Alpine Village TREE-EETS!"

The crowd parted for a chubby young yodeler wearing Lederhosen and a feathered hiking cap over blond curls. The two pig-tailed women flanking him wore dirndl dresses straight from the Bavarian Alps. Each Fräulein carried woven baskets filled with chocolate-covered treats.

"Petits fours?" one asked Franco.

"*Danke schön* there, Gretel." He popped a square into his mouth and smiled politely. "Yummy."

"Come on," I said, tugging his leather jacket, and we started walking—until I saw the black banner, red swath, and fine gold lettering of Valrhona Chocolat.

As my steps slowed, the cinnamon stick of a man in brown formalwear approached me (probably because he saw me staring with rapt wonder).

"My name is Christof, mademoiselle, and it would please me if you would sample our Grand Cru chocolates."

"Oh, if you insist," I said.

The man's young assistant lifted a shiny black box containing a dozen dark squares resting on red velvet and tiny doilies of gold paper. Using delicate gold-plated serving tongs, Christof lifted a perfect, shiny square.

"We were the first house to pioneer Grand Cru chocolates," he said. "Indeed, our mission is to enflame a passion for premium chocolates with origins and taste profiles as complex as fine wines."

"Or fine coffees," I noted.

"But of course!" Christof's head bobbed in complete agreement, then he turned with slight hesitation to my shaved-headed, leather-clad companion. "And one for you, monsieur?"

"*Merci. Il semble délicieux,*" Franco replied.

Christof's smile widened. "Oh yes, they are delicious!"

I might have taken a bite of my Grand Cru square if I hadn't been gawking at Dirty Harry speaking careful French. The detective smiled at me.

"*J'ai vécu dans un quartier haïtien,*" he explained.

"You grew up in a Haitian neighborhood?"

Franco nodded. "Brooklyn is a country all its own."

"Ah, yes. That would explain your accent," Christof noted, then turned back to me. "You are about to sample

Guanaja, by the way, a chocolate of Honduran origin, seventy percent cacao and dark as sin." He winked.

My other four senses went on hold as the fragrant square melted like dark, sweet butter over my tongue, blocking out the noise, the bright convention-hall lights, and pretty much all reason for living except to chew and swallow. When my wits returned from their transcendent food trance, Christof was gone.

"Seventy percent cocoa?" Franco said. "Tastes like *all* chocolate to me."

"When a chocolate has seventy percent cocoa content, it simply means seventy percent of that bar is chocolate, the rest are other ingredients like sugar, milk, flavorings, and additives."

"There can't be much sugar in this," Franco said, making a face. "Tastes a little bitter, but good bitter, like a dark beer."

"Exactly. More cocoa equals less sugar—and more complex flavor. Stout beers have chocolaty flavor notes, just like some of our coffees, and they're pretty heady together, too. You should taste my Mocha Cake with Chocolate Guinness Glaze. Mike loves it."

"Coffee, chocolate, and Irish stout in one bite? Sounds like a party in my mouth . . ." He finished off the dark square. "This is definitely more potent than the stuff I grab at the drugstore counter."

"That's because in America, the FDA allows a milk 'chocolate' bar to have as little as ten percent cocoa."

"That's it?"

"In Europe, a product like that isn't even allowed to be labeled chocolate."

"Yeah, well . . . as interesting as the dark stuff is, I wouldn't want a steady diet of it. I mean, chocolate *needs* milk and sugar."

"That's how you feel about coffee, too."

"Hey, c'mon, don't you think a guy like me needs something light and sweet to balance out the dark?"

"You wouldn't be talking about more than chocolate and coffee, would you, Detective?"

"Believe me, Coffee Lady, the darkness we see on this job makes you cherish light wherever you find it."

I stopped and stared. "You know, that's sort of profound."

"Yeah, it is. But they're not my words. I was quoting somebody."

"Thomas Edison?"

"Mike Quinn."

Franco smiled at the slightly stunned look on my face. "Why so surprised?"

"I don't know . . . I shouldn't be I guess. Mike's favorite Blend drink is a sweet latte."

"C'mon now, Clare, you know he wasn't talking about coffee."

"No?"

"No." Franco studied me. "So, when are you two tying the knot, anyway?"

Oh brother. "Did Joy put you up to asking me that?"

"No."

"Mike?"

"No." He shrugged his leather-covered shoulders. "I just wondered . . ."

"Well, we're not getting hitched *today*, okay? So give me a second here . . ." I waved the guide. "We're in the right aisle, but I need a booth number . . ."

When I looked up again, I found Franco flirting with a young brunette dressed as a canary-yellow box of Milk Duds.

"Oh, sure, Milk Duds are chewy," Franco was saying as one hand raided her sample bag. "But I love the Dud because it's just like me. It's sweet, has a surprisingly soft heart, and lasts a long, long time."

The perky girl-in-a-box giggled, letting him help himself to her goodies. I wandered over.

"I see you've gotten over your disappointment at missing Joy."

Franco grinned. "A little harmless flirting goes a long way on this job, Coffee Lady. You like Duds?"

"No. Never did."

He popped a few more into his mouth.

"At least you're enjoying yourself now," I said.

"Free Duds are like rainbows and lollipops."

"Childhood memories, huh? Like Proust's madeleine?"

"Corner candy store. Owner's daughter ran the counter. She was *almost* as incredible as your daughter. Her name wasn't Madeline, though. It was Maria." He sighed. "Her Duds were always fresh."

Suppressing a smile, I tugged his lapel. "Let's go, Detective. I found the booth number—"

"Yodel-AYYY-eee-OHHH! Swiss Alpine Village TREE-EETS!"

Once again Franco reached for his holster. Embarrassed, he caught himself. "Somebody ought to bury that guy in an avalanche, along with Heidi and Pippi Longstocking."

"Hey, I loved Heidi and Pippi!"

"Fine, Heidi and Pippi get stays of execution. But not the yodeler."

"No argument."

Twenty-six

Nutrition Nation's expo footprint was big and flashy with a sparkling disco ball spinning overhead. Inside the booth's resin walls strobe lights flashed on displays packed with products geared toward sports nutrition, bodybuilding, and toning.

"What are these guys doing at a candy fair?" Franco asked. "Nutrition Nation is nothing but a slop shop."

"A what?"

"A 7-Eleven for Red Power Ranger Go-Go Juice. Every 'roid head on the job shops at their stores."

"You're referring to steroids? Aren't they illegal?"

"Science is faster than the law. Nutrition Nation peddles anabolic steroid alternatives, stuff that doesn't turn into a steroid until it's ingested. That technicality allows them to skirt the law—for now."

While Franco drifted off, checking product labels and shaking his head disapprovingly, I spied a familiar face: Maya Lansing, actually a life-sized cardboard standee of the fitness queen.

This Maya wore more clothing, spandex mainly. With

sculpted arms flexed, she clutched a ten-pound weight in each hand. At her Adidas-clad feet sat skin toners and diet powders in packaging bearing her smiling face.

"Excuse me," I called to a man in a black leotard. He was crouched down low, fiddling with an extension cord. "I need to speak to someone in charge."

Muscle Man rose to his full height. He wasn't that big—if you considered the average New York delivery truck. And his craggy middle-aged face wasn't all that wrong for his hyper-pumped frame. (My family scrapbooks contained an old photo of my *nonna* sticking her head through a cut out of Charles Atlas taken at Kennywood Park. There was a surprising re-semblance, although Nonna didn't have a walrus mustache.)

"If you're the replacement girl, then you're late," he snapped.

"Excuse me?"

"What agency sent you over?" he asked, checking me out. "You're fine, I guess, except for your age . . ."

"I'm not a model."

"Oh! Sorry about that. I'm Vince." His hand pumped mine. "I thought you were my replacement booth bunny." He winked, looking me over with a whole new interest level. "One of the three girls I hired bugged out at the last minute, claimed she dyed her skin green and couldn't get the stuff off. Crazy, huh?"

"Uh . . ." Out of the corner of my eye, I noticed Franco watching us, but he kept his distance, pretended to be checking out the booth's products.

"So, are you a fan of Maya Lansing? Interested in her stuff?" Vince asked, gesturing to the standee. "She came by yesterday for a meet-and-greet. You should have been here."

"Really? Did you happen to give Maya an umbrella? A big golf umbrella with your logo on it?"

"I did indeed. But I'm sorry to tell you, honey, those aren't freebies. They're for Nutrition Nation associates and national wholesale buyers only. You're welcome to purchase one online for thirty-five dollars."

An amplified voice interrupted him. "Vince to the stage, please. Two-minute warning . . ."

"Time for the show. Grab a spot up front." He winked again. "You'll get plenty of free samples."

Vince walked to a raised platform and climbed a few steps, where he picked up a wireless microphone. A recorded drum roll began, and the disco ball over his head spun wildly. Drawn by the drumbeat, a crowd formed and moved to the edge of the stage. I grabbed a front row view before it became impossible. Franco joined me.

"Ladies and gentlemen, welcome to Nutrition Nation, your source for a better body," Vince said, electronic voice booming.

With the familiar *bink-bink* opening to "Tainted Love" by Soft Cell, the curtains parted and a bevy of svelte women in neon spandex, retro hot-pink leg warmers, and spotless white headbands "dancercised" onto the stage.

"Why are you laughing?" I asked Franco.

"Fond memories," he said. "My oldest sister's Jane Fonda workout videos were late-night viewing in my troubled youth."

"How many siblings do you have, anyway?"

"Too many." He smiled. "But I love them all."

For a "hard case," this guy really did seem to have a soft, chewy center. It gave me hope.

Meanwhile, Vince continued his spiel.

". . . and founded in 1980, Nutrition Nation has been helping you reach your personal best for three decades with innovative new products that fit the changing needs of our times."

The dancing girls dipped for a few push-ups. When they jumped back onto their feet, each clutched a silver-blue candy bar.

"You wonder why bulk-up and nutrition bars taste so bad? So did we! And our answer is a new line of nutrition bars that tastes as good as they work. Containing European-style dark chocolate and a proprietary mix of ingredients, each of our new candy bars target areas of the body with specific nutrients to add bulk and strengthen muscles."

Franco glanced at me. "Candy bars for bodybuilders?"

"Now we know why they're at the ICE show."

"Here to prove how effective the new, delicious Triple-Triceps for Men bars can be, straight from Asgard, home of the Norse gods, it's the Thor of Triceps!"

A blond bodybuilder clad in fake fur and a ridiculous horned helmet emerged from behind the curtains carrying a huge stone mallet. He flexed his sculpted arms and mugged for the crowd. Behind us, female whoops and wolf whistles erupted. This audience appeared to know this show well—many of its members were wearing smocks and costumes from other show booths.

Vince's voice boomed once more. "Here to demonstrate the proven results of our new Bionic Biceps Power Bar, straight from his Saxon homeland, it's the Beowulf of Biceps!"

No more faux fur. Now we got spandex stitched to resemble medieval chain mail. This Beowulf had a long, brown ponytail and clutched a rubber sword that flopped rather limply (in my opinion). The ladies didn't seem to mind. They applauded and cheered for more.

Unfortunately, the detective at my side didn't agree. He hid his face behind his hands. "Let me know when this is over."

"And now, from Mount Olympus, the Sun God has come down to earth to introduce Ultra-Abs for Men. Here he is, shining down on us all . . . the Apollo of Abs!"

A single spotlight highlighted a third bodybuilder. Clad head to toe in a yellow velvet bodysuit with shiny gold tassels, only Apollo's face and rock-hard midriff were bare. A crown made of gold plastic flames topped his head, and his long sideburns were dabbled with shiny gold sparkles.

His marblelike abdominal muscles were certainly impressive, but it was Apollo's face that was unforgettable. In fact, the last time I saw the man who called himself Dennis St.

Julian, he was sprawled across a hotel bed, a phony butcher knife sprouting from his well-developed chest.

"That's him!" I whispered, shaking Franco. "The Apollo of Abs is Dennis St. Julian, the phony corpse from the hotel!"

Franco lowered his hands and peeked at the gyrating male bodybuilder through one squinting eye. "I don't know, Coffee Lady. That picture in your purse is pretty unspecific where it counts."

"Open *both* eyes and take a good look. It's him, I'm sure of it."

Reluctantly, Franco obeyed. Meanwhile, I unfolded the picture and discreetly displayed it to him.

"Okay, I can see the resemblance around those skinny muttonchops," he said. "But you don't have anything near as good as a mug shot so . . ."

While we debated, the Thor of Triceps disposed of his mighty prop hammer, picked up his bag of sample goodies, and headed for the excited women. The Beowulf of Biceps put down his floppy sword, picked up another goodie bag, and did the same. Both were mobbed in seconds.

"Come on."

I pulled the detective up onto the low stage, and we quickly approached the Apollo of Abs just as he was picking up his bag of goodies.

"Let me do the talking," I told Franco.

"Mr. Apollo," I said. "My associate and I would like a word with you?"

The Sun God took one look at the shining gold shield dangling around Franco's neck, dropped his goodie bag, and leaped off the stage.

"Stop! Police!" Franco yelled, turning more than a few heads.

So much for your low profile, I thought.

Of course, the Apollo of Abs kept right on going. The yellow velvet bodysuit with golden tassels elbowed its way through the audience and vanished in the convention floor crowd.

Franco took off after him—and I took off, too.

"Hey, honey!" Vince's amplified voice bellowed. "Where's that cop going with my Sun God?"

Franco pulled ahead of me fast, and I lost sight of him. A moment later I heard a familiar cry, this time cut violently short.

Yodel—AAY-eee—YOWWWWLLL!"

Lederhosen pinwheeled over the crowd, then the yodeler crashed into a gourmet jelly bean table. Apollo's plastic crown rolled along the floor and came to rest on a pixilated rainbow of sugar.

Now I knew how to locate Franco. Follow the chaos!

"So sorry!" I called, racing by the jelly bean–covered Bavarian.

I heard another crash and saw a tray of chocolate-chunk cookies fly into the air. Finally, I spotted Franco, taking a hard right into a big enclosed booth. I followed him, passing under a *Sparta's Greek-Style Sweets and Snacks, 300 Varieties* (of course) banner. Their logo was even a bearded Leonidas grinning behind his Spartan helmet.

I moved through an aisle displaying boxes of Baklava Bites and Greek yogurt candies when Apollo grabbed me from behind.

The man's rocklike forearm slammed my face as it hooked around my neck. My nose stinging, I tried to scream, but he couldn't have that, so he tightened his hold to cut off my air, pulling me back so quickly he nearly gave me whiplash.

As the pressure on my throat increased, my vision began to redden. I could no longer breathe. I tried not to panic, but my fate was terrifyingly clear: if I didn't do something fast, the Sun God was going to put my lights out.

Twenty-seven

~~~~~~

My arms flailed, clawing at Apollo's eyes, but he bent backward, just out of reach, lifting short little me in the process.

Great! Now my feet are off the floor!

Trying to break free, I banged my elbows into my captor's guts, bruising little more than myself (the Sun God really did have incredibly hard abs). When the pressure eased a bit, I realized my backup had backtracked and finally spotted us. I sucked in air when my toes touched the floor. As my vision cleared, I recognized the expression on Detective Franco's face—pure rage. But the detective quickly masked his anger, approaching us with a calming voice.

"Hey, dude. Stay cool now. The lady and I just want to ask you a few questions . . ."

Apollo reared backward, lifting me again. "Don't come any closer!"

Franco stopped midstride. "Easy. Take it easy, okay?" He raised one peaceable hand, spread his fingers wide, showing it was empty while slowly moving the other into his jacket. He was going for the handgun in his shoulder holster!

No! I thought. *I don't want anyone shot!*

Desperate times, desperate measures! I bent one knee back, bringing the heel of my shoe up as hard as I could. I was aiming to kick Apollo's shin but missed, connecting instead to a place where the Sun God never shines.

The strongman howled and released me. I dropped to the ground limp as a melted Milk Dud. Maneuvering into a sitting position, I rubbed my bruised nose. My hand came away red.

That bastard gave me a bloody nose! Okay, now I'm pissed!

While Apollo danced away, clutching his groin, Franco jumped over me, body-slamming the bodybuilder.

Thank you, Detective!

Both men stumbled backward and crashed into a huge plastic bin of yogurt-covered pita chips, which scattered like ice-covered leaves. Apollo got back to his feet and threw the first punch. *Big mistake.* Franco easily dodged the telegraphed blow, grabbed Apollo's wrist, and used the man's momentum to slam him down into the carpet of white pita chips. The bodybuilder hit the floor with a deliciously satisfying crunch.

Still gripping Apollo's fingers, Franco straddled the big man and twisted his arm behind his back, punishing the fingers until Apollo howled again.

"Leave me alone!" the Sun God bellowed. "I didn't do anything!"

"You ran from an officer of the law," Franco calmly replied, "and then you put your big yellow hands on this nice Coffee Lady, which hasn't exactly put the officer in a *sunny* frame of mind."

Franco ground the bodybuilder's nose into the crunchy white chip carpet. The smell of sugary yogurt rising from the floor became cloying. Apollo seemed to go limp in surrender, but when Franco reached for his handcuffs, the Sun God started struggling again. In response, the detective bent Apollo's fingers until the man with perfect abs screamed like a little girl.

"Don't hurt him!" yelled an actual girl.

I recognized the voice. It belonged to my long-lost Blond in Black—and her familiar deer-in-the-headlights expression was back on full display.

Apollo spit pita. "Get—PHAAACK—out of here, Vanessa!"

But the woman did not budge, even when I got to my feet and stepped up to her. Despite my bloody nose, she recognized me instantly.

"I know you!" she cried, pointing.

"Right back at ya," I said, ignoring the throbbing bruise that was my face. Pulling up the bottom of my henley, I tried to staunch the bleeding.

Apollo lifted his head, his face half coated with the clownish white of crushed yogurt.

"Don't talk to them," he warned the blonde.

"That wouldn't be polite," Franco said, pulling the man to his knees. "Not after all the trouble we went through to meet you."

Several members of the Javits Convention Center's security team moved in, Taser guns at the ready. When Franco flashed his shield, I could see the relief on their faces. One guard informed Franco that an NYPD sector car was on the way. Then they retreated a respectable distance to execute "crowd control."

"We can share here or at the precinct," Franco told the bodybuilder. "Let's start with your name, Dennis—"

"Who's Dennis? I don't know who you're talking about—"

Franco interrupted with a loud, theatrical sigh, eyes directed at the heavens. "No cooperation. What's a Boy Scout to do?" With his free hand, Franco patted Apollo down and found a wallet tucked into his velvet bodysuit.

"Hey!" Apollo protested.

"Oops, looks like your wallet fell during our scuffle, Mr. St. Julian," Franco said innocently. "Let me retrieve it for you."

"My name is Talos, Troy Talos. I don't know anyone named Dennis!"

"Well Mr. Talos, Troy Talos, you've got a whole lot of business cards with the name 'Dennis St. Julian' printed on them." Franco continued rifling the wallet. "Ho, ho! And what's this? A parole card from the state of California. Wonder if the board knows you've traveled out of state? And did you stop by the NYPD and declare your status as a parolee?"

Troy cursed.

Franco shook his head. "Nah, I didn't think so." He glanced at Vanessa. "Are you a parolee, too?"

"No," she said. "I'm just Troy's girlfriend."

"Okay, now, Troy . . ." Franco noticed me trying to staunch my bleeding nose. He handed me a folded handkerchief. "Why don't you get whatever's bothering you and the lady off that overdeveloped chest of yours?"

But Troy clammed up.

I touched Franco's arm. Lifting his handkerchief to my bloody nose, I made sure to shield my lips. *Let me*, I silently mouthed.

Franco nodded. He understood my strategy and seemed happy to play along. Even though these two weren't yet arrested and Mirandized, Franco was still a cop. If he asked questions, there were legal implications. But if I asked questions, well, I was simply a witness having a conversation that he happened to overhear . . .

"We know you tried to drug Alicia Bower in her hotel room the other night," I charged, voice muffled by the hanky. "What drug did you give her? She's an older woman in frail health. You could have killed her!"

Troy paled. "She was never in any danger. You can't prove it—"

"Oh, yes we can! Alicia dumped half of your cocktail into her hotel room's vase, and that sample is being tested by an NYPD crime lab. We'll have proof against you soon enough, with or without your cooperation."

"I'm telling you, Alicia was never in any danger! I knew

her weight, her age, and I mixed the cocktail up especially for—"

"A roofie's a roofie," I said, "and administering one is a crime."

"I just wanted to scare her," Troy insisted. "Make sure she didn't attend that product launch party. I tried to get her to come away with me, go on a last-minute romantic getaway to the Hamptons—but she was so obsessed with that stupid party she couldn't think of anything else!"

"So you drugged her?"

"It was harmless, just part of an act, a stage show. I wasn't going to take advantage of her. I was just trying to scare her."

"With drugs?"

"Look, lady, I was desperate, so I went with a con I'd pulled a few years ago on the wife of some CEO in Palm Springs."

"Is that what earned you the parole card?"

"No. I had a pharmacist's degree, till I got busted for distributing steroids."

Franco glanced at me with a half smile. "A muscle-head using steroids? I'm shocked . . . shocked!"

"That's what I'm trying to tell you," Troy said. "I had a license. I've got the knowledge. I didn't mean Alicia any harm. I mixed up a cocktail with enough juice for her to sleep the full eight and wake up fuzzy enough to buy my butchered boyfriend act—"

"And believe she might have done the butchering," I said.

"That's right," Troy replied. "I even gave myself a zombie cocktail."

"A what?"

"Something I created. It's a mix of drugs that slows the pulse, makes the skin cold to the touch, plus a sedative and muscle relaxant to help me play dead."

"There's really a mix of drugs that can do all that?"

"What? You never heard of *Romeo and Juliet*?" He smirked. "I woke up right on time, too. When I heard you in the hotel room, talking on the phone, I knew the whole thing was blown. I took off right after you left."

I faced Vanessa. "And you were supposed to pretend to be his girlfriend? His wife? Someone to convince Alicia she'd better get out of town before the police arrived—and leave you some money for a lawyer before she left?"

"Yes, that's all there was to it," Vanessa said.

"So what's your position at Aphrodite's Village Online?" I asked.

She shook her head. "I'm and actress/model. I don't work for that company."

Boy, I liked that answer. "So . . ." I glanced at Franco, feeling pretty proud of myself. "Someone *hired* you to do this. What was the payoff?"

"Nothing," Vanessa replied. "Just promises, that's all. Only she can't deliver on those promises. Not now."

I blinked behind the hanky. "Why can't she deliver?"

Vanessa stared at me with dead eyes. "She promised us big parts in her new Web series. Troy. Me. We were going to be rich Internet stars—and most likely cable television, too. All we had to do was make that stupid witch miss her launch party."

"Maya promised you all this?" I asked.

"Maya?" Vanessa said. "Who the hell is Maya?"

Oh God, I thought as the truth dawned. All the dots were there to connect. The California link. The lead role in a Web series. None of that pointed to the fitness queen, Maya Lansing.

"It was Patrice Stone who hired you, wasn't it?"

"Yes," Vanessa said. "We met her at an audition about a month ago. Patrice said she knew our work and would find something for us." A shadow crossed her face. "What Patrice really knew about was Troy's criminal record."

"And Patrice made you an offer." I coughed into the hanky. "Why? Patrice was a golden girl. The sky was the limit for her."

"Not according to what Patrice told me. She said Aphrodite was real tight with Alicia Bower and that radio doctor, Sherri Sellars. Back in college, Aphrodite and Sherri were in the same sorority or clique or something, and Alicia was their professor. Anyway, Aphrodite is planning an exit strategy. In another five years, she's going to promote a replacement to head her company. Patrice wanted that spot. Her only other real competition was Sherri and Alicia—and Alicia was the one who'd come up with a really lucrative product, so she's the one who needed to be taken down a peg."

"So Patrice knew about your crazy plan?"

"No. She didn't care about the details. She just wanted Alicia kept away from the launch party."

"Only something went wrong."

"Yes, Troy screwed up, and Alicia made the party," Vanessa said. "I went to Patrice's hotel room this morning, to beg for another shot. That's when I found out . . ."

"Patrice Stone was murdered last night."

"What?" Troy cried.

Vanessa turned to him. "I was just coming to tell you. Patrice is dead."

Four uniformed NYPD officers arrived in time to hear Troy curse a blue streak. Franco pulled him to his feet, greeted two of the cops by name.

"Take this pair into custody and Mirandize both of them." He leaned close to my ear. "Not that they have much more to tell us, thanks to your curious mommy act. I can see why Big Mike is sweet on you."

"You want them at the Sixth, right, Detective?" one of the uniforms asked.

Franco shook his head. "The One Seven. The Fish Squad is going to want a nice, long sit-down with Vanessa and the Sun God."

OUTSIDE the convention center, the sky was clear, the weather balmy. The sun was shining so brightly, it made my nose sting even more.

"Who knew Candy Land could be so much fun?" Franco said, still shaking pita crumbs and yogurt bits out of his jacket.

I continued to dab my bloodied nose with his hanky as I

watched a handcuffed Troy Talos being placed into a sector car. Another NYPD vehicle idled at the curb with Vanessa already in the backseat. Franco noticed my nonresponse and gave me a strange look.

"Are you feeling okay, Coffee Lady?"

My ponytail was undone, my nose felt raw and swollen, and the front of my henley was splashed with my own blood. I shook my head.

"I think I'm in shock."

"Then let's get you to an ER."

He took my elbow, but I shook my head.

"It's mental. I'm still trying to process what Vanessa told us."

"What part?"

"That Patrice Stone, my innocent victim, wasn't so innocent after all."

"Oh, that . . ." Franco squinted at the cloudless sky. "Do this job long enough, and you'll find out there's no such thing as an innocent victim."

"Not true," I said. "And that's an awfully cynical way to look at the world."

Franco smiled. "She's baa-aack! Now that's the Clare Cosi I know."

"Yeah, well . . . what I know isn't cheering me. I'm almost certain my former mother-in-law is in business with a murderer."

"Alicia Bower?"

"I'm betting Alicia discovered that Patrice Stone was really behind that fake-corpse setup at the Topaz Hotel—and that's why she killed her."

Franco nodded. "That's a motive, all right."

"And on the night of the murder, I saw Alicia returning from the rain-soaked Garden alone. What was she doing out there?"

"You tell me."

"She was looking for the security cameras! Alicia wanted to check the location of each lens so she could use an open umbrella to hide her identity."

"Yeah, this is starting to sound premeditated," Franco said, his tone encouraging.

"Alicia's planning didn't end there. Killing Patrice wasn't enough. She tried to frame Maya Lansing, too, by using the fitness queen's umbrella—a neat trick to dispose of two rivals in one night."

"That's one tough old dame, but it sounds like you figured it all out."

"It makes perfect sense."

"Sure, it makes perfect sense," Franco replied. "But where's your proof?"

My shoulders sagged. The answer to Franco's question was simple. I didn't have proof. Not yet. But now that I was sure of Alicia Bower's guilt, I was certain I could find some kind of evidence to hand Lori Soles and Sue Ellen Bass.

Fortunately, a germ of a plan was forming in my head. All I needed was the proper tool, and I knew exactly where to find it—with the rest of Joy's childhood things in the closet of my duplex.

Twenty-Eight

⟳⟳⟳⟳⟳⟳⟳⟳⟳⟳⟳⟳⟳⟳⟳⟳⟳⟳⟳⟳

The next twenty-four hours melted away faster than a white chocolate truffle on a sun-baked sidewalk. Time chilled only twice for me—first when I put our dinner together and next when Mike and I were finally alone.

I'd invited Quinn to join us for a very good reason, other than I wanted to see him (which was nothing newsworthy; I always did). I was more concerned with Sergeant Franco's vendetta against that Jersey drug dealer.

I wasn't about to rat the guy out, especially after he'd backed me up so brilliantly, but since he and my daughter gave Mike so much *agita* the night before, I thought breaking bread around a communal table would benefit everyone. (And with a full stomach and a little *vino*, Franco might even feel sanguine enough to come clean with Mike privately, work out some kind of cop compromise.)

So I pulled out my cutting board, my knives, and my large sauté pan. I warmed the extra-virgin olive oil, put pasta water on to boil, and began putting together what I'd come to think of as my Italian mole.

Yes, I know: this was Manhattan, land of 24/7 takeout.

But I'd promised Sergeant Franco a home-cooked meal, and I aimed to deliver.

My grandmother's pasta sauces simmered for five to six hours. I had only one. But I refused to sacrifice flavor. The trick was layering in fresh ingredients, intensify their essence with vibrant spices, and finishing with the velvety melting of a fine, dark secret: chocolate.

The resulting mushroom-wine sauce was like an excellent coffee blend (not to mention my idea of the perfect man)— exhilarating complexity with a robust body, smooth finish, and the lingering feeling of rich, warm depth. (I planned to serve it over fat fettuccine noodles—and since sizable men came with sizable appetites, the menu would also include butter-basted Rock Cornish game hens with lemon and rosemary, Caesar salad, and fresh garlic bread.)

Joy offered to help, but she was a salaried stove-jockey now, and I wanted to give my girl a break—frankly, I needed one, too, and that's what cooking was for me.

The rote routine of slicing mushrooms felt quietly calming. The faint scent of soil evoked relaxing visions of pastoral farms and lovingly tended gardens. The act of stirring was practically Zen meditation; and when the ingredients came together, the room was saturated with an aromatic air-bath more invigorating than a day spa.

Such were my private musings. I seldom shared them— not in an age when most people ate with the press of a button, be it microwave or speed-dial call to a pizzeria. Then again, most people weren't raised by a woman born in the rural hills of Italy, where bread was baked in outdoor ovens; cycles of planting and harvesting inspired rituals that stretched back millennia; dreams held powerful portents; and miracles were not only possible but seen and felt every day.

My grandmother's name was Graziella—Italian for Grace. "God put beauty in everything," she'd say, "if you take the trouble to see it . . ."

Like a vanilla bean in simmering milk, she infused my

world with the sweetest essence, showing me the magic of rising yeast breads, the music of snapping green beans, and the gardener's palette of ripe-red tomatoes, dark purple egg-plant, yellow-gold zucchini flowers, and pale orange peppers.

Not that my childhood had been a blithe, pain-free play. At seven, I saw no beauty in my mom leaving my pop for a salesman on his way back to Miami. Tears had been the cul-mination of that act. Tears and fear and confusion. But then Nonna stepped in.

Day in and day out, she'd been there for me, just as she'd been there for the customers of her little grocery—just as I wanted my coffeehouse to be there for my customers when they stopped by for a warm cup of something that would reassure and renew.

That's why time in my kitchen always made me feel closer to Grace—and Joy, because I'd raised my daughter to believe what my grandmother believed: that simply taking, taking, taking made you a sucking void, hollow, "like a dead per-son." But preparing a meal was an act of giving, and giving was evidence of living. That's why cooking meant so much to the likes of us. It was more than love. It was life.

I could only hope Joy's future husband would see that in her and love her for it. I knew it was one reason Mike loved me. Not that he'd explicitly stated it. But the man's routine rendezvous with the Grim Reaper needed continual remedy, and the true-blue flame of my gas stove always lightened that darkness.

I would have enjoyed Mike's company in my kitchen that evening with his jacket and holster shed, his shirtsleeves rolled up, but he was running late, so when Sergeant Franco arrived, I opened a bottle of Pinot Noir, poured off eight ounces for my recipe (with a little taste of that cherry-oak velvet for myself), and sat my daughter and her roughneck suitor in the duplex living room with a crackling fire and the rest of the bottle.

I left the room with a kind of clueless buoyancy, pretend-ing they were about to have a stimulating discussion about books, film, music, art, but (of course) one glance back revealed lips and tongues engaged in something other than discourse.

I sighed, wondering what was wrong with me anyhow. When Mike and I first started dating, we didn't talk about art, either—and we certainly didn't need Mocha Magic.

When Mike finally arrived, I unfurled my favorite tablecloth of Florentine lace, lit two tapers in crystal holders, and the four of us settled ourselves around the Spode Blue Italian pattern (Madame's third best china) in the duplex's small dining room of porcelain antiques and polished mahogany. More wine was poured; my food was eaten with smacking lips (on Franco's part), kind compliments from my daughter, and Mike's occasional thrilling moan of taste bud bliss.

Mike and Franco never talked work, although an exchanged wordless glance or two suggested secret understandings. I might have been put off if Joy and I hadn't engaged in a few private looks of our own.

Dessert and coffee went quickly, thanks to Franco's inhaling of my fresh-baked cookies. I'd contemplated making an easy, self-saucing Chocolate-Chip Cobbler, or my quick Chocolate Crostada, but I had two kinds of dough already chilling in the fridge. The first was my secret recipe for "Pure Ecstasy" Chocolate-Chip Cookies.

With brown butter, espresso powder, homemade brown sugar, and two kinds of chips, my version of the time-honored American cookie produced a toffee-like gourmet treat with mouthwatering notes of buttery caramel. Naming them was easy: Mike never failed to make his man-in-ecstasy noise when he consumed them. (Actually, he said they qualified as a drug.)

The other dough I had chilling was a classic peanut butter.

Franco rivaled Elvis in his love of peanut butter. (This I knew from the Five-Borough Bake Sale.) And since an ICE chocolatier handed me a promo bag of sixty percent cacao chips, I decided to create a "surprise" cookie center of dark chocolate. The result was a sweet and tender peanut butter cookie with the kind of ooey-gooey chocolate heart that grown men swooned for.

My daughter liked the cookies okay, but her swooning was for Manny. Eager to be alone with him, they departed to go "clubbing"—in the East Village, they assured us, not East Jersey.

Just before they headed out, I noticed Quinn murmur something to Franco (in a seriously dangerous tone) about GPS tracking. The young sergeant looked fairly cowed on that front. Then again, I speared the man with the kind of motherly glare that warned: if you even *think* about taking my daughter across the Hudson, you won't see another sunrise.

Alone again with Mike, the fireplace newly stoked, I settled into the sofa beside him. With our hot mugs of coffee and a fresh plate of warm cookies, time stretched luxuriously again, like that fine square of Valrhona dark chocolate melting on my tongue (or, in this case, the gooey chocolate centers of my Peanut Butter Surprises).

"Sweetheart, these are . . ."

I think he said outstanding. His mouth was too busy chewing to tell.

"Freezing the dough balls before baking is the secret to successfully stuffing a cookie with chocolate," I said, absently channeling an old *In the Kitchen with Clare* column. "Not that you need to know that in your line of work."

He laughed, leaned back, and put his arm across the sofa back, coaxing me to tuck into his long, strong body. (I didn't need coaxing.)

"Actually, I made them for Franco," I confessed, snuggling closer, "a foodie token of thanks for backing me up today."

Mike fell silent after that, a somewhat sullen silence it seemed to me.

"Okay, what's wrong?"

"You got a bloody nose," he said. "Franco shouldn't have let that happen . . ."

We'd recounted the story at dinner—Franco and I took turns telling it (although I left out the part about the Incredible Hulk Vince checking me out, and Franco left out the Milk Duds girl).

"You're missing the point," I said. "Troy Talos was cutting off my air. If Franco hadn't doubled back and body-slammed the jerk, I would have had more than a bloody nose. I would have had brain damage."

"You're the one missing the point, Cosi. Franco shouldn't have taken Joy across the Hudson last night—and today you and he both should have called Soles and Bass."

"Oh, please. Do not equate what I did with what Joy did. I phoned Lori Soles. I got her voice mail. I only went to the ICE show to see if Nutrition Nation was giving out black umbrellas. Then Alicia's Candy Man dropped in as the Apollo of Abs and . . . well, it just snowballed!"

"Take it easy. I'm not looking for an argument."

"Neither am I . . ."

I shouldn't have been surprised at Mike's criticism of Franco. Mike was his supervisor, after all, responsible for his actions and well-being. On the other hand, I'd seen Mike bend the rules, even bend the truth if it would help him get the job done, because like all good detectives, Quinn was as much Odysseus as Dudley Do-Right. He was valiant but he was wily.

Well, so am I . . .

With long sips of my dark, rich (still-unnamed) coffee blend, I let the silence stretch between us until the man's inner Odysseus emerged again.

"So what happened?" Mike finally asked (as I knew he would). "I mean after Franco sent the One Seven your convention-center cargo? What did Soles and Bass tell you?"

"Not much I didn't know already. They did find out how Troy pulled the stabbed-to-death routine."

"Fake knife?"

"Not exactly. The carving knife was real but the blade was sliced off, the bottom bent into a ninety-degree angle. Flesh-

colored latex sealed the flat end to the man's chest in an upright position and all that fake blood camouflaged the latex.
That and a sedative with a zombie cocktail to slow his heart-
beat and cool his skin and the illusion was complete."

"Clever."

"It was. And it almost worked, too. Vanessa was all ready
to play the part of Troy's wife, pounding on the hotel room
door to confront her cheating husband—only to find him
stabbed to death and Alicia the likely suspect."

"I get the scam. Alicia should have opened the door fuzzy
from a drugged martini, hysterical from waking up next to a
corpse—and, therefore, amenable to Vanessa's suggestions."

"Like give me some money and get out of town fast," I
said. "Then Alicia would have missed her own product
launch party, which would have damaged her standing with
her boss, Aphrodite, especially with Maya Lansing swooping
in to steal the show along with a big chunk of the Mocha
Magic profits. And that's exactly what Patrice Stone
wanted—to bring Alicia down a peg and move herself up the
game board, closer to becoming Aphrodite's successor."

"So is the Fish Squad picking up Alicia Bower for an interview?"

"No."

"No?"

"Their lieutenant doesn't think the case is strong enough.
No physical evidence has turned up to implicate Alicia—not
yet. They're still looking."

"Yeah," Mike said on an exhale. "I've been there, all
right . . ."

"As Sue Ellen put it to me: 'Even a half-wit of a defense
attorney could pull apart a case of circumstantial evidence.'"

"It's true . . . especially if there were others at that party
who had motive."

"On the other hand, Lori said this new development has
moved Alicia up their persons of interest list. Troy and Vanessa have solid alibis for last night: They were working the
ICE show with plenty of witnesses. And they admitted that

Patrice paid them for a criminal 'prank' against Alicia, which would have given Alicia a very strong motive for murder. The whole thing narrows the field for the Fish Squad's investigation."

"It also narrows the field for the detectives analyzing the crime scene."

"You mean they'll start looking to match physical evidence to Alicia?"

"That's how they'll build the case against her. They'll find something. And when they do, they'll secure warrants, uncover what they can to get a confession. It's barely been twenty-four hours. You just have to—"

"Wait. I know. It's what detectives do."

"You're usually pretty good at waiting."

"Not in this case."

"Why?"

"Well . . ."

I paused, took a breath, and raised my mug for a long, strong sip of fortification. I didn't want to ruin the evening, but I had to bring this up—

"Alicia's product," I said. "The Mocha Magic powder . . ."

"What about it?"

Mike shifted on the sofa, suddenly uncomfortable—which didn't make me all that comfortable, either. Leaning forward, I put distance between us, enough to see the truth in his midnight blues.

"You suspect already, don't you?"

He glanced away, stared into the fire, and silently sipped his own coffee.

"Mike?"

"You have to be the one to tell me, Cosi, because I'm not working right now."

That's when it hit me. My ex-husband had been right. Mike already knew. *Oh God.* "I really don't want to believe Matt. But he thinks . . ."

I let my voice trail off, waiting for Quinn to jump in, admit what he thought, and just make the accusation already. But he refused, just sat there in silence waiting for me to make the decision.

"Finish your sentence," he finally said. "What does Matt think?"

"He thinks Mocha Magic has something in it that's a lot more powerful than herbs and spices. He thinks I should have it tested, and we were hoping you'd help us with that."

"Clare . . ." Mike rubbed the back of his neck. At last, he met my eyes. "Are you *sure* that's what you want?"

"Look, I'd rather have you tell me there's an illegal narcotic in our product than we find out through class action lawsuits or a lawyer from the FDA."

"All right, then. I'll have it tested, let you know."

"Thank you. I mean it. Thank you for helping me."

"You're welcome."

I put my arms around his neck. "And thank you for trusting me."

It was hard to believe, given Mike's commitment to his work, but the man's inner Odysseus was actually ready to look the other way, let me break the law if that's what I wanted. But it wasn't what I wanted, and I was glad we got that straight between us.

I began to pull away, but Mike held my arms in place. Then his big hands moved to splay across my back, urging my heart closer to his. I shut my eyes, inhaled the citrus aftershave of his freshly shaved cheek, the earthy aroma of his leather holster, the faint scent of java on his breath . . .

He put his lips to my ear. "Are we done working now, Cosi?"

"Yes," I replied, a thrill going through me as his lips found mine. *Oh yes . . .*

At first, Mike's kisses were light and teasing, tasting of cookies and coffee, but soon they deepened, their sweetness darkening into something much sultrier. When his hands left my back, I felt momentarily bereft, mourning the loss of that satisfying contrast of soft breasts against hard chest.

Then I realized why he'd put the space between us: he was undoing my buttons.

"Mike," I whispered, "the dirty dishes . . ."

"What about them?" he rasped, slipping his hand inside my blouse. With one sure flick, he unhooked the front clasp of my bra. I inhaled sharply as his rough palm cupped a heavy breast; then his callused fingers found ways to make me sigh and moan and forget how to say the words *dirty dishes*.

For a moment, I recalled our young guests, Joy and Franco, locked together on this same sofa. I nearly laughed as I realized that being a hostess has its advantages.

"Want to finish our coffee upstairs?" I managed to whisper between heavenly gasps.

"Absolutely . . ."

Twenty-nine

The sound of an ambulance siren woke me from a light sleep. A soft glow lit the master bedroom. The fireplace had burned down to cinders, but a small lamp next to the four-poster was still burning. I glanced at my alarm clock—3:45 AM. Beside me, Mike was breathing in the steady rhythms of deep sleep, his arms curled possessively around me.

Mike's lovemaking tonight had been languorous and dreamy; his touches tender; his words caring; and the way he drank in my less than perfect curves made me feel as desired as Titian's Venus.

I kissed his head when we finished, told him to get some rest. Then I cracked a book along with the front window, determined to listen for Franco's car pulling up, my daughter coming safely home.

Nice plan. But Mike's sweet, regular exhales soon lulled me into oblivion. Now I was worried. Had Joy come home or was she still out clubbing? Had Franco heeded Mike's warning to stay on our side of the Hudson?

I'd already thrown on my oversized T-shirt, now I tied a

bathrobe around me and shoved my feet into slippers. Down the hall, I quietly pushed open the guest-room door.

Joy was tucked cozily under the bedcovers. A rush of relief washed over me when I saw her long, dark hair spilled over the white pillow, a little smile on her angel face.

I smiled, too, recalling my sleeping beauty at sixteen, at twelve, at six, at two, and just born. *The years* . . . They went by so slowly and so fast. Feeling tears well, I turned to descend the steps.

As I headed for the kitchen, a flash of pink caught my eye. A small paper gift bag sat on an end table in the dimly lit living room, right next to the sofa where Joy had thrown her red jacket.

Looking at that glossy little bag, I felt my heart stop. Slowly, I walked toward it, dreading what I'd discover inside. *Oh, please,* I prayed, *for Matteo's sake, please don't let me find an empty ring box in here!*

I peeked inside. "What the . . . ?"

"Clare . . . what are you doing?"

I turned. Mike had trailed me. He'd thrown on a pair of sweatpants. His sandy hair had boyish cowlicks; his powerful chest and arms were bare. My body's reaction to a half-naked Quinn was practically autonomic. I ignored it (or tried to) and held up what I'd found.

"Is that women's lingerie?"

"Baby-doll pajamas—a gift to Joy from Franco."

"How do you know?"

"They're Hello Kitty pj's."

He scratched his head. "Isn't that a little girl thing?"

"It was Joy's thing when she was a little girl. Franco knows it." I sighed and put the pajamas back in the little pink bag. "This is major."

"How do you figure?"

"Mike, this isn't a bustier or a thong—something a young woman would wear with a lover. It's the kind of cutesy thing a girl would sleep in when she's alone."

"So?"

"So don't you get the message? Franco wants Joy to wear these when she's back in Paris. He wants her to remember him when she goes to bed every night."

"That's kind of sweet. Don't you think?"

"Matt can't know about this."

"What? The pajamas?"

"No! That they're in love!"

"In love?"

"Didn't you notice how they acted at dinner? How they finished each other sentences?"

"Now that you mention it. I did. And the salt thing . . ."

"Oh God, the salt . . ."

When Franco had reached for the saltshaker, Joy laid her delicate hand on his big arm. Like a magic wand, her light touch was all it took to paralyze him.

"Remember what I told you?" she said quietly. He instantly put the shaker down again, tasted his food, and whispered, "You're right. Doesn't need it."

One end of Mike's mouth quirked up. "Yeah, Franco is into Joy. That's clear."

I wrung my hands. "Don't you think it will pass with him? I mean . . . when Joy's away, back in Paris. He has a roving eye, right?"

Mike shrugged. "Up to now, Franco's had nothing but hit-and-run bedmates. Joy's the first young women he's maintained a friendship with."

"That's what Joy told me when I asked: 'Franco is just a friend.' Well, I didn't want to admit this, but when she asked about us getting married, I wondered whether she was thinking about that question for herself. But she's way too young to consider it—and Matt would strangle Franco before he'd let his little girl walk down an aisle with him."

"Let's table the discussion on your ex-husband, okay? I want to talk about something else. Something important—at least to me."

"You mean those cold-case files? The ones that involve the Village Blend and Matt's mother? Did you read them yet?"

"No. I'm still waiting on archived files."

"Then what do you want to talk about?"

"Joy's question—the one you don't want to talk about."

"You want some hot cocoa? Because I do . . ."

"Clare . . ."

I led Mike into the kitchen and stopped in shock. I'd expected to find a sink overflowing with dirty dishes, pans, and cutlery. But the place was spotless, not even a crusted fork sat in the sink.

"It's all cleaned up," I whispered.

"Must have been a good fairy," Mike said, behind me.

"A fairy named Joy."

Grateful, happy, proud (and still worried she was in for massive heartbreak with Franco), I reached for a saucepan and put some whole milk on the burner to warm.

"Okay," I said, pulling out the squeeze bottle of dark chocolate syrup I'd made from Voss's bittersweet. "What do you want to talk about?"

Mike sat down, ran a hand through his sleep-mussed hair. "Clare, answer me straight, okay? Why do you have reservations about making a commitment?"

"That's not a fair way to characterize it."

"Then what is?"

"I just have reservations . . ."

"About me?"

"No."

"Are you sure? Because most of my days are spent digging the truth out of a steaming pile of equivocations, and it certainly sounds to me like you're trying to break it to me gently."

"Break what?"

"The fact that your feelings for me . . . that they have limits."

"Mike, I love you. I love you with all my heart."

"Then what's your problem?"

"It's not my problem. It's yours. I'm sorry Joy brought this question up, because whether or not you want to admit it, you don't want a wife—"

"Hold it right there—"

"Look, maybe *want* is the wrong word. *Need* is a better one—what you need and what you don't need."

He folded his arms.

"You need your freedom, Mike, a pass to come and go, to put your work first. And that's okay with me. You don't need the burden of a wife waiting for you to show for dinner every night, expecting you to hold up your end of a conventional relationship."

"I don't follow your argument. I'm *very* happy in a relationship with you. And I thought you were, too. I don't see how you can argue that what we have now isn't working, because it is."

"You're not hearing me. I'm saying the opposite. What we have now is working. And that's why I want to keep things the way they are. I love my life, too . . . and I'm not about to change on you, but if our relationship changes, our lives change, and I'm not ready for that . . ."

"Clare, please . . ." He massaged his forehead. "Explain to me exactly: *Why* would our lives have to change?"

"Why?" I threw up my hands. "You're the one who nearly resigned his position this week! You don't think that would change everything? If they reassigned you to a precinct in southern Brooklyn or eastern Queens, I would never see you."

"That's crazy."

"Okay, I would *hardly* see you."

"I would simply commute to a new precinct."

"With the hours you keep? The commitment you have? I'd have to move with you to keep our relationship going. Uproot from this place, this life . . ."

"You do realize this is a theoretical argument?"

"So? Most of your days are spent finding and proving some theory of a case, aren't they?"

"That's work. Law and procedure; cold, concrete crime solving. What I'm talking about is practically the metaphysical opposite—and I *know* you know that."

Did I? I looked away, not sure what to say . . .

Mike spoke again, his voice quiet. "You're a worrier, Clare, but worrying isn't going to solve anything. You have to learn to trust."

"Trust you?"

"Trust yourself. Your decision. Your choice. Trust that things will work out . . . and if they go off track, you'll find a way to get them back on again."

"I just . . ." With a deep breath, I turned off the burner under the milk, moved to sit with him at the table. "I want things to stay the way they are. Is that so bad?"

Mike fell silent. He met my eyes. "You're telling me it's my turn to wait?"

Another man might have said those words with brittleness, with sarcasm. Mike said them with calm, quiet comprehension. I loved him all the more for it.

Leaning closer, I took his hands in mine. "I just need time, Mike."

"How much?"

"I don't know. Enough to be sure we're on the same path, enough to make certain that a wedding ring won't end up feeling like a locked handcuff, on either of us."

He took a breath. "I guess we both know waiting is a state I'm acquainted with."

"Thank you. I mean it."

"You don't have to thank me, Clare. I love you."

"I love you, too," I said. "And I'm here for you. That I promise you."

"A promise is all I'm after."

THIRTY

~~~~~~

THE next day my coffeehouse was filled with small actors (literally).

Up the street, auditions were again under way for the new musical sequel to the *Wizard of Oz*, and (like the Wicked Witch coven before them) the vertically challenged citizens of Munchkin Land designated us their java bean outpost.

Our morning regulars fell silent as the front door opened and sixteen little people paraded across our floor. Most were middle-aged, a few older, every one of them less than four feet tall. As the group approached the counter, my newest, youngest barista didn't even blink.

"Good morning," Nancy Kelly said with a practiced smile. "What can I get you?"

I bit my cheek as Esther threw me a deadpan stare. "Looks like Dorothy is finally getting the hang of not being in Kansas anymore."

I arched an eyebrow. "Except she never mentioned living in Kansas."

"Hey, given all the places that girl is supposedly from, I'm sure it was a stopover."

Tucker Burton's boyfriend, Punch, was back at our coffee bar, too. Like Nancy, the lean Latino didn't bat an eyelash at the new rush of customers. He stopped sneering at the concept for this new musical, too. Now he was complaining there were no parts for him.

"I've already missed the witch call," Punch said with a sigh. "And I do *great* green-skinned drag. I would jump in today, but I'm too tall to play a member of the Lollipop Guild."

"Oh, come on. It's a big show," Tuck said in his usual upbeat tone. "Check the audition schedule at HB Studio. I'm sure you'll find a chorus part."

"This is my first audition," one of the little people announced. In his late twenties with a square-jawed handsome face, the wannabe Munchkin waited patiently for me to pull him a double. "That's what I'm hoping for—a part in the chorus. You got to start somewhere."

Tuck nodded. "Good attitude! Remember, there are no small parts, only small—"

Esther and I froze, Punch's eyes bugged in horror, and Tuck's mouth suddenly snapped shut.

"I'm . . . I'm so sorry," he stammered.

All of the little people burst out laughing.

"I've heard that line ever since I got my Equity card," an older actor shouted out. "The only funny thing about it is seeing big people like you swallow their tongues."

The little people laughed even harder.

"Yo! Boss!" Esther called an hour later.

By now, the Munchkin rush had slowed considerably. Some had left with cups in hand, but most were still relaxing at our café tables.

"What it is?" I called.

"Your apron has been beeping for the last fifteen minutes. Do you have a clue when it's going to explode?"

"Sorry, that's my cell." I looked up from the inventory

spreadsheet on the countertop. I'd hung up the apron before taking a break. "Would you mind handing it to me?"

I set down my pen and gently touched my tender nose. Fortunately, the bruise from my scuffle with the Apollo of Abs was healing fast. By the time I'd opened the Blend this morning, only a little tenderness remained, but something pained me even more—the cloud Alicia Bower had placed over this shop.

"Here you go, boss."

"Thanks." I punched up the voice mail message and scowled. *Don't speak of the devil,* my *nonna* used to warn, *or he may appear.*

In this case, the devil was a she.

"Clare, it's me. Listen up," Alicia began in her imperious tone. "I've dispatched Daphne with a set of instructions. It is *crucial* that you follow them *to the letter.* I'll be unavailable for a call back from you, but we will speak soon . . ."

God, it was difficult to swallow that tone from the woman who could put this landmark shop out of business. And "out of business" for the Blend meant more than breaking my heart by breaking up my cozy little family of baristas. It meant Madame would lose her life's work, Matt his century-old family trade, and my daughter her legacy.

Gritting my teeth, I tried to focus on the spreadsheets again when Esther interrupted. "Look who's here, boss." She jerked her thumb toward the door. "The Mod Couple."

I swiveled my stool to find Daphne Krupa and Susan Chu walking toward me. Given their colleague's untimely death less than forty-eight hours ago, I would have expected the two young women to be wearing black, but apparently, mourning did not become them.

Garbed again in sixties retro chic, both girls wore shift dresses in dynamic colors. Susan's was a hot-pink design. She also wore sunglasses with pink frames. Daphne's print was teal—and she'd swapped her chili-pepper red cat glasses for little round ones with blue frames.

Both dresses displayed plenty of leg, each encased in

opaque tights that matched the dress. Their little backpacks matched, too; Daphne's was over her shoulder, Susan's strapped to her back.

"Hey, guys," Daphne said with a chipper wave.

"Remember us from the other night?" Susan called, equally perky.

Tucker and Nancy smiled big. "Hey, there!"

"What's up?" Esther called flatly.

"Welcome to my Village Blend," I said. "How are things going? I mean, given Ms. Stone's death."

"It's not so bad today," Susan said, "although yesterday morning was seriously unpleasant."

Daphne nodded. "Patrice handled our event planning, so there was a lot of confusion. Aphrodite had to cancel two back-to-back promo events that we had scheduled for last night."

"But I'm sure Aphrodite was upset, right?" I asked. "I mean, Patrice had been her assistant for a long time. She must have been emotional."

"Oh right," Susan said. "We were all very sad."

Were, I thought. *A past tense on grieving already? It sounds like Aphrodite is more broken up about canceling two PR events than the news of her former assistant being bludgeoned and drowned.*

"Things are back on track now," Susan added. "Alicia Bower stepped right in and took control of the schedule for Aphrodite. That woman is a machine!"

"A machine? Really?"

"For sure! She booked out a whole floor at the Topaz and called in staff from our Long Island offices. Aphrodite is really grateful—"

"So, anyway," Daphne interrupted, "we're here to tell you that everything's still on schedule for Sherri Sellars's big 'Love Doctor' yacht party tonight."

"Yes," Susan said, switching to a practiced tone of corporate speak. "We're all very excited about her Smooth Sailings for Couples project! We're sure your team will do a great job with the beverage service tonight."

"And at the Garden of Aphrodite grand finale gathering on Saturday," Daphne added. "Alicia says not to worry about the Mocha Magic samples. She'll make sure there are plenty at both parties for us to push."

Yeah, I thought, *and given the product's likely inclusion of a narcotic, "push" is the appropriate term.*

"Will there be a public funeral for Patrice?" I asked.

Susan's corporate grin fell. "Ms. Stone's body will be laid to rest in Iowa, where her parents live."

"But Aphrodite *is* planning a little moment-of-silence thing before the Garden of Aphrodite product pitches kick in," Daphne said.

"It will be brief. We don't want to depress anyone."

Daphne nodded. "'Getting over' is good. That's what Sherri says. And the fastest way to do that is a return to normal."

"'Normal' as in we're back to gofering our buns off," Susan said. "We've had messenger duty all morning. I was uptown then down then east then west!"

"And I just got back from Brooklyn," Daphne added.

"Where did you go in Brooklyn?" Esther asked. "My boyfriend lives in south Brooklyn."

"I went to Voss Chocolate."

"Lucky girl," Esther replied. "I love that place."

"It was my first time there. Williamsburg is so cool and artsy. And the shop is awesome. Gudrun Voss makes the chocolate right there on the premises, so it smells amazing. Gudrun even had one of her assistants give me a tour."

"Your place smells great, too," Susan told Esther. "Like freshly roasted coffee."

Daphne's head bobbed. "And that fireplace looks so cozy and warm."

"I'll bet this is the original plank floor, isn't it?" Susan said.

Daphne pointed. "And those circular wrought-iron stairs are fabulous!"

Esther glanced at me. "Wow. These two could turn the world on with a smile."

"Hate to disappoint you," Daphne shot right back. "But the only way I'd throw my Mary Richards cap in the air is if a television network paid *me* a hundred thou an episode."

"My kind of girl," Esther said.

"What's in your Mocha Diablo?" Susan asked, pointing at the chalkboard.

"Espresso, chocolate sauce, cinnamon, steamed milk, and a devilish pinch of chipotle powder."

"Yum! I'll have one."

"Cappuccino for me," Daphne said.

"What size?" Esther asked.

"Large, I guess, or . . ." Daphne stared at the board. "What the heck is a *King Kong*?"

My cell went off on the counter. I picked it up.

"How are you, Cosi?" Lori Soles began, sounding upbeat.

"Good morning, Detective. Thanks for calling back."

"I know you're anxious," she said. "But I don't have any news for you."

Seeing Daphne and Susan staring at me, I lowered my voice and swiveled the stool. "No physical evidence yet?"

"No, but thanks to Ruben Salter, we've got a new view from another camera, actually from a neighboring building—"

"Did you get a look at the killer?"

"The high-angle security cam shows the umbrella moving under the podium's canopy. Two minutes later Patrice Stone's body plunges into the pool. I say *body* because the autopsy found no water in the victim's lungs, which means Stone was dead before she hit the reflection pool."

"It was the blow to the head that killed her?"

"Two blows. The first from behind, and the second above the left eye when the victim was on the ground."

The details were grisly enough to make me cringe.

"Hang in there. We've got a digital expert working on those recordings. Something will turn up. But listen, I have a question for you."

"For me?"

"Yeah, we just sent some Nutrition Nation umbrellas to

our CSU. They'll run tests, try to verify whether the heavy handle could have been used as the murder weapon."

"Did you ask Maya about it?"

"She and her husband admitted to bringing the umbrella, but they couldn't produce it in the cloakroom. They claimed it was taken."

Exactly what I thought. Alicia is trying to frame her!

"Anyway," Lori continued, "you were very helpful with that umbrella angle, and my lieutenant thought you might have some ideas on that note we found in the raincoat pocket—do you remember the word on the note?"

"Laeta?"

"Yes. Have you heard anyone mention it?"

"No. Not yet, but I'll be sure to let you know if I do."

"Thanks, Cosi. Got to run now. Talk to you again," Lori promised, right before the line went dead.

"Are you okay, Ms. Cosi?" Daphne asked as she sipped her cappuccino. "You look kind of pale. Did you get bad news or something?"

"It was a private call."

"From the police?"

"Excuse me?"

Daphne shrugged. "Sorry to be so nosy, but my boss, Sherri Sellars—she asked me to find out." She lowered her voice. "At the Mocha Magic party, she saw you come back with those two lady detectives. She said you were pointing people out for the police to speak with, that you were working with them."

"Well, if you remember, I was the one who found Ms. Stone's body, so they asked me to help. And I'm pretty sure the police spoke to *everyone* who attended the party, not just the ones I pointed out—"

"Ms. Bower told us you're some kind of investigator," Susan cut in. "And your boyfriend has some kind of big-deal special position with the New York Police Department?"

"Don't believe every piece of gossip you hear, ladies. I'm just a coffeehouse manager—"

"Boss!" Tuck called from behind the register.

"What?"

He pointed to the front window and sang. "You've got company."

I swiveled around again to find two unmarked police cars pulling up fast in front of our shop. Both had red bubble lights going on their dashes.

Mike walked in, radio in hand, dressed in his usual brown suit. In lock step behind him were two young detectives—a man and a woman. Both moved to an empty table and sat.

Like the Fish Squad, I'd served these two detectives many times. They worked at the Sixth, but today they weren't wearing blazers and pressed slacks. They were dressed like neighborhood regulars in jeans and light Windbreakers.

"I need to speak with you," Mike said, grim faced. "Privately."

As I excused myself, Daphne displayed a smirk. *Told you!*

Thirty-One

~~~~~~~~~~~~~~~~~~~~~~~~~~~~~~~

"**What's** with all the little people?" Mike asked when we reached my tiny office on the second floor.

"*Return to Munchkin Land* flash mob," I said. "Short people need caffeine, too."

He met my eyes. "I read the files this morning."

"The cold-case files? That's what all this is about?"

"It's not good, Clare. You better sit down."

Crap.

I settled into my rickety office chair, and Quinn pulled up another.

"Years ago, your former mother-in-law was brought before a grand jury. She'd been involved romantically with a police detective who frequented the Village Blend. Sound familiar?"

Oh my God.

"Are you sure she never mentioned anything like this to you?"

"Of course, I'm sure! What happened?"

"This detective, Cormac Murphy 'Murph' O'Neil, he was dirty, on the take. Mrs. Dubois probably didn't know it at the time—at least, I hope she didn't. Anyway, as it all went down, he and his partner were questioning a major drug dealer in the field when shots were fired. The partner and the dealer were killed, the dealer's money went missing, and so did your former mother-in-law's dirty boyfriend."

"What do you mean 'he went missing'?"

"He disappeared. Mrs. Dubois was called before a grand jury and asked to testify all she knew about her boyfriend. She answered questions about their relationship, explaining how they'd met, how long they'd been involved. They asked her if he'd made any statements about leaving town, if he ever contacted her, what he said, but she refused to answer any questions that might give away his intent or locations. The judge put her in jail."

I closed my eyes as a memory came back to me. "That's when it happened . . ."

"What?"

"That time Tucker had been falsely arrested, accused of murder, Madame mentioned that she'd been arrested herself. She wouldn't say anymore, but I assumed it was over some war protest or something. Nothing like this!"

"Clare, if Mrs. Dubois knows anything about her former boyfriend's whereabouts or anything he may have said about that crime, the money, the shootings, *anything*, she needs to give it up now. This killer cop, O'Neil—the PD has a source that tells us he's surfaced again. The theory is he used the money to start a new life, a new family, and now that he's up in years he doesn't want to take any chances that his family can be found out. He's very dangerous, Clare, and he'll be especially dangerous to your mother-in-law. He'll most likely want to tie up loose ends."

"What does that mean?"

"It means, if given the chance, he'll make sure she stays silent forever."

FOR the next ten minutes, Mike continued to fill me in. As we finished our discussion, he assured me the Village

Blend would be watched 24/7. He already knew about "Scar-face" following us to the ICE show—Franco had informed him—and when he pulled out a file photo of this killer cop, I must have turned pale.

"This is the same man, isn't it?"

I nodded. "He sat right downstairs at our counter, intro-duced himself as Bob. He's much older now, of course. His hair is silver-white instead of brown. And that terrible scar across his cheek is new, but I'm almost certain it's the same guy."

"Well, if you see him again, do not engage him in conver-sation. Do you hear me? You alert my detectives, or you call me, right away. Okay?"

"Okay. But what about Madame? If she's in danger—"

"Already taken care of. We have detectives watching Mrs. Dubois' penthouse until we get this cop killer in custody."

"Does she know any of this?"

Mike put a hand on my shoulder. "Only if you want to tell her. That's your call, sweetheart. I don't care either way—as long as you get the information."

"Mike, I can't promise you she'll talk to me!"

"Look, you and I both know we could pull her into an interview room. First Deputy Commissioner Hawke could have done that himself. But he's a smart man, a good cop. He knew the case. He knew Mrs. Dubois would likely clam up again. So he put me on the job, hoping I'd figure out an angle—and, sweetheart, you're it."

"*Me?*"

"Yes, you. You're my best bet." He gave me that Odysseus half smile. "In more ways than one."

MIKE swept out and, true to his word, left his young un-dercover team behind. I returned to the coffee bar—more than a little distracted. Daphne had to touch my shoulder to get my attention.

"Ms. Cosi? Sorry, but I have to go, and I need to give you this."

She pulled a manila envelope out of her backpack and placed it on the countertop. It was then I remembered Alicia's message about Daphne bringing me a note.

Addressed to me, the label commanded: *OPEN IMMEDIATELY. All caps,* I thought, *just like Alicia's tone.*

The envelope was unsealed, just loosely fastened. Inside I found a plain folder holding final catering instructions for tonight's yacht party on the East River. Paper clipped to that folder was a separate typewritten note with one of Alicia's new business cards attached to it. I instantly recognized the Mocha Magic logo of Alicia's card—a diner-style coffee cup with rising steam forming a floating heart.

> *Clare,*
> *Maya Lansing and I have decided to settle our differences.*
> *We have agreed to meet in Aphrodite's big tent at Socrates*
> *Sculpture Park this afternoon at three o'clock. We have also*
> *agreed that you should mediate our discussion and help us*
> *come to terms on the Mocha Magic issues. Present this letter*
> *to the guard at the security gate and he will admit you, and*
> *only you, so please come alone.*
> *Alicia*

Great, I thought. It wasn't enough that I was supposed to charm an octogenarian clam into giving up her tightly held pearl. Now I was supposed to sit between a platinum-haired Amazon who threatened to beat me up and a business associate whom I was trying to put behind bars—and my job was to help them work out their problems?

"Daphne," I said, "this note tells me I'm supposed to go to Socrates Sculpture Park today."

"Really? Why?"

"It's a long story. Have you been there yet?"

"No, Ms. Cosi," she said. "That grand finale setup is top secret. I have to wait until Saturday to see it, just like everyone else. But maybe Susan's been there."

Daphne swung around. "Hey, Susan. Have you seen the big tent yet at Socrates Sculpture Park?"

"No. I'm not scheduled to work the tent until Saturday morning."

"You'll love that park, Ms. Cosi," Nancy piped up. "I was just there last week. Dante Silva was helping a friend install some sculptures, and I wanted to check it out."

Esther rolled her eyes at me. "More like she wanted to check Dante out."

"It's super easy to get there," she said, grabbing a napkin. "I'll draw you a map."

"Phone call, Clare," Tucker announced just then.

Stepping behind the counter, I picked up the store phone. "Clare, this is Gudrun."

Gudrun Voss, aka the young Chocolate Nun. I knew at once why she was calling. She'd received the last-minute catering instructions just like I had.

"I just have one question," she said.

Her voice was so small, I could barely hear it. "Speak up, please, Gudrun. I've got a shop full of excited Munchkins."

"Excuse me?"

"That's better."

"Listen," she said, "answer me straight. What's wrong with my Raspberry-Espresso Flowers?"

"I'm sorry . . ." My head was still spinning from everything I'd learned. I tried harder to focus. "I need more."

"At the launch party two night ago, you and your servers chose not to put out my Raspberry-Espresso Flowers. Why?"

I was about to answer, but the question itself struck me as odd. We offered such a lovely variety of treats at the party. It seemed unlikely anyone from Aphrodite's Village would have complained about missing them.

"Gudrun, how did you know about that?"

"I was there."

"You were there? At the launch party? Why didn't you introduce yourself?"

"I often attend events incognito. That way I can hear what people really think about my chocolate."

"Well, there was nothing wrong with your flowers per se. The problem was you grease-penciled *REF* on the box. Someone in the kitchen threw it in the refrigerator. When they came out, near the warm ovens—"

"Oh, damn! Sugar bloom?"

"Yes?"

"Fine. I'll mark it differently next time."

"Wait," I said. "Would you answer some questions for me? When did you get there exactly? And when did you leave?"

"I'm sorry, Clare. I'm very busy today. We have an event tonight on the yacht, you know. I'll see you there."

"You're coming?"

"I said, 'I'll see you there!' "

I tried to ask again, but on a *whooshing* noise of exasperation, Gudrun killed the line between us.

BACK at the coffee bar, Daphne and Susan were saying their good-byes.

"Thanks for the coffee, everyone," Daphne called.

"Totally delish," Susan agreed. "Hey, Daph, you want to meet for dinner?"

"Sure. Where are you headed now . . ."

The girls separated on Hudson. Then Gardner Evans burst in to start his shift, proudly waving his new CD mix for our sound system. Nancy Kelly waved good-bye, and Tuck waved the phone again.

"Matt wants to know when he should stop by to discuss the seasonal delivery schedule."

"Tell him to be here at two o'clock sharp," I replied. "And tell him to bring a car."

"A car? Why?

"Because I need to be in Queens at three. And he's going to be my backup."

Thirty-Two

THE sun is strong today. Too strong! Too much light!

She whipped closed the window curtains, anxious to bring back the cool, shifting shadows of her underworld. Her heart was beating so fast now, her lungs laboring, her skin beading with perspiration.

Calm down, *she counseled herself.* You have plenty of time . . . plenty of time . . .

She would prepare for this event the way she always did—like a machine. First she selected her clothes. Black again . . . black for mourning, black for death . . .

Next she found the mask.

Her masks existed in many forms, but for this performance, she went to a closet and dug out the plastic kind—a copy of the one she'd used on Bay Creek's bridge, above that snaking canal of water that carried away her old self, which spanned the distance that led to this new one.

After laying out everything on the bed, she sunk to her knees, smirking with a thought: Years ago, that woman had gone down on her knees in a bedroom, too. But not to pray . . .

With a deep breath, she lifted the mattress and groped around for the cold steel shaft. Fingers closing on hard metal, she pulled, letting the mattress fall with a muffled thud.

Feeling the weight of the weapon, she smiled. Here was something better than prayer. Here was power. *The power to defend life and exact death. The power to make three women's lives a living hell.*

The same way they did for my mother . . .

She stroked the dark trigger, so cool and smooth, recalled the joy of pulling it, only once before—on her mother's persecutor.

I showed him what *premeditated* really was, didn't I?

First she'd bought the gun, so easy, just a weekend drive away. Then she'd stalked him, all the way from Long Island, waited for him to leave the restaurant, then his club, finally the bar. At last, he came back to the Manhattan parking garage, tipsy, distracted . . .

She'd dressed with perfect irony—a young mother, cradling an infant. Hera breast-feeding Hercules. Only this son of Zeus had a belly full of bullets, and when the gun discharged in the chilly gloom, light flashed like the light from Hera's breast to create all the stars of the Milky Way.

She cackled, recalling the man's shocked face; his fat, falling body; the light of life leaving his eyes. Such a brilliant lawyer! Such a brilliant mind! How dazzling are you now? In your coffin? In your grave?

The getaway had been easy. No one saw her. No one stopped her. But she learned a valuable lesson the next day, watching those idiot news people report the execution.

Beware of all-seeing eyes. They record everything: comings and goings, sins and secrets . . .

The gods of the underworld had been with her that night. The police ignored the security camera's image of a bundled up mother, her face obscured as she carried her child. Instead, they focused on more promising suspects: a young punk with a mugging rap sheet; a vagrant with mental problems; a worker on parole.

From then on, she remembered to look out for those all-seeing eyes—or find a way to trick them. All-seeing people were another matter. People like Clare Cosi.

That woman just wouldn't stop prodding and probing; pushing and snooping. The stupid Coffee Lady might even be smart enough to unmask her. Which is why she must die this afternoon. And once that nosy barista is gone, I can begin my grand finale . . .

Thirty-Three

That afternoon, three impatient horn blasts shattered the tranquillity of my coffeehouse. I glanced out the front window to find a military vehicle idling on Hudson.

"I think Mr. Boss has arrived," Esther announced, "unless we're hosting a reunion for Desert Storm vets."

The Hummer was massive; its exterior dabbled in the chocolate-chip brown of army camouflage. When I reached the sidewalk, Matt waved me forward.

"My God," I said, "are we going to Queens or invading a small country?"

"Get in and we'll decide."

I slung my heavy handbag full of tricks over my shoulder. It clattered as I climbed into the cab. I swear I felt the monster engine rumbling in my chest.

"Breanne's magazine rented this prop for a fashion photo shoot," Matt explained.

"What to wear when the Joint Chiefs drop by?"

"Apparently, military-style wraps are a Best Bet for a Fall Favorite. Anyway, she had the thing parked in our building's garage, so I thought, 'What the hell?' More fun than her wimpy hybrid, don't you think?"

That's when Matt took a closer look at my face—and his smile vanished. "What happened to your nose, Clare?"

"Oh, that . . ." I touched the bruise. "It's nothing—"

Matt's expression darkened. "Did Dudley Do-right do something wrong? Because if he did, he won't know what hit *him*."

"Matt—"

"I mean it. I'm *pretty* sure I can take that guy, armed or not."

"Thanks, but Quinn had absolutely nothing to do with this. I ran into a door . . ." *A big canary yellow door with a rock-hard forearm.* "And with enough makeup you can barely see the damage."

"A door?" Matt repeated. "So what's the name of this 'door' and where can I find him?"

"I'll explain on the way. Let's get going. Here—" I passed him the napkin. "Nancy drew me a map."

He waved it away. "I've got all the directions I need right here." With affection, he patted a GPS device fitted to the dashboard. "We're 6.9 miles, twenty-eight minutes, and one toll away."

"Thank R2D2 for me."

Matt slipped on a pair of Ray-Bans and eased the Hummer into traffic. With his new longish hairstyle and dark goatee, he looked like he was driving to an all-night jam session at the Blue Note—or a Mexican bank robbery.

"Matt," I said, trying to keep my voice light. "I have a quick question for you."

"Shoot," he said, then smirked. "Not literally. I mean, Quinn hasn't given you his gun, has he?"

"Did your mother ever date a cop?"

"You're kidding, right?" Matt snorted. "My mother trusts cops about as much as I do."

"Since when?" I challenged. "She never said anything to me about not trusting the police."

"I'm not surprised, given what your boyfriend does for a living. Around you, she obviously kept her opinion to herself."

"So you don't recall her mentioning dating a detective?"

"What's this all about?"

"Did she ever mention a man named Cormac O'Neil? Maybe she called him Murphy or Murph?"

"No, Clare. That name doesn't ring any bells. Now why are you asking?"

"I'll tell you about it—later."

"Well, at least tell me why I'm driving you to an outdoor art space in Queens."

I took a breath. "Aphrodite has taken over the park for a PR party to launch a new line of home furnishings. The event is scheduled for Saturday, but at three o'clock today, I'm supposed to meet Maya Lansing and Alicia Bower on the grounds to mediate their peace conference."

Matt rubbed his dark goatee. "Isn't Maya that half-naked fitness queen who threaten to end you? Maybe we should buy pepper spray. I can stop by the Queens Spy Shop. They've helped me before—"

"No. I don't need—"

"On second thought, Maya is pretty buff. Maybe you should bring a Taser. The nose is good, though you'll look tougher with a battered face. Intimidating, you know?"

"This is supposed to be a peace conference."

"So was the Munich Agreement. Eleven months later Nazi tanks rolled into Warsaw."

"You're the one who brought the tank!"

"That's not the point." Matt's eyebrows knitted. "How did this all come about?"

Waving the letter from Alicia, I delivered a carefully edited version of my trip to Nutrition Nation—leaving all of Franco's involvement on the cutting room floor. By the time I was finished with my update, we were through the Midtown Tunnel and inside the borough of Queens.

"So you're telling me our new business partner isn't just a drug pusher. She's also a—"

"Murderess." I swallowed hard. "Yes, sorry, but Alicia had motive and opportunity. And she also framed Maya Lansing for the crime."

The light changed, and we drove past a public housing project and into a distressed industrial area made up of junk-yards, warehouses, and garages. Most depressing were the shuttered businesses: Laundromats, delis, bodegas. Their deteriorated signs were half rusted, their windows dark.

But then Matt made a right turn onto Vernon Boulevard, and the world around us suddenly transformed. Vernon paralleled the East River, and between the sun-kissed chop of that flowing water and the wide road we were on, stretched a lush, green swath of parkland.

A block later, I recognized the walls of the Noguchi Museum, a building with ten art galleries on two floors. I'd spent a glorious day here a few years ago, viewing the works of Japanese-American artists as well as the lamps and furniture designed by Isamu Noguchi.

My tension eased as I remembered the simple tranquillity of the open-air sculpture garden within those walls—an example of the miracle that was New York City.

As challenging and rocky as life often became on these urban streets, sometimes all you had to do was turn a corner to find yourself in a better place, one filled with imagination, vision, beauty, and hope.

"We're here," Matt said, one eye on his GPS screen. "Socrates Sculpture Park is on our left, past this big box store."

"Pull into the store's lot," I said. "Nancy warned me there was no other place to park around here."

We swung into Costco's sprawling acreage, past its automotive garage and discount liquor store. Matt found a spot big enough to accommodate Bree's fashionista prop, a space facing the East River, a channel of water that led directly to the Atlantic Ocean.

Matt cut the engine and powered down the windows. Fresh sea air swept in along with the cry of seagulls and the sweet scent of Italian roasted peppers from a nearby concessions area.

In front of our Hummer, a narrow sidewalk paralleled the jagged shoreline. Two African-American teens, an older Greek man, and a Hispanic father and son sat among the damp rocks, dangling fishing lines hopefully.

Across the treacherous river the Manhattan skyline rose up like the shimmering walls of a mythic city—one of the most breathtaking views of New York I'd ever seen. *And in a Queens Costco parking lot. Who knew?*

"Okay, Clare. What's your plan, and why do you need me?"

"I'm going to blackmail Alicia Bower."

Matt peered over his sunglasses. "That's a crime."

"So is murder. I'm going to inform Alicia that I've figured out she killed Patrice. I'm going to lay out my evidence and threaten to go to the police unless she cuts me in for a big piece of the profits on Mocha Magic."

"Alicia won't like that," Matt said. "And Maya Lansing won't, either. And the fitness queen is very big and very buff."

"I'm going to inform Maya that Alicia tried to frame her by using her Nutrition Nation umbrella when she committed the murder."

"You're going to start a cat fight, and you'll be in the middle!"

I pulled a digital recorder from my purse. "I'm going to document the entire conversation. When I tell Alicia I want money in exchange for my silence, I'm sure she'll incriminate herself."

"So what?" Matt threw up his hands. "That recording will be made without consent, so nothing you get will be admissible in court."

"Doesn't matter. If I can establish Alicia's guilt without doubt, I can turn over the recordings to Lori Soles and Sue Ellen Bass. Those two detectives are trained interrogators. In an interview room, they'll be able to break Alicia down and get a confession."

"Not if she shuts her yap and hires a lawyer."

"I'll be a witness to whatever she says. So will Maya. They'll get her, Matt."

"That still doesn't explain why I'm here."

"You're my backup."

"How can I back you up if you're supposed to come alone and the security guard at the gate won't let me in?"

"Now comes the genius part of my plan." I dug into my handbag and pulled out Joy's old baby monitor. "My super-secret weapon."

I handed Matt the device's receiver while I kept the actual monitor.

"This thing is battery operated and voice activated, too. And it's got a great range. You'll be able to hear me, so I can narrate what's happening. You can't talk to me because the monitor only works one way. But if you hear trouble on my end, you go right to the gate and alert the guard."

"Clare, this thing is an antique! You probably haven't given it a real workout since Joy was an infant."

"Wrong. I used it through most of our daughter's adolescence."

"This I've got to hear."

"When Joy was fifteen, I caught her trying to sneak out of our Jersey house past midnight. So while she was at school the next day, I dug this out of my closet and hid the transmitter in her bedroom. After that, I could hear everything she said when she was on the phone with her friends. When Joy made plans to go out and party without permission, I was always there to thwart them. She never managed to sneak out, not once, all the way through graduation. So believe me, this works." I held it up, smiling wider than an infomercial babe. "Guaranteed."

"Clare, you're diabolical."

"I'm a mother."

"Well, I'm glad you weren't *my* mother. I never would have had any fun."

Thirty-Four

~~~~~~

Ten minutes later I stood a few yards from the park entrance, baby monitor and digital recorder tucked inside my bag. Before approaching the gate, I glanced over my shoulder at my ex. He gave me a thumbs-up.

Matt had already repositioned the Hummer under the fire escape of a crumbling warehouse across the street. Now he stood beneath a rusted sign, pink baby monitor to his ear.

"Okay, one more test," I said. "If you're receiving me, raise your right hand and wave."

Matt flashed the proper signal.

"Now get back inside the Hummer. I don't want the guard to see you lurking around."

When Matt was out of sight, I pulled out Alicia's letter to present to security and crossed a gravelly stretch. Aphrodite's people had erected a chain-link fence that completely blocked the park entrance. A Parks Department notice warned the public that the area was closed all week for "a private event." A sign over the gate had been draped with a scarlet banner. *Live Like a Greek Goddess!* it exhorted the city's women.

I found a buzzer for deliveries and pressed it. Waiting for a response, I peered through the chain links. Unfortunately, the view was blocked by eight-foot partitions painted to resemble Doric columns.

Since the exhibition was just days away, I assumed I'd find more activity. But there was no sign of people going in or out, and after a full minute passed, still no guard arrived to admit me.

Meanwhile, a roiling mass of clouds crossed paths with the spring sun, and the formerly luminous afternoon turned unsettlingly gloomy.

Impatient, I finally rattled the gate and discovered it wasn't locked. I waited for a guard to show, but all I heard was the sound of canvas flapping in the wind and the cry of more seagulls.

"There's no guard," I told Matt. "But someone left the gate unlocked, so I'm going in . . ."

I stepped between a gap in two of the partitions and into an enclosed, grassy area wide enough to accommodate our Hummer and then some. The path was bordered by high plywood walls painted with reproductions of art found on Greco-Roman urns and mosaics. I'd been instructed to meet Alicia in the big tent, and like a culturally enlightening cattle chute, the walkway led right up to a white party tent two stories high.

"This has to be the place," I told Matt. "I can't imagine anything bigger would fit inside this little park."

The interior was cast in shadows, and I paused before entering, troubled by the lack of activity.

"There should be someone here," I said. "A security guard to watch the stuff at the very least. And where are Alicia and Maya? It's time for their summit meeting, but so far the place looks deserted . . ."

Suddenly, I heard the hum of electric generators. One by one, floodlights high in the tent's steel-framed rafters sprang to life. A broad red carpet, running down the center of the enclosure, was now illuminated with intermittent pools of light.

The tent's interior had been partitioned off into smaller spaces with banners dangling over each entrance. All these spaces were dark, save one at the farthest end of the carpeted corridor. There the light was so bright it spilled into the makeshift hall, infusing the carpet with an almost neon red glow.

"I think I'm being played here and I don't like it," I told Matt. "But if Alicia thinks spooky lighting is going to intimidate me, she's mistaken."

Secretly, though, I found the whole thing creepy, and I could imagine Matt's reaction. Right now he was probably pounding his head against the Hummer's steering wheel, shouting things we both knew I couldn't hear like, *Get the hell out of there, Clare!*

"Sorry, Matt. I want to find out what's going on . . ."

I walked down the aisle, following the pools of light as if they were stepping stones across a shallow creek. I reached the first exhibition space, where a banner touted *The Minotaur Collection*, with the tagline *Furnishing His Man Cave.* Inside I spied pool tables, wet bars, display cases, even gun racks.

I continued forward, passing myriad displays: the Athena Collection: Bed and Bath for the Discerning Woman, and Gaia's Garden: Outdoor Furnishings to Complement Mother Nature. The Spartan Collection was touted as "an edgy minimalist style experience," which apparently meant IKEA-style stick furniture and uniquely innovative designs for uncomfortable-looking chairs.

At last I arrived at the brilliantly lit exhibit for the Perseus and Andromeda Collection; *Boudoir Beauty for Classic Couples*, its banner promised.

"This has to be the place, but I still don't see anyone . . ."

Instead of going in, I paused at the entrance, waiting for the invisible hand that led me here to reveal itself once more. I didn't have long to wait. Behind me the pools of light went out, one after the other, until the only illumination inside this night-black tent was directly in front of me.

I crossed the threshold. Three steps in, I found myself surrounded by an array of bedroom furnishings. The most impressive piece was a massive bed with four Doric columns supporting a sea-blue silk canopy. The bed itself was raised high off the floor and framed by twin nightstands with matching lamps. A tall Japanese-style screen completed the decor.

The imposing bed was backed by a tall mirror, its silvered glass framed by a bone-white ceramic frieze depicting Perseus battling Medusa, the female demon with the serpent hair who turned men to stone with her deadly gaze.

According to myth Perseus outsmarted Medusa by using the reflection on his polished shield to avoid her lethal stare. Guided by that trusty mirror, he used his sword to cut off the she-devil's head without being turned to stone.

True to the story, the sculpted frieze portrayed the warrior hero with shield raised, his eyes averted from the menacing gorgon. I was so intrigued by the frame's artwork that at first I didn't notice a word scrawled in red letters across the mirror itself.

SEVERA.

Was it the designer's name? Curious, I climbed up two of the three platform steps, toward the foot of the massive bed then cried out. Someone was on the mattress—Maya Lansing sprawled facedown, three bloody holes stitched across her back. Her head was turned, and when I saw her wide, sightless eyes, I knew the fitness queen had gone through her final cooldown.

She was shot in the back, I realized, probably while she was reading the word scrawled on the mirror . . .

Now I was the one looking into that mirror—just in time to spot the reflection of a figure stepping out from behind the Japanese screen!

Clad neck to toe in black, the figure's face was hidden behind a virgin-white Kabuki mask. The stranger clutched something in a gloved hand. I realized what it was a split second before I threw myself onto the floor.

The gunshots that followed shattered the mirror instead of my skull, and a shower of shards cascaded over Maya's corpse.

"Gun!" I cried to Matt. "Someone's shooting at me!"

With the killer behind me, I rolled sideways across the floor until I slammed into the love seat. Bullets chewed the carpet, and when I hopped over the couch, the last shot punched a hole through the back of it, filling the air with an explosion of stuffing.

Hearing an empty click, I prayed the shooter was out of ammo. I peered through the hole in the shattered love seat and spied the black silhouette near the broken mirror. The shooter was fumbling to reload.

This is my chance!

I raced for the exit. Within seconds, I heard more pops. Bullets came so close I felt the shock waves. A vase exploded and then a sink, another mirror and a ceramic swan!

Suddenly, I heard a loud crash, followed by the chugging roar of a vehicle engine and the sound of breaking glass. Finally came the earsplitting blast of a familiar horn.

Matt!

Seeing the headlights rushing toward me across the red carpet, I ran toward the Hummer, waving my arms. The vehicle came to a skidding stop right beside me. I reached for the handle, but the passenger's door was already open.

"Get in!" Matt yelled.

I entered with a single leap. "Alicia's trying to kill me!"

"That's Alicia?" Matt said, eyes forward.

I peered through the windshield and saw the white Kabuki mask glowing in the tent's eerie gloom. Then I glanced away in time to avoid being blinded by the stab of a brilliant scarlet light.

"She's using a laser sight!" Matt cried, pushing me onto the floor. Glass rained down on me when the passenger window exploded.

I screamed. "I thought Hummers had bulletproof glass!"

"This is a prop Hummer! Not a real—oh, never mind!"

Matt slammed the vehicle into reverse and punched the gas. The wheels spun, shredding the red carpet for a moment before gaining traction. Then the big car lurched, and we were on our way.

Matt's head turned, so he could drive backward, which meant he couldn't see the red laser dot coming to rest on the side of his skull. Lucky for him, I did.

"Get down!" I yelled. Grabbing a handful of Matt's long hair, I pulled as hard as I could.

Matt howled, but his big head moved just in time—the window blew out a second later. He didn't slow down. We exited the tent and kept going, through the cattle chute and back toward the street. The fence and the gate were already in ruins, shattered when Matt drove in.

As we hit the street, he slammed the brakes—too late, unfortunately. A limousine had rolled into the intersection behind us, and the Hummer smashed into its front grill, a rear-end collision in reverse.

"God, Matt! I hope no one was hurt." I pushed open the door.

"Stay down, Clare! Help is on the way. I already called 911!"

Heedless of the danger, I jumped out of the Hummer and raced to the car we'd struck. The hood was crumpled, the hissing radiator belching steam. I could hear approaching sirens, too. Lots of them.

The other driver, a Sikh with a full beard and turban, emerged from his smashed Town Car, shaking his head with exasperation. Then the man opened the passenger doors, and two women climbed out. Both were shaken but unhurt.

One of them was Madame. The other was Alicia Bower.

THIRTY-FIVE

∘∘∘∘∘∘∘∘∘∘∘∘∘∘∘∘∘∘∘∘∘∘∘

DAMN her! Damn her straight to hell!

Face sweaty behind the mask, she bolted from the dazzling light. Safe in the shadows of the tent, she ripped away her white face, peeled off her midnight togs. Beneath, more clothes clung damply to her skin, yet another self.

She pulled out the Go Green! *shopping tote, stuffed everything inside—the gun, the mask, the laser site. The black disguise came last, topped with a decoy box to bury all the evidence.*

In the distance, sirens wailed. Hugging the tote, she dropped and rolled. The tent bottom gave as she moved against it, birthing her into the fresh-cut grass.

Out on the street, a car horn blared, voices shouted, traffic screeched, but she remained invisible. Hidden by the canvas mountain, she ran for the edge of Socrates Sculpture Park.

At the shoreline, the river shimmered, tempting her with a watery escape. If only she could swim across! But the current was too treacherous, the very act suicidal. Given her performance on the Bay Creek bridge, the irony nearly made her cackle.

Another bridge beckoned now, down river—the Queensboro. She had to reach it, as fast as possible. Slipping down the damp rocks, she moved to the river's edge, hurried for the property line. Now trees and shrubs would be her shield as she climbed back up the embankment. Finally, on a steadying breath, she stepped into the open.

The Costco lot was vast and crowded—exactly what she needed. Slinging the tote bag over her shoulder, she wandered out as stupid and glassy-eyed as the shoppers before her: mommies struggling with toddlers, families fumbling with carts, couples bickering over needs and receipts. Invisibly, she slithered among them. None bothered the lone woman snaking by their minivans, economy cars, and SUVs; and if they glanced into her tote, all they'd see was a box of Pampers.

When she reached the store's busy exit, she flowed with the crowd and began her search. In almost no time, she saw it—a dark sedan moving slowly, like a shark. The livery driver had disgorged his fare, appeared hungry for a new one. She waved him over. He pulled up and she ducked in back.

"Manhattan," she said, hearing the pathetic quiver in her voice. She swallowed hard, tried again: "No hurry. Take your time . . ."

As they headed for the main road, she chewed her lower lip. Her fury had given way to fear and, for the first time, an admission . . . failure. But she would not stop. Not now. Not ever. She just had to get clear of this place.

"Some kind of car wreck up here," the driver warned. "Big backup. Lots of police . . ."

"Can you get around them?"

"I'll try."

As the driver turned the car, she held her breath. Soon he found a new exit, and she was on her way again, heading down river, into the shadow of that towering bridge.

Sitting back, she closed her eyes. Once again, she was invisible. No one would suspect her, and that's how she would win. That's how she always won.

Striking from the shadows, she'd get them all, one by one, including that stupid little witch who'd ruined today's performance. The very thought nearly brought a giggle to her lips. Clare Cosi may not know it yet, but she had been judged and sentenced.

And won't you be surprised, Ms. Cosi, when you find *me* your executioner!

Thirty-Six

❧❧❧❧❧❧❧❧❧❧❧❧❧❧❧❧❧❧

"**I** am *not* a murderer!"

Hands on slender hips, Alicia Bower met my eyes, incensed and defiant.

I pointed to the lovingly battered café chair directly across from mine, the one from which she'd dramatically leaped. "Sit down."

The four of us—Alicia, Madame, Matt, and I—were positioned like points of a compass around the table. We had our privacy up here on the Blend's closed second floor. What we didn't have was peace. We'd barely settled in before Matt blurted out, "Until you two rolled up in your limo, Clare thought *Alicia* was the shooter."

"I am outraged! Outraged!" Alicia cried.

"There's no use getting emotional, dear." Madame picked up her cup and saucer. "Clare's right. Sit. Drink your cappuccino. It's quite delicious . . ."

Tugging on the lapels of her pinstriped blazer, Alicia stood firm a moment, then tossed her perfectly coiffed flapper hair and returned the seat of her skirt to the seat of the chair.

"You called to tell me you were sending over instructions. What was I supposed to think?" I asked Alicia.

"I sent over the catering instructions, that's all," Alicia replied. "I had nothing to do with that fake letter."

Suddenly Matt sprang up. "I need another double!"

I wasn't surprised. The man had downed his first *doppio* faster than Quinn's fire-haired cousin knocked back Irish whiskey. Either my ex-husband really needed more caffeine, which was easy to believe, or he wanted an excuse to regroup after Alicia's tantrum (even easier to believe).

"Ladies? Anything else?"

We shook our heads, and Matt headed for our corkscrew staircase.

Of course, the police had interviewed us at the crime scene. They processed us further at a Queens precinct, taking our statements, our photos, and our letters. Yes, *letters* plural.

Alicia had received a typewritten note similar to mine, summoning her to the park tent. Her memo had been from Aphrodite (supposedly), and Susan Chu had been the one to deliver it. The police discovered a *third* summoning message in the stiffening fingers of Maya Lansing's corpse, this one also purportedly from Aphrodite. God knows who delivered Maya's letter. Daphne? Susan? Yet another of the Aphrodite's Village gofers?

The whole thing made my head spin, and in just a few hours, my staff and I were expected at the Twelfth Street Pier. I'd signed a contract, agreeing to cater another PR event for Aphrodite's Village—this one on a yacht for relationship expert Sherri Sellars.

I'd accepted their advance, purchased inventory, and scheduled my people. Aphrodite's contract carried stiff financial penalties for dropping the ball at the last minute (and she was known to be litigious), so I was loath to back out now. But the police had yet to find today's shooter, and I wasn't too keen on becoming that killer's target dummy for the second time today. Consequently, I ordered (yes *ordered*)

Alicia, Madame, and Matt to come back to the Blend with me. *It's time we hashed everything out,* I'd told them. *Everything.*

"Why, in heaven's name, did you think I would want to shoot you?" Alicia demanded.

"Because I'm a key witness in the murder of Patrice Stone—"

"That doesn't explain a thing!"

"It *will* if you allow me to *finish*. I've been helping the two lead detectives on Patrice's case nail *you* as the primary person of interest in her murder."

"You *what*?" Now Madame joined Alicia for a duet of outrage. (I didn't blame them.)

"Just listen to the whole story," I said, "because the circumstantial evidence against Alicia is overwhelming . . ." I laid out the tale, finishing up with the truth about Alicia's Candy Man, Troy Talos. By the end, both women's mouths were slack. "And here's the biggest shock of all: the person who hired Talos to seduce Alicia away from her own launch party was Patrice."

Alicia's face blanched. "Patrice Stone?"

I nodded.

"My goodness," Madame said. "In heaven's name, why?"

"Ambition. Patrice wanted the top spot at Aphrodite's Village after Aphrodite retired, and Alicia was stiff competition for it, so Patrice tried to take her down a notch."

Madame sighed. "How puerile."

"That's not the worst of it," I said.

"What is?" Alicia whispered.

I met her gaze. "Think it through: if you discovered or even suspected that Patrice was behind that criminal prank, then you would also have a highly plausible motive for murder."

"But I didn't kill Patrice!" Alicia wailed. "And I didn't know she'd hired Dennis!"

"You mean Troy, dear," Madame corrected.

Alicia covered her eyes. "Whatever that man's name was, I can tell you he was a pro at turning on the charm . . ."

That was easy to believe. "Troy Talos is a wannabe-actor

parolee who ran gigolo scams in the past. I'd say *pro* is the right word."

Alicia held her head. "Oh God."

"Listen up, okay?" I touched Alicia's arm. "I have to ask you a question. It's an important one so look at me."

Frowning, Alicia glanced up.

"The night of Patrice's murder, you put on your raincoat and went into the Garden. Everyone was inside by then. I understand you told the lead detectives that you were simply checking the weather, but I don't believe it. Why did you go out there, Alicia?"

"I . . . I left something . . ." She looked away.

"If you don't tell me the truth, I can't help you."

She smirked. "So now you're going to *help* me?"

I folded my arms. "Believe me, lady, if you *want* to twist in the wind, I'll be glad to let you."

As I sat back, Madame leaned forward, closing still-strong fingers around Alicia's wrist. "If I were you, dear, I would tell my daughter-in-law the truth."

Stiffening like an ice sculpture, Alicia cast her eyes downward, fixing her gaze on the old scars in the wooden tabletop. "I went out to the Garden," she said, voice barely there, "to rifle the files on Patrice's smartphone."

"You what?" Now Madame and I were the duet.

Releasing her wrist, Madame sat back, and I leaned forward. "Why did you do that?"

Alicia wrung her hands. "I know it sounds awful. But I noticed Patrice had left it out there after her speech, on the shelf under the podium. When the storm hit and everyone rushed inside, I saw it as luck—an opportunity to watch my back."

"So you did suspect Patrice was trying to undermine you?"

"Not Patrice—but I heard gossip that other Sisters in our Village were angling for control of my Mocha Magic product. I needed to find out who my enemies really were. So I skimmed Patrice's e-mails."

"What did you find out?"

"Not much. There were messages from Maya, Aphrodite, and Sherri Sellars, as well as Patrice's assistant Susan Chu. The e-mails from Maya were the most incriminating—but you already know what she was up to. You witnessed our argument at the party. What I didn't know was that Patrice's words of support for me that night were a total lie. She was two-faced, a good little actress."

"And now she's a *dead* little actress." Matt walked toward us from the top of the stairs.

"Matteo, that's awful," Madame scolded.

"It's the truth, Mother." He moved to the table but refused to sit. "And speaking of truths, now is a good moment for another one. Don't you think, Clare?"

I speared Matt. *Don't you put this all on me or you'll be the next corpse!*

Catching my drift, he folded his arms and shifted his gaze to the woman of the hour. "What's in the Mocha Magic, Alicia?"

"Excuse me?" She frowned. "Didn't you read the press packet?"

"Humor me. What's in it?"

"Village Blend coffee—*obviously*. Voss chocolate and a proprietary combination of imported herbs and spices."

"Come clean, honey. What *drug* did you add to that herbal mix? A narcotic? A controlled substance? What?"

"My boy—" Madame's voice was stern. Clearly, she didn't care for Matt's tone, yet she paused, trusting her son enough to give him some latitude. "What are you suggesting here?"

"I'm *suggesting* that the 'magic' in that Mocha Magic is going to sink us all." He looked to me. *Okay, Clare, now you're on.*

I took a breath, braced myself. "I asked Mike Quinn to help us out. I gave him a sample. He's having it tested."

Once again, Alicia went into jack-in-the-box mode, flying into another tantrum—lots of "What nerve!" and "How dare yous!" But she soon ran out of gas, and Matt and I were ready for her.

"If the product ingredients are kosher, then you have nothing to worry about, do you?" I said.

Matt nodded. "Either you're lying to us or you're duped, too. Which is it?"

Alicia sank into her chair. She looked to Madame and both admitted an odd fact. Although the two had sampled plenty of the Mocha Magic product during its final stages of development, neither imbibed at the launch party.

"I *did* eat the chocolates and pastries," Alicia said, "and so did your mother."

Matt shook his head. "As a flavoring agent, the active ingredients are diluted. When you drink the stuff, you feel the effects. I promise you."

I turned to Madame. "Why didn't you drink the Mocha Magic at the party?"

"Frankly, dear, I'm no fan of instant coffee. Compared with other instants, I found Alicia's product acceptable, even superior. I *did* feel a *slight* boost of euphoria when I sampled it weeks ago, but nothing like a *drug*."

Matt glanced at me. "I don't want my mother putting that stuff into her system. But Alicia needs to try several cups of it *now*, in front of us all."

I nodded. "I'll have Esther bring some up."

"Thanks."

I stood but didn't leave. Matt had interrupted our discussion before I could make things clear to Alicia on the Patrice Stone murder.

"What is it, Clare?" Madame asked.

"I want to make sure you both understand this. After we're through here, Alicia should call her lawyer. She needs to go up to the Seventeenth Precinct and amend her statement. She's got to tell the police the truth about what she really did in the Garden on the night of the party."

"Yes, fine," Alicia said, waving her hand. "I'll take care of it."

"Good," I said, relieved, and headed for the stairs.

"HOLY smokin' rockets! It's just smoke . . . and a rocket," Nancy complained as I moved toward our espresso bar.

"Exactly," Dante replied.

Dante Silva, my *artista* barista, appeared to be showing Nancy Kelly a series of pen-and-ink drawings from one of his sketchbooks. I knew Dante was scheduled to relieve Esther any minute, but I was surprised (and a little upset) to see Nancy here. She had had a shift earlier today and left once already. She wasn't scheduled to work again until our catering gig tonight.

Slipping behind the counter, I asked Esther to prepare four servings of Mocha Magic and take them to the second floor.

"No problem," she said, pulling out a tray.

I tipped my head toward Nancy and Dante. "I've been trying to keep them apart on the schedule. What is she up to with him?"

Esther rolled her eyes. "She's paying him to create an original tattoo for her . . ."

"I see."

"But if you ask me, *he's* the one paying for it."

"I don't get the whole rocket thing," Nancy said, obviously agitated.

"I turned your phrase into an image," Dante calmly explained. "The smoke. The rocket. It's signature Nancy, so I thought it would make a great tattoo. You can pick out the colors, of course . . ."

I moved closer, glanced at the drawing—an art deco rocket with curlicue smoke belching from its tail pipe. The design was charming, but Nancy appeared stressed out by the very idea.

"Okay . . ." Dante buried the sketch, scratched his shaved head, and found another.

A few rejected designs later, Esther was ready to head upstairs with the Mocha Magic samples, and I was pulling myself a badly needed espresso shot. "Tell Matt I'll be right up, okay?"

"Sure, boss . . ."

"Here's a great one," Dante told Nancy. "The Greek philosopher Plato believed that a serpent devouring its own tail was the first living thing in the universe, the origin of all life. This design is a Norse version of the concept."

Nancy frowned. "Why is the snake biting its own butt?"

"It's symbolic for the circle of life—the snake who devours its own tail."

"Yuck. Who would want a ringworm for a tattoo?"

"Fine. What do you think of a unicorn?"

"I think it's uni-*corny*!"

"How about an ankh?"

"A what?"

Dante touched one of the colorful tattoos on his own ropey arms—a cross with a loop on top. "It's an ancient Egyptian symbol."

"It's called the Key of Life," interjected Barry, one of our most loyal customers.

"Yes, it's very spiritual," agreed Jung-Min, another regular. "It looks cool on your arm, too."

Dante smiled at the pretty, young grad student, now leaning over his shoulder. "Thank you."

"Oh, you're welcome," Jung-Min said, grinning back. "When do you start pulling shots, Dante? I love your latte art!"

He checked his watch. "Fifteen minutes."

A friend of Jung-Min's wandered over (another coed, of course). "Would you show me some of your sketches, too, Dante?"

"Excuse me!" Nancy glared at the girls. "Dante is working with *me* now. Some privacy, please?"

Jung-Min and her friend blinked, shrugged, and found an empty table.

With an exhale, Dante closed his sketchbook. "How about a dolphin? All girls love dolphins, don't they?"

"What's *romantic* about a fish? I want something *personal*. From *you*."

Dante visibly tensed. *Finally*, the boy got a clue. I bit my cheek and sipped my espresso. The earthy warmth felt as though it were spreading into my very bones. *God, I needed that . . . and this break from the Tantrum Queen. Now I know why Matt slipped away . . .*

"How about a flower?" Nancy continued, reaching across to take Dante's hand. "A rose with a heart around it—and your signature. I've got to have your name etched into my skin."

"Oh, man . . ." Dante pulled back his hand. "I don't think that's such a good idea . . ."

"Why not? You sign your paintings, don't you?"

Dante's reply was drowned out by three loud voices— Alicia's, Madame's, and Matt's. As they descended the staircase, Matt's gaze found mine behind the counter. Looking pleased, he gestured as if he were drinking, then flashed a thumbs-up sign.

Setting down my demitasse, I hurried to catch up with Alicia, but she was already out the front door. Turning, I faced Matt and Madame.

"Where is she going?"

"To dress for this evening's yacht party," Madame said. "Which is where I'm going, too." She pecked my cheek. "I'll see you on the boat, dear!"

As Madame moved to the sidewalk, arm up, a cab pulled over and she was gone.

I turned to Matt. "Doesn't Alicia understand how much trouble she's in with the police? She needs to go up to the Seventeenth Precinct *now*, with a lawyer. She needs to amend her previous statement and straighten things out with Detectives Soles and Bass!"

Matt shrugged. "Alicia doesn't seem to think it's so urgent. She said she's putting it off until the morning. She's a lot more upset about what Gudrun Voss did to her product. And so am I."

"What happened up there?"

He smiled down at me. "Score."

"You got through to her?"

"Alicia drank a single cup of the Mocha Magic and admitted we were right. She started cursing like a sailor, ranting that Gudrun changed the product profile."

"Why would Gudrun do that without telling her?"

"I don't know. But Alicia swore she'd have it out with the little chocolatier on the boat tonight. I'm looking forward to seeing that."

Given the "Sisterly" confrontations I'd witnessed this week, I wasn't at all sure I was. Frowning, I checked my watch and glanced across the coffeehouse floor. Quinn's two undercover sentries were still settled in our corner, nursing large lattes. Matt still didn't know about them—or Quinn's cold-case assignment or Scarface.

The bizarre story of his mother's old flame being a cop killer had taken a back seat to the hot water we were in with Alicia and her Village people. Frankly, I was glad Matt was here. If something went down, I wanted someone around who could handle chaos, and Matt's third-world travails—from African uprisings and Bangkok brawls to Indonesian tsunamis—had tempered him well.

Given the shooting gallery we'd gone through a few hours ago, I was glad he was coming tonight, too. But now I was the one slipping away. I had plenty to do before this yacht party started.

I just hoped to God it didn't end with a bang.

Thirty-Seven

As we exited the cab in front of the Twelfth Street Piers, Joy dropped the first bombshell of the evening.

"Mom, I can't reach, Franco!"

"What do you mean?"

"I left him five messages since this morning. He never returned one."

In less than an hour, the 240-foot-yacht *Argonaut* was scheduled to depart. Tucker and Nancy were already aboard, preparing a coffee and chocolate service for one-hundred-plus guests.

As I mulled over my daughter's complaint, I felt Joy's eyes on me. "What?"

"Have you heard from Mike?"

"Not since this morning. He's on the job. Probably the same job Franco is working. That's the life, honey."

Joy shook her head, retied her ponytail. "Well, I hope nothing happened to Manny. It's not like him to ignore my calls."

I could see the worry on her face, and I wondered whether she could live every day in the shadow of that anxiety, because that's what a relationship with a police officer meant, especially in this city.

On the other hand, I knew very well there could be another reason the sergeant hadn't called my daughter. A tasty distraction might have crossed his path, like that Milk Duds girl. But if that's the kind of dog Emmanuel Franco truly was, Joy was better off finding out sooner than later.

Still, a mother's duty was to provide a place of comfort not chaos, so I squeezed Joy's hand. "I'm sure Franco's fine. Mike gets tangled up all the time and can't call back . . ."

Joy looked relieved—that made one of us.

As we entered the terminal building, I warily eyed the crowd of strangers surrounding the yacht.

"I'm still not happy with your decision to help out tonight," I said.

"Oh, Mom, stop worrying. Look!" She pointed to the base of the gangplank where security had set up a metal detector. "Everyone has to go through a scanner before they board. It's safer on that yacht than it is in our coffeehouse."

Joy had a point—and she didn't even know about Scarface. Neither did she know that two undercover Queens detectives would be on board, waiting for Maya's killer to expose herself (at least, that's how their lieutenant put it to me earlier). Left unsaid was the ugly truth: "exposure" for a killer like this could very well mean another dead body.

The thought had me speed-dialing Matt.

"I'm on my way," he assured me. "Ten minutes from you."

"Your father's coming. Let's board."

After Joy and I passed through the scanner, we climbed the gangplank. A pair of hulking, square-jawed private security officers greeted us. They searched our bags, asked for photo IDs, and checked our names against a list on a laptop screen. That's when I realized Matt's name had to be added to my staff list.

Rather than explain the situation to the A-team, I looked for a familiar face. Thankfully, I saw two: Daphne Krupa and Susan Chu. The Mod Couple, once again dressed in 1960s-style psychedelic colors, stood with heads bent together in a secretive conversation.

I sent Joy off to find Tucker and approached them.

". . . and what are you going to do?" Susan whispered.

"Oh, hey, Ms. Cosi," Daphne said, loudly cutting off her friend. "Did . . . did you check in okay?"

"I did, but I have to talk to you about a staff substitution." I explained about Matt.

"I'll take care of it," Susan said, and left for the registry desk.

I turned to Daphne. Curious what they'd been chatting about so intensely, I fished. "How's your boss holding up? Is Sherri ready for her big night?"

"She's totally frantic," Daphne whispered, looking more than a little stressed herself. She began fidgeting with her pink-and-orange polka-dot scarf. "It's gotten worse since the night Patrice . . . well, you know . . . and then Maya this afternoon."

"Believe me, I know what happened to the fitness queen. I had a front-row seat."

"My gosh . . ." She shook her head then leaned closer. "Ms. Cosi, you really do work with the police right?"

"What's on your mind?"

"I found something—"

"Good evening, one and all!" Sherri Sellars loudly sang as she arrived at the top of the gangplank. Fit and trim in a beautifully tailored off-white suit, she exuded enough glamorous energy to power the Upper West Side. Her light brown hair, freshly sun-kissed by a salon colorist, was once again worn loosely to her shoulders, giving off that casual California style, while her rimless glasses reminded us all that we should take her seriously, too.

I noticed Daphne had stepped away from me, as if we hadn't been speaking. I played along. A moment later, Sherri climbed the stairs to an upper deck without even glancing in our direction.

"What's wrong?" I asked.

"I'm scared, Ms. Cosi . . ." Daphne's usually upbeat voice sounded strangled. "This afternoon, Sherri told me to print something out, but I opened the wrong file on her laptop. The note was about Patrice, and something that happened the night she died. I think Sherri—"

"All fixed!" Susan interrupted. "Mr. Allegro won't have any trouble coming aboard." As I thanked Susan, she handed an envelope to Daphne. "And here's Mr. Laurel's press pass."

Daphne glanced at me. "Sherri's been wooing John Laurel for weeks," she explained. "She really wants a lifestyle piece in the *Times*. Anyway, I'm supposed to meet this reporter, escort him around personally." Worrying the envelope in her hand, she looked to her friend, who made an odd face.

What do these girls know? What did Daphne find?

"Excuse me," Susan said. "I've been summoned by Aphrodite."

Daphne nodded in understanding—as if an actual goddess had called Susan for an audience.

Daphne began to continue with her tale when she glanced over my shoulder and tensed. "We'll talk later," she whispered. "Don't approach me. I'll find you."

A second later, a hand touched my arm. I jumped.

"You seem tense, dear," Madame said.

Alicia stood beside her, hands tightly fisted. "Our chocolatier Gudrun Voss is on board. We'll have our private meeting with her before we leave this ship."

A rolling swell from a passing sanitation barge slammed the *Argonaut*, but the happily buzzing crowd barely noticed the motion. With the night beautifully balmy and clear, the city's skyline provided a dramatic backdrop for Sherri's stage, on the yacht's top deck.

As we sailed up the East River, the view was split. On our left gleamed the towering skyscrapers of Manhattan, the glare of headlights on its FDR Drive creating a bright string of pearls down its riverbank. On our right, a lesser glow pulsed from the outer boroughs with their low-rise buildings and row houses, the pale yellow of distant headlights flickering more like backyard fireflies.

My baristas moved among the partygoers with trays of real Voss chocolates and faux Mocha Magic.

(Matt and I refused to serve the drug-laced stuff so we secretly swapped it for our Mexican Choco-Lattes. Historically, chocolate, coffee, and cinnamon were all considered aphrodisiacs, so it wasn't a total dupe.)

Tucker ran things without a hitch—well, maybe one small one. We had no room for our frozen staircase tonight, so I'd ordered a Venus duo for dramatic impact.

"Weren't we supposed to have two ice sculptures?" I asked.

"One Venus to a customer, I guess," Tuck quipped.

Nancy Kelly appeared to be performing well. "How are you holding up?" I asked her as Matt snatched a dark-chocolate-mint truffle from her tray.

"Gosh, Ms. Cosi. Joy and Tucker think I'm going to pass out or something just because I got sick at Rock Center." Blushing, she rattled a plastic bottle in her apron pocket. "Tuck even gave me seasick pills."

"It could be worse."

"I know! Esther could be here!"

Above the humming boat motor, swish of waves, and salt-laced Atlantic breezes, Sherri Sellars's amplified voice echoed across the dark river as she welcomed her guests.

"In the sweep of life, love can be a glorious dream. But that dream will come true only for those who are open and ready, like budding flowers . . ."

Sherri cupped her hands. Then she slapped them closed, like a trap. "People who entomb their hearts like turtles in their shells miss the magic life has to offer. My desire, my fervent wish, is for all people to emerge from their shells and blossom in each other's light. That's why my late-night LA radio show, *Smooth Sailing in Relationships*, is going into national syndication this summer!"

Sherri nodded her burnished head, accepting the requisite applause. Since taking the microphone, her voice had been flawlessly modulated, her dulcet tones and perfect pitch ideal for radio. Yet every time the relationship specialist dropped a new nugget of mixed-metaphor wisdom, my ex-husband groaned audibly.

"In my years as a partnering counselor, I've heard the same refrain from other specialists. You have to work at a relationship, they all say. It's not easy. You must knuckle down; pick up a paddle and row, row, row; put your nose to the grindstone." Sherri paused. "No wonder young people shy away from marriage. It sounds like a second job!"

The crowd laughed, some applauded.

Sherri raised her index finger. "I have a thought. Instead of working at relationships, let's *play* at them." She grinned. "I mean, if it isn't fun, why have a relationship at all, right?"

More light applause.

"So, ladies, instead of meeting your man at the door with a pout on you lips and that tired old line 'We have to talk,' why not greet him wearing a big smile and nothing else!"

Some of the men hooted.

"That's right. Hand him a cup of Mocha Magic—a 'miracle brew' that's guaranteed to put the magic moments back into your relationship. Then hit the bedroom! Play now, talk later. Or maybe not . . . Maybe you won't have to talk ever again. And won't he be happy!"

The crowed laughed; men applauded.

"Seriously . . ." Sherri held up her finger once more. "In relationships, we must remember the three B's. Keep things beautiful, bubbly, and buoyant . . ."

Matt glanced at me. He was smirking.

"What?"

"In Africa, there's a shrub with a small red fruit that causes sour substances to taste sweet. They call it the miracle fruit."

"And?"

"The glycoprotein in the juice fools the tongue, so you

keep eating the bitter, thinking that it's sweet, until you get sick."

"What's your point?"

"Couples can drink all the 'miracle brew' on the planet, but they'll still wake up the next day in the same crappy marriage."

"Aren't you being a little hard on her? Aphrodisiacs have been around for thousands of years."

"Yeah, but not pop-psychology panaceas."

"You think she's full of hooey?"

"What else would you call those quick-fix ideas?" He folded his arms. "I think she's peddling a drug, Clare, and you know what a drug does, right? It makes the sour in your life taste sweet. The problem is you have to keep taking it. Great for the dealer's bottom line—not so nice for your next-day reality."

"Wow," I said. "Pretty profound for a former cocaine addict."

"The key word being *former*."

A burst of applause broke through our conversation, and I realized Sherri had finished her presentation. Stepping down from the low stage, she began moving through the crowd, greeting audience members.

My ex shot me another odd look.

"What now?"

"A suspicion. I'll be right back . . ."

I held my breath as Matt moved up. He firmly shook Sherri's hand. I couldn't hear what he said, but it was obviously something complimentary because Sherri laughed and nodded.

"What was that all about?" I whispered when he returned.

"Just wanted to find out something."

"Well, something occurred to me while you were shaking her hand. This is supposed to be a PR event for her radio show, right? Yet she's doing a hard sell on the Mocha Magic. Why? What's in it for her?"

"She must be cut in for some control of it," Matt said.

"Or she's angling to, just like Maya."

I tensed, thinking of the fear and panic in Daphne's voice. Sherri Sellars appeared together and successful, intelligent, and accomplished. But so did Patrice Stone. *What if Sherri has a dark side? What if—*

I was about to tell Matt about my theory when I realized a striking pair of blue eyes were staring at me from under a black, broad-brimmed fedora.

The stranger wore a long, dark coat; a white shirt with no tie; and a full, silver beard with two sidelocks hanging down at his temples. He turned away quickly, but not before I felt a shock of recognition. This man was Scarface! I was sure of it! I'd never forget the penetrating cop stare of those steel blue eyes.

"Matt," I rasped. "Do you see that guy over there?"

"The rabbi?"

"He's dressed like a Hasidic Jew, Matt, not a rabbi."

"What? You have the Mossad after you now?"

"I doubt that man is even Jewish! The first time I met him he said his name was Bob."

Matt scratched his goatee. "He's wearing a press pass. He's probably from a Borough Park newspaper. Maybe his name is Job and you misheard."

"Please."

"What? You're not making a whole lot of sense, Clare."

"Trust me, okay? Do not approach him. Do not talk to him. And do not let that man get close to your mother. According to Mike Quinn, he might mean her harm."

Matt's eyes narrowed. "Then if he gets near Mother, Joy, or you, I'll take him out."

"I hope it won't come to that," I said as I speed-dialed Mike Quinn. I got his voice mail, just as I had earlier. I told him where I was and that the Scarface man we'd spoken about was on board. Then I dialed the Sixth Precinct and left an emergency message for him.

I hated going through the precinct. They'd radio Mike,

which was extreme because so many other cops would hear the call, but this was police business, not personal, and I knew he'd want me to do it.

I'd hardly closed the phone when Madame and Alicia waved me forward. I tucked the phone away and squared my shoulders.

The time had come to confront our crafty chocolatier—Gudrun Voss.

Thirty-Eight

Madame and I followed Alicia down several decks, low enough to feel the spray off the black water. We passed through a large hatch, into a hallway with royal blue carpeting and recessed lighting. Three doors opened onto the corridor, all closed except one at the far end.

One of Aphrodite's young assistants stopped us, a petite nymph dressed in flowing spring green. Minthe was her name. She had delicate features, celadon eyes, and wavy golden hair. I nearly checked her back for wings.

"We're here to see Gudrun Voss," Alicia said.

"Aphrodite is still speaking with her," she said breathlessly. "Wait here, please."

Minthe disappeared through the open door. A minute passed. Then two. As Alicia paced, I glanced at Madame and pointed. She gave me a little smile. *Go!* she mouthed. I returned her smile and nodded then began to creep toward the open door.

"Clare!" Alicia rasped in alarm. "Where are you going?"

"To snoop," I said. "Wait here."

Hugging the wall, I moved along the corridor, as close as

I could to the open door. Finally, I heard voices. Two women were speaking, one arguing passionately, the other calm. I closed my eyes and focused, straining to make out their words over the throb of the yacht's engine.

"I told you I can't meet your schedule without compromising quality. Voss is a boutique company with a small, highly trained staff. We don't operate twenty-four hours a day . . ."

That's definitely Gudrun Voss! Though we'd never actually met, I'd asked the chocolatier to speak up so many times over the phone I'd recognize her too-timid voice anywhere.

"You want me to double my output," she continued, "but when you changed the formula, I had to readjust the recipe . . ."

Changed the formula? Alicia's formula?

Flattening myself further against the bulkhead, I felt the engine thrum at the base of my spine as I inched closer to the door.

"You've ignored my e-mails and you won't take my calls," Gudrun said, "so I've come here tonight to tell you face-to-face: it can't be done."

Aphrodite's silence was frustrating us both, but only Gudrun was in a position to complain about it—finally, she did. "Do you understand what I said, Aphrodite? Has anything I've said gotten through that Hellenic wall you've erected against reality?"

The response was completely devoid of emotion, almost robotic. "Yes, I heard what you said."

I risked a peek around the corner. Aphrodite remained stubbornly out of sight, but I spied Gudrun. The famous "Chocolate Nun" was dressed in chocolate, too—not her signature black chef's jacket but a simple cocoa pantsuit. Like Alicia, she was slender with pale skin and dead-straight black hair, although hers fell well past her shoulders—and she was much younger, of course. Alicia was in her fifties, at least; Gudrun in her mid to late twenties.

"You've 'heard' what I said!" Gudrun repeated, obviously annoyed. "What is that supposed to mean?"

"You have your instructions, Ms. Voss. The enhanced formula has been delivered, now produce the product."

"Fine-quality chocolate can't be churned out like a fast-food burger. It has to be roasted. Ground. Aged. Tempered."

"Making the schedule is your problem, not mine," Aphrodite said.

"It's impossible. I can't do it. You can sue me."

"I don't have to sue you. I own you."

Gudrun cursed and whirled. Before I knew it, she burst through the door, black hair lifting on an evening breeze, pale cheeks ruddy with anger. She moved down the hall so rapidly I don't think she realized I'd been eavesdropping.

Alicia tried to block her. "Wait, Gudrun! I want to speak with you."

"Get out of my way!" she cried, pushing Alicia roughly as she rushed out the open hatch.

Alicia stumbled on her heels, then recovered and tossed her flapper hair. "Well, I never——"

The nymph reappeared at the door. "Ms. Bower, Aphrodite would like to see you and your friends. *Now,* if you don't mind."

As we entered, Aphrodite dismissed her assistant with a backhanded wave. In her midthirties at most, the self-styled goddess lounged on a white velvet couch under a window with a panoramic view of the Manhattan skyline. Her legs were up on the couch, her feet shod in Roman-style leather sandals in the same icy blue as her silk pantsuit. Petite and small-boned, I doubted the Web mistress was much taller than my own five-foot-two frame, despite a rather bizarre, high-fashion upsweep of platinum hair that added inches to her height.

"This is my lifelong friend, Madame Dubois, and her daughter-in-law, Clare Cosi," Alicia said. "Clare manages the Village Blend and roasts the beans for our Mocha Magic powder."

She stood and I took Aphrodite's proffered hand. It held all the warmth of a dead fish. Her gaze remained on the carpet, never once lifting to meet mine. Aphrodite moved from me to Madame as if she were sleepwalking. Madame and I exchanged glances. She mouthed two words—a name, a legend, and one of my idols: *Andy Warhol*.

Decades ago, when Madame was running the Village Blend, Warhol, Edie Sedgwick, and a motley crew of hangers-on from Warhol's famous Factory often visited her coffeehouse.

Madame once told me how Edie and the others would behave outrageously while Warhol sat in the corner and quietly watched them, impassive behind his thick glasses, invisible under his own signature mop of platinum hair.

Was the creative genius painfully shy or was it something else? Maybe the enigma was part of the persona, or maybe, once crowned, a "visionary" monarch didn't need to make an effort.

Aphrodite certainly fit the latter theory. While she might have been a powerful force on the World Wide Web, in the flesh this slight, soft-voiced woman presented herself as so unengaged she seemed hardly in the room. Yet from what I just overheard, this woman was fully in charge.

"Why did you want to speak with Gudrun?" Aphrodite quietly asked us.

Alicia cleared her throat. "Well, *Ms. Cosi* here has brought a problem to my attention."

"Problem?"

"Yes, a problem with the Mocha Magic. The production samples seem to be much more powerful than the small-batch product we tested." Alicia paused. "I believe another ingredient might have been added by Gudrun Voss . . ."

Aphrodite's sigh was loud and sustained. She touched her temple and bowed her head. When she spoke again, she sounded close to tears.

"Alicia, I cannot believe that you're troubling me with this, after all that's happened this week. First Patrice . . . Poor Patrice. And then today, Maya . . ." Her voice caught, she swallowed, touched her eyes. "Half our events canceled. The tent wrecked. Police everywhere . . ."

Alicia jumped in, immediately solicitous. "I'm so sorry, Aphrodite, perhaps this can wait for a better time—"

"No," I said. "This can't wait. We need answers and we need them now."

As if a switch had been flipped, Aphrodite's anguish instantly vanished. For the first time, her eyes met mine. I stared hard into those icy orbs—they held no emotion beyond a cold fury at being challenged. The effect was chilling, but I squared my shoulders.

"I overheard your conversation with Ms. Voss," I confessed. "Clearly, you were the one who altered Alicia's formula, not Gudrun Voss."

Alicia gasped then sputtered. "Clare, you . . . you must have misheard!"

"I know what I heard," I said, and was about to continue when—

"No! Please, no!"

The terrified shout was followed by a piercing scream, then—

SPLASH!

I hurried to the door. The corridor was empty, Minthe gone.

Where is Minthe? Where did she go?

The hatch to the outside walkway was open wide, night air flowing in. Alicia, Madame, and Aphrodite followed me across the carpeted hallway. Once outside, I saw a crumpled form on the deck. The ladies behind me gasped.

I dropped to my knee and checked the woman for a pulse. She moaned when I touched her then turned her face to the light.

"It's Susan Chu!" I glanced at Madame. "Get help, find a doctor!"

Madame nodded and hurried off, leaving Alicia and Aphrodite behind. I touched the back of Susan's head and felt blood. Her eyes fluttered open.

"Daphne! Where's Daph?"

"She's not here, Susan."

"But she was. She *was*!" Clutching my arm, she looked around, eyes pools of fear. "She was right here, with me. Daphne was telling me she'd found something on her boss's computer. She said Sherri was furious and going to *end* her. Then Daph pointed behind me. She looked horrified, confused . . ."

She touched the back of her head, pulled away fingers stained with red.

"What happened next?" I asked. "Susan! What happened?"

Susan stared mutely at her bloody fingers, began sobbing hysterically. I looked up and down the deck for Daphne. Where was she?

Alicia and Aphrodite didn't appear to care. They weren't even looking at me, or poor Susan. They stood with mouths gaping, staring at a word spray-painted on the bulkhead.

RUFINA.

"It's from your college thesis," Alicia told Aphrodite in a voice of shock and dread. "But who would remember? They're dead. Everyone is dead!"

That's when I noticed Daphne Krupa's pink-and-orange polka-dot scarf, caught on the deck railing a few feet away. I rose and looked over the side. One long end of the brightly colored silk was now trailing in the deathly dark water. Remembering that loud splash, I felt sick to my stomach.

"Help!" I yelled. "I need help! A woman's been thrown overboard!"

I heard fast footsteps along the walkway. A young Korean-American couple led several crewmen to our aid. I'd seen this man and woman in the crowd, but I thought they were members of the press. Now I blinked in surprise when they flashed their gold shields—these were the undercovers from Queens!

"A woman was thrown overboard," I told them. "A young woman named Daphne Krupa."

Soon after, bells sounded and a voice came over the PA system. "Passenger overboard. Passenger overboard . . ."

The *Argonaut* lurched as the engines shifted tempo, and the yacht began the careful process of turning around in midchannel.

As Susan Chu was helped into a state room, the male detective cornered Alicia and Aphrodite, and herded them away. The woman detective approached me. "Let's talk."

TWENTY minutes later I was staring at the espresso-colored water that was churning into foam in the wake of our passing.

The *Argonaut* had long since sailed over the area where Daphne had been lost. Rescue helicopters and several boats still circled the perimeter, their searchlights playing across the river's glassy surface. I hadn't given up all hope, but I doubted Daphne had merely been tossed into the drink. Just like Patrice Stone, she'd probably been bludgeoned before she was dumped over the side.

I told Queens sergeant Grace Kwan all of that and more, replying to her many questions. Shortly after my interview ended, she consulted with her male partner, who'd interviewed Susan Chu. Before we returned to the pier, Sherri Sellars was taken into custody.

"Why would I kill Daphne?" Sherri cried as the two detectives cuffed her. "I protected that poor girl! I trained her to be my Web master. Why would I do anything to harm her?"

I agreed with Sherri. It didn't make any sense, despite the things Daphne told Susan. Could poor dead Daphne have been fooled by false evidence on Sherri's computer?

As the yacht steamed back toward its home, Matt and Madame rejoined me. I asked after Joy, and Matt said she was helping Tucker break down the catering stuff. According to Madame, Alicia was still being questioned by the police.

I told them about Sherri's arrest. Madame was shocked, but Matt wasn't surprised. "When I shook Sherri's hand, I saw her dilated pupils, her flushed complexion. Take it from a guy who knows, the Luv Doctor has a special relationship with white powder, and tonight she was coked to the gills."

"That must be why she couldn't produce any witnesses for her whereabouts when Daphne was attacked," I said. "She slipped off to feed her habit."

Matt nodded. "She sure looked like she needed a fix after her talk. And when you need cocaine that much, you're just about crazy enough to do anything, including toss your assistant over the side."

"That doesn't sound like the kind of calculating killer who sent phony letters to entrap Maya, Alicia, and me. And you need self-control to paint a word over a bulkhead after you've beaten two girls down and thrown one over the side."

"What are you saying, Clare?"

"I think Sherri is being framed."

As we approached the pier, the captain warned us over the PA system that everyone would have to wait until police business was concluded before we would be permitted to disembark. Despite that directive, all the guests assembled on the lower deck, close to the exit, as the *Argonaut* berthed.

I noticed a lot of activity on our dock. Not a shock, considering all that had happened. But I was surprised to see two familiar faces among the crowd. As soon as the gangplank dropped into place, Manhattan detectives Lori Soles and Sue Ellen Bass led a foursome of uniformed officers aboard.

I tried to speak to them, but the Fish Squad quickly disappeared below deck. Moments later, Sherri Sellars was escorted down the plank by Detective Kwan and her partner.

Two minutes after that, Soles and Bass reappeared. Alicia Bower was now walking between them. Her head was down, her hands cuffed behind her back.

I ran up to them. "Lori! What's going on?"

Alicia turned when she heard my voice. "Clare! Help me!"

"Quiet," Sue Ellen barked.

Lori Soles stopped to speak with me while Sue Ellen and

two other officers proceeded down the ramp. As Alicia was pulled along, she called over her shoulder. "Bay Creek Women's College! Find Aphrodite's thesis. Find it, Clare!"

"You have to let me speak to Alicia!" I begged Lori.

"That's not going to happen, Cosi."

"But—"

"We got a nice print from a piece of the victim's smartphone that the killer tossed off the Garden's rooftop. It took time, but we found it—and matched it with a print on file in Long Island. We now have a solid case against Alicia Bower for the murder of Patrice Stone."

"Listen to me! There's a perfectly reasonable explanation for that print. Ask Alicia. She'll tell you—"

"Alicia will have her day in court," Lori said before turning away.

Matt appeared beside me, put a hand on my shoulder. "You know, Clare. You *did* think Alicia was the murderer."

"Because that's what the killer wanted me to think. But Alicia's not a murderer—and I don't think Sherri is, either. Someone went to great lengths to frame Alicia and Sherri. Someone wanted to frame them both."

"Clare's right," Madame told her son, lips tight. "Alicia is *not* a murderer." She faced me, her violet eyes welling. "We have to fix this. We have to help her."

"We will." I took her hand in both of mine. "I promise."

Matt pointed over my shoulder. "Why don't you start by asking Dudley Do-Right here for some advice."

"Mike's here?" I spun to find Quinn's long legs striding across the deck. In his wake were Sully and a uniformed officer. Mike paused, scanned the crowd, and walked right over to the Hasidic man in the broad-brimmed hat. He paused to stare into the older man's eyes while Sully took hold of the man's arms and pinned them behind his back.

With a brush of his hand, Mike knocked away the hat, pulled at the false beard. As it fell away, I saw that terrible bone-white scar.

"Cormac Murphy O'Neil, you are under arrest for the

murder of a New York City police officer. You have the right
to remain silent—"

Madame heard the man's name and blanched. "It can't
be . . ." When she turned to look, their eyes met. Matt and I
had to move quickly. We caught her in our arms before she
sunk to the deck.

Thirty-nine

~~~~~~

KEEP your head down. Stay quiet. Don't give yourself away . . .

God, it was hard. The giggles were bubbling up again, threatening to expose her. But it was just too perfect: Seeing Alicia and Sherri led away in handcuffs.

Now they knew what her mother felt: Fear. Dread. Humiliation. Now they would go through a public trial, be shunned by so-called friends, torn from their families, suffer living vivisections by a rabid press.

Have fun, ladies! Enjoy having prosecutors dissect your lives, examine every blemish, exhume every personal secret . . .

Yes, this was what she'd dreamed of, all those years ago: to watch this show, watch them suffer! She bit her cheek, made it hurt, then swallowed down the laughter.

Only one more act to go now. Like the judge and prosecutor, this monster's fate would end with an execution. And if that little snoop, Clare Cosi, dares get in my way again, I'll end her, too.

FORTY

~~~~~~

"**H**OW'S she doing?" Mike Quinn asked.

He pulled me aside when he noticed Madame's reaction. Cormac O'Neil had been led away by now, escorted down the gangplank, and placed in Mike's unmarked vehicle.

"A doctor on board is checking her over to make sure she's okay. Matteo and I just need to get her home."

Quinn nodded. "Have you spoken with her yet about the past? Her grand jury appearance?"

Shaking my head, I considered explaining what kind of day I'd had, but this wasn't the time or place to start unloading. Mike's own day was far from over, and he didn't need more baggage from me. So I simply said—

"If Madame needs to talk when we get her home, I'll listen. Otherwise, I'll broach the subject tomorrow morning."

"Tomorrow's fine. Don't stress her. O'Neil surfaced for a reason, and I'm guessing he'll give it up easily." He lowered his voice. "What about you? How are you holding up?"

Feeling Quinn's heavy hand on my shoulder, I closed my eyes, still amazed that a simple touch from this man was all the aphrodisiac I needed. Like a warm espresso, it woke up every part of me.

"I'm fine. Long day, that's all . . ."

He cupped my cheek. "You don't know how much I'm looking forward to its end."

"Me too."

Mike moved his hand back to my shoulder—his grip felt firmer. "I have to ask you something, Clare. Has Sergeant Franco tried to contact you?"

"No."

"Do you know if he's been in contact with Joy?"

"He hasn't, and she's left plenty of messages for him. What's the matter? Is Franco in danger?"

"He's not in danger. He's in trouble."

Aw, no . . . "It's the dealer again, isn't it? The case he couldn't let go."

Mike nodded. "Franco defied orders, trailed that scumbag from Jersey, and arrested him in Manhattan. Hawke found out. He and Franco had words . . ."

Mike's public mask was rigid but not unreadable, not to me. His dark blue eyes had narrowed slightly, deepening the crow's feet at their edges. His mouth looked tight.

"Hawke's really angry, isn't he?" I said. "What's he forcing you to do?"

Mike exhaled. "He wants Franco's badge and gun."

"For heaven's sake, what's the sense in that? Didn't the man simply do his job?"

"Following orders is part of the job, too, Clare."

"I'm sorry, but this stinks like office politics—another big boss with a big ego."

"I don't like it much, either, but the chain of command can't be broken without consequences."

"And what if the top of that chain is *wrong*?"

"Franco's done a good job for me, for my squad. I want to save his career, but he has to help himself now. He has to come in."

"It's just . . . Mike, it's not right, and you know it."

Quinn looked away, rubbed the back of his neck. His expression went from stony to openly grim, as if he were trying very hard to control anger—or pain. "If he contacts Joy or you, try to convince him, okay? Tell him to call me. We'll work it out."

"Can you really work it out? Or is it too late?"

"Honesty, I don't know. I'll do what I can . . ."

An hour later, I was sitting in Madame's penthouse apartment near Washington Square. Her live-in maid had greeted us at the door. Like a doting mother, Consuelo fussed and clucked, tucking Madame into bed, plumping her pillows. Consuelo brought her a cup of cocoa, too, even fixed a tray for me and Matt before retiring herself.

"Okay, she's resting comfortably," my ex-husband said, striding out of his mother's bedroom. "She insisted on calling a lawyer for Alicia, but she's finally settled in. Now talk to me, Clare . . ."

"Sit down," I told Matt, cradling the warm cup. The rich, heady aroma of fine European chocolate reminded me how Madame had fussed and clucked over me during my pregnancy. The drink tasted of everything that was sweet and comforting and good. "Have some cocoa."

Matt remained standing. He folded his arms. "I want to know *who* this man O'Neil is, *why* he was arrested, and *why* my mother fainted when she saw him on that yacht tonight!"

"Lower your voice—I'm going to tell you. But I want you to sit down first. This is liable to be a shock . . ."

When Matt finally settled on the sofa, I explained it all: how Mike Quinn got involved, how he read the police file, how Madame was thrown in jail for protecting a cop killer.

"I can't believe she did that . . ." Matt was holding his head now, just as shocked and upset as I knew he'd be. "When did this happen exactly?"

I gave him the dates.

"I remember that time . . ." He sat back, gaze going glassy. "About a year after my father died, Mother arranged for me to spend six months with the Gostwick family—they were good friends of my father's, and they owned a coffee farm in Costa Gravas."

"I know the Gostwicks, Matt. You and Ric are best friends . . ."

"I'm just trying to explain. I missed my dad so much back then. I was failing out of school, getting into fights . . ." He shook his head. "It must have been extremely difficult for my mother. You know, I didn't even think about it then. I only thought about myself, my own grief. But now that I'm a father . . ." His voice caught. "I think it must have been very hard for her to send me away like that. Maybe it screwed up her judgment."

"Maybe. But I'm sure she hoped the change would be good for you."

"Oh, it was. I learned so much over those months. Ric's father taught me about the coffee business from the bottom up, and we traveled, too, because the family loved to sail. They showed me Jamaica, Haiti, much of the Caribbean. We even motored through Central America. I came back to New York fluent in Spanish and Creole French, feeling ready to take on the world."

"And you did . . ."

Just a few years later, Matt went off alone to backpack Europe. I was staying with relatives, studying Renaissance art. We met in Italy. One chance encounter on a beach, and our lives changed forever.

"Well," I said, "if you were in Costa Gravas that long, it explains why you don't remember this character O'Neil. He must have duped your mother into the relationship because, according to the police file, Cormac O'Neil was one dirty cop."

"Cormac O'Neil was one *good* cop."

Madame's voice was fixed and strong. She stood in the doorway to her bedroom, a white silk robe wrapped elegantly around her, her bearing as regal as ever.

"Cormac was also a righteous man. The best. I'm sure he still is."

I set down my cup. "That's not what the police file says."

"And I was not *duped* into a relationship with him. Our love grew out of friendship. And our friendship grew from trust. Cormac protected me, and he saved our Village Blend . . ."

Matt and I exchanged glances. Was this guy a devil or a saint? He couldn't be both. Could he?

Matt stood. His voice was soft. "I'd like to know everything, Mother. I think you better start from the beginning."

Forty-one

~~~~~~~~~~~~~~~~~~~~~~~~~~~~~~~~~

Ten minutes later, we had heard most of her story—a completely different version than the one on file with the NYPD. According to Matt's mother, Detective Cormac O'Neil came into her life about the same time as Alicia Bower.

"You said Alicia worked for you as a barista," Matt reminded her.

"That's right. She'd been raised with quite a lot of money and status on Long Island, but her family lost everything when her father was caught running an investment scam. The fallout was terrible for her. She was finishing up her senior year at New York University—suddenly, she had no money to her name, and she badly needed work.

"Alicia loved our Blend. She was there all the time as a customer, with her books, between classes—so I hired her. I trained her as a barista, and she really took to it. She worked so much and so well, I even made her my assistant manager. I came to trust her like you two trust Tucker."

"I get it," Matt said. "But why don't I remember her?"

"Because, by the time you came home from Costa Gravas, she was accepted into a graduate program at the school she mentioned tonight—Bay Creek Women's College. She earned her doctorate and was offered a position as an assistant professor. But not before she helped me get through what became one of the best and worst summers of my life . . ."

"Because of O'Neil?"

"It didn't start with him. It started with a couple of young punks who decided to run a criminal enterprise from a corner table of our second floor."

Matt looked stricken. "Why didn't you tell me?"

"Oh, it was over by the time you came home. Everything was. And back then Greenwich Village was a much different place than it is today."

"I remember," Matt said.

Even I knew that. New York had gone through a devastating fiscal crisis in the seventies. The early eighties weren't much better. Crime exploded, graffiti covered everything, dealers sold drugs openly, and the Village . . . well, it was a much less polished and picturesque place.

Because rents were lower, artists, musicians, actors, and writers were still living here in great numbers amid the cobblestone streets and Federal-style walk-ups, but so were druggies and vagrants. Eclectic, offbeat shops were more prevalent, too, and so were empty storefronts and crumbing property facades.

"Cormac came in for coffee every so often," Madame continued. "We'd never spoken beyond polite greetings, but suddenly, I needed help. I didn't want the police to think I was profiting from the loan-sharking and drug dealing those men were engaged in, so I told Cormac about my problem. Within a week, he set up a sting and had them arrested."

I glanced at Matt—so far, this guy didn't sound dirty.

"Cormac became a regular after that. Since I refused to take his money, he insisted I go out to dinner with him. He was a proud, quiet man, but he knew about loss and pain, and . . . he was a good listener."

She turned toward her son. "I was still grieving for your father, and Cormac could see that. But he helped me work through my sadness over those months when you were gone, and . . . we fell in love."

I picked up my cup and took a long drink of warm chocolate. This was a sweet and poignant story, but I knew it was about to take a bad turn. Swallowing hard, I braced myself.

"Cormac and I were happy. We'd settled into a routine, began making plans for the future, and I didn't think anything could hurt us, but . . . as the summer progressed, he became tense and even more quiet than usual.

"One night, he confided in me. There were dirty cops in his precinct. He wasn't sure how to handle it because he didn't know where in the chain of command the corruption stopped, and he needed hard evidence and solid witnesses for the charge.

"Soon after, I received a phone call. Cormac was frantic. He'd been on an apartment building rooftop, arresting a dealer when a young patrolman appeared out of nowhere and blew the perpetrator's head off."

"Oh my God."

"I'm sorry, dear, but that's what happened."

Matt leaned forward. "What did O'Neil do?"

"He drew on the uniform, and there was a shootout. Cormac's partner was killed, and Cormac jumped from the roof—he landed on a fire escape and got away."

"Why did the patrolman do that? What was he trying to accomplish?"

"This young police officer was on the payroll of organized crime. His buddies discovered Cormac and his partner were working on a case against them, and they ordered them both killed. This patrolman had a superior officer ready to back his version of events. They made Cormac out to be the corrupt one, the dirty detective who killed his partner, murdered the dealer, and ran off with the drug money."

Matt rubbed his goatee. "Sounds like your guy was an Irish Serpico . . ."

To older New Yorkers, Detective Frank Serpico was more than just the subject of a Hollywood movie. Serpico's near-death experience at the hands of fellow officers was legend, and his testimony about widespread police corruption led to the Knapp Commission, which cleaned up much of the NYPD.

Madame nodded. "Corruption was certainly rife in the early seventies. The Knapp Commission helped, but it wasn't a cure-all. Cormac told me this particular patrolman was well connected. He had a few relatives high up on the force. Cormac intended to bring his story to the Justice Department—and that meant he had to disappear for a while."

"Did he go to the Feds?" I asked, hopefully.

"I assume he did, but I don't know what happened after that. I thought he would come back for me . . ." She shook her head. "I hoped he would, but he never did. And when that corrupt patrolman was never brought up on charges, but instead promoted as a hero, I came to believe they got to Cormac. I thought for sure he'd been killed."

"What about the grand jury?"

"Before he disappeared, Cormac implored me not to say a word to anyone about what I knew, not even to a judge or jury. What could I say? I couldn't prove anything—and the corrupt cops would have known I was a threat. The possibility of my being murdered for exposing it all—with no evidence, mind you—was just too great. I wouldn't risk making Matt an orphan. I vowed to stay silent to protect my son. So I refused to answer their questions, and the judge sent me to jail."

"Jesus," Matt whispered.

"Alicia was the one who saved me. She was a tower of strength, so efficient and fearless, like a machine. She took over the Blend, ran it in my absence. She found a lawyer for me and the means to bail me out. She continued to prop me up and run the coffeehouse even after I was released from jail, until I was emotionally able again.

"Alicia was even the reason for my subsequent happiness. When she met Pierre Dubois at a Long Island charity dinner, she absolutely *ordered* him to drop by my coffeehouse for the very best cafés au lait and *sablés* in the city. I never would have met Pierre otherwise. I owe her so much . . ."

I looked at Matt. He exhaled hard. Finally, we understood.

"If not for Alicia," Madame said, "I never would have held on to the Blend or gotten through losing her the way I did . . ."

Madame's gaze was downcast. It was so late now, and I wasn't sure I'd heard her right. "You mean, losing *him*? Cormac?"

"No . . ." She took a breath, let it out. "I lost my daughter. Our daughter. I had a miscarriage in jail. Cormac didn't know I was expecting. I didn't think I could anymore . . . I was going to name her Clare—after the younger sister he'd lost in his childhood . . ."

Matt appeared shocked. Neither of us knew what to say.

"Life may take from us, but God gives back, in His own time. A few years later, when Matt came home from Europe with a young woman named Clare, who was pregnant with a daughter . . . well, I knew it was meant to be." She turned to me. "I knew you were a gift from God the moment I heard your name. The daughter I'd lost came back to me."

I put my arms around her, blinked back tears. "I can't believe you've been carrying that around all these years . . ."

Matt swallowed, his voice hoarse. "No wonder you never trusted the police."

"My darling boy, it wasn't that I didn't trust them. I simply needed to get to know them before I could judge which cops were good and which weren't."

She paused, met my eyes.

"Mike's a good cop," I said quietly.

"I know he is, dear. Officer Quinn saved your life and Joy's." She squeezed my hand. "I don't know why Cormac is back again, after all this time. But I have to trust that your blue knight will protect him from men like that deputy commissioner Hawke. If Cormac gets a fair hearing, I'm sure everything will turn out all right."

I shifted on the sofa, suddenly queasy. "What did you say about Hawke? How do you know him?"

Madame blinked. "Didn't I say? Larry Hawke was the name of the corrupt patrolman. The young officer who appeared on the roof, shot the dealer, Cormac's partner, and tried to kill Cormac. Hawke was the cop who framed him."

Shaken to the core, I sat frozen a moment. Finally, I rose and quietly excused myself.

In Madame's bathroom, I sat on the edge of the tub, ran my fingers through my hair. In my bones I knew that Madame was telling the truth. But her facts ran completely counter to the police file.

Will Quinn believe me? Or will he claim Madame is just trying to protect her old boyfriend, like she did before?

I recalled the words we'd had at the dock about Franco. What would Quinn do? Side with me and Madame? Or with the towering command structure he'd trusted for his entire career?

I checked my watch. It was past midnight, but I had to call him, try to explain. I fumbled in my pocket, found my cell. A voice mail was waiting for me. Mike hadn't rung through. He'd sent a silent message.

"Clare, listen to me carefully. This cold case has gotten complicated . . . and a little dangerous. I'm going to be out of touch. I'm not sure how long. You won't be able to reach me through my cell or the police radio. Sully and I need to follow a few leads. For our own safety, we can't be traceable. I can't say more to you now, except . . . well, I think you'll understand this. I'm about to pull a Franco . . ."

Oh my God.

"Try not to worry . . . and, please, do not tell anyone what I've just told you. It could put our lives in danger. Just . . . I don't know, say a prayer for me today. I'm going to need it . . ."

Praying was the first thing I did, asking God to keep Mike and Sully and Franco safe. Then I squeezed my eyes shut, realizing in a whole new way what Madame must have felt all those years ago.

How do I make sense of this?

Did Mike hear the same story from Cormac and believe him? Were they trying to gather evidence and go to the Feds together? Or had Mike confronted Hawke, just like Franco? Did Hawke try to take Mike's badge and gun? Or was it even worse? Did he try to take his life?

What in heaven's name is happening?

I closed my eyes, bowed my head, and lost track of time. When a soft knock sounded on the door, I rubbed the back of my neck.

"Clare?"

I'd spent so long in the bathroom that Matt had grown concerned. I opened the door, moved into the hall.

"Are you okay?" Matt asked.

"I'm staying here with your mother tonight . . ."

"You look like hell," he whispered, opening his arms.

I stepped into them.

Matteo's body felt as strong as ever, as strong as his spirit, and I let him lend me that strength. Holding on tight, I let myself break, felt the hot tears dampen his shirt.

"Did Mother's story upset you that much?" he whispered.

I wanted so badly to spill more than tears, tell Matt about the call, about Franco, Hawke, everything. But I felt bound by Quinn's request. Just like Madame, I had no evidence of Hawke's guilt, none. The only thing I *could* do for Mike Quinn was what he'd asked—not tell a soul what was happening. Not even my family.

"Please don't cry," Matt whispered, stroking my hair. "It'll be okay . . ."

"You don't know that."

"No. But I find if you say it enough times—and click your heels—sometimes it is . . ."

"What are you? Glenda the Good Witch?"

"Naw. The good witch auditions aren't till next week."

I pulled away, swiping at my eyes. "Better tell Punch then. He's willing to do drag to get into that show . . ."

Matt touched my wet cheek. I squeezed his hand. "Check on our daughter, okay? Let her know I won't be back to the coffeehouse until late tomorrow."

"Where are you going?"

"Your mother and I may not be able to help Cormac O'Neil or Mike Quinn, but we can do something to help Alicia Bower—and that's what we're going to do . . ."

Forty-two

~~~~~~

I rented a car and drove us east, toward the brightly rising sun. Bypassing the city's gritty borough of Queens, we headed for the north shore of Long Island, land of quaint waterfront villages, pedigreed horses, and exclusive yacht clubs.

Over a dozen institutes of higher learning were located on the Island east of New York City. Bay Creek Women's College was not among them—and for good reason. A decade ago, the school had gone coed, changing its name to Bay Village College.

According to its Web site, the campus's Essen Library held the archives for student theses, and that was our destination. But we had a problem: neither Madame nor I knew Aphrodite's real name.

I'd searched the Web, read her Wiki bio, her Facebook page (three million likes!), but Aphrodite had reinvented herself so aggressively, I had no clue where she was born or who she really was.

Fortunately, scholarly papers are generally cross-referenced by subject, so I was hopeful that any thesis referencing Laeta, Severa, or Rufina would be listed in the card catalog.

I didn't think the paper itself would clue us to the killer's identity. The real lead would be found on a lending card of some sort, the kind that listed all the people who'd accessed the thesis, hopefully stretching back years. If I found a familiar name—one who had motive and opportunity to frame Alicia and Sherri—that person would zoom to the top of my suspect list.

Now, as we crossed the lush green of the manicured campus, Madame openly admired the main library's High-Victorian Gothic style. We quickly checked the brass plaque for the architect's name and I noticed the building was a national landmark, which housed the college library, a collection of rare first editions, and the Juliana Gregg Saunders Archive and Reading Room.

Madame pointed at the plaque. "Who knew Juliana Saunders had a philanthropic bone in that venal body of hers?"

"You know the woman?"

"I'm afraid so. She's one of Otto's more disagreeable clients—and in oh-so-many ways. Last year she bid on a Chuck Close self-portrait because 'it was just the right size' to fit her two-story Park Avenue living room and the colors matched her brand-new Aubusson."

"Ouch."

"Thank goodness she lost the auction."

"Yes . . ." I was smiling now but not because of the story. I realized Madame's acquaintance with Ms. Saunders might be the miracle we needed, right when we needed it.

The Essen Library, a private institution at a private college, required a student or faculty ID to enter. Rather than try to explain ourselves at the dean's office, I thought my work-around would save us valuable time.

"Do you think you can channel this Juliana Gregg Saunders? Imitate her mannerisms? Her attitude? Convince people you're the real deal?"

"Why would I want to do that?" Madame suppressed a shudder.

I pointed out the security issue, and Madame agreed. As

we ascended the steps to the library's entrance, she slipped into her role and boldly took the lead.

The student working the front desk didn't bother to look up from her iPad as we approached. "ID, please," she said, hand extended.

Madame squared her shoulders. "My good woman, one does not need a common ID when one's name is on the door!"

The girl looked up. "Excuse me?"

Madame tapped a manicured nail on the polished desk. "My name is Juliana Gregg Saunders, and I wish to see my room!"

"Room?"

"The Juliana Gregg Saunders Archive and Reading Room, young dolt. I pay a steep annual stipend for the privilege, and because the room bears my name, I would like to see it . . . *Now.*"

"Oh . . . oh! I'm so sorry Mrs. Gregg—I mean Saunders, er, *Mrs.* Saunders."

Madame sniffed and the student jumped to her feet. "You can go up right now. It's almost lunchtime, but I'm sure Ms. Themis will be happy to give you a tour."

"Announce us," Madame said. "Immediately."

"Of course!" The girl lifted the receiver and with shaky hands dialed a three digit extension. She waited. "Ms. Themis isn't picking up. She's probably working in the stacks. If you want, I can escort you—"

"I'm capable of following directions, if they are accurate."

The girl appeared relieved. "Okay. Take those stairs one flight up, to the second floor. Then make a left."

"Come, Clare. Let's see how this institution spends my largess!"

A wide staircase behind a granite arch led upstairs. Halfway to the top, Madame sighed. "That was quite distasteful. Imagine going through life behaving in such a ghastly manner. It's so taxing . . ."

"Don't drop your newfound nasty just yet. We're not out of the woods."

I opened a heavy door and we entered the archive. The walls were lined with darkly stained shelves packed with volumes thin and thick. A half-dozen reading tables, arranged to take advantage of the western sun streaming through the tall windows, were empty now. In fact, we saw only one occupant—an elderly woman with wild gray hair, sorting books beside a wheeled cart.

Madame cleared her throat. "Excuse me—"

Without facing us, the woman raised a hand for silence. With her other hand she fished a pair of false teeth out of a Mason jar and slipped them into her mouth.

"I'm sorry," she said, facing us at last. "I can't say a comprehensible word without my teeth. Someday I'll be gone from this room, but these choppers will still be in that jar, chattering away like the voice of the Cumaean Sibyl!"

The woman approached us, her teeth roughly in place, which gave her a crooked, toothy smile. Not much younger than Madame, she had that same spark in her eyes and spring in her step. Dressed appropriately tweedy, her jacket actually had leather patches on the elbows. But her outspoken attitude and wild gray-white hair were far from retiring.

"I'm Miss Themis, the head archivist. But please call me Phoebe," she said, extending a hand.

"I'm Juliana Gregg Saunders," Madame said solemnly. "And this is Clare, my personal assistant."

"Now that's odd," Phoebe said, "because the Juliana I know is just now rolling out of bed with a bad hangover and worse disposition."

The woman leaned close and lowered her voice. "And between you and me, after a typical evening in her cups, the last thing Juliana would *ever* do is visit her reading room."

My knees felt suddenly shaky. Madame paled. Phoebe simply cackled and slapped her knee. "Look at you two! Your faces are white as whippletree petals!"

"Whippletree?"

"Dogwood. Part of Chaucer's nomenclature from "The Knight's Tale." Did you know Boccaccio was the source of that tale? His was an epic, of course, and old Geoffrey changed the genre to romance, although, inspired by Boethius, he added an undercurrent of philosophy."

"I see."

"Too much information?" She cackled again. "Oh my. Why so serious?" she leaned close. "Nothing to fear. Your secret little masquerade is safe for now. But, of course, with good scholarship, most secrets are revealed, sooner or later."

"Sooner is better," I replied, offering my hand. "My name is Clare Cosi and this is Mrs. Dubois. We apologize for crashing your reading room, but we need information. It's a matter of life or death—"

"Tea!" Phoebe exclaimed. "Earl Gray. There's nothing better than a strong tea served hot with a story well told."

"We don't have time for—"

"Sounds *delightful*," Madame cut in, squeezing my elbow. I forced a smile. "Thank you so much."

MINUTES later, tea was served under a tall, open window, in the warmth of the noontime sun. A flowering laurel tree stood just outside, swaying in the spring breeze. The sea-tinged air flowed in off the manicured quad along with sounds of laughter from passing students.

The cups were cardboard, the sugar in little packets, but the hot tea, freshly brewed from imported loose leaves, could have raised the dead, and the home-baked mini chocolate-chip scones, rich with butter and cream, were perfectly balanced—the lighter flavors rescued from complete obliteration by the judicious control of the chocolate's darkness.

When we were all settled in, Madame tactfully explained our quest. "We're searching for a thesis written by one of your alumni. Unfortunately, we don't know the author's name. We only know the subject."

Phoebe patted Madame's hand. "Never fear, Mrs. Dubois. All of our papers are cross-referenced."

I jumped in. "This paper mentions words or perhaps

names. One of them is Laeta, another is Severa—" I was ready to spell them out, but Phoebe was way ahead of me.

"Laeta, Severa, and Rufina. You don't have to be coy, ladies. If you wanted to see 'The Romance of the Vestals' by Thelma Vale Pixley you need only ask—the dean of the college, that is."

Aphrodite's real name is Thelma Vale Pixley?

Phoebe rose and fetched a thin, worn volume from a shelf. "Once upon a time, this notorious thesis was referenced each and every semester," she said. "That's not true anymore. Time has passed, and the school has done its best to make everyone forget."

Madame arched an eyebrow. "Forget?"

The archivist stood at my shoulder, volume in hand. "I'm not supposed to show this to anyone but students or alumni. Not without the express permission of Dean Parnassus."

I felt a pressure in my chest. *So close. Are we dead?*

"Oh, what the Hades!" Phoebe declared.

She placed the volume on the table in front of me, and I turned immediately to the lending sheets attached to the inside back cover. As Phoebe spoke, I rapidly scanned the names of those who'd looked at this thesis in the past eleven years. None looked familiar—and I felt crushed.

"That paper is a real potboiler," Phoebe said. "As scholarship it's rubbish, but as fiction it's worthy of Anne Radcliffe."

"I adored Anne Radcliffe when I was a girl," Madame said. "I do believe I married an Italian man because I read *The Italian* at too impressionable an age."

"Well, my guess is Miss Pixley was reading Henry Miller," Phoebe said. "Or perhaps the Marquis de Sade, because the girl turned a tale of intrigue and injustice from the late Roman Empire into a Dionysian tragedy of sinister lust—complete with erotic passages. Of course, much of Greco-Roman mythology was driven by amorous desire."

She tipped her head to the swaying branches beyond the open window.

"My beautiful laurel even has her roots in such a tale—a nymph transformed into a tree, the answer to a prayer as she ran from the clutches of a lustful god. 'A heavy numbness seized her limbs, thin bark closed over her breast, her hair turned into leaves, her arms into branches, her feet so swift a moment ago stuck fast in roots, her face lost in the canopy. Only her shining beauty was left.'"

Madame sighed. "So much yearning, desire, and heartbreak. The young live in Puccini."

"Oh, Puccini! '*Mi chiamano Mimì*' is one of my favorite arias."

"I have it as my ringtone."

"Did you know the libretto for *Gianni Schicchi* is based on an incident mentioned in the *Divine Comedy*?"

"Which one?"

As the newfound friends continued talking, I paged through the long paper. Finally, I interrupted: "Excuse me, but what was Miss Pixley attempting to explore here? An Apollonian versus Dionysian philosophy?"

"Oh, nothing so deep as that, I'm afraid." Phoebe tipped her head to the campus quad. "And yet her dissertation became so popular among the other girls, she was made something of a campus celebrity."

"But isn't this supposed to be a scholarly study?"

"There's some scholarship involved," Phoebe said. "The trial and execution of the three innocent Vestals occurred in AD 213, as in the thesis. And Emperor Caracalla, the man whose lust for them led to their death sentences, was as brutally handsome as he was murderously brutal. But the rest of it is a fiction that sprung from the fevered, postpubescent mind of Thelma Pixley."

"What happened to the author?" I asked.

Phoebe's teeth rattled. "*That* story is quite a potboiler, too. And it also ends in an execution. It was back when this college was exclusively a girl's school. With that notorious paper circulating throughout the student body, Miss Pixley became a ringleader. She spearheaded a pagan revival.

Thelma and her friends formed a secret sorority, complete with Dionysian rites."

Phoebe lowered her voice. "These were daughters of affluence, you understand, so recreational drugs were easy to purchase. But this was a school for girls, so there was a dearth of men around with whom to practice their rites."

"Then who did they target?" I asked.

"Male faculty members. Thelma focused her lust on one man in particular, a literature professor with a promising career ahead of him. Dr. Victor Temple also had a wife and a young daughter."

Phoebe set her cup on the desk. "Dr. Temple was a fine educator and a good man. But in the end he was just a man, and he fell into bed with young Miss Pixley."

Phoebe paused. "Not long after that, Dr. Temple's wife, Dora, discovered the affair and shot her husband to death."

Madame gasped and I blinked. *Aphrodite lured a respected, married professor into an affair—one that ended in murder?*

As Phoebe continued talking, I returned my attention to the library lending sheets. After searching the names carefully, I pointed: "I see a Temple listed here. A woman named Olympia Temple accessed this paper five years ago. Do you know who she is?"

Phoebe nodded. "Olympia Temple was the only daughter of Dora and Victor Temple."

"Was?" Madame repeated.

"Yes, past tense is appropriate, I'm sorry to say. Olympia crossed the Styx by her own hand."

"Suicide?"

Phoebe nodded. "The year her mother died in prison, Olympia jumped to her death from the Bay Creek bridge."

"Will you tell us more?" I asked.

"I will—and I'll give you an even more knowledgeable source for future reference."

FORTY-THREE

~~~~~~

"Can you tell me what actually happened?" I asked.

Madame and I were now sitting in the cramped offices of the *Bay Creek Village Chronicle*. Phoebe Themis had suggested we speak with Mr. Kenneth Jeffries. According to our helpful librarian, he'd done the most thorough reporting on the case.

"What *actually* happened?" Mr. Jeffries barked a laugh. "Really, Ms. Cosi, for any trial, that's a Rashomon sort of question, isn't it?"

With the late afternoon sun streaming through his window, Mr. Jeffries's hair looked as gray-white and crumpled as the old newsprint piled around him. He'd been an AP stringer during the years of the Temple murder and subsequent trial. Now he was editor in chief of the *Chronicle*'s struggling, three-man operation. The grizzled veteran appeared pleased to hear his stories were remembered, though his tone tended to drift into the land of smug.

"What *actually* happened is entirely dependent on with whom you speak. In the prosecutor's view, the murder was premeditated, and Mrs. Dora Temple was a cold-blooded killer."

"And what did the defense believe?" I asked.

"The murder was accidental. Mrs. Temple wanted only to frighten her husband's young mistress by pointing the gun at her. She never expected the struggle to follow. The fatal wounding of Dr. Temple was sheer accident."

Madame arched an eyebrow. "And what did you believe, sir? Or don't reporters have opinions?"

Jeffries blinked, as if waking up to a sharper mind than he'd expected. "Touché, ma'am."

"No offense," Madame said.

"None taken. Like politics and jelly doughnuts, the good stuff is usually found in the middle, isn't it?"

Madame sighed. "Objectivity *is* a rare thing these days."

"Well, I'll tell you this . . ." Jeffries sat up a little farther in his seat, the condescension gone. "I heard *every* bit of testimony, interviewed all the witnesses, and I think my conclusion is the right one . . ."

According to Jeffries, Mrs. Temple surprised her husband by dropping by his campus office. "A professor named Alicia Bower was standing in the hallway outside, speaking with one of her students—a Sherri Sellars. Mrs. Temple pushed past them both and burst through her husband's door. She found her Victor half naked with one of his students, Thelma Vale Pixley. She drew the gun and aimed it directly at Thelma. Alicia and Sherri rushed in and tried to wrest the weapon away from Mrs. Temple. During the struggle, Dora pulled the trigger, and Dr. Temple was struck in the groin. He bled to death en route to Bay Village Hospital."

Madame glanced at me. "Now that *does* sound like premeditated murder."

Jeffries nodded. "She brought the gun and she pointed it. The prosecutor believed it was premeditated, too, and he was aggressive. Alicia and Sherri were friendly with Mrs. Temple. They didn't want to testify against her, but they took their sworn oaths seriously and told the truth as they saw it.

"The prosecutor compelled them to testify for his side— including a statement they overheard Mrs. Temple make during the struggle. 'I swear I'll end them both.'" He snapped his fingers. "Those two sealed the deal. The scandal with all the requisite publicity ruined them at the college, of course. Alicia resigned her post and went off to be a free-lance writer. The jury found Mrs. Temple guilty of all charges. She showed no remorse, and the judge sentenced her to twenty-five years to life."

"And she died in prison?"

"After seven years, Mrs. Temple applied for early parole. The board denied her request. She still hadn't shown any remorse, and she'd physically assaulted a female guard. When she heard her parole was denied, she hanged herself in the prison laundry."

"Dora had a daughter," I said. "What happened to her?"

Jeffries's buoyancy flagged suddenly. "Olympia Temple. Now there was a tragedy."

"How so?" Madame asked.

"Olympia hardly knew her father, but she was close to her mother. Mrs. Temple made bail, and for two years before the trial, that girl listened to her mother rail against the prosecutor, the judge, the friends who had 'turned on her' to testify against her. When her mother was sent to prison, the daughter was devastated."

"Do you have a photo?" I asked.

Jeffries found only a few. Olympia was young during the height of the trial—around thirteen years old. She was a slender, Caucasian girl with long, dark blond hair, which she used to cover her face when cameras began snapping her photo.

He tapped the image on screen. "Several years after Mrs. Temple was sentenced, I wrote a piece about her life in prison. A few days after that article was published, I started getting poisoned-pen letters. Then someone slashed the tires on my car."

Letters followed by violence? Madame and I leaned forward. "What did you do?"

"I turned the letters over to the police. They believed

Olympia was responsible. When I heard that, I couldn't bring myself to press charges, but they spoke with her, hoped to frighten her into stopping. She didn't. The tire slashing was repeated after I wrote an article about Mrs. Temple's parole being denied."

"There was no one else who could have done it?" I asked. "An angry cousin, an uncle, a sister? The Temples must have had close friends."

"Dr. Temple and his wife were transplants from Maine. They had no relatives in the area. None that I could find, and I looked, too. Their friends were connected to the college, and when the scandal broke, most of them distanced themselves from Dora Temple—understandable since they had upstanding reputations to maintain and Mrs. Temple couldn't escape the bad publicity. When Mrs. Temple went to prison, her daughter was taken in by guardians, not related, an elderly couple also connected to the college."

He shook his head. "After all Olympia had been through, I didn't wish to press charges against her, and the harassment did stop after she vanished."

"You mean after she killed herself."

Jeffries scratched his head. "I'm not so sure she did."

"But Phoebe Themis told us there were witnesses. They heard a scream, saw something plunge off a bridge. Dora's belongings and a suicide note were found on top of that same bridge. She'd worn her mother's wedding gown for that jump and shreds of it washed ashore."

"And no *body* was ever recovered."

Prickles iced my skin. "Are you certain?"

"Are you hungry, Ms. Cosi?"

"Excuse me?" *Oh no,* I thought. *I hope he's not hitting on me for a dinner date.*

"I suggest you stop by the River View restaurant, just outside of our village. Ask for the head waiter, Freddie. Tell him I sent you. Freddie has an eyewitness opinion about what happened."

"We'll do that," I said, rising.

"And try the bay scallops with saffron risotto." Jeffries kissed the tips of his fingers. *"Délicieux!"*

By the time Madame and I arrived at the River View, dinner service was under way. In the parking lot, we paused to admire the sweeping view of the "river"—really a long, wide inlet of the Long Island Sound with strong currents shimmering between thickly forested cliffs.

"That's where Olympia Temple jumped," Madame said, gazing at the high bridge, where a commuter train was now rumbling across.

Inside, Madame and I grabbed a snack at the bar and asked to see the head waiter. After our wine was poured and fried oysters served, the bartender introduced us to Freddie—really Fredrick Lloyd, a round, bald little man with a charming accent, who told us he was born in London and raised in Oxford.

"Oh, sure. I was there the night of the jumper," he said. "Me and Connie, who died last year. Most everyone else is new."

He leaned close, glanced at his watch, and nodded in the direction of the railroad bridge, just visible in the gathering dusk through the large bay windows.

"Keep your eyes on that bridge," he advised.

We did and within a minute the lights came on, illuminating the entire span. One central light was much brighter than the others. Like a spot, it shone all the way down to the inlet's rippling waters.

"See that big light. The jump came from right there. I heard this scream, and then some of the guests pointed. Then everyone was screaming and running about. But not Freddie."

He tapped his temple. "I was feeling nostalgic, so I kept on watching the girl."

"Nostalgic?" I asked. "What do you mean by that?"

"When I was a boy, me and me mates had an annual ritual. Every May first we rose early and showed up for the Bridge Jumpin' Festival at Magdalena."

"Oh, the bridge jumping!" Madame nodded. "If memory serves, students from Oxford have been jumping off that bridge for more than a century. Am I correct, sir?"

"You are indeed, ma'am. But me and me mates, well, to be honest, we were there to watch the girls jump into the Cherwell. It was a long time ago—lots of pretty hippie girls around with their flowered dresses. Those dresses would balloon up, and we pimply faced boys would catch our first glimpse of bloomers, er . . . beggin' your pardon, ladies."

"No apologies necessary," Madame assured him. "Boys will be boys. I have a son myself . . ."

Yes, I thought, *one who's made a global study of glimpsing girls' bloomers.*

"Like I say, I was no stranger to seein' girls in dresses jump from bridges. And I watched that jumper's white dress balloon up just fine, but the whole way down it was the same."

Freddie pressed his arms to his side and stood erect, making like a chubby Oscar statue. "She was stiff, you know? Like an ice sculpture. She never moved once the whole drop."

He leaned in, lowered his voice. "That's a big, bright light there, and that bridge is plenty higher than the Magdalena. Yet I didn't see any bloomers, and I don't recall seein' any legs. None at all."

TWENTY minutes later, we stood by our rental car while I took one last look at the railroad bridge and the dark, treacherous depths below it. Our day of inquiry was over, and it yielded a crucial conclusion.

"Olympia Temple isn't dead," I said. "She faked her death and created a new identity to get even with the people she blamed for her mother's imprisonment and suicide."

"The judge and prosecutor?"

"Yes, they were killed outright. But a quick death wasn't

vengeance enough for Olympia when it came to Alicia Bower and Sherri Sellars. Those women had testified against her mother, and Olympia wanted to see them suffer—not in one quick instant before death, but for years."

"So she framed them for murder."

"Exactly."

"But who is Olympia?"

"Someone close to Alicia and Sherri. Someone who knew about the friction between the Sisters of Aphrodite and exploited it. She sent those fake letters, right? So it had to be an inside job."

"Her age should help give her away."

"Olympia Temple would be in her twenties. Like Nancy Kelly, our youngest barista. The killer would have attended the party at Rock Center, and the Sherri Sellars PR event on Aphrodite's yacht . . ."

I closed my eyes, replaying my walk up the *Argonaut* gangplank, the look of our coffee and chocolate display, the meeting with Aphrodite, the scream, the *splash*.

Freddie's voice came back to me: *"She was stiff . . . like an ice sculpture."*

"Stiff," I whispered, like the roots of Phoebe's laurel tree. *Her face lost in the canopy. The nymph transformed.*

That's when I knew.

FORTY-FOUR

〜〜〜〜〜〜〜〜〜〜〜〜〜

NIGHT dropped her veil on Manhattan, turning the bright maze of city streets into a shadowy underworld. As I rolled home, the tall, spotless windows of my coffeehouse shone like welcoming beacons in a wine-dark sea. The golden glow cheered me for a moment—but only a moment.

"Where's Mother?" Matt asked from behind the counter.

"Safe with Otto. I dropped her at his gallery. Don't worry."

"Worrying is all I'm doing, Clare. All I've *been* doing."

"That makes two of us."

Feeling down but not out, I settled in at my own marble-topped bar. I still hadn't heard from Quinn—and Joy hadn't heard from Franco, or so she had informed me the last time I'd phoned her.

Matt slid me a fresh *ristretto*, took the stool next to me. "Find out anything that will help Alicia?"

I held up a finger, knocked back the strong elixir. "We found out plenty. It will help Sherri, too." I brought Matt up to speed on what we'd discovered.

He sat dumbfounded a moment. "You *have* been busy."

"The ride home was just as productive. Your mother drove part of the Grand Central so I could have a long cell phone conversation with Lori Soles."

"Wait. Didn't Lori cut you off at the dock last night?"

"She did, but I don't blame her. All the evidence pointed to Alicia—except for one thing. And that's why she listened to me tonight. This morning, the crime scene people finally came up with a solid forensic image off a hidden security camera. The date and time stamp made the evidence irrefutable."

"I'm all ears."

"Remember those fake Greek columns at Rock Center's Garden? They were lit from inside."

He nodded. "I remember."

"Well, their glow turned the rain puddles into mirrors—and one of the building's hidden cameras picked up a clear reflection of the killer's legs as she moved to and from the podium to bludgeon Patrice Stone."

"You're telling me a photo of legs will ID the killer?"

"No, but they are exculpatory for Alicia because she wasn't wearing opaque red stockings that night, and my killer was—or, rather, the young woman I believe is really Olympia Temple."

"So what's Lori going to do?"

"She and Sue Ellen are starting to run background checks, follow up on that thread. I hope they come up with something, before Olympia strikes again . . ." I dug into my bag for my cell, checked the messages. "Why won't she call me back?"

"Who?"

"Aphrodite. She's next on Olympia's hit list. I'm sure of it. What I don't know is what she's planning—an outright murder or another frame job. And if she's planning a frame job, I can only guess who she's going to kill."

"I take it you called Aphrodite to warn her."

"Of course. I warned Lori Soles, too. I don't know if the police have gotten in touch with her yet, but so far Aphrodite is ignoring me, just like she ignored Gudrun." I closed my eyes. "Mike hasn't called me, either. Not since leaving a message last night."

"You need a cop that bad?"

I need Mike that bad. I took a breath, tried not to ache for him, and opened my eyes. They felt wet.

"Clare?"

"It's a cinch," I said, swiping at my cheeks. "My own personal cop would come in handy right now."

Matt touched my arm. "Look, as long as Dudley Do-Right is MIA, I'll be your cop, okay?" He formed a gun with his finger and thumb, took aim, fired, even blew on the finger barrel. "No kidding. I'll help any way I can."

"Help!" Esther squeaked, eyes wide.

Matt and I turned to find her hanging up the store phone.

"What's wrong?" I asked.

"Nancy has gone off the deep end!" Esther came at us, hands flying like the Scylla monster. "That crazy girl drugged Dante!"

"What!" Matt's eyes bugged. I covered mine, and Tucker misplaced his latte pour. Half the steamed milk ended up on the work counter.

"Is this *your* typical day, Clare?"

"Esther," I said, "who exactly was on that phone?"

"Dante," she replied. "Calling from Beth Israel's ER."

"Is he *poisoned*?"

"Dante's fine. Apparently, it was Nancy who got sick."

"Explain, please!" Tucker demanded, wiping up the latte foam. "Narrative, narrative!"

Esther folded her arms. "Dante went over to Nancy's place to show her more tattoo designs. He told me he knew she was crushin' on him, but he figured it would be okay because she has two roommates. But, of course, Nancy arranged to be alone when he arrived, and she slipped him a massive dose of Mocha Magic in a mug of hot cocoa!"

"The definition of date rape," Matt said, rubbing his goatee. "It's also a felony."

I held my head. "Oh brother."

"Dante claimed he was in control of his libido—and then he wasn't," Esther said. "But Nancy got dizzy before they got very far and threw up all over him." She rolled her eyes. "Serves Baldini the Barista right. I warned him to steer clear of that lovesick girl! Now she's just sick."

"Wait," I said. "Why is Nancy sick?"

"Apparently she drank the stuff, too—and it gave her a temporary bout of hypertension," Esther tapped a finger on her chin. "Or was it *hypo*tension. Anyway, the doctor said it was a reaction to siden-daffodil, or siden-dafquil—"

"Sildenafil," Tuck said a bit sheepishly. "That's in Viagra. You know, the little blue pill."

"If that's what Aphrodite put in our Mocha Magic, it's definitely a controlled substance," I said. "I can't believe she jeopardized people's health like that. What was she thinking?"

Matt spit an ugly word about Aphrodite. Then he cursed in French, long and hard.

"So where's Nancy now?" I asked.

Esther took a breath. "Dante stayed with Nancy at the ER for three hours, but he had to leave her—he's late now for a gallery event with some of his own paintings."

I reached for my sweater. "I'll go get her—"

Esther stopped me. "Sorry, Mr. and Mrs. Boss, but it gets worse. Nancy is convinced Gudrun Voss is responsible for that crap in the Mocha Magic. She told Dante that as soon as she's discharged—which is any minute now—she's going to hop a train to Williamsburg and give the chocolatier a piece of her mind."

I reached for my cell and speed dialed Nancy. After several agonizing rings, an electronic voice told me to leave a message.

I turned to Matt. "I couldn't reach her. She must be in the subway already. There's no signal down there."

Matt had calmed a bit—or at least he'd stopped cursing.

"Listen," I said, grabbing his arm. "We have to go to Voss Chocolate. I feel partially responsible for this. That poor girl is lovesick and just plain sick. She's not thinking straight, Matt. We have to get to Nancy, explain it's not Gudrun's fault, and bring her home."

Matt began a new string of curses, this time in Portuguese. I had no clue what he said, but it sounded very rude.

Esther waved her hand. "Take me! Take me! If you're going to Chocolate World, I will be *happy* to ride shotgun. Mr. Boss can stay here."

"Oh no you don't," Matt said. "I've been slaving away all day behind that counter. Even a drive to Brooklyn in Breanne's crappy hybrid sounds like a vacation."

"Fine," Esther said folding her arms. "But I'm giving you both my chocoholic shopping list."

"**Matt!** That's Aphrodite's town car. I recognize the vanity plates."

"Eros, huh?" Matt snorted. "That woman is a walking cliché."

My ex-husband's foot was as heavy as Esther's list was long, and we'd made it to Williamsburg in record time. But progress slowed in the maze of narrow, one-way streets in this waterfront district, so it was after ten when we arrived.

A *Voss Chocolate* banner hung like a medieval standard from the walls of a century-old, three-story building on the edge of the river. It was past closing time, and all the doors and windows were shuttered with steel gates, including the tiny retail outlet on the ground floor where Aphrodite's car was parked.

Matt edged our sedan into a spot next door, in front of a plywood-walled construction site. I jumped out before he cut the engine.

My heels echoed hollowly as I ran to Aphrodite's vehicle. A boat whistle sounded, the lights on the towering span of the Williamsburg Bridge winked between a pair of ancient marine warehouses, newly transformed into trendy stores and pricey co-ops for the affluent hipster.

The windows on the late-model town car were tinted, but I could see a Mocha Magic press kit on the back seat.

"Oh, yeah," I said, "this is Aphrodite's ride."

"So?"

"So I've been trying to reach her all evening, warn her she's in danger. Obviously, she's inside now with Gudrun."

"We're here to find our wayward barista. Not rescue a drama queen."

"Calm down, Matt. You're getting angry again."

He grunted.

"This is a working factory," I told him. "Deliveries arrive at all hours, There has to be a way in . . ."

The building was unadorned and had few windows. It housed a full-scale chocolate factory, along with facilities where Gudrun mixed her cocoa with the Blend's coffee beans and Alicia's powder to create the Mocha Magic syrup. The mocha concentrate was then bottled and sent to Long Island City where another facility freeze-dried and packaged it.

As I hugged myself against a chilly wind whipping off the water, I noticed a hand-scrawled sign beside one of the smaller gates: *Late-Night Deliveries.* Over that sign I found the doorbell and intercom. I hit the button and a buzzer sounded deep inside the building.

"What are you doing, Clare? Let's go back to the car and wait for Nancy to show up."

"But Nancy is probably inside already."

"Clare, she took mass transit. You know how lousy subway service can be at night. Nancy might not even be in Brooklyn yet."

"She's had plenty of time to get here." I said, buzzing again. Stubbornly, I pressed a third time, then a fourth. Finally, I reached for my purse and phone—only to discover I'd left them in the car.

"Matt, go back to the car and grab my purse from the front seat. I have Voss's number on speed-dial. I'll call Gudrun and tell her to stop ignoring the doorbell."

Matt was halfway to the car when the intercom crackled. "Who is it?" The voice was soft and electronically garbled.

"Gudrun? Is that you? It's Clare Cosi."

"You're looking for Nancy, your little lost barista." I heard a sound. *Was that a giggle?* "Nancy is here with us. Would you like to come in?"

Matt heard the intercom and turned. But Gudrun sounded odd and I sensed there was something wrong, so I waved him back.

The noise of grinding metal startled me as a hidden mechanism raised the shutter. I glimpsed movement through the glass door. Two figures were silhouetted against the blinding lights inside the factory. Blinking against the glare, I realized one of the figures was pressing a very large handgun to the other's head.

"Come in, Clare Cosi. *Now*, or your little friend Nancy dies," the soft voice taunted through the intercom.

Gudrun Voss is Olympia Temple? Good God, how could I have been so wrong?

Matt saw me tense and moved forward. I swung one hand behind my back and made a gun out of my thumb and index finger, pumping the thumb a few times to stress my point.

Please, Matt, see my finger gun! Figure it out!

As I moved toward the door, I risked a sidelong glance at my ex. He watched, openmouthed, until I was almost inside. Then he turned and ran back to the car with an urgency that told me he'd gotten the message.

Matt will call the police. He'll tell them there are hostages, and they'll send a SWAT team. Everything will be okay . . .

I'd hardly pushed through the glass door when the steel gate descended again. My heart took off, my brow grew damp with perspiration.

Heaven help me, I'm locked in with a stone-cold killer . . .

The scent of chocolate permeated the air. A machine roared dully somewhere on the factory floor. I watched Gudrun remove a Blue Tooth headset and toss it aside.

"Step forward," she commanded in a voice louder than Gudrun's usual meek tone.

I took three steps—not quite lunging but fast enough to rattle my adversary. She stepped backward, onto the factory floor, dragging her silent, struggling hostage with her. Was it Nancy? I couldn't see the girl's face! A burlap sack covered her head. I couldn't see Gudrun's face, either. I recognized her signature black chef's jacket, but her features were obscured by her long, dark, loosely hanging hair.

Nancy (if it was Nancy) hardly struggled and never spoke. The burlap hood muffled her frightened whimpers as she docilely followed Gudrun's lead.

Piled up around me were large, fat burlap sacks, all stuffed with dried and fermented cacao from Madagascar, South and Central America, and the Ivory Coast of Africa.

Gudrun had hollowed out the center of the building, and I could see all the way up to the roof and its massive glass skylight. Roasters, winnowing machines, grinders, mixers, and vats of chocolate liquor lined the brick walls.

"Where's Aphrodite?" I demanded. "I know she's here."

"You know, do you?"

Gudrun's voice was much too forceful, and I finally realized that I'd been played—and I'd been *right*.

"I know a lot of things," I told the killer. "I know you're *not* Gudrun Voss, for instance. And I know you're not *Daphne Krupa*, either. Your name is Olympia Temple."

The hostage began to struggle, and her captor cuffed her with the butt of the gun. Alarmed, I stepped forward, and Olympia leveled the weapon at my heart. With a sharp laugh she tossed her head, and the black wig fell away, revealing her pixie hair.

"I know everything, Olympia. And Soles and Bass—the policewomen I've been helping—they know everything, too."

"Everything?" she cried. "What do they know? What do *you* know?"

I know the SWAT team is on its way, I thought. Only a minute or so had gone by, and I had three or four to wait, maybe more. The police wouldn't be using sirens, so I wouldn't hear them coming, but I needed time for them to get to us, and that meant I'd have to keep this maniac talking.

"I know you used an ice sculpture to fake your suicide," I told her. "The ice hit the water like a body, then melted away so authorities would find shreds of your clothes and no sign of an artificial dummy. You used the same trick on the yacht—with our missing Venus ice sculpture—to fake your own murder."

"How can you know that?" Olympia said, her tone clearly shocked.

"I know that—and I know how you got off the boat without getting caught . . ." While I spoke I searched for a way out, or a way to strike back. "Like the nymph in Ovid's *Metamorphoses*, Daphne transformed into a laurel—not a tree this time, but a *man*. You became John Laurel, the reporter whose press pass you got from Susan Chu."

"Poor Susie, she never figured anything out, never saw it coming when I hit her. I would have killed her, too, but I needed a witness to tell everyone I was dead. So I hit her from behind, painted the name Rufina, then screamed to get everyone's attention before throwing the ice sculpture overboard and slipping away to transform again."

I nodded my head, feigning admiration. "A stroke of genius. You had us all fooled. You were too smart."

"You figured out a lot—for a glorified deli-counter girl."

"But not everything," I said, reigning in my fury. "I never figured out where you hid that umbrella. The one you used to bludgeon Patrice to death. Or the raincoat that kept blood splatters from staining your party clothes."

"You actually helped me that night," she said. "You and Mrs. Dubois knocked over that fiberglass Greek column and broke the interior light. The hollow tube was dark, so I stuffed the umbrella inside, along with my raincoat."

I nodded again, like an impressed protégé. "You played us all."

Olympia flashed a twisted smirk. "People are fools. Tell them what they want to hear, show them what they want to see, and they'll follow like lemmings."

"Is that how you lured Aphrodite tonight? Did you tell her what she wanted to hear?"

"Close enough. I waited for Gudrun's closing time and took her hostage. Then I used Gudrun's e-mail account to send a message to Aphrodite. 'I'm going to the press with the truth about the drug in Mocha Magic unless you meet me at my shop at once.' Worked like a charm. Dressed as Gudrun, I waved her inside and slammed the gates. Aphrodite and her little golden-haired assistant, Minthe, walked right into my trap."

I was walking, too. Every few seconds I'd take a small step forward. Without realizing it, Olympia was backing away from me.

"But your plan tonight," I said, desperate to keep her talking. "I can't make sense of this . . ."

"Because you're too stupid," she said. Olympia squared her shoulders, clearly proud and pleased to have an audience, someone who could appreciate her masterful plan. "These women, these Sisters, condemned my mother to a cage, like some kind of animal. A place so horrible there was only one escape possible—"

"Suicide."

"Now Alicia and Sherri will spend the rest of their days caged like animals, too."

"And Aphrodite? Will she spend the rest of her life in prison?"

"That whore? The one who *ruined* my life?" Olympia shook her head. "Oh no. She dies here. Tonight. Thanks to the e-mail I sent, the police will think Aphrodite came here to murder Gudrun."

"Why?"

"Because she threatened to reveal the truth about that drugged-up mocha powder of yours. And after Aphrodite shoots Gudrun, she'll burn this place to hide the evidence.

Of course, some of you will be trapped here in her fire—and because Aphrodite didn't count on your interference, she'll be knocked unconscious before she can escape, too. The police will find the gun still in her hand." Olympia smiled. "Death by fire—a fitting fate, don't you think? A whore on her way to Hades."

As I continued moving slowly forward, Olympia kept backing up. Now she stood beside a metal shelf holding cellophane-covered buckets of dark mocha syrup.

I heard a moan coming from the other side of that shelf. I risked a peek and saw Aphrodite sprawled on the floor but stirring. Gudrun lay nearby, stripped down to her black brassier and slacks. My breath caught when I spied *Nancy,* lying right next to them, eyes closed, arms curled.

Oh my God, Nancy! Is she still alive?

I choked down my fear, my rage. "I know something else, Olympia. I know that's not my barista you're threatening. Why don't you let the poor girl go?"

Olympia faked surprise and pushed the girl to her knees. Then she ripped the sack away. Minthe's puppy dog eyes blinked up at me.

"My mistake," Olympia said. Before I could react, she pressed the gun against Minthe's head and pulled the trigger.

The blast was deafening. One second Minthe's thin, pale face was there—and then it wasn't. The body flew sideways and struck the plank floor with a hollow thud.

"You crazy bitch!" I screamed.

Then we both heard a crash loud enough to cut through the gunshot still ringing in our eardrums. Shards of shattered skylight rained down. Along with the glass came a figure clinging to a thin black cord

"POLICE! SWAT TEAM! FREEZE! WE'RE ARMED! DROP YOUR WEAPON! GIVE IT UP!

Unfortunately, it wasn't a real SWAT team—it was Matt, all alone. He'd heard the shot, freaked, and taken a reckless chance. For a moment he hung suspended above the factory floor, yelling that he was the police, the army, SEAL Team Six, and whatever else popped into his head. Then, suddenly, whatever he'd used for a rope snapped under his weight, and Matt plunged straight down.

"POLICE! PUT YOUR HANDS UP! YOU'RE UNDER AR—*ooopb!*"

Matt landed on a stack of Madagascar cacao. The hard landing shut his mouth and eyes. *The fall knocked him out!*

Olympia was rattled, then raging. She approached my unconscious ex, gun extended.

Oh no you don't! I rushed her. Reaching up, I yanked a pail of mocha syrup off the shelf, dumping it over her head.

As Olympia knocked the pail away, I grabbed her wrist with both hands. She fought me, eyes closed, blinded by the brown goo. She was strong, but I was determined, and it came down to a battle of wills.

As we struggled over the gun, Aphrodite ran by us, on her way to one of the factory's windows and a fire escape beyond.

"Help me!" I begged. "Grab the gun, Aphrodite! Do something!"

But she kept going, her only interest saving herself! With a single heave, she lifted the big window and crawled through onto the metal fire escape. Night air whipped her flowing dress as the river's black water roiled below.

Olympia could see by now—enough to realize her prize prey was escaping. Enraged, she kicked me hard, sending me backward.

"Die! Die! Die!" she howled as she pumped three shots into Aphrodite's back. The goddess swayed in the wind, then tumbled into the water below.

Olympia whirled to face me. But I was ready with another bucket of Mocha Magic—and this time I swung it like a club. Again and again, I bounced the metal pail off Olympia's head. The chocolate-covered monster finally dropped without a sound, and I kicked the gun out of her limp hand.

"Matt! Matt!"

I ran to my ex and dropped to my knees beside the pallet of cacao beans. He wasn't moving, and it didn't look like he was breathing, either. I brushed aside his shaggy hair, touched his cheek—and his eyes opened!

"I think I hurt myself . . ." He moaned.

"You big, dumb, stupid hero! You could have killed yourself!"

"Oh, man, the dog was worse than the fall."

"Dog?"

"A very fast German shepherd guarding the construction site next door. I climbed that building to jump to this one. But not before that damn shepherd bit me in the butt."

Tears stinging my eyes, I hugged him—then I jumped and Matt bolted upright when a controlled explosion blew the steel gate off. Ropes fluttered down from the shattered skylight, too, followed by armed and armored men. Boots hit the plank floor all around us. More men stormed through the blasted gate, weapons raised.

A SWAT team—a *real* one—had finally arrived.

"What took you so long," Matt groused.

A tactical officer in black armor emerged from behind the metal shelf, Nancy Kelly in his arms. Pale and shaken, my barista touched her bruised head. But her buoyant inner Nancy returned when she saw me.

"Holy smokin' rockets, boss. What the heck hit me?"

FORTY-FIVE

~~~~~~~~~~~~~~~~~~~~~~~~~~~~~~~~~~~~~~~

TWO days later things were back to normal at my coffeehouse—"normal" being a relative term, considering Village life.

"Remember, Punch," Tuck said from behind our counter, "the part you're auditioning for today is the *most important* role in *Return to Munchkin Land*."

"But it's only the chorus, Tuck, just a small part."

"Punch! *What* do I always say?"

The lean Latino put down his cup and sighed. "There are no small parts, only—" He suddenly froze, glanced around.

"You can relax," I assured him from the next stool. "There are no *small actors* in here today." (Since we'd opened six hours ago, I'd served a steady stream of hulking, hairy men.)

"Exactly," Tuck said. "And where would the Wicked Witch be without a dependable army of Flying Monkeys?"

"Ha!" Nancy cut in, arriving for her lunchtime shift. "She wouldn't need them if she had a flying Matteo!"

"More like a *plunging* Matteo from what I heard," Esther cracked.

"Matt was *very* brave," Nancy said, eyes glazing as she tied on her apron. "He saved my life. I'll be forever grateful to him."

Esther stared at Nance a long moment. "Oh no."

Nancy turned to Tucker. "When is Matteo coming back to the Blend, do you think? Will he be working as a manager again, the way he did the other day? That was a *great* day! He's *such* a good manager!"

"Oh, boss!" Esther sang.

I glanced up from Matt's revised delivery schedule. "What?"

She leaned down. "Did you hear that?"

"Matt's flying to Costa Rica next week," I said. "Let's hope Ms. Kelly is over her new crush by the time he gets back."

"I guess we should look on the bright side," Esther said. "At least she's over Dante."

"Nancy's lucky he's not pressing charges."

"Speaking of charges," Esther said, "did you check out New York One's *In the Papers* segment this morning? We're still the top story across the city."

I nodded.

Tuck moved toward us. "You know, I can't decide which headline was my favorite. *Chocolate-Covered Serial Killer Gets Licked, Spider-Man Saves 3 in Willy Wonka Hostage Drama,* or *Cocoa Kook Goes Loca for Mocha.*"

"Well, *kook* is certainly the right noun," Punch said.

"No doubt," Esther said. "That sicko actually smiled for her mug shot."

"I know!" Punch cried, smoothing the monkey hair on his arms. "That girl is cray-zee!"

"But not crazy enough for an insanity plea," I pointed out, glad of it.

Olympia Temple was no longer the wayward little girl hiding behind a curtain of hair. The media had discovered a brand-new sinister star, and she shined darkly for them. But Warhol's famous fifteen minutes had begun ticking away already, and Olympia would soon learn what every convicted criminal knew—the brief clock of fame winds down to interminable years behind prison walls.

"You know something I can't stop thinking about?" Tucker confessed. "Olympia called herself Daphne and escaped off the boat as Laurel. Anyone who knows Ovid or a bit of basic mythology could have connected the two. It's as if she wanted someone to discover the clues."

"From what Soles and Bass told me, serial killers tend to take pride in their work. Olympia Temple made killing her art. On some level, she wanted it to be appreciated."

"What? The art of murder?"

I nodded. "Sociopaths get high on power, control, and manipulation. They also crave pity. I guarantee you, Olympia sees herself as the victim in all this, the star of her own sick show."

Tucker's eyebrows rose. "Sounds like my little directorial pep talks to the disparate citizens of Oz. Every actor, no matter the size of his role, is the star."

"Exactly, and given what we now know about the late Ms. 'Aphrodite' Pixley—from her antics in college to her setting employees against each other—that woman was probably a sociopath, too."

"Yes, well . . . I'm sorry Aphrodite is dead, but I'm not sorry we're all free of her."

"You and me both."

"So, no more Mocha Magic?" Esther assumed. "It's dead?"

"Kaput," I assured her. "The only reason Madame signed that contract was to help an old friend."

"Doesn't Alicia care about selling the powder?"

"Not anymore. And she's finished with Aphrodite's Village, too."

"I'm not surprised," Esther said. "I mean how does an ex-professor end up working for a Web site like that, anyhow?"

"A job's a job," I said. "After Alicia left Bay Creek Women's College, she couldn't find another academic position, so she began to travel and write, which included freelance restaurant reviews and eventually food writing. Thelma was always looking for smart new writers and editors. Apparently, they reconnected on—"

Esther held up her hand. "Don't tell me. Facebook."

I shrugged.

Tuck leaned against the counter. "One thing I don't get. Why would Aphrodite want to put a controlled substance into Mocha Magic, and how could she think she would get away with it? The FDA would have found her out eventually."

"Alphas," I said.

"Am I supposed to understand that?"

"Alphas are important to marketers because they're the kind of customers who influence other customers. That's what all these parties were about—Aphrodite was marketing to alphas: reporters, bloggers, food and beverage critics, wholesale buyers. If she could impress them with the potency of an adulterated product, then they'd spread the word. After the Mocha Magic took off, she'd remove the drug. By then, she was hoping the product would sustain itself via placebo effect."

"Sounds like your basic bait-and-switch," Punch said.

"You're right. It was unethical—and the woman who created it, Alicia, had scruples. That's why Aphrodite altered the formula behind her back."

"So what's Alicia going to do now?" Tuck asked.

"Travel, eat, write . . ." I smiled. "She's going to have enough money to retire early."

Esther smirked. "She won the Powerball?"

"Better. Alicia's lawyer discovered that Aphrodite was behind Patrice Stone's hiring Troy Talos to seduce her away from the Rock Center launch party."

Tucker, Esther, and Punch hooted. I didn't blame them. It was a real bombshell.

"Apparently, Aphrodite wanted Maya Lansing, the fitness queen, to be the spokesperson for Mocha Magic. Aphrodite knew Alicia would never agree to that. Her solution was to keep Alicia away from her own launch party and allow the fitness queen to take the spotlight. Alicia's product hadn't even hit the market, and Aphrodite was conspiring to undercut her."

Evidence on Aphrodite's computer made it clear that she knew and approved of Patrice's plan to hire parolee Troy and his girlfriend, Vanessa, which gave Alicia grounds to sue the Hades out of the woman's estate and company.

"The attorneys are working out a big, fat settlement as we speak," I told them. "Soon Alicia will have enough of the Love Goddess's money to do whatever her heart desires."

THE lunch crowd came and went, the flying monkeys with them as the Broadway auditions wound down for the day. Madame stopped by. I was happy to see her and immediately pulled a fresh espresso.

"Have you heard from Lieutenant Quinn yet?" she quietly asked as I slid the demitasse across the blueberry marble.

I shook my head, unable to trust my voice. The news was good otherwise, and I tried to focus on that. Sherri Sellars was released, the charges against her dropped, and Alicia Bower was a free woman who'd soon be stinking rich. But I couldn't stop counting the hours since I last heard from Quinn (sixty-three going on sixty-four). Late last night, alone in bed, I had broken down and tried his cell, but as he warned, I only reached his voice mail—and I cried myself to sleep.

"Try not to worry, dear," Madame said.

"I don't know how to do that . . ."

"Focus on what's in front of you. Live each hour, each day, one at a time . . ."

I nodded, unable to speak again. I could tell from her answer that Madame wasn't hopeful. This was starting to feel like Cormac O'Neil all over again.

"Mom! Mom!"

I whirled, panicked at the sound of fear in Joy's voice.

"Honey, what's wrong?"

"I was upstairs, watching the local news. I heard something *terrible*. I think it's about Franco."

I gripped her arms. "What did you hear? Tell me."

"Arrests were made by the Internal Affairs Bureau—arrests of officers, some of them high ranking! The mayor's holding a press conference in a few hours."

Oh God . . . I turned to read Madame's face. She looked as stricken as I felt. Was this Larry Hawke again? *He must have pulled the trigger on Franco and trumped up charges against Mike and Sully . . .*

I would have stumbled, even fallen, if I hadn't been more concerned about propping up my daughter. When the bell over our front door rang, I didn't care. All I wanted to do was close the shop and turn off the lights.

"Joy? You okay? What's wrong?" Manny Franco stood five feet away wearing a navy blue suit, his shaved head clean, his rugged face strained at the sight of my daughter's tears.

"Franco!" Joy rushed the man so fast and hard, the mountain of muscle nearly tipped over. He held her tight as she showered him with kisses.

"J'étais ainsi inquiété," she cooed.

"Mais je suis bon, ma joie," he said, his accent rough. *"Tout est bon!"*

"Franco, what happened?" I demanded. "We thought Hawke had you arrested."

The sergeant's smile got bigger. "Other way around . . ."

As Franco told the story, he'd gone rogue for one reason: to prove that Larry Hawke could be bought.

Apparently, the New Jersey dealer that Franco had arrested—counter to Hawke's orders—was the nephew of a mob boss. The reason Hawke didn't want him touched was not to turn the file over to federal officers but to bury it completely. The boss had reached out to Hawke, paying him to protect his relative.

"I had some friends in the bureau," Franco said, "even more in the boroughs. I asked around, put some things together, and went to Lieutenant Quinn. Turns out, he was interviewing this old-timer who'd gathered some pretty serious evidence against Hawke, too. So we all went to Internal Affairs, and they came clean with a case they'd been building against Hawke and some of his associates throughout the department. Damn good thing we came forward, too, because IAB was getting suspicious of our meetings with Hawke. They were starting to suspect me, Mike, and Sully of being just as dirty."

The bell rang again and we all turned.

An older man stood there, tall and stoic. He had silver hair, sharp blue-gray eyes, and a bone-white scar across his ruddy cheek. Smartly dressed in a twilight blue suit, he searched the shop, finding and focusing on a single person sitting at the counter—Blanche Dreyfus Allegro Dubois.

He didn't move and neither did we.

Slowly, Madame rose to her feet. She crossed to him and stood staring for the longest time. Then her gently wrinkled hand touched his scarred cheek.

"Hello, Mac."

"Hello, Blanche."

"You look like you could use a cup of coffee."

Cormac swallowed and paused, as if he couldn't trust his voice. "I could, Blanche. I could."

She laced her fingers in his and led him to the bar. I blinked back tears as he took Mike's seat, settled in as if he'd never left. Then Madame slipped behind the counter and began to fix his drink.

Instinctively, we backed away, let them have their privacy. Joy and Franco excused themselves, heading up to the closed second floor, arm in arm. I breathed a sigh of relief. Wherever Quinn was, I knew he was okay—at least I prayed he was. In fact, praying wasn't a bad idea.

I closed my eyes and that's when I heard it. The bell rang one more time.

"Got something hot for me, Cosi?"

I took a breath, opened my eyes.

Mike Quinn was standing in front of me, wearing a full-on smile.

EPILOGUE

"**THAT** man is the most persistent, pigheaded Irish cop I ever met . . ."

Upstairs in the duplex kitchen, Mike Quinn and I were sharing a fresh pot of coffee and fat, decadent slices of my Chocolate Blackout Cake (based on the original Brooklyn recipe). We had a lot of catching up to do, given his past few days of blackout.

"It took him ten years," Mike said, "but O'Neil learned everything he could about the world of finance. Once he knew how to follow money, he worked to connect Larry Hawke to the secret bank accounts where his dirty payoffs were hidden. Then he found the accounts of some of Hawke's pals, and the rest is front page news—this week, anyway."

I refreshed our cups and sat down again. "I wonder what Madame and O'Neil are talking about downstairs."

"I'm sure he's trying to explain what happened all those years ago."

"Do you mind telling me?" I didn't want to exploit a confidence, but I was desperate to know. "Why did he leave her like that? Without even letting her know if he was dead or alive?"

"From what I gather, O'Neil believed the less Mrs. Dubois knew, the safer she'd be. He was right, obviously. She made it through just fine."

"But if he was worried about her safety, why didn't he stick around to protect her?"

"You don't understand. O'Neil couldn't even protect himself. He went to the Feds, and they relocated him in witness protection, but two killers came for him within the first few weeks. He got lucky or he wouldn't have survived at all. That scar"—Mike swept his hand along his own cheek and across his throat—"is from the botched hit. He knew any wife of his would have been killed, too. At that point, the man had no choice. He really disappeared, created another identity and another life in Australia."

"That's all there was to it?"

"Well . . ." Mike looked away, as if weighing whether to keep talking. "From what I gather . . . he loved Blanche deeply, but he also knew what was important to her . . ."

He paused, turned to meet my eyes.

"Go on . . ."

"This coffeehouse, Clare—it was more than a business to her. It was a legacy. She felt it was her duty to keep it thriving, to pass it down to her child. How could he ask her to leave it?"

I took a breath. Mike was talking about more than my mother-in-law, and we both knew it. Reaching for my cup, I realized my hands were shaking. I couldn't read him. Not on this particular truth. I had no idea how he felt.

"So . . ." My voice was weak. "O'Neil really just came back to get Hawke?"

"He built a life in Australia—a wife, children, grandchildren. But he told us he'd reached an age where he couldn't die without trying. So, yes, he came back to get Hawke, to clear his name—and to see Blanche again, try to explain what had happened all those years ago."

I glanced out the kitchen window, thought it over. "O'Neil is such a tough guy, so brave. He came all this way—thousands of miles after three decades. Why did it take him *days* to face the woman he loved and tell her his story? I don't understand that."

"I do. It's not easy to admit, but . . . as a man, I understand completely . . ." Mike's gaze fell into the dregs of his cup. "He couldn't find the nerve."

Quinn couldn't stay. The mayor's press conference required his presence, and he had a few other "very important things" to do, but he promised to come back for dinner. As night fell, I turned on the true-blue flame of my gas stove.

According to Punch, the word *mole* came from the Aztec *molli* meaning "concoction." Growing up in Spanish Harlem, he claimed every mama had a different combination of ingredients, a secret mix that made it her own. This particular recipe was new for me, something I came up with given this week's crazy concoctions. I hoped Mike would like it.

I warmed the oil first, sautéed the onions, added the peppers, and the Guinness stout. Aromas rose from my pot and I inhaled deeply . . . the garlic and ginger, cumin and coriander, fennel and cinnamon.

They say a dish like this is an acquired taste—not unlike living in a crowded, competitive city, where cultures and cuisines continually clash. It certainly wasn't for everyone. Like most things in life, the key to making it work was keeping the blend balanced. Not too spicy but not too bland, either, and always tempering the bitter with the sweet.

As I stirred in the Mexican chocolate, watched it sensuously melt, I felt an arm slip around my waist, warm lips at my neck.

"Hi, Clare."

I smiled as Mike nibbled me. "You looked very handsome on television."

"You could pick me out in that sea of faces?"

"I could."

"Want to hear something funny?"

"Absolutely."

"I saw Soles and Bass at One PP, and they are royally pissed at you."

"Why? Because I screwed up their case against Alicia?"

"Not even close. They're angry about the wedding gifts."

"Excuse me?"

"Apparently, the night of the Rock Center party, your baristas served aphrodisiacs to half the detectives in Midtown."

"That's right. They did."

"Within two days, three of those guys proposed to their girlfriends and two reconciled with their ex-wives. Lori and Sue Ellen will be going to weddings for the next six months."

"Sounds to me like cupid helper isn't always a bad thing."

"As me sainted grandmother used to say, 'A little bit o' crazy flavors the stew.'"

"That reminds me, Detective . . ."

"What?"

"You and I never did take that *loco* mocha out for a test drive."

"Oh, sweetheart . . ." Mike's lips moved to my ear, his breath hot as he promised, "Cupid won't need any controlled-substance help in our bedroom tonight."

I turned in his arms, expecting a kiss—and found instead a small white box, the kind that held a ring.

"Don't panic," he said. "It's not a diamond."

I snapped opened the lid.

"It's an Irish friendship ring. We call it a Claddagh."

The circle was polished silver, beautifully wrought. Two small hands held a crowned heart between them. The shape of the design came to a gentle point.

"When a woman wears it on her right hand, pointed away from her body, it means she's not romantically involved. If she wears it pointed toward her, it's a sign that her heart is taken—in someone else's hands."

I waited for Mike to say more, but he didn't. He waited, like he always did, because waiting was a state he knew so well; waiting was an act he trusted. And now he trusted me to make the choice.

Andy Warhol once said that "fantasy" love was much better than "reality" love. "The most exciting attractions," he wrote, "are between two opposites that never meet."

Warhol was right about a lot of things: the modern phenomenon of instant fame; the commerce of art and the art in commerce. But he was wrong about love.

At Joy's age, Matteo Allegro had been my fantasy love, not to mention my very attractive opposite. I'd tried to make it real, tried to make us fit. But we didn't fit. Now I was twice Joy's age, and I knew the difference between fantasy and reality, between magical thinking and practical acceptance.

Quinn was an Irish firefighter's son turned cop; I was an art-school dropout turned coffee pro. He was nearly six five. I was barely five two. But we were alike where it counted, in the silences, in the heart.

I took a breath, deep and long, and gazed at the crowned heart in the ring he'd given me, held aloft by clasping hands. There were no guarantees when you loved someone—especially when that someone carried a shield, a gun, and a whole lot of baggage. Maybe I should have felt anxious or afraid at seeing the ring's hands connecting, but all I felt was love, all I wanted was here.

With deliberate care, I slipped on Mike's circle of silver. I thought of my nightmare and those handcuffs, but there was no lock here, no force now. The fit felt good. The ring was heavy with quality, yet the burden was light.

Lifting it higher, I smiled, wanting Mike to see the direction I'd given it. Like a sterling compass, it pointed with hope toward my own heart.

Recipes & Tips
from the Village Blend

Visit Cleo Coyle's virtual Village Blend at
www.CoffeehouseMystery.com
for even more recipes including:

* Clare's Brooklyn Blackout Cake (for Mike)
* Chocolate-Glazed Hazelnut Bars
* Chocolate-Dipped Cinnamon Sticks
* Cappuccino Kisses
* Chocolate-Chip Cobbler
* Mocha-Glazed Rum Macaroons
* *Gianduia* Brownies and Chocolate-Hazelnut Fudge
* Tiramisu Bars (based on Canada's Nanaimo Bars)
* Triple-Chocolate *Budini*
* Quick Chocolate Crostada
* and many others . . .

RECIPES

~~~~~~

Believe me, there's no metaphysics on earth like chocolates.

—FERNANDO PESSOA, POET, WRITER,
PHILOSOPHER

Aphrodisiac Brownies

With Alicia's Mocha Magic off the market, Clare Cosi developed this recipe for her coffeehouse customers. As usual, NYPD Detective Mike Quinn was her first taste tester. "These should hit the spot," she told him. "Possibly more than one." The reason? Three of Clare's ingredients have long been considered aphrodisiacs . . .

Chocolate, *of course, is the classic Cupid consumable. The Aztecs were probably the first to make the connection between amorous feelings and the cocoa bean. The emperor Montezuma was said to have fueled his romantic trysts by ingesting large amounts of the bean.*

Coffee *contains caffeine, a stimulant that is also considered a perk in the department of amorous desires. Historically, when coffee was first introduced to the Turkish culture, husbands were expected to keep their wives well supplied. If the husband could not provide daily coffee for his wife, it was a legitimate cause for her to divorce him. Even if you don't care for coffee, don't skip this ingredient. It enhances and deepens the chocolate flavor in the brownies.*

Cinnamon *is a fragrant and stimulating spice. The Romans* *believed cinnamon was an aphrodisiac. Cleopatra famously used it to arouse her many lovers. In these brownies, the cinnamon works hand in hand with the brown sugar to layer in depth of flavor that's subtle yet spicy—sure, it may drive your lover crazy, but as Mike said, "A little bit o' crazy flavors the stew."*

Makes one 8- or 9-inch square pan of brownies (about 16–20 squares)

12 tablespoons (1½ sticks) unsalted butter
4 ounces unsweetened chocolate, chopped
1 teaspoon ground cinnamon
1 teaspoon espresso powder
2 large eggs
1 egg yolk
1 cup granulated sugar
½ cup light brown sugar, packed
½ teaspoon salt
¾ cup all-purpose flour
½ teaspoon baking powder
¾ cup semisweet chocolate chips (about 5 ounces)

Step 1—Prep the oven and pan: Preheat the oven to 350°F. Line bottom of an 8- or 9-inch square pan with parchment paper or aluminum foil, extending the paper or foil beyond the pan to make handles (this will allow you to lift the brownies out of the pan while still warm). Lightly coat the paper or foil with nonstick cooking spray.

Step 2—Make the chocolate mixture: Place the butter and unsweetened chocolate in a microwave-safe container and heat in 30-second increments, stirring between each session, until the mixture has melted. (Or warm the butter and chocolate in a small saucepan over very low heat. Be sure to stir continually to prevent scorching.) After the chocolate mixture is melted and smooth, stir in the cinnamon and espresso powder. Set aside.

Step 3—Create batter and bake: In a large mixing bowl, whisk the eggs and egg yolk. Whisk in both of the sugars and the salt. Whisk in the chocolate mixture from Step 2. Switching to a spoon or spatula, stir in the flour, baking powder, and chocolate chips. Blend enough for a smooth batter, but do not overmix or you'll produce gluten in the flour and toughen the brownies. Pour the batter into the pan and bake about 30 minutes. Underbaking is smarter than overbaking. The brownies are done when the top surface has become solid and displays small cracks. Remove from the oven and allow to cool in the pan no more than 5 minutes. Using the parchment paper (or foil) handles that you made in Step 1, carefully lift the entire brownie cake out of the hot pan and allow to finish cooling on a rack. Cut into small or large squares and eat with joy!

Chocolate Zombie Clusters

When Clare Cosi isn't dreaming of Mike, she's dreaming up recipes. From the moment Detective Sue Ellen Bass mentioned zombies on Eighth Avenue, Clare couldn't stop thinking about the challenge of creating a chocolate recipe that was so easy a zombie could make it (no-bake, natch!) and so delicious it would send the eater into a food-bliss trance. Maybe a cross between a cookie and a candy, hmm . . .

For inspiration, she did a little research into real zombies. Historically, the most famous "zombie" case was discovered in Haiti. A man was made into a zombie with a "zombie powder" that contained plants with spines and toxic resins, puffer fish, and ground bones.

Ground bones! she thought. That's it! Her cookies needed to have a satisfying zombie bones crunch to them. Spying the Nutella chocolate hazelnut spread on her counter next to a container of nuts, she snapped her fingers, pulled out her saucepan, and Chocolate Zombie Clusters were born.

Makes about 3 dozen cookies

*2 cups coarsely chopped nuts, toasted (walnuts, pecans, hazelnuts,
peanuts, or any combination)*
¾ cup Nutella
2 teaspoons vanilla extract
8 tablespoons (1 stick) butter
2 cups granulated sugar
¼ teaspoon salt
½ cup whole or low-fat milk
¼ cup cocoa powder

Step 1—Prep: Later in this recipe, you will need to add the following ingredients very quickly, so get them ready now. Measure out the roughly chopped nuts (toast them first for better flavor; see how at the end of this recipe). Set the nuts aside. In a small bowl, mix the Nutella and vanilla and set aside. Line two large baking sheets with parchment or wax paper. This is where you will drop the hot, no-bake cookie dough.

Step 2—Cook up the batter: Place the butter, sugar, salt, milk, and cocoa powder in a nonstick saucepan. Bring this mixture to a boil while frequently stirring to prevent scorching. Boil for 2 minutes. (Be sure to boil for the full 2 minutes to get the best result.)

Step 3—Remove from heat and finish: Remove the pan from the heat. Wait 2 full minutes for the boiling to subside and the mixture to cool off a bit. Stir in the Nutella-vanilla mixture and the chopped nuts.

Step 4—Drop and cool: Drop the cookies by the tablespoon onto the lined baking sheets. As they cool, they'll harden. To speed up the hardening process, slip the pan into the refrigerator. Then pick one up, take a bite, and become a chocolate zombie!

How to Toast Nuts: Toasting nuts brings incredible flavor out of them, and the process is so easy it's truly worth that extra step. Preheat the oven to 350°F. Spread the nuts in a single layer on a baking sheet and bake in for 8–10 minutes. Stir once or twice to prevent scorching. You'll know they're done when your kitchen air become absolutely redolent with the flavor of warm nuts.

Frozen Mexican Choco-Latte

With Gudrun Voss on board as the Village Blend's new chocolate supplier, Clare added a Mexican Choco-Latte to her coffeehouse menu. The drink proved so popular she tried to imagine some novel variations. The food muse was quiet for a while, and then Clare went to sleep. After she woke up in a cold sweat, she imagined this drink: there's nothing like a nightmare about a homicidal ice sculpture to inspire the creation of a new recipe.

Makes two 6-ounce servings

½ cup brewed coffee or espresso (for 6 coffee ice cubes)
½ cup low-fat milk
½ cup vanilla ice cream
½ teaspoon unsweetened cocoa powder
¼ teaspoon ground cinnamon
Sweetened whipped cream, optional
Chocolate shavings (or sprinkling of cinnamon), for garnish

Method: Fill an ice tray with the coffee and freeze. Place the coffee ice cubes in a blender. Add the milk, ice cream, cocoa powder, and cinnamon. Pulse the blender to chop the coffee ice cubes into fine particles. You can either create a very icy drink (like a frozen margarita), or run the blender full speed until the mixture is liquefied and smooth. Pour the coffee mixture into two glasses. To finish with flare, crown each glass with a dollop of sweetened whipped cream and top with chocolate shavings and/or a light sprinkling of cinnamon. Drink with joy!

Joy Allegro's Milk Dud Thumbprint Cookies (for Sergeant Franco)

When Joy found Franco's leather jacket pockets stuffed with Milk Duds, he finally came clean about flirting with the Milk Duds booth bunny at the Javits Convention Center. Joy didn't get angry—she got busy, coming up with this recipe for a caramel-stuffed chocolate cookie. One bite of this Milk Dud–inspired treat with its chocolaty nest and chewy, sweet chocolate-caramel center made Franco decide to put chocolate bunnies behind him for good.

Makes about 2 dozen cookies

For cookies:

> 1½ cups all-purpose flour
> ½ cup unsweetened cocoa powder
> ½ teaspoon salt
> 1 cup (2 sticks) butter, softened
> ¾ cup white granulated sugar plus ½ cup, for dusting
> 1 teaspoon vanilla extract
> 1 large egg

For caramel filling:

> 25 caramels (store-bought is fine)
> 5 tablespoons heavy whipping cream (or half-and-half)
> 5 tablespoons semisweet chocolate chips

Step 1—Create batter: In a mixing bowl, whisk together the flour, cocoa powder, and salt. Set this dry mixture aside. In a second bowl, combine the butter, ¾ cup sugar, and vanilla. Using an electric mixer, beat until creamy. Add the egg and continue beating until well mixed. Add dry ingredients and continue beating on low until a smooth batter forms.

Step 2—Chill and prep: Cover the bowl with plastic and chill the dough for about 15 minutes in the refrigerator (no more than 15 minutes). This will make the dough easier to roll. When ready to bake, preheat the oven to 350°F and cover a baking sheet with parchment paper or silicone sheets. (*Note:* Use the parchment paper not to prevent sticking but to ensure bottoms do not burn before cookies are finished baking.)

Step 3—Roll and sugarcoat: Place ½ cup of white granulated sugar in a shallow bowl. Using clean fingers, roll the dough into balls of about 1 inch in diameter. Drop the dough balls in the bowl of sugar and lightly coat. Place balls on the prepared baking sheet, leaving room for spreading. Gently press your thumb into each dough ball, making a nice-size indentation. (Take care not to tear the cookie ball or press all the way down to the baking sheet.)

Step 4—Bake and cool: Bake for 15 minutes. Cookies will be fragile until they harden so wait a few minutes before moving them to a cooling rack. If using parchment paper, simply slide the entire sheet of paper to the rack; otherwise, use a spatula with care.

Step 5—Make caramel filling: As cookies are cooling, melt your caramels, cream (or half-and-half), and chocolate chips in the microwave by heating in 1 minute increments (stirring between each heating session). Or heat the caramels and cream in a saucepan over low heat, stirring often. When the caramels have melted, add the chocolate chips and stir until smooth. Spoon into each cookie's thumbprint. (Use two teaspoons—one to scoop up the mixture and the other to scrape it off and into the thumbprint.) If the mixture hardens during this process, simply reheat. Warning: Do not taste any of your cookies until the filling has cooled completely. If the caramel is still very hot, it will burn your mouth! Allow to set, and eat with joy (and Franco)!

Tip: When making cookies, always allow your baking sheets to cool before putting more dough on them. A hot baking sheet will cause any cookie to spread immediately and alter its proper baking time. You can speed up the cooling process by running cool water over the back of your baking sheets. (Dry before continuing to use.)

Clare Cosi's "Pure Ecstasy" Chocolate-Chip Cookies with Beurre Noisette and Homemade Brown Sugar

Beurre noisette *(brown butter), two kinds of chocolate chips, a bit of espresso powder, and a step where you essentially create your own brown sugar (using molasses), make Clare Cosi's gourmet version of the chocolate-chip cookie one to die for. When Detective Mike Quinn first tasted them, he told her they nearly qualified as a drug. With toffee-like notes of buttery caramel, this mouthwatering cookie is in a class by itself. (And when Mike consumes them, he makes an extra-long "man-in-ecstasy" noise—sans little blue pill, too. Not bad!)*

Makes about 2 dozen cookies

12 tablespoons unsalted butter, melted and browned
(see end of this recipe)
1¾ cups flour
½ teaspoon salt
½ teaspoon baking soda
½ teaspoon baking powder
1 cup granulated sugar
5 teaspoons molasses (unsulphured, not blackstrap, such as
Grandma's Original)

2 large eggs, lightly beaten, room temperature
1 teaspoon vanilla
½ teaspoon espresso powder (to deepen chocolate flavor)
¾ cup good-quality semisweet chocolate chips
½ cup good-quality bittersweet chips
(such as Ghirardelli 60% cacao chips)

Step 1—Make brown butter: Create your melted and browned butter (see end of this recipe). Set aside to cool.

Step 2—Mix dry ingredients: In a separate, small bowl, whisk together flour, salt, baking soda, and baking powder. Set aside.

Step 3—Mix wet ingredients and make dough: Into a large mixing bowl, measure out the granulated sugar. Add the molasses and stir well. (You have just made your own light brown sugar.) Add in the eggs, vanilla, espresso powder, and the brown butter that you made in Step 1. Mix with a whisk or fork until well blended. Switch to a spoon or spatula and stir in your dry ingredients from Step 2. Mix only enough until a smooth dough forms. (Do not overmix or you'll create gluten in the dough, and your cookies will be tough instead of tender.) Finally, fold in the chocolate chips.

Step 4—Chill and roll: Cover the mixing bowl of dough with plastic or foil and chill in the refrigerator for 30 minutes. This will make the sticky dough easier to handle. (You can also wrap the dough tightly in plastic and chill overnight.) Preheat the oven to 375°F. Line a baking sheet with parchment paper or silicone sheets, or lightly coat with a nonstick cooking spray. Pinch off pieces of dough and lightly roll into Ping Pong ball–size rounds (about 1½ inches in diameter). Do not overhandle and feel free to use a cookie scoop (or small ice cream scoop) instead. Set the dough balls on a baking sheet, allowing room for spreading. You can either bake the cookies as dough balls or flatten them slightly with the palm of your hand. The flattened cookies will bake up slightly crisper (and flatter, of course!); the dough balls will bake up softer, chewier, and a bit thicker.

Step 5—Bake: Bake for 9–11 minutes. You're looking for the raw dough to cook completely but without the bottoms scorching. If you find your cookie bottoms browning too much or even burning, try lining your baking sheets with parchment paper or silicone sheets, which not only prevent sticking but help cookies bake more evenly. When cookies come out of the oven, use a spatula to carefully transfer them from the hot pan to a cooling rack. Before baking a new batch of cookies, make sure the pan has cooled off or the cookies may spread too much. These cookies are amazing—eat with joy!

How to Make Brown Butter: Joy Allegro calls it *beurre noisette,* literally "nut butter," because of the beautiful walnut color the butter turns when you make it. Here's how you do it: Simply add the butter to a skillet set over medium-high heat. Swirl the pan as the butter melts. As it cooks, it will start to foam. Continue cooking and watching carefully for a few minutes. What you're doing is caramelizing the butter's milk solids. When you see the butter turn a deep golden brown color and notice a delicious nutty, caramel aroma, the butter is ready. Pour the brown butter out of the hot skillet and allow it to cool a bit before adding it to the recipe—you don't want to cook the egg with hot butter!

Roasted Rock Cornish Game Hens with Rosemary and Lemon Butter

An elegant yet easy entrée, Clare Cosi cooked up four of these Rock Cornish hens in about an hour—all the time she had to prepare that promised "home-cooked dinner" for Sergeant Franco, Joy, and Lieutenant Mike Quinn. This quick-roasting method produces a crispy, buttery skin. The lemon infuses the moist meat with tangy brightness while the herbs tickle the tongue. These elegant little birds usually weigh in around 2½ pounds each, so plan on one bird per person for your service. These hens also make a wonderful complement to Clare's Fettuccine with Italian Mole (Mushroom Wine Sauce), which she prepared for that same special dinner. See the next recipe for instructions on making that dish.

Makes 2 servings

2 Rock Cornish game hens
Sea salt and ground white or freshly ground black pepper
2 medium lemons, quartered
6 tablespoons (¾ stick) butter, softened, for paste, plus 2 tablespoons
butter, melted, for basting
3 tablespoons chopped fresh rosemary (or 3 teaspoons dried)
3 tablespoons chopped fresh thyme (or 3 teaspoons dried)
4 toothpicks (for closing cavity during roasting)

Step 1—Prep hens: Preheat the oven to 450°F. (*Tip:* Many ovens need extra time to reach this temperature. Don't trust the preheat beeper. Give your oven a full 30 minutes to properly preheat.) Lightly coat the rack of a roasting pan with nonstick cooking spray. Remove the giblets from each hen's cavity, rinse each hen, and pat dry. Salt and pepper the inside cavity. Stuff each game hen with ½ tablespoon of the fresh rosemary, ½ tablespoon of the fresh thyme (if using dried herbs, use ½ teaspoon of each), and 3 lemon quarters. Place the two hens on the rack of the roasting pan.

Step 2—Make butter paste: Place the softened butter in a bowl, and using a fork (or clean fingers) mix in the remaining fresh (or dried) rosemary and thyme until you've made a nice herb-butter paste. Slather each of the game hens all over with the butter mixture. Sprinkle each game hen with salt and pepper. To prevent lemons from falling out during roasting, draw together excess skin on either side of the open cavity. Drive toothpicks through the skin to secure (2 toothpicks per bird should do it).

Step 3—Roast the meat: Place the roasting pan in the oven and roast for 30 minutes. Baste the hens with melted butter and return the hens to the oven for another 10 minutes. (*Tip:* Encase the wing tips in aluminum foil to prevent scorching.) Baste the hens a second time and return to the oven for the final 8 minutes of cooking. Remove from the oven, tent foil around the birds to keep them warm, and allow them to rest for 10 minutes before serving. If you skip this resting period, when you slice into the meat, the juices will run out and the meat will taste dry. Allowing the meat to rest gives the juices a chance to re-collect and the meat to remain moist.

Clare Cosi's Fettuccine with "Italian Mole" (Mushroom Wine Sauce)

This delicious mushroom wine sauce served over fat fettuccine noodles combines two of the many vibrant cultures that Clare lives among in New York City. Mushroom sauce and pasta may be an idea with culinary roots in Italy, but the spice mix and finish of chocolate are borrowed from a classic Mexican mole. This unsweetened chocolate (also known as "bitter" or "baking" chocolate) isn't something you taste in the sauce; it's a subtle secret ingredient that adds a rich, meaty depth of flavor that suggests it was cooking for many hours instead of less than one (about all the time Clare had to prepare dinner for her daughter, Franco, and Mike Quinn).

Makes 6 servings

1 pound fresh mushrooms, chopped
A few glugs of olive oil
3 garlic cloves, smashed
¼ cup vegetable stock
½ cup dry red wine
⅛ teaspoon allspice
⅛ teaspoon ground nutmeg
½ teaspoon sea salt
⅛ teaspoon white pepper
¼ cup brewed coffee
1 tablespoon butter
1 teaspoon unsweetened chocolate, chopped
1 pound fettuccine noodles,
cooked according to package instructions
Grated Pecorino Romano or Parmesan cheese (to garnish)

Step 1—Prepare and cook mushrooms: Gently wash the mushrooms (any variety or combo you like), pat them dry, and chop them. Cover the bottom of a nonstick pan with olive oil and lightly sauté for 3–5 minutes. Transfer cooked mushrooms and any juices to a bowl and set aside.

Step 2—Make sauce and cover: Add more olive oil to the pan and sauté the garlic until soft and translucent. Then return all the mushrooms to the pan, along with any juices. Add the vegetable stock, wine, allspice, nutmeg, salt, and pepper. Simmer for 3 minutes. Add the brewed coffee, cover, and simmer for 10–12 minutes.

Step 3—Uncover and reduce: Uncover the pan and continue cooking for another 6–8 minutes until some of the liquid evaporates and the sauce thickens a bit.

Step 4—Add butter and chocolate: Stir in the butter. When the butter is melted, sprinkle the chopped chocolate over the sauce and stir. The heat of the sauce will melt the chocolate's darkness into goodness, allowing it to blend with the many different flavors for the very best result. Toss well with 1 pound of cooked fettuccine. Plate and garnish with freshly grated Pecorino Romano or Parmesan cheese.

Madame's European-Style Hot Chocolate

Makes 2 servings

1½ ounces bittersweet or semisweet chocolate,
grated or finely chopped
1 cup milk
Granulated sugar, optional
Whipped cream or crème fraîche (see tip at end of recipe)

Method: Grate all of the chocolate, reserve 2 teaspoons, and divide the rest in half, putting each half in a separate mug. Place a saucepan over medium heat and warm the milk, stirring continuously. *Do not let the milk boil or you may get a scorched taste in your hot chocolate.* When the milk begins to simmer, remove it from the stove and divide it between the two mugs. Stir the milk and chocolate until the chocolate completely melts. Top with whipped cream and a teaspoon (per mug) of the grated chocolate you reserved at the beginning of the process.

How to Make Crème Fraîche: Crème fraîche is a thick, tangy French sour cream. It's delicious on top of sweetened berries. Try mixing it with herbs and using it as a potato chip dip or adding a dollop on potato pancakes. (See Esther's Roasted Garlic and Herb Latkes recipe in the Coffeehouse Mystery *Holiday Grind*.) Crème fraîche can even add the complexity of tangy brightness to buttercream frosting.

In a saucepan, combine 1 cup heavy whipping cream with 3 tablespoons buttermilk. Warm carefully over medium heat—just to the touch, no more. Pour the liquid into a glass jar or bowl, and cover lightly with a clean towel (do not seal). Let stand at room temperature (about 70°F) for 10–24 hours. You're watching for it to thicken. Stir it well, then seal and refrigerate. (Use within 10 days.)

Madame's Sablés

Like a French shortbread, this tender, buttery little cookie is very simple to make yet an elegant addition to any coffee or tea tray. Sablé actually translates to "sand," the name coming from the crumbly texture of the cookie (again, like a shortbread).

The French have many variations (lemon, orange, almond). They dip them in chocolate and sandwich them together with jams. But Clare's favorite flavor is praline—for very good reason. Praline sablés were the cookies Madame baked for Clare during her pregnancy. No surprise: they're Joy's favorite, too.

Makes about 3 dozen cookies

Basic Vanilla Sablés:

> *1 cup (2 sticks) butter, softened*
> *½ cup confectioners' sugar*
> *½ cup granulated sugar*
> *1 large egg*
> *2 teaspoons vanilla extract*
> *2 cups all-purpose flour*

¼ teaspoon salt
1 egg white (for wash)
⅓ cup coarse finishing sugar, such as sparkle, demerara, or turbinado
(Sugar in the Raw)

Step 1—Make the dough: Using an electric mixer, cream the butter and sugars. Add the egg and vanilla and beat until smooth. Add the flour and salt, and stir with a spoon or spatula, until the dry ingredients come together into a sticky dough ball—but do not overwork the dough or your cookies will be tough instead of tender.

Step 2—Form logs: To make the dough easier to work with, chill it for 15 minutes. Divide in half and form two 8- to 9-inch logs on separate sheets of wax paper, using the paper to shape and smooth the logs. Wrap tightly and chill in refrigerator until very firm (at least 3 hours or overnight). Logs can be refrigerated for up to 1 week or wrapped a second time in foil and frozen up to 1 month.

Step 3—Bake: Preheat the oven to 350°F. Line a baking sheet with parchment paper or a silicone sheet. On a separate sheet of wax paper, lightly brush each log with egg white wash and roll in (or heavily sprinkle with) coarse finishing sugar. Using a knife, cut the chilled dough into ¼- to ½-inch slices (your choice). Bake for 15–20 minutes, rotating pan once for even baking. Cookies are finished when edges are light brown but centers are still pale.

PRALINE SABLÉS:

Follow the recipe above, but in Step 1 fold ½ cup Crushed Praline (recipe follows) into the dough before shaping and chilling. When Madame makes the praline version, she also replaces the ⅓ cup coarse finishing sugar (in Step 3) with ½ cup or more crushed praline, pressing lightly to make sure particles stick to the egg-washed dough logs.

Crushed Praline
(and Foolproof Almond Brittle!)

Praline is a brittle confection made of almonds (or hazelnuts) and caramelized sugar. A popular ingredient of French pastry chefs, it can be served as candy; ground and used as a flavoring; or even sprinkled over ice cream or on top of tarts, custards, and cakes.

Makes 2 cups

⅓ cup water
¼ teaspoon lemon juice (to prevent caramel from crystallizing)
1¼ cups white granulated sugar
1⅓ cups slivered almonds, toasted
(see How to Toast Nuts on page 334)

Cover a baking sheet with parchment paper. To make caramel, combine water, lemon juice, and sugar in a 2-quart saucepan. Place over high heat, and stir constantly with a wooden spoon or silicone spatula. After 10 or so minutes of continual boiling and stirring, the mixture will turn light golden. Just as the color deepens to a darker golden, remove pan from heat (if it darkens too much it will burn). Add almonds and stir well. Carefully pour this very hot mixture onto prepared baking sheet. Flatten into an even layer. As it cools, it will harden. (You have just made a delicious almond brittle!) Break into pieces. Place pieces into a resealable plastic bag and crush into a coarse powder with a rolling pin, meat mallet, or bottom of a heavy mug. (Who needs anger management?) For easy cleanup, fill pan with water, add utensils, and boil to melt crusted caramel.

Clare Cosi's Moist Mocha Cake with Shiny Chocolate Guinness Glaze

"Like a party in my mouth," said Sergeant Manny Franco upon tasting Clare's super-moist, chocolate-glazed mocha cake. The cake is wonderfully spongy so it soaks up the rich, chocolate glaze beautifully. As Clare mentioned to Franco, the flavor notes of coffee and malt (from the dark beer) intensify the chocolate. You hardly taste the coffee in the cake or the beer in the glaze; you simply enjoy a deeper, more satisfying chocolate experience.

Makes one 8-inch round, single-layer cake

½ cup granulated sugar
½ cup light brown sugar, packed
⅓ cup unsweetened cocoa powder
1 cup cake flour (if using all-purpose flour, see note at end of recipe for proper amount)
1 teaspoon baking powder
1 teaspoon baking soda
¼ teaspoon salt
½ cup buttermilk, low fat is fine (to make your own, see end of recipe)
1 large egg, lightly beaten
2 tablespoons vegetable or canola oil
1 teaspoon vanilla extract
½ cup black, brewed (and cooled) coffee
Chocolate Guinness Glaze (recipe follows)

Step 1—Prep the pan: Preheat the oven to 350°F. Cut out a round of parchment paper and place it in the bottom of an 8-inch round layer-cake or springform pan. Lightly coat the paper and sides of the pan with nonstick cooking spray. Set aside.

Step 2—One-bowl mixing method: Place both sugars, cocoa powder, flour, baking powder, baking soda, and salt in a large mixing bowl and whisk to blend. Add in the buttermilk, egg, oil, vanilla, and coffee. Whisk again until the ingredients are well blended (but do not overmix or you'll create gluten in the flour and your cake will be tough instead of tender). Pour the batter into your prepared pan.

Step 3—Bake: Place the cake in the center of the oven and bake for 30–35 minutes. The cake is done when a toothpick inserted in the center comes out clean (with no batter clinging to it). Cool the cake in the pan on a wire rack for at least 20 minutes. Run a knife around the outside of the pan, place your serving plate over the top and carefully flip to remove. Peel off the parchment paper. You now have a flat and even top to your cake! To finish, pour the warm Shiny Chocolate Guinness Glaze (recipe follows) all over the cake top, allowing it to drip down the sides and soak into the spongy cake. Let the glaze sit for about 30 minutes to set. Then serve and eat with joy!

Note on Cake Flour: I highly recommend using cake flour for this recipe for the best result. Cake flour is milled finer and lighter than regular all-purpose flour and will give you a more tender cake. If you've never bought cake flour before, look for it in boxes (not sacks) in the grocery store aisle where all-purpose flour is sold. If I still haven't convinced you to use cake flour, and you want to use all-purpose flour for this recipe, then make sure to reduce the amount of flour by ¼ cup.

How to Make a Buttermilk Substitute: Buttermilk adds a wonderfully bright tang to recipes, deepening the complexity of flavor beyond plain milk. To make your own sour milk replacement for buttermilk, simply place 1 tablespoon lemon juice (or white vinegar) into a measuring cup and fill it with milk (whole or low fat) until the liquid reaches the 1-cup line. Allow this mixture sit for 10 minutes at room temperature, and then use it as you would buttermilk in any recipe. (Note: Clare's Moist Mocha Cake recipe calls for only ½ cup buttermilk.)

Shiny Chocolate Guinness Glaze

Clare Cosi is always on the lookout for things that might make her favorite Irish cop happy. Guinness stout in the glaze of a chocolate cake? Perfect. "When using beer for a recipe," she warns, "allow it to sit and warm to room temperature. Of course, beer foams when you first pour it. You'll need to let the foam settle before measuring the beer or simply spoon off the foam and measure the liquid. To keep the extra beer from going to waste, you might want to invite someone who likes beer to join you in your kitchen." (And, in Clare's case, it's no mystery who that someone is going to be.)

Makes about ¾ cup of glaze, enough to cover one 8- or 9-inch round or square cake

¼ cup Guinness stout (measure beer only, not the foam)
2 tablespoons light corn syrup
¼ cup confectioners' (powdered) sugar
½ cup semisweet chocolate chips (3–4 ounces)

Step 1—Cook glaze: Combine the corn syrup and stout in a small saucepan and bring to a boil. Stir in confectioners' sugar until well dissolved. Remove from heat and whisk in the grated chocolate until it melts and the glaze appears shiny and smooth.

Step 2—Finish cake: For good pouring consistency, be sure to use the glaze while it's still warm. To make pouring easier (and give you more control over where the glaze lands), transfer the warm glaze to a container with a spout, such as a glass measuring cup. Pour slowly over the top of your cake, covering the surface completely and allowing the glaze to drip down the sides. Tilt the cake plate a bit (if necessary) to help even out the distribution of the glaze. The glaze will set in 15–30 minutes.

Note: You can always double the recipe and serve the extra on the side, pool it on serving plates, or try it as an ice cream topping. (It tastes like hot fudge!) To reheat extra glaze for serving, simply pop it in the microwave or warm it on the stove, and whisk until smooth.

Chocolate Espresso Saucers
(Flourless Mocha Almond Cookies)

Why are these flourless cookies called Espresso Saucers? Because these strange and amazing mocha-almond cookies bake up as round and flat as the saucer of a demitasse in which an espresso is traditionally served. Sweet, crispy, chewy, and chocolaty, these treats are an exotic edible—perfect for a murder mystery. They are also made without one bit of flour so their texture is unique. They'll practically melt in your mouth.

Makes 18–20 large, flat cookies

> 4 cups confectioners' sugar
> ½ cup unsweetened cocoa powder
> ½ teaspoon salt
> 1 tablespoon espresso powder
> 4 large egg whites, room temperature
> 1 tablespoon vanilla extract
> 1 cup slivered almonds, toasted (see toasting tip on page 334)

Step 1—Prep the oven and pan: Preheat the oven to 325°F. These cookies will stick to your pan so make sure to line a baking sheet with parchment paper and coat the paper with nonstick spray.

Step 2—Make the batter: In a large mixing bowl, whisk together the sugar, cocoa powder, salt, and espresso powder. Stir in the egg whites and vanilla to create a batter. Fold in the almonds (be sure to toast first for better flavor).

Step 3—Bake: The cookie batter will expand and flatten quite a bit so keep plenty of room between each mound of batter. Drop by heaping tablespoons onto the parchment lined baking sheet. Bake for about 15 minutes. You're looking for the cookie to expand and the surface to firm up and crack. *Important:* These cookies will break apart easily while still warm. To cool, carefully slide the parchment paper off the hot baking sheet and onto a cooling rack (or use a spatula to carefully transfer one cookie at a time). Once cool, these cookies will harden up nicely.

(No-Bake) Ganache-Dipped Chocolate-Chip Cookie Dough Bites

Made without eggs, this "raw" chocolate-chip cookie dough is not only safe to eat but heaven on your tongue. Dipped in chocolate ganache and rolled in finely chopped nuts, each little ball of dough becomes a tiny ice cream sundae on a toothpick. A fun, retro dessert for a party and an adorable treat for any coffee or tea tray.

Makes about 30 cookies

For Cookie Dough Bites:

4 tablespoons (½ stick) butter, softened
¼ cup light brown sugar, packed
2 tablespoons white granulated sugar
1 teaspoon vanilla extract
⅛ teaspoon salt
2 tablespoons brewed coffee
½ cup sweetened condensed milk
1 cup all-purpose flour
1 cup (about 6 ounces) mini semisweet chocolate chips
30 toothpicks

For Double Dipping (optional):

1½ cups walnuts, toasted and very finely chopped
(see toasting tip on page 334)
¾ cup Chocolate Ganache (recipe follows)

Step 1—Make dough: In a large bowl, cream the butter and sugars with an electric mixer. Beat in the vanilla, salt, coffee, and condensed milk. Add in the flour and chocolate chips, mixing until the dough comes together and is well blended (do not overmix).

Step 2—Chill, roll, and freeze: At this stage, the dough is too sticky to roll. Cover your mixing bowl with foil and chill in the refrigerator 15–30 minutes (or wrap dough in plastic or foil and chill overnight). Pinch off pieces of dough and roll into bite-size balls (about 1 inch in diameter). Set balls on a baking sheet lined with parchment or wax paper (be sure to line the baking sheet or the dough will stick to the pan). Sink a toothpick into each of the dough balls. (Warning: If serving to young children, do not use toothpicks.) Freeze until firm, 1–2 hours.

Step 3—Double dipping (optional): Place toasted walnuts in a sealed plastic bag and hammer with a rolling pin or large spoon until the nuts are very finely chopped. Or grind the nuts in a blade grinder or food processor. Place them in a shallow bowl and set aside. Make the Chocolate Ganache (recipe follows). Remove cookie dough balls from the freezer. Pick up each dough ball by its toothpick, dip top half of each ball into the chocolate ganache, followed by a dip in the bowl of finely chopped walnuts. Place the double-dipped balls back on your lined baking sheet. When the sheet is full, return it to the freezer for another 20 minutes or until the ganache hardens into a delicious chocolate shell. Store your finished Chocolate-Chip Cookie Dough Bites in the refrigerator or freezer in a plastic container or sealable plastic bag.

CHOCOLATE GANACHE

Makes about ¾ cup

1½ cups semisweet chocolate chips
6 tablespoons heavy whipping cream

Method: Place the chocolate chips into a microwave-safe container. Heat in the microwave for 30 seconds. Stop and stir. Repeat again until the chips are completely melted. Add the cream and stir continually until smooth and shiny. If vigorous stirring does not produce smooth results or if the ganache begins to harden, return the bowl to the microwave for another 30 seconds and stir again.

Note: When making large batches, note this ratio for double dipping. For every dozen Chocolate-Chip Cookie Dough Bites, you'll need ½ cup of finely chopped and toasted nuts plus ¼ cup of ganache—which can be made with ½ cup semisweet chocolate chips and 2 tablespoons heavy cream.

Chicken Mole with Guinness Stout (for Mike Quinn)

Based on a recipe from Punch, who claimed every mama in Spanish Harlem had a secret combination of ingredients that made the mole her own, so it is with Clare's version.

The name for mole, the rich Mexican sauce often served with chicken, came from the Aztec word molli *meaning "concoction." Clare's version, heavily influenced by New York City's melting pot of cultures, truly lives up to that Aztec etymology. She plumbed her Italian heritage for ingredients like fennel but gave the biggest nod* to Mike's Celtic heritage with the addition of the dark and malty Guinness stout.

Mole is an acquired taste and certainly not for everyone. The key to making this wild range of ingredients work as a whole is to keep the blend balanced. Not too spicy but not too bland, either, and always tempering the bitter with the sweet.

Makes 6 servings

4 chicken breasts (skin on, bone in) or 1 pound cooked and
shredded chicken (about 3 cups)

2½ cups Guinness stout

Salt and freshly ground black pepper, to taste

2 tablespoons canola or corn oil

water

½ pound bacon, chopped

2 large red onions, chopped

2 large yellow onions, chopped

1 Spanish onion, chopped

6 garlic cloves, smashed

2 bell peppers, chopped (approximately 1 cup)

½ jalapeño pepper, seeds and veins removed, chopped (for a hotter
mole, use 1 jalapeño, or leave it out completely for no heat)

2 tablespoons chili powder

1 teaspoon dried oregano

1 teaspoon dried thyme

½ teaspoon ground cumin

½ teaspoon ground cinnamon

½ teaspoon ground coriander

½ teaspoon fennel seeds

2 tablespoons ground almonds (or 1¼ teaspoons almond extract)

1 ounce semisweet chocolate, chopped

2 tablespoons sesame seeds, for garnish, optional

Step 1—Poach the chicken: You can poach the chicken just before making the mole or a day in advance. Place the 4 chicken breasts in a large pot or Dutch oven, skin side up. Ideally, they will sit in a single layer or overlap only a bit. Pour 1½ cups of the Guinness, the salt and pepper, and the oil into the pot and fill the rest of the way with water. The liquid level should be high enough to cover your chicken by 1 full inch. Bring the pot to a boil, and then turn the heat down to a simmer. Half cover the pot, cooking for about 15 minutes. Then turn off the heat and cover the pot fully, leaving the chicken to finish cooking in the hot water for another 15 minutes. Remove chicken from the poaching liquid. When cool enough to handle, discard the skin and shred the meat into pieces (discard bones). Set aside the shredded chicken. (If making a day in advance, place in a plastic container and refrigerate.)

Step 2—Cook the bacon and prep the veggies: Take out a separate, large pan, and slowly cook the fat out of the chopped bacon. Do this over low heat, about 15 minutes, stirring occasionally. Cook only until the fat is rendered; the bacon should not be crispy.

Step 3—Cook the veggies: When the bacon fat is rendered, add the chopped onions, garlic, bell peppers, and jalapeño. Cook slowly over medium heat until the onions are translucent and the peppers soft, for 10–15 minutes.

Step 4—Create a spice mix: Pour the remaining cup of Guinness into a mixing bowl and add the chili powder, oregano, thyme, cumin, cinnamon, coriander, fennel, and ground almonds. Pour this aromatic mixture into the pan with the bacon and vegetables. Stir well to blend. Using a hand immersion blender, chop and blend the ingredients into a smooth sauce. When well blended, add the chocolate, stirring until melted and velvety smooth.

Step 5—Add the chicken and finish: Add the chicken to the sauce and continuing cooking until thick, for 25–30 minutes. Plate the chicken mole and sprinkle sesame seeds, if using, over the finished dish. Serve hot with plenty of warm flour or corn tortillas for dipping in this amazingly flavorful sauce!

Peanut Butter Surprises (Peanut Butter Cookies with Ooey-Gooey Chocolate Hearts)

Sergeant Franco rivals Elvis in his love of peanut butter. (This Clare knew from the Five-Borough Bake Sale that took place in Roast Mortem.*) With her promo bag of chocolate chips from the ICE show, she decided to create this "surprise" treat for him—a sweet and tender peanut butter cookie with the kind of ooey-gooey chocolate heart that grown men swoon for—and the perfect, home-baked thank-you for body-slamming that scumbag Sun God.*

Makes 18–20 big, stuffed cookies

1 cup (2 sticks) butter, softened
1¼ cups peanut butter (standard creamy, *not* sugarless)
1 cup granulated sugar plus ½ cup, for dusting
1 cup light brown sugar, firmly packed
2 large eggs, lightly beaten
2 teaspoons vanilla extract
2 cups all-purpose flour
1 teaspoon baking powder
1 teaspoon baking soda
¼ teaspoon salt
1 cup semisweet (or bittersweet) chocolate chips (6–8 ounces)
Confectioners' sugar, optional

Step 1—Make the dough: Using an electric mixer, cream the butter, peanut butter, and sugars in a bowl until light and fluffy. Add in the eggs and vanilla and blend well. Finally, add in the flour, baking powder, baking soda, and salt, and mix only enough until a soft dough forms.

Step 2—Form and stuff: Pinch off generous pieces of dough and roll into big, golf-ball-sized rounds. Cradle the cookie ball in one hand. Use the thumb of your opposite hand to make a deep indentation in the center of each cookie ball. Fill the hole with about a teaspoon of chocolate chips and then seal the chocolate inside the dough ball. Gently roll the balls in white, granulated sugar for a finished look.

Step 3—Freeze: Place the cookie balls on a wax-paper-covered plate in the freezer for 30 minutes. (The wax paper will prevent the dough from adhering to the plate.) Do not skip this freezing step. This is the key to a successful cookie. If you don't freeze the cookie dough before baking, the cookie may break while baking and the chocolate may ooze out instead of staying in the center of the cookie.

Step 4—Bake: Preheat the oven to 350°F. Place chilled cookie balls on baking sheets lined with parchment paper, keeping the balls a few inches apart to allow for spreading. Bake 20–30 minutes. The cookies are not done until they flatten out, so be patient and wait for this to happen. The chocolate should stay inside. A nice "cover" for a cookie with oozing chocolate is to gently dust with confectioners' sugar. (Yes, a bit of sweetness and light once again rescues the day—and the cookie.)

Note: Hot cookies are fragile. Allow them to cool before picking them up or they'll break on you. And allow your baking sheets to cool before putting more dough on them.

"Fudge Factor" Cupcake Tops

"What I can't swallow is fudging," Mike told Clare, "as in fudging statistics, fudging results, fudging the truth. Mathematicians call it a fudge factor—putting an extra calculation into an equation just so it will work out as expected . . . It's what we law-enforcement types call a scam."

After Clare finally discovered the "fudge factor" in Alicia's Mocha Magic powder, she contemplated a "fudge factor" goodie, one that was packed with chocolate flavor but without an excessive amount of butter in the ingredient list.

These fudge brownie–like rounds are the result. They'll delight your taste buds with the sultry flavor and aroma of chocolate, and when frosted, you'll think you're eating the top of an old-fashioned fudge cupcake. But here's the best part—with Clare's "fudge factor" in place, these treats use far less butter than similar recipes. Can you find the "fudge factor" in Clare's ingredient list?

Makes about 20 rounds

4 tablespoons (½ stick) butter
2 tablespoons cocoa powder
4 ounces semisweet chocolate, chopped
¼ cup hot brewed coffee
1 cup ricotta cheese (whole milk)
1 cup light brown sugar, lightly packed
½ cup granulated sugar
1 large egg, lightly beaten
1 teaspoon vanilla extract
1 cup all-purpose flour
Pinch salt
½ teaspoon baking powder
Fast Mocha Frosting (recipe follows)

Step 1—Create the mocha paste: In a small saucepan, combine the butter, cocoa powder, chocolate, and coffee.

Over low heat, melt everything together into a mocha paste, stirring constantly to prevent scorching. At no time should this liquid boil, or you'll get a terrible burnt taste to the chocolate. If that happens, discard and begin again. (You can also microwave these ingredients. Use a microwave-safe bowl and heat in 30-second bursts, stirring between each burst to avoid burning the chocolate.) Set aside to cool.

Step 2—Mix up the dough and chill: Using an electric mixer, beat ricotta cheese and sugars a minute or so. Add in the mocha paste, egg, and vanilla. Blend until smooth. With the mixer set to low, mix in flour, salt, and baking powder. Do not overmix or you'll produce gluten in the flour, and your rounds will be tough instead of tender. Chill dough at least 1 hour in the refrigerator before baking. You must do this to harden up the dough and also to allow the flavors to develop. (During this hour of chilling, the chocolate will richly penetrate the ricotta cheese).

Step 3—Bake, cool, and frost: Preheat the oven to 375°F. Line a baking sheet with parchment paper and spray with nonstick cooking spray. (Yes, spray the paper! These "cupcake tops" are lower in fat than cookies and cakes with lots of butter and will have a greater tendency to stick. The parchment will also protect the bottom of your rounds from browning too much.) Drop a heaping tablespoon of dough per round onto your the baking sheet and cook for 10–13 minutes. Do not overbake. The finished round will feel spongy to the touch on the outside but with a somewhat firm structure. The inside should be fudgy, moist, and a little underbaked. The rounds will be too soft to pick up when they first come out of the oven. Slide the entire sheet of parchment onto a wire rack and allow rounds to cool before lifting or moving. They will harden as they cool—and they'll taste deliciously fudgy, filling your mouth as you chew with the sultry flavor and aroma of chocolate. Once cool, frost with Fast Mocha Frosting (see below).

How to Make Fast Mocha Frosting: In a nonstick saucepan, melt 4 tablespoons butter over medium-low heat. Add 4 tablespoons cold brewed coffee, 4 tablespoons unsweetened cocoa, and 1 teaspoon vanilla extract. (Do not boil or you may get a scorched taste.) While stirring, add 2–2½ cups confectioners' sugar, a little at a time, until mixture is melted and smooth. (You be the judge on the consistency you prefer. The amount you need may vary depending on the humidity or your altitude.) Remove from heat and work quickly to frost the cooled cupcake tops. The frosting hardens fast. You can always reheat, stir, and add a bit more coffee to soften again.

Phoebe Themis's Mini Chocolate-Chip Scones

The scone is the UK equivalent of an American biscuit. They're delicious with tea or coffee, slathered with butter while still warm, or split and served with clotted (or unsweetened whipped) cream and fruit preserves. The scone originated as a Scottish quick bread. According to Madame's new favorite librarian, "The name came from the original Stone of Destiny, known as Scone, which was the place where Scottish kings were once crowned." For further reading, Phoebe Themis suggests The Stone of Destiny: Symbol of Nationhood *by David Breeze, Chief Inspector of Ancient Monuments, and Graeme Munro, Chief Executive, Historic Scotland, published by Historic Scotland, 1997.*

Makes 12 scones, of 2 to 2½ inches in diameter

2 cups self-rising flour
1 teaspoon baking powder (yes, with the self-rising flour!)
½ cup (1 stick) butter, well softened
⅓ cup granulated sugar
¾ cup mini semisweet chocolate chips
¾ cup whole milk (for a richer scone, use half-and-half or light cream)

1 large egg, lightly beaten
1 ½ teaspoons vanilla extract
Turbinado sugar (Sugar in the Raw), for dusting, optional

Step 1—Prepare the dry ingredients: Preheat the oven to 400°F. Lightly grease a baking sheet or line it with parchment paper. Place a sieve in a bowl and measure the flour and baking powder into it and then lift the sieve and sift the two together into the bowl. Add the (softened) butter. Use your fingers to work the butter completely into the flour until the mixture is mealy and crumbly. Fold in the granulated sugar and chocolate chips.

Step 2—Prepare the wet ingredients: In a separate bowl, whisk together the milk and egg. Reserve 4 tablespoons of this mixture and place it in a separate cup. (You'll use this reserved liquid to coat the scones before baking.) Whisk the vanilla into the remaining egg mixture.

Step 3—Marry the dry and wet: Using a fork, begin to combine the egg mixture with the dry ingredients, a little at a time. A sticky dough will form.

Step 4—Knead gently and stamp out your scones: Form the dough into a ball and move it to a floured surface. If the dough is especially wet or sticky, add a bit more flour until you can work with it. Using floured hands, shape and pat the dough into a very thick circle of about ¾- to 1-inch thick. Stamp out the scones with a round biscuit (or cookie) cutter that's around 2 inches in diameter. For best result, dip the cutter repeatedly in flour between applications to the sticky dough. Gather up the scraps and repeat until all the dough is used up. Using a pastry brush, coat the top and sides of each scone with the milk-egg mixture that you reserved in Step 2. Sprinkle the tops with turbinado sugar (optional).

Step 5—Bake: Place your pan on the top rack of the oven and bake for 10–15 minutes, depending on the size of your scones. To ensure even browning, rotate the pan once during baking. They are done when the tops have turned a golden brown. Remove and cool on a wire rack. (To reheat scones, wrap loosely in foil, and warm in a preheated 350°F oven for about 10 minutes.)

CLARE'S BROOKLYN BLACKOUT CAKE (FOR MIKE)

~~~~~~

WHEN Mike had to become untraceable for his own safety, Clare went a little crazy. To keep as busy as possible during this blackout period, she decided to make her Blackout Cake.

The Blackout is a rich and decadent chocolate cake with fudge pudding slathered between each of the three layers. The entire cake is then frosted in chocolate and covered in cake crumbs. The original recipe was developed in Brooklyn, New York, during World War II, and is named after the blackout drills performed by the Civilian Defense Corps.

Because the dessert is time-consuming to make and complicated to assemble, Clare found it the perfect distraction from her continual worries about Mike's safety. Even better, when Mike finally appeared, safe and happy, she had this incredible cake ready to help them celebrate.

The recipe for this cake, along with photo illustrations on how to make it, can be found at my Coffeehouse Mystery Web site. Visit me there at www.CoffeehouseMystery.com to download a free PDF of this recipe. If you have any questions, I also have a message board.

Cook with joy!

—Cleo

Don't Miss the Next
Coffeehouse Mystery by Cleo Coyle

*Join Clare Cosi for a double shot of danger
in her next coffeehouse mystery!*

For more information about the
Coffeehouse Mysteries
and what's next for Clare Cosi
and her baristas at the Village Blend,
visit Cleo Coyle's Web site at
www.CoffeehouseMystery.com